CW01270510

THE DOVE UPON HER BRANCH

A Novel Portrait of Christina Rossetti

DM Denton

ISBN: 979-8-9883353-0-6
Library of Congress Control Number: 2023942429

Cover designed by DM Denton
Interior art by DM Denton

Too late for love, too late for joy,
Too late, too late!
You loiter'd on the road too long,
You trifled at the gate:
The enchanted dove upon her branch
Died without a mate;
The enchanted princess in her tower
Slept, died, behind the grate;
Her heart was starving all this while
You made it wait.

From *Bride Song* by Christina Rossetti

In the case of the Rossettis, the biography of any one individual may very well
seem 'only an episode in the epic of the family' …
from *The Rossettis: Dante Gabriel and Christina* by Elizabeth Luther Cary

Dedicated to my late mother, father, and brother
What are brief? Today and Tomorrow.

PART ONE

Sing, that in thy song I may
Dream myself once more a child
~ from *Maude* by Christina Rossetti

CHAPTER ONE

A storm had passed through and left the room broken.

Christina insisted there wasn't any truth in the tantrum that pulled down draperies and took a hammer to a table, chair, and the mirror positioned over the mantel. She would never have done something so ambitious, let alone difficult to mend.

It wasn't surprising Gabriel depicted her as a maniac even though twice she had been his choice to model for the Virgin Mary. His talent for caricatures couldn't resist speculating on Christina's reaction—regression—when *The Times* compared her poetry to Jean Ingelow's.

It was just a cartoon, almost forgivable as a playful reminder of when they were both as naturally wild as the inhabitants of the Zoological Gardens up the road from the first Rossetti address on Charlotte Street. In those days, the northern end of Regent's Park was a place for scientific study, a scruffy work-in-progress. A tunnel connecting its east and west ends was ideal for shouting to cause an echo and running the risk of an official reprimand. Whether owing to Mama sincerely apologizing, Papa gushing over his *"bambini brillanti,"* or those bright youngsters pleading for themselves, they were never prevented from enjoying the zoo's other attractions, which included a striated monkey, armadillo, sloth, parrot, and even a bear, lion, tiger, and elephant. There were fewer animals than after it officially opened to the public, but, with contributions from Windsor and the Tower, enough to fill the enclosures, buildings, cages, and a few hours on Saturday afternoons.

Before wombats took the stage, the star for the Rossettis, even more popular than the Egyptian giraffe added when Christina was six, was an antelope. A placard on wrought-iron fencing, in agreement with Gabriel's copy of *Peter Parley's Natural History*, identified the graceful beast as a West African Sing Sing.

"Sing, sing antelope, sing, sing," Papa called every time he saw it, Gabriel performing the ritual when his father wasn't there.

Of course, the creature never sang, but Christina always giggled and believed it might yet.

Her mood could quickly change due to her sudden shift from viewing the animals as entertainment to feeling their longing to be less sheltered.

"Cheer up, baby sis. At least they don't have to eat each other to survive."

Later, in art, Gabriel's hand would revere and mock her. In

childhood it tightly held hers through the streets, park, zoo, and up Primrose Hill. For children who didn't mind being blown about, the broad meadowed mound was a welcome departure from the city while keeping it in view. Appropriated by Henry VIII, it still offered pursuit, not of wolves, boars, or deer, but, as a Tutor king must have also enjoyed, fresh air, exercise, and feeling on top of the world.

"Will the ground tremble?" little William wondered when he heard there was a plan to tunnel trains under it.

Like Christina, he didn't remember much about Number 38 on cobbled Charlotte Street and trusted the agreement of Maria and Gabriel that Number 50 was a better fit and more fun. The narrow three-storied residence, in a mainly Italian neighborhood with lodging houses, a tailor, bootmaker, coach builder, and rag-and-bottle merchant, looked onto a cab-rank and public house. Constant coal-fire smoke and a messy mix of residents and pedestrians, including tradesmen, barristers, clergy, academics, and artists, challenged their mother's efforts to maintain a clean and organized household. She never knew what exile or misfit their father would bring into it. If anyone could remain level, disciplined, and respectable in such circumstances, it was Frances Mary Lavinia Polidori Rossetti.

It was also fortunate Mama was forgiving, as her patience was often tested by Christina's need to get her way and displays of temper when she didn't.

Sometimes trying a different tactic, little sister relied on big brother to make good enough arguments for her demands. Gabriel might, but he also refused to, perversely amused as Christina stamped her feet and wept.

"I want to watch it."

Not for the first time the Punch and Judy show was setting up in the street in front of their house.

"You know Mama doesn't want us to." Maria didn't look up from reading.

"Why not?"

"It's crude." William glanced at their mother, who nodded.

"We could sneak out and back in."

"God help us when you grow up, Christina."

"I pray he will, Mama."

"I have an idea." Gabriel took their mother aside to tell her what it was. Whether he had her approval or not, he went outside and used his easy smile to turn the Punch and Judy performance towards their front parlor.

"All right. But no opening the window."

Mama didn't mind them finding ways to satisfy both her objectives and their own. She tempered the moral directive of "if we cannot have what we like, we must like what we have" with "if we cannot do all we like, let us do what we can." She had to be as creative as Papa, the family they had made as challenging as he was. At least there was a balance, if not in each of the children, then between them. Just as her husband's exuberance and egotism was offset by her measured and modest ways, the calm of their first- and third-born offered relief from the chaos of their second and last.

In Christina's experience, the line between the better and worse behaved Rossetti siblings wasn't neatly defined. Maria's bossiness and jealousy sabotaged her saintly status. William was consistently compliant but would prove rebellious in his eventual atheism.

The boys were favored as the fiscal future of the family, and also its public persona, which was why Gabriel was soon a concern, although given a pass because of his artistic potential. The girls' talents weren't ignored or discouraged but protected from the pressure of earning anything other than their dignity. It was expected they would be taken care of with or without husbands. Mama's sisters were unmarried and led safe, respectable, comfortable—in Aunt Charlotte's case, luxurious—lives. As Papa was healthy and ambitious and Mama's role was to care for her family at home, Christina, the beloved baby, couldn't imagine a better life. Eager to begin each day, she and her siblings would make a race out of waking, washing, and dressing, before having breakfast with their parents. Once *il professore di Italiano* left for work, without complaint for the long walk or the-stop-and-go jolting ride on the omnibus to King's College, Mama was as content with the position of schooling her complicated, capricious brood.

She had her hands full with four youngsters to keep track of, discipline, educate, and encourage, but there was never any doubt her heart was, too, with constant love for them. Her revival from exhaustion at the end of another long day was obviously because Gabriele Rossetti returned with the reasons she had chosen him over a stable, stolid Scottish colonel.

Papa was also the bearer of sweets he knew would delight everyone except the protector of fledgling teeth and highly-strung temperaments. Mama might ration the toffee, fudge, jelly babies, bonbons, or marzipan, but she couldn't fault her husband's patience with juvenile chatter and games, communion and clashes, displays of pure gall and genius. Even if working on some literary project, he would take the time to tell stories, recite poems, and sing in his beautiful baritone voice.

He was a father to be adored, who gave his children strawberries that reminded him of *Napoli*, was attentive to what they had to say, were learning, drawing, or writing. He encouraged their imaginations and intellects to flourish.

They grew to realize how much older he was than their mother. His hair was thinning, and he put on weight. He spent less and less active time with them and more of the evening lying on the rug in front of the hearth, a cat curled beside him. Mama's figure was still lissome, her hair as lusciously brown as when she first set sparkling eyes on the man who'd had so little and so much to offer her.

At their first meeting, Mama's thoughts might have looked ahead to children inheriting their father's garrulous, generous, poetic, affectionate personality. That her own papa, the robust Tuscan, Gaetano Polidori, already loved Gabriele Rossetti as a son was enough to sanction the match.

***

How many children could say their home hosted the humblest and highest at the same time, on any given evening invaded by expatriates their father never hesitated to invite in. *Un cercatore* or *un seccatore*, beggar or bore, Papa satirized them. Through the back door he welcomed a bookseller, organ grinder, biscuit maker, macaroni man, and one called Galli who thought he was Christ. Others entered that way with a Masonic knock and handshake. Through the front, disgraced Italian counts and generals made as officious entrances as a small house on Charlotte Street afforded. Mama blushed every time she spoke of the visit from Nicolò Paganini, "all in black, without his violin but boasting the long hair he tossed about when he performed."

A regular caller, the artist Signor Pistrucci finally fulfilled a promise to Mama and did portraits of all her children.

"Such a pretty little Christina. Such a perfectly still and dull Christina has never existed." Even as a boy, Gabriel didn't doubt he was the bona fide artist in the family and, therefore, the opinion that mattered.

"He caught her wide-eyes and the softly determined jut of her chin, I think," William quietly offered.

"Unimaginative work, Will," Gabriel responded. "Where is the thought in her eyes? The words on her lips? The breath from her nostrils? He didn't capture her truth."

"Well, no question he honestly depicted my ugliness." Maria's eyes dared anyone to agree.

Christina lived it all again through the unreliability of her own memory and the detail of William's, which recalled everything, including that which he was told later. There were many stories, but only a few material reminders, like the locket some excited prince had given Christina, holding inside a faded picture of *la Madonna* that, at the time, made her tremble.

There had been a box containing small dolls, marbles, spinning tops, puzzles, and wooden soldiers and animals brought at Christmas or for birthdays along with confections by some of the less beggarly visitors who felt obliged to return the Rossettis' hospitality.

"I remember helping Mama," Maria reflected, "to cut whatever bread there was into as many pieces as possible. We barely buttered it, if at all. Jam only when it had been a good preserving year. Rarely, there was cake."

"I wanted to help," Christina lied.

"We didn't trust you wouldn't eat more than you prepared," Maria playfully scolded.

"Oh, such a wayward little Christina." Gabriel winked.

"Such a hungry little Christina." She was always emboldened by his attention.

CHAPTER TWO

"No, Chrissy. We must wait," nine-year-old Maria insisted.

"Why, Moony?"

"They shouldn't be picked until ripe."

"How long?"

"I don't know. Maybe tomorrow. Or the day after."

"What if I ate one now?"

"It wouldn't be juicy ... or sweet."

"How do you know?"

"*Nonno* says they should be fully red and soft to—"

Maria's firm grip thwarted the impulse of her little sister's outstretched arm.

The following day, on the same edge of their grandfather's garden, Christina again burst into tears, this time denied the fruity feast wildly cascading down a hedgerow bank because every ripened strawberry was wounded. Slugs had done the damage, a few still clinging to their victims.

"We weren't meant to have any. As Mama says, it never hurts to practice patience and self-restraint."

"Yes, it does." Unlike Maria, six-year-old Christina didn't look for sensible instruction in disappointment.

Maria reminded her of the currant bushes that grew upright and less prone to slimy invasions. They could provide an alternative snack and filling for a pie Aunt Eliza might be persuaded to make.

***

Holidays a world away from London were repetition to look forward to: first stagecoach to Uxbridge, second to High Wycombe, local transport halfway to Amersham letting them off at the crossroads to Holmer Green. It became apparent why they packed light: it was a long walk for short legs down a pretty lane into the village and another to *Nonno's* Cottage, its gardens, orchard, pond, pigsty, and spaniel named Delta.

Eventually, Christina would accept the house was small and ordinary. While it belonged to *Nonno* and her imagination's infancy, she found the property vast and full of uncommon experiences. Pure air, bird song, a look up to the sky, the shifting of sun and shadows, a honeysuckle-scented breeze, even a soot-less splash of rain was magical for the city child. Her hands swung free of others' fears and her legs moved at a quick pace to see cows out to pasture, frisky lambs, and a shepherd lad leaning on his crook as if waiting for her.

One day in the country was worth a month in town and better than Christmas, her birthday, or even Papa saying she was like the moon risen at the full.

As the strawberry incident demonstrated, Maria was more concerned with denial than gratification. If it was up to her sister, Christina would have spent most of the holiday shriveling in the darkened room of their ever-ailing grandmother. What impressionable, inquisitive, unsophisticated little girl wouldn't have preferred Gabriel's good looks, charm, and offers of adventure, as long as she had a sympathetic brother like William to retreat to when their older one was horrible?

"He said they would come to life again. But they didn't, Will, oh, they didn't."

Gabriel had netted several frogs because she wanted to hold one. He kept them out of water in the sun until their skin cracked and their croaking stopped, all floating belly up once he finally returned them to the pond.

"Just like for Jesus, you have to believe they'll be resurrected."

"How ridiculous, Gabriel."

"Maybe, Will. But does she have to be such a baby? As Papa says, we could fill bottles with her tears."

Emotion often poured out of Christina, "a serious flaw" that would "interfere with her contentment." She meant to heed her mother's words but her original temperament, or "original sin" as *Nonno* playfully called it, was hard to give up.

Christina loved thinking about Grandfather Polidori: his hearty greeting, busy mind and hands, scent of ink and linseed oil but not so much the rotten eggs smell of gunpowder that brought another unlucky pigeon to the dinner table. Some people, only a few, were easy to forgive.

He was a man of many talents, from translating Milton in the depths of his soul and study to working with wood and mosaics in the chaotic shed where he aided her concealment during a game of hide and seek. She liked to think he did so because she was his favorite grandchild, the same reason he invited her to sit on the bench beside him as though to participate in what he was crafting. He didn't seem to mind her chatter while she sanded a piece of wood she believed would end up an integral part of a bird house or feeder, chair, or table.

"*Avrà più spirit che tutti.*"

"What does it mean, *Nonno*?"

He told her to ask Maria, "To test her *Italiano*."

She found her sister picking parsley and pulling scallions in the kitchen garden. "'She'll have more spirit than us all.' I say, a warning more than a compliment."

"It's not fair. No one tells Gabriel to be different than he is."

Maria gripped Christina's hand to lead her in the direction of their grandparents' house. "I'm sure Aunt Eliza could use your help. Or Uncle Philip might need some sorting his books. You know how confused he gets. And *Nonna* will be wondering why you haven't sat with her today."

"No." Christina tugged herself away and ran as if escaping terror, tears streaming again, her life ending before it had begun, her little legs not taking her fast enough to get lost in Penn Wood.

The peach tree she had to pass before scaling the southern wall of the garden—something she had never done without Gabriel giving her a boost and William on the other side to catch her—was laden, some of its fruit hanging low enough for her to reach. She turned, but Maria had, for the time being, given up on her.

"One each for my brothers," she laid two peaches on the ground, "and for Moony and me. The biggest and juiciest are for *Nonna* to … to … have … with her tea." She picked two more.

On her way back to the house, Christina detoured to her grandfather's workshop, the peaches she held in her skirt rolling out. She picked them up and checked for bruises. *Nonno* wasn't in his shed. She heard a shot and "*maledirà*" and was momentarily relieved. She left a peach for him, covered her ears, and prayed for his target as he fired again.

Holmer Green was where Christina learned to take the good with the bad. It was there she first studied a rosebud swelling with dew, drooping in the rain, lifting in sunshine to become a perfect flower only to wither soon after. She also experienced the rewards of exploring rather than following, so she discovered her own interests, especially the smallest things that were more precious for being overlooked. Beetles and caterpillars were often in her hands, gently examined and returned to the grass, branch, or leaf she had lifted them from. William informed her that spiders were fragile and could perish with the gentlest touch. With patience no one thought she had, she watched them dangle, move up and down by a thread, or weave their magic that sparkled, swayed, and survived beyond belief. When an impulsive poke caused a frog to cover his head with his feet, she tried a soft stroke, which persuaded it to show her its eyes. She and Gabriel were alike in some ways, but she couldn't intentionally cause any living creature harm.

She was guiltless but acutely sad when she noticed a lifeless mouse in the dust and debris of the orchard. After trying unsuccessfully to revive it, she buried it in a shallow hole with a moist, mounded covering, kneeled, prayed, and intended to be back the next day with a handful of what her mother called "Mary's daisies." They were everywhere around her grandparents' cottage, across its lawns and creeping through its pathways, opening to the sun, closing to the rain. Mama had shown her how to weave them together in chains for her wrists, hair, or around her neck, Gabriel promising to paint a portrait of her "adorned with them."

Christina's return to a mouse's mossy grave was delayed because of frequent showers and sniffles that didn't develop into as bad of a cold for her as others. Mama was already experiencing poor health, the reason she had spent much of the year at Holmer Green with only two children at a time, except for a few weeks during summer when they were all there.

Maria was even sicker, although Gabriel insisted he was. William put aside his own discomforts to take care of everyone else.

Christina felt a foot taller all alone on her way back to a rodent's final resting place, expecting to experience the reverence of church when she knelt to place flowers there.

A scream, she didn't at first know was her own, shattered the ceremony, daisies scattered around a large, black, worm-like insect emerging from the grave. She gasped for breath and stumbled as she ran back to the cottage and into William.

"Where have you been? *Nonno* was the first to realize you were gone."

She couldn't answer with the truth or a lie, noticing Delta sitting at the other end of the hall, wagging his tale. When she reached him, she dropped to the floor, threw her arms around his neck, and looked up, a long way up, to her grandfather, who had somehow avoided being even just a little sick.

"Why is there death, *Nonno*?"

"Hmm." He frowned and tapped his head. "Well. Let me think. Ah, yes. Manzoni wrote 'Death is the great peacemaker.'"

Later she would learn Manzoni was a poet, a novelist, the writer of *The Betrothed*, *I Promessi Sposi*, a masterpiece, especially when read in Italian.

"Death is too cruel, horrible insects feeding on it." She couldn't stop picturing what she hadn't seen.

"Now, now." *Nonno* stroked her disheveled hair. "Better you should forget and smile than remember and be sad."

***

Eventually, Holmer Green belonged to strangers. Christina missed its specific sweetness of air and brightness of greens, the clean mists of its mornings, its star-studded nights, and darkest ones, too. She longed for prowling alone and doing nothing, which in the country was never boring. She didn't, however, miss *Nonno*, because she had him close all the time, within walking distance. Holmer Green might have gone from anticipation to memory, but in exchange there was a new playground. Maria decided the stucco Italianate villa at 15 Park Village East, on the edge of Regent's Park, should be named Myrtle Cottage, after the legendary Trojan Polydorus, who was turned into a myrtle tree. Christina called it the house that looked both ways, prompted by her grandfather claiming he chose it because one side was in the town and the other in the country.

"We are creatures of both."

There was the delight and annoyance of sooty trains rattling and whistling by its front window and, at its rear, the pleasure and peril of running down the sloping garden to almost slide into the canal. She no longer had to leave London for choirs of frogs, searches for bird nests, picnics, swimming, rolling in leaves, sledding, snowball fights, and, if it was cold for long enough, skate-less ice skating, all in her grandparents' backyard.

Even *Nonna* Polidori was accommodated with more than just another gloomy room and sick bed, what Christina's father branded "her warlike spirit" entertained by soldiers' drills in the military barracks she could view from her voluntary confinement.

Like Holmer Green, the Park Village house was crowded with Polidoris and always welcome to Rossettis, especially the youngest. The main interior attraction was its library full of volumes for a change from their father's obsession with Dante Alighieri and their mother's insistence on religious stories. It catered to their cravings for adventure, gothic melodramas and horror, and tales of knightly chivalry. Among their very favorite books were their uncle's criminal underworld Newgate novels.

Nonno once again had a shed for "making useful things," but this one revolved around a small iron printing press that, with the help of Sicilian compositor *Signore Privitera*, published Gaetano Polidori translations, poetry, and prose, and was set to reveal such talents in his grandchildren.

CHAPTER THREE

"Today's your natal day, sweet flowers I bring ..."

Mama's opinion was the one that haunted Christina the most. Getting her way wasn't as gratifying as hearing her mother say, "Good girl" and, even better, seeing approval in her eyes. They were glowing and moist as Christina held out a forget-me-not posy and began reciting her first poem—the first she admitted to.

"Mother accept I pray, my offering ..."

"Of course, my darling." The flowers were in Mama's hands. "Go on. I know the best is yet to come."

How does she? Christina wondered if Gabriel had given the surprise away as he had threatened, not only that there was a poem but, also, the very words that comprised it. She went on anyway. "And may you happy live, and long us to bless ..."

Mama carefully laid the flowers in her lap, so she could make use of the handkerchief tucked in her sleeve.

"Receiving as you give," Christina's own eyes welled up, "great happiness."

"And the rhymes all your own. I heard you wouldn't have any help with them."

"Who told you?"

"Please, do not pout."

"I'm sorry, Mama."

"Let poetry be your expression."

The faint scar on Christina's upper left arm was a reminder of when she had used scissors instead.

"Oh, yes, Mama, I think that is how to save myself."

***

In church and her conscience, Christina began to seriously consider her sins. However, trying to be and do better faltered whenever Gabriel blew through bragging about his misadventures, almost every day since he and William attended King's College. Papa's professorship had granted the first son free admission, the second reduced tuition.

Maria looked forward to sharing in their books and lessons. Christina was captivated by their tales of junior school and its bullies, reversing her regret at not being a boy.

"Be glad you don't have to endure it, Chrissy."

"Gabe's right," William too quickly agreed with his brother to be insincere. "It's no place for the likes of us. A rude shock. Every day there's some nasty boy who wants a fight."

"How does Papa teach there?"

"He's in a position to punish them."

"How does he do that?"

"Well, I hope, not by throwing books at their heads." Gabriel laughed.

"That happened to you?"

"Ah, Chrissy. Do you think I might deserve it to?"

"Yes."

"So I did. But I ducked, and it hit the poor sod sitting behind me."

"Who threatened 'to ruin your pretty face.'" William turned Christina's amusement to fear.

"And yours, too." Gabriel slapped his brother's shoulder. "This horrid going to school business is almost worth it for the walk there and back. Oh, you know it is, Will. Especially, the return. A busier part of the day—"

"No, Gabe." William moved as if to cover Christina's ears. She pushed him away.

"—on those streets where Jenny lifts her skirt."

"Who's Jenny?" Christina stood on her toes.

"No one." William's cheeks colored pink into red.

"Lazy, laughing, languid Jenny," rolled out of Gabriel's smirk.

"I wish I could meet her."

Gabriel continued to entice his little sister back to naughtiness by bragging more about his own. He even performed his cripple act, from his pocket pulling the coins it had solicited on the streets before his scam was realized.

William entertained her, too. "I couldn't keep up with our lazy, laughing, languid Gabriel Charles running away."

***

Christina and Maria only ever played at dancing, taught by one of Papa's visitors, *Signore Parodi*, who, in William's words, spoke "a curious lingo, compounded of Italian, English, and whatever else." That neither sister was very good at the specific stepping, swaying, twirling, and flirting their instructor declared "all respectfully hopeful young ladies should have in their best attributes arsenal" was the least of Mama's worries. A dismissive shake of her head wasn't her response to anything that threatened Papa's professional reputation. Her panic was palpable the evening her sons' schoolmaster unexpectedly called and stepped into the parlor where the Rossetti siblings were rolling on the floor as though with excruciating belly aches. Did he think it was the fault of her cooking, or, as the children laughed at his reaction, did he consider their mother an accessory to their horseplay and, worse, disrespect? Even when Papa explained no offense was meant by his "clever children acting out the battle of Clan Alpine from Sir Walter Scott's *Lady of the Lake*," there remained the chance that a report would reach the higher-ups at King's College deeming her husband unfit to continue teaching there. It might even put off his private students, also necessary to his income.

The schoolmaster had gone when Gabriel wielded a chisel as a prop for his Othello enraged with Desdemona, who Christina, until that moment, had been happy to play, as she was usually denied significant roles in Rossetti home theater. Both sisters gasped with relief as Gabriel agreed not to risk hurting Christina, and horror when he wielded the carving tool against himself.

"No harm done." Gabriel unbuttoned his shirt to show a distinct scratch on his chest.

He often influenced how they entertained themselves, and not always in crazy ways that embarrassed their mother or threatened their wellbeing.

"I propose each of you write a novel I'll illustrate. Imagine. Like a troop of word acrobats." He was an irresistible salesman with his long chestnut curls, shimmering eyes, and persuasive patter. *"La grande famiglia Rossetti* will do amazing, heart-stopping feats with the dexterity of their imaginations."

"And hands." William never ceased to be fascinated with his brother drawing.

They all admired Gabriel's ability, even Maria who thought it was her mission to tell anyone who might not know and remind those who did that her eldest brother was born to be an artist. She especially loved to relate how the milkman witnessed six-year-old Gabriel drawing a rocking horse, "exhibiting a talent that proved he was either a midget or prodigy."

"I think, Moony, I would rather be celebrated as a poet than an artist."

"I suppose that's why you've been signing and dating all your pictures."

"Just in case. When I'm poet laureate someone might be interested in them."

"And why we all will make sacrifices to send you to Sass's."

"I'm the one making the sacrifice."

"You?"

"Wasting my time staring at bones and draperies, dotting squares, constantly sharpening my pencil and erasing with moldy bread while standing up to my ankles in crumbs."

"All worth it when you're accepted to the R.A."

"Or not."

Maria wouldn't let up on him, insisting art was his true vocation. "There are enough literary scholars in the family."

"I won't be left behind by a moon-faced muse in a pinafore." Gabriel credited her for irritating him out of his usual procrastination by racing him to be the first grandchild worthy of *Nonno's* printing press.

Gabriel tried not to seem pleased when Maria's poem, *On the Death of Lady Gwendoline Talbot*, didn't print well in thirteen foolscap pages of *piccolo*.

Christina saw her grandfather's "machine" as more than the whir of its wheels, slide of its rollers, and click of its plates. The magic it made from the pump of his foot and rhythm of his hand feeding and retrieving resulted in a permanency of expression that, even when formed in the wrong font or smeared, fed her growing desire to write.

She felt further pulled into the same inevitable purpose by Gabriel's way with words, especially on paper where he serenaded in troubadour fashion. His writing was richly romantic and adventurous, surprisingly noble and tender, reflective of a past that was his through Italian Medieval lyricists. Also, in language and subject, there was the influence of Dante Alighieri, a blessing and curse in the Rossetti consciousness since Papa had reincarnated him through obsessive research, painstaking translations, eccentric theories, and in the name of his first-born son. Whether by coincidence or prophesy, Gabriel Charles Dante Rossetti grew into a young man donning the 13th and 14th Century poet's persona and pursuits like a flamboyant costume to hide and reveal him.

Christina knew she couldn't write like Gabriel any more than she could become a young woman with the confidence he had and liberty he was allowed on his journey towards adulthood. What she did have, and hoped she always would, for life and art, like a second mind, pair of eyes and ears, and alternative heart, was imagination. It was a playful, expectant, consoling companion for her childhood and a necessary refuge from what came next when adolescence began with their father's failing.

"I feel tired in every limb," Papa would say, so the family knew better than to expect hugs, sweets, games, and interest in their activities and accomplishments, although the cat might still get his napping partner in front of the fire until *Professore Rossetti* made his way to bed earlier than his youngest child.

One evening, in addition to *"Buona notte"*, Christina heard, "I fear

I'll not live much longer."

"I don't like Papa to talk that way."

"He'll be all right." Mama stood at the bottom of the stairs.

"You know, for you have told us," Maria seemed older than their mother, "sickness and suffering are sent to correct us."

"But I never expected ... so soon ...."

Papa didn't sleep well, that night or many others. At best Christina heard him conversing with Mama or shuffling in the hall, talking to himself in Italian. At worse he interrupted everyone's sleep with retching. When Mama explained he was diabetic, which caused him to feel weak and weary, have fevers, nausea, and trouble with his eyesight, Christina began to fall into gloomy moods that didn't find relief in crying, foot stamping, or holding her breath, the last rarely used since she was two or three.

CHAPTER FOUR

"Are you ready to test your poetic prowess?" William always began the game with the same question.

Christina was sitting on her bed, the candle on the table beside her burned down to more smoke than flame. She crumpled the paper she had been writing on.

William offered another piece that looked as if it had been torn from a notebook. "To be fair, Maria came up with the list. I thought a sonnet in an hour. A breeze for you. A scramble for me. You'll need another candle."

"There's one on the dresser."

Christina assumed William wanted her to write something floral and fluid, clever, even comical; if serious, thoughtful but not too pious. He was looking for the little sister who said what was on her mind, showed what she was feeling, and was only ever upset for trifling reasons. The one who filled the house with impulses and questions, who never thought about growing up, and yet promised to be a bright star when she did.

Christina missed her, too.

So much was different and difficult since Papa was ill. On leave from his professorship, potentially never to return, private students reduced to those who could come to him, his pride was also wounded by Mama having to find work. Even worse, his self-worth had been shaken by the rise of the younger political exile Mazzini, the withholding from publication of his *Amor Platonico*, and the belittling of *La Beatrice di Dante*.

Reports from Mama in Hastings cautiously hoped Papa's health and mental state were improving. Christina had attempted a letter to him in Italian, which ended up mainly apologetic for its linguistic errors. She was glad to switch to composing in English following the rules for *bouts-rimés*, a game accidentally invented by Dulot, described by Gabriel as "the blank sonneteer." The 17th century poet claimed to have written three hundred sonnets when all he had come up with were their end rhyming words.

The competition began where Dulot's effort ended — at least, paused and never moved on. Christina's sonnet, without any mention of God, beat William's in, as he insisted, substance, certainly in speed. Still, twenty minutes wasn't a record; Gabriel had been known to do one in ten.

***

"Who opened a window in here?" Aunt Margaret closed it. "I won't have anyone sickening under my watch." She had good reason to be concerned on another wind- and rain-chilled early June afternoon.

"I think it was the housemaid. She said the parlor felt stuffy with Rossettis confined too long," Maria joked.

"Oh, look what's come in the post." Christina noticed their aunt was holding an edition of *Hodge-Podge*. "It's all raggedy. Why didn't Mama just bring it home with her?"

"Because they're off to Paris now."

Christina was immediately anxious. "Maybe they'll never come back."

"Of course, they will." Maria had her mother's homemade periodical in her lap, smoothing it out before she lifted and began to read it. "Mama is all about our well-being, wishing we could go to the seaside or the country."

"Can't blame them if they abandon us." Gabriel acted as if he was unaware of interrupting her. "Aye. Here she blows." He waved a handkerchief towards his younger sister.

Christina refused it, easily turning off her tears. She sat next to Maria on the sofa, draping her right arm over her sister's left shoulder and resting her chin against it. She silently read what Maria did out loud, loving Mama's writing about *the beauties of rural scenery, the cock's clear call, lazily crowding cows,* and *the dewey scent of spring in burgeoning greens and flowers.* Her point was to remind them how to survive London's *smoke, noise, and hustle, and expressions of weariness.*

Maria continued reading out loud, "'Rather than give into your sluggishness, rise at sunrise, wash your faces with cold water, and dress for exercise rather than vanity. After a light breakfast, set off to walk through Regent's Park and even up Primrose Hill, where the air is somehow unaffected by smoke-spewing chimneypots. Then your spirits will be renewed.'"

Day after day the sun didn't appear, and the threat or actuality of rain persisted. Aunt Margaret's protests of any action that might cause "sickening" meant there was no sallying forth outside of filling their time, minds, and collaborative *Illustrated Scrap-book.* As with previous editions, Gabriel added self-proclaimed "choice sketching specimens" and was almost as generous to Christina, pronouncing the "poetic effusions" she offered, especially *Rosalind,* and *Corydon's Lament and Resolution,* particularly good. Maria was of two minds about whether she wanted her *Vision of Human Life* included, finally accepting Gabriel's commendation, and forgetting pride was a sin. William continued to work on his drawn-out *Ulfred the Saxon*, even though he didn't think anyone wanted to continue reading it.

"Its interest increases with every installment. Can't leave it dangling. It must go in, Will."

"If you think so." William seemed more resigned than convinced. "What are those blotches on your face?"

Gabriel shrugged, more interested in Aunt Margaret, who had entered the parlor with a book and look around the room she may have hoped to have to herself. "So, what are you reading, Auntie?" he asked. "Nothing Faustian, or pirated, I hope." He went on to reproach her for reporting to Paris that he was writing and reading indecently. "I'm sure Mama understands Shelley is a must for me."

A few hours later, he had erupting blemishes all over his arms and face and complained of a headache like "the devil setting my head afire."

The same physician who had suggested their father leave London for a while urged Gabriel to also find relief by the sea. He was much better by the time he left, revived by the chance to fulfill a long-standing invitation to Boulogne as the guest and student of Papa's compatriot and friend, the painter Maenza.

Christina annoyed Maria by asking every day when Mama and Gabriel would return. William offered to help pass the time with rhyming or chess or taking their mother's advice and his barely younger sister to Primrose Hill. If their walking also took them down Albany Street to Park Village East, there were reminders in daisy-less lawns of long-ago places and imposing houses that nostalgically tested what they had learned from their mother's instruction on the difference between Ionic and Corinthian columns.

Their grandfather might be found in his shed. On one occasion, he handed Christina a page from Gabriel's ballad *Sir Hugh the Heron*. "Not a word in your correspondence. It's a surprise for when he returns." When he returns. If he returns. He must return. Gabriel was only fifteen, not yet finished at Sass's and soon to apply to the Royal Academy for free admission. Papa was the most anxious for him to do so, a requisite step on his way to being a successful artist without straining his parents' resources. Christina was more concerned about Gabriel being on his own in France. Strangers might put up with him for a while, but they weren't family to offer a refuge from the misunderstandings society, even bohemian society, would make about him.

"Of course, *Nonno*," William's soft voice brought her back to the brother who was there. "And when will we see Chrissy's in print? Even Moony has admitted she is to be the poet in the family."

"Is Maria still copying them?"

Christina had no idea *Nonno* knew. It was around her twelfth birthday, a Sunday afternoon, when Maria pronounced a poem of Christina's to be first-class and suggested she put it and all others in a notebook. Christina's view of her sister softened as Maria's plump hand inscribed the title page: *Poems by C.G. Rossetti.*

***

Love reigneth high and reigneth low and reigneth everywhere. The line came to Christina on the way to Albany Street's fort-like yet gracefully towered Christ Church, the plane trees and elms dropping the last of their littering leaves, the air brisk enough to taste. She was going to worship with Mama as if there had never been a Sunday without her.

Maria returned Reverend Dodsworth's greeting with a perfunctory nod, while continuing into the church through a shallow, pillared portico.

Mama and the minister courteously competed in discussing Mr. Rossetti's health.

"We thought we had him back. He was as good as cured. Then overnight ...."

"Oh, Mrs. Rossetti. So I heard. What a shock. But he is a little better?"

"He can see hazily in one eye, almost not at all in the other, but, perhaps, from this—"

"He will also recover."

"Yes, yes."

Christina reached for her mother's hand.

"We will offer prayers."

"I prefer you not mention him, us, by name, Reverend."

"Of course." Reverend Dodsworth squinted at Christina, who provided him with something more to say. "During the summer, your girls came every Sunday, even in the rain. Also now and then in the week, for confession, although such angels had little reason for it." He embarrassed Christina. "Haven't seen your lads for a long while."

"Gabriel Charles only just returned from France."

"But, Mrs. Rossetti, he still isn't here."

"He will come soon."

When he can get himself up early enough, Christina thought.

"And the other one?" Reverend Dodsworth asked before his attention was diverted by the arrival of more of his congregation. Christina gently but urgently pushed by her mother into the church.

"Why won't Will come, Mama?" Christina whispered once they were sitting in their reserved pew, the fair cost of which had persuaded her mother to switch her spiritual allegiance from Holy Trinity,

Marylebone to Christ Church, Camden. It wasn't often Christina saw Mama lose her temper, but the ever-increasing seating rents at Holy Trinity had sparked her Polidori indignation. Reverend Saxby Penfold had been visibly shocked at her accusation of his profiting from those genuinely seeking salvation, while Christina had been impressed her mother could be as perfectly rattled as she was usually restrained.

"You may ask him. I won't." Mama, by her tone, was irritated, but not enough to confirm in words her displeasure with her youngest son.

The morning sunlight sprayed into the church to exaggerate dust floating and settling, the austerity of its walls, the cracks in its marble floor, and the lines around Mama's eyes.

Maria lifted her head from prayer, "Our zeal is not his," and immediately bowed again.

Zeal? It was a word Christina liked for its implication of passionate commitment. She was threatened by it, too.

Other young men went to church, like one Christina repeatedly noticed sitting on his own, which suggested he was there willingly. Eventually, James Collinson was someone to nod to because Gabriel, who recognized him from Sass's, did.

Gabriel finally made it to church with an ego to be served rather than a soul to be saved. Both Mama and Maria shushed his assertion that he would one day improve Christ Church's decorations with some of his own.

Mama further admonished him on the walk home.

"If you really want to accomplish such a proposal, I suggest no more telling Mr. Cary you were absent from class because you 'had a fit of idleness,'" Mama said in her inimitably tactful way of implying there wasn't any choice in her suggestion. "Those reports of your disobedience, even disruptiveness, are most disturbing to your poor papa. He's afraid you'll spoil your chances of getting into the Academy. As if he doesn't have enough to worry about."

Gabriel almost immediately succumbed to her well-measured concern and, not for the first or last time, genuinely made a promise he couldn't keep.

CHAPTER FIVE

While William rubbed ink on the elbows of his jackets and mourned the death of his plan to become a doctor, Gabriel made shabbiness a signature of his look as a poet and artist the world was waiting for. A loosened collar, colorful scarf, cheerful whistle, and unwillingness to sacrifice were all he needed to avoid the solemnity and duty the rest of his family had undertaken since its patriarch was indisposed to earning a living and their smiles.

Circumstances weren't the worse they could be. *Nonno's* advance on Mama's inheritance meant they weren't yet on the verge of bankruptcy and Christmas a few weeks after Christina's thirteenth birthday was less meager than it might have been. The loan hardly went far enough to allow Maria, when she turned seventeen the following February, to refuse the position, procured by Aunt Charlotte, of nursery nanny to the brother of the Marquis of Bath.

As usual, Gabriel offered unhelpful advice. "I say, Moony, you don't have to be bullied out of your life to earn pittance and put up with beastly, uppity brats."

"Says he who costs much and earns nothing." William didn't always hide his resentment of being denied his desired career.

As was her calling, Maria was ready to shame them all. "I thank God I may help with the burden Papa has shouldered without complaint for so long."

"All he does now is grumble." Gabriel said what Christina wanted to.

"Even the hardest things can be borne through necessity, self-denial, and faith."

Christina heard her sister crying the night before she was to go away. Christina's heart broke for her, but mostly for herself. After an exchange of cheek kissing in the brisk morning, she was amazed at Maria's composure as she barely lifted her dark woolen skirt and worn-white petticoat to step into the elegant Longleat carriage where Aunt Charlotte was already bundled. With the closing of the door by the impeccably costumed and indifferent driver, nosy neighbors likely confused at such a display of affluence, the sister who had been Christina's essential adversary and advocate disappeared into the fog of growing up all at once.

Christina suffered the loss of Mama, too. During the day, Frances Polidori Rossetti went to pupils' homes to give lessons in French and Italian. When she was at home, domestic doings, correcting papers, an ailing husband, and exhaustion stole her from mother-daughter conversations, reading and praying together, and comfortable silences. William was also mostly unavailable, still attending King's College School and, in the evenings, either studying, or out somewhere with Gabriel.

Caring for Papa was a heavy, suffocating cloak cast over Christina, blinding her with his blindness, sickening her with every ailment he had or imagined, defeating her because of his failures. She never wanted to add to his distress, even as she resented him shrinking into insignificance and frailty, knowing he couldn't help it. She tried not to let him spoil every moment. Relief might be as simple as sitting with needlework mostly idle on her lap until, preferably, a purring cat was. She would read or write poetry or prose. If her father was in one of his better moods, they might play chess, his appreciation of her skill not extended to her winning. Visits from *Nonno* gave her and Papa something to look forward to in the endlessness of being confined together, but only as rarely as Gaetano Polidori put aside frugality and hired a cab to bring him. He encouraged conversations others were afraid to attempt with Papa for fear he would rage or sink further into his death wish. *Nonno* was able to calm Papa's histrionics, and revive his interest in politics and publishing, art and poetry, especially his Dante obsession. Christina learned to have patience, knowing from experience that her dear *Nonno* would allow time for their usual *tête-ê-tête*, which involved a look in her poetry journal at its newest entries. If there were gifts, he wouldn't reveal them until he was about to leave, like a small parcel of homemade confections from Aunt Eliza, a book from Uncle Philip's library, or a satiny ribbon to tie in her hair.

She kept it in her sewing box, its pristine condition implying it had rarely contradicted her drab dress-sense.

There was always an open invitation to 15 Park Village East for dinner on Sunday after church. At least once a month Mama accepted. She might allow Christina to go when she didn't, but only with one of her brothers, preferably William, who, to avoid Mama's hope that he would be, like Gabriel, a now and then church goer, wouldn't agree to anything that might take him near its red door.

"Uncle Philip could meet me at Christ Church and after dinner bring me home."

Mama hardly considered that option. "No. Philip isn't … well, reliable. He might have one of his spells and I won't have you walking the streets alone or cause your grandfather to waste more money on a cab."

Christina wanted to cry, except her conscience wouldn't let her, Mama's forbearance and calm stretched thin in managing Papa's emotional and too often unkind outbursts. If Christina did resort to any of her old devices, it would be to cajole, even nag, William until standing in proximity to Christ Church was less threatening to his principles than the loss of his sister's good opinion of him.

Dear William. Christina could never think badly of him. If anything, that he didn't need religion to practice devotion and humility proved he was more self-regulated and even of better character than she was. From an early age, seemingly doomed by having to leave school at fifteen and a half for the bottom of the Excise Office ladder, he diligently took on the responsibility of caring for them all. Christina didn't hold back her tears on learning his fate, running to console him, to implore him not to throw his talents and dreams away. She saw his sad eyes and didn't want to make it more difficult for him "doing what was right" as he later defined his "vocation." She was upset with as much as for him, until it was obvious he hadn't discarded his talents and dreams but reorganized them.

***

Christina didn't have linear remembrance of those years—1843, 1844, 1845 and beyond—that tunneled through the despair of growing up. She emerged for air and sunshine in flashes back and forth. A visit to the Reads of Finsbury Pavement, Islington while they were summering in the country offered the ambiguous delight of seeing Maria again, who was their governess after leaving Lord and Lady Charles Tynne's employ. Christina was pleasantly frustrated by backgammon, a board game that would never usurp her pleasure of playing cards or chess. She rode a horse named Jack who, she was promised, would take her for a gentle trot, but with one wrong tug it turned into a wild ride that terrified her until her feet were on the ground and the stable boy commented how bonny she looked. She found a companion in one of Maria's charges, a sweet girl who insisted on being called Bessie and begged her not to leave, as Christina wished her sister had.

She was relieved Maria didn't mind her friendship with Bessie, surprised she actually encouraged its continuation with the idea that Christina send stamps for the girl's collection.

And, for whatever reason, keep up a correspondence with her. You need to look beyond that dreary house, and Bessie can only benefit from acquaintance with you, Maria wrote once Christina was back home.

Christina spent hours carefully peeling postage off current mail and going through bundles of older letters, not only hers, which weren't yet abundant, but, also, after requesting permission, her mother's. William offered stamps and so did Gabriel, although he needed reminding until it seemed he would never supply any. Christina knew Bessie would especially appreciate the foreign ones that had sent news of family and friends, a few from France and Germany, many more from Italy, *Nonno* contributing the oldest. Christina wished she could have witnessed Bessie's delight over the rarity from Spain in commemoration of Goya.

The package wasn't complete until a poem was included, an entreaty, a declaration, an offering of more than *one hundred humble servants* in *their livery of red and black*. Odd that so many stamps were in those colors, especially the English ones, so she couldn't help dressing her poem rather soberly with them. It was her intention to delicately describe a girl she had hardly begun to know but had immediately seen how *gravity and gladness* mixed in her, a bane and blessing Christina knew too much about. Was that not why they had become fast friends, quickly sensing each other's similarly complicated temperament, enough to overcome shyness and social status?

Thought here, smiles there; perfection lies betwixt, Christina could still hear her own sigh because of the satisfaction of coming up with that last line, perfection only as it related to *Dear Elizabeth*. It was acceptable to assign it to someone else, never oneself.

Christina would have felt fortunate to have one friend outside of family, but somehow, and despite feeling locked away, she made another. Amelia Barnard first stepped into Christina's society as the bride-to-be of Dr. Heimann, who, a few years earlier, had exchanged Italian lessons from her father with German lessons for his children. Amelia was pretty and pleasant, her olive-skinned and dark-eyed Jewishness exotic. She was conservatively elegant, a sapphire sheen to the gray cloth of her dress, wide and almost frilly lace on her collar and cuffs that Mama, Maria, or Christina would never wear.

Amelia had been almost schoolgirlish looking through the Rossetti siblings' scrapbooks she gave more importance to than their being strewn about the house did.

"Might I write to you?"

Christina hesitated, because she doubted she would have anything interesting to express in reply.

Amelia's wish to further their acquaintance wasn't deterred. "And you must visit. Once I'm married." She noticed her betrothed approach and reached out to his hand and desire to please her. "Don't you agree, Adolf?"

"Anything, if you say so, my dear." The German was as genial as ever, even when what he had taught his Rossetti pupils one lesson was forgotten by the next.

"We'll reside in George Street. Only a few miles away."

An amiable young woman with the kindest intentions couldn't release Christina from being too young, poor, melancholic, and impossible to have a social life. Still, miraculously, their friendship began and continued, comforting and companionable, mostly through correspondence, but those visits that at first seemed unlikely would be constant, too.

CHAPTER SIX

Leeches were suggested as treatment for her lack of monthlies, Christina horrified while joking that faced with her flesh, they would flee for the door.

She was fourteen when amenorrhea was attributed to the over-stimulation of her mind by poetry. Dr. Hare also prescribed cupping, but again her mother refused to let the "already fragile body and psyche" of her youngest be "so violently assaulted." Instead, Mama drew more money from her inheritance to bring in London's best physicians. Dr. Locuck, Dr. Watson, and Dr. Latham repetitively prescribed bloodletting, tinctures, exercise, and that the patient be kept cheerful. Christina risked her mother's disapproval when she rolled her eyes at the idea that long days shut up with her father's debilitation and moods could ever be happily habitable, certainly not while his obsession with dying encouraged her own.

Christina began to believe she would, within a few years, be part of the statistic of girls who never made it to womanhood. She worked herself into a panic writing poems, obsessing over her failings of temperament and heart, and not having enough time to prepare herself for eternity. She might have given a passing thought to what she would miss of marriage and motherhood or the regret or relief of neither being granted her. Ambition to display her cleverness worried her more, not because she might never have a chance to fulfill it, but that she wanted to. So many things needed correcting before she was short-lived. For instance, she liked to hear her verses praised, but should not seek congratulations. Philippians 2:3: *Do nothing from rivalry or conceit, but in humility count others more significant than yourselves.* Did she think too much of herself? She wasn't very tolerant of other people, too little time being left to spend irritated or, worse, bored by them. And what about her resistance to what was required of her? She was far too rebellious, and when she was, or, at least, tried to be, obedient, often was resentfully so.

You wouldn't last a week as a governess, Maria wrote to her, more to confess than accuse. *I'm surprised I have.*

"I think you've chosen illness over doing anything but poetry." Gabriel knew her so well.

"Who would want to be ill?" Christina countered, while thinking how not being robust offered immunity from responsibilities, prospects, and, especially, needlework.

"Doctor Hare called it hysteria." William shook himself as though to ward off the condition.

"Don't worry." Christina could still come up with a witty retort. "It's only catching to girls."

Dr. Hare would be her regular physician for years. She decided she didn't like him once she found out he told Mama and Papa she was out of her mind. They didn't seem to believe him. She was very much in her mind: examining it, purging it, perfecting it, aligning it to her spirit moved by intensifying faith from disorder to discipline. It wasn't religious mania but spiritual sanity. Dr. Hare noted she appeared listless, at barely fifteen looking twenty, her brunette hair and complexion lacking luster, although her conformation was good. His reference to her body's development seemed to imply that, despite sensations of choking and chest pains, she wasn't on a premature march towards death.

Gabriel did irreverent sketches of Dr. Hare in caricature of the animal that named him. Despite her disputes with some of the doctor's conclusions, Christina became attached to his treatment of her being ill-prepared for life as it was supposed to be waiting for her. Other girls would be looking forward to expectant introductions and dizzying dinners and dances, wearing lovely clothes and their hair in silly, stylish ways to make them prettier than their futures needed them to be. Aunt Charlotte was able to provide Christina with second-hand dresses finer than family funds allowed for the purchase of new ones. Even with altering, they would never fit her. Like her mother and sister, by some perversion of conscience, Christina preferred to appear colorless, unadorned, white lace barely showing at her collar and cuffs, footwear sensible and sturdy.

She was only ever tempted to finery by Lady Isabella Howard's generosity. One of the many daughters of the Earl of Wicklow, she had been Aunt Charlotte's pupil, the younger Christina charmed by the loveliness of her character after one brief meeting. Aunt Charlotte's wish to get Christina out and about arranged the visit to a tall, sparkling-white, pillared house the Howard family lived in when the House of Lords was in session. Isabella insisted Christina choose any or all of the dresses displayed on the deep mattress of her bed. The softness of Isabella's voice and touch of her arm, the sincerity of her intention, and the generosity in her blue eyes made it impossible to refuse.

"Just one." Christina satisfied her conscience, too. "I couldn't possibly ever need more."

"You are more likely to go somewhere than you think."

Christina remained adamant that a single dress would do.

"Well, then this one, seeming the simplest, certainly the subtlest in styling and trimming, its ruching very fine. Without a doubt the sweetest. I have worn it as day and night wear, the latter to a friendly informal supper or recital or ... if for somewhere like the opera, it can be fancied up."

Christina never wore it. At first there wasn't any occasion for the color of a cloudless summer sky, rustle of satin, and trembling of tassels in her uneventful life. Then there was no life left for Isabella. Aunt Charlotte's letter said the eighteen-year-old's *decline was sudden and swift, an infection of some sort that showed no mercy, not even for youth and beauty.* Before she folded and put the dress away, Christina appreciated it as Isabella had, with its skirt sprayed out and long sleeves crossed upon the point of its bodice. She thought about her own decline, inevitable and unenergetic, giving her more time to prepare for its outcome, which she needed as much as the noble Isabella had not. Surely the dearly departed had never acted spoiled or willful, resorted to tantrums, or tried to manipulate others with her tears. Isabella appeared to have been the epitome of goodness, her soul spotless, her spirit pure; there was nothing to make waves on her way to Heaven's shores. Christina, in a leaky boat on troubled waters, envied Isabella's easier escape to the land of sure repose.

Calmly there she lay. All pain had left her; and the sun's last ray shone through upon her, warming into red.

At least Christina's envy was elegiac, but, nevertheless, another sin to make amends for. At the rate she was seeking absolution only to create the need for more, she feared she must live longer than her innocence could survive.

***

Morbidity and melodrama were a poet's best companion. That was what Bryon and Shelley told Christina in leather-bound hauntings. Around the same time Christina buried a mouse in a grave that worms showed no respect for, her old-soul sister Maria decided the point of poetry by writing an epitaph for a song-singing thrush who may have eaten too many snails. Gothic tales had long been dramatizing and darkening Christina's imagination. She kept less company with books than the rest of her family, even managing to postpone plunging her fragile sensitivities into Dante until she was eighteen. Her early reading was typical for her age: *Robinson Crusoe, The Arabian Nights, Ivanhoe,* a Shakespearian play now and then, preferably not the history ones, and romances by Anne Radcliffe, especially the exotic, supernatural, brooding, terrorizing *Mysteries of Udolpho,* and, of course, *The Italian.* Maturin, the Irish Huguenot, gave Christina a favorite Faustian-like novel, *Melmoth the Wanderer,* and out of one of William's school books, she copied a magnificent eulogizing of Princess Charlotte of Wales who at twenty-one died during childbirth. *Life is full of death; the steps of the living cannot press the earth without disturbing the ashes of the dead – we walk upon our ancestors – the globe itself is one vast churchyard.*

It wasn't a certain kind of reading that caused her world of light to shape into something shadowy. More than one medical opinion mentioned that personality changes were often found in girls who were both overly emotional and intellectual. Or was it a certain situation, as common as it wasn't? She couldn't tell whether she was to blame or just shouldn't think of it, something not clearly remembered she could never forget.

Papa wasn't well, and neither was she; being left behind and confined together strained, altered, and confused their relationship. It was said Christina was growing into looking like her mother, so in his wife's constant absence and considering his waning sight and position as patriarch, a daughter might dutifully go beyond helping him sort and proof his papers and reading his writing back to him.

"Your voice is truly Rossetti," he declared. "Intensely musical."

"But you know I can't sing, Papa."

"I know what I hear," he said, not for the first time indicating that his ears had become his eyes. "Your music is the written word. Your genius, too."

She was surprised by his praise, not heard for so many years, and spontaneously stroked his arm. He, in turn, made a mistake himself, an unnatural one, which she apologetically corrected, but it was too late to preserve the papa who spoiled her by delighting her innocence rather than taking it away.

Suddenly she couldn't look him in the eyes, afraid she would see his shame or, worse, that he had none. There was silence between them, even when they spoke to one another. She understood little of what had happened, except it was shocking. She might want to but couldn't avoid him, being alone with him. There was only one servant for cooking, cleaning, and laundry, Christina required to make sure her father got his meals and medicine. Most mornings she had to help him down the stairs and into the parlor. Within a few hours, struggling with reading and writing and being forgotten, he was more occupied with frustration, self-pity, a worsening temper, and, to Christina's relief, sleep. He insisted the curtains were closed so day was night and the house was even more of "a tomb," as Gabriel put it. Except for a few hours in his bed, a meal, and arguments with his father that were disrespectful but understandable, her eldest brother escaped into his excitement for life. Even William's civilly employed existence offered him a way out of what had become a graveyard for Papa's disappointed past and present and his youngest daughter's life.

When Dr. Hare was summoned yet again, there was no longer talk of amenorrhea or hysteria, but, instead, a suggestion regarding Christina's health of body and mind that gave her reason to almost like him. She must go to the seaside, take long walks on its beach, collect souvenirs, build a sandcastle, even do some bathing, although she "mustn't get her hair wet or linger long in her costume afterwards."

"Please, Mama. I long to see the sea ...." *before I die*, she only thought.

"Oh, dear. You can't go alone. I can't accompany you and who will be at home during the day for your papa?"

It was decided that Aunt Charlotte, given leave from her duties to the Marchioness of Bath, would accompany Christina to Folkestone. On the morning they were to set off, Aunt Margaret, shrugging and frowning and carrying a small satchel of clothing and a large bag of knitting, arrived to stay with her brother-in-law.

"'Where's Christina? Where's my pretty genius? Why has she abandoned me and left me with this shrew?'" Aunt Margaret reported him shouting. Or "'She's never coming back. I know it. She is disgusted by me as I am by myself.'"

"With good reason, I told him," Aunt Margaret went on without knowing what the reason really was. "Your father is disgruntled, unkempt, and otherwise offensive, hardly the company a young woman should be keeping."

Christina surprised herself by wanting to contradict her aunt, at least express a little sympathy for Papa's distressing descent into old age. It must have been that a few weeks away and the restorative power of the sea had made forgiveness more possible.

Late August on the coast of Kent was oppressively hot. For Christina it was a fresh chance to burn bright again. She couldn't get enough of the sun's shining, not tempted to join the crowds under gaily colored canopies hung between light poles. She didn't even take a parasol as she walked the strand or waded in rockpools and the incoming tide. She needed her hands free to investigate miracles of loveliness the sea offered. She found shells quaintly curved, spotted, and spiked, more rarely storm-stranded starfish, sea horses, and anemones, and, on shingled stretches, she was spoiled for choice of differently shaped, sized, and colored pebbles. A basket borrowed from the landlady of the rooming house Mama had chosen in consideration of cost but Aunt Charlotte thought "plebeian and shabby," held enough of them, along with shells and samples of seaweed, for the aquarium Christina decided she must have at home. She would enlist Gabriel's support, certain he would be for it.

Towards the end of the holiday there were some days shut out from heaven by heavy clouds, the sea moaning and fretting against the shore. It was hard to tell whether the mist came off its foam, from the overcast sky, or her once again darkening thoughts.

Why did she always go from gladness to gloom? The day she arrived the view of the channel was clear and calm, swallows swirling, dipping, and squealing with a sense of freedom and fun. The morning before her departure, they were silently, somberly flying away from the pier, because of the fog soon out of sight over the sea that separated England from France and churned up the divergent parts of herself. Aunt Charlotte calling was the vocal reminder that her sabbatical from a dreary, chilly existence was short-lived, although she harbored a little hope, which, for the time being, none but her muse could hear: *Come again, come again, come back to me, bringing the summer and bringing the sun.*

***

Returning to reality was a little better than expected. Mama was glad to see some color in Christina's cheeks and a lightness to her step. Maria was home for a few days and happy to be the older and wiser sister. William was eager to compare the *bout rimés* he and Christina had done together while apart. Gabriel was in favor of an aquarium, or, as he humored her further, "a pond in the parlor."

She began to fear his interest would wane, for it took months to find one that had a cover and they could afford. Finally, he and William clumsily and, to Mama's dismay, profanely carried it into the house. Cast iron heavy, its mismatched Grecian pillared frame and cabriole-legged stand needed cleaning and painting, but its glass was intact. Christina's Folkestone aquatic collection of goldfish and koi fish were added to its cool water and aesthetic appeal, making a pleasant distraction, if not enough of one, through more interminable days of caring and not caring for her nearly blind and toothless, cantankerous, repentant father.

> *Tell me not there is no skill*
> *That can bind the breaking heart,*
> *That can smooth the bitter smart,*
> *When we find ourselves betrayed,*
> *When we find ourselves forsaken,*
> *By those for whom we would have laid*
> *Our young lives down …*

PART TWO

Her eyes were like some fire-enshrining gem,
Were stately like the stars, and yet were tender;
Her figure charmed me like a windy stem
Quivering and drooped and slender.
~ from *House to Home* by Christina Rossetti

CHAPTER SEVEN

Christina sat at the high narrow desk by the front parlor window, wintry and candle light mingling while she proofed for Papa in between writing for herself. As was often the case, she tried to ignore his mutterings, less successfully his dribbling ink because he forgot to use the pen wipers she kept him in supply of. Before cleaning up the mess he had made of more than his fingers, she scribbled a few lines about compassion and imagining the rug beneath her feet was the Brussels-weave Mama had always wanted.

"I'm sorry, dear. The sooner I'm dead, the better."

"Don't say such a thing." She was weary of the repetitiveness of the exchange.

A corked condiment bottle containing lemon juice, as suggested by their Irish servant girl Betsey, was kept inside Christina's desk along with a rag that had attempted to erase ink splashes too many times already. She used it anyway, rubbing Papa's latest mishap into faint stains that matched many others on the carpet.

There was a knock at the door.

"Yes. He's at home, sir."

The man Betsey brought to the parlor was tall, his face flushed, eyebrows bushy, and chin square, his jacket, cravat, waistcoat, and trousers artistically mismatched and well-worn. He seemed expectant, then confused, his searching, sapphire gaze scanning the room. He removed his green velvet feathered hat, implying his impression of Christina with a broad smile and slight bow. She felt, and probably appeared, cross because she was unprepared to greet anyone she didn't know.

Christina lowered her face and hurried back to her desk.

"I've come to see the Art Catholic." The visitor's voice revealed he was Scottish.

"Who?" Papa grumbled.

Christina could have told her father what he didn't know. She had helped collect some of Gabriel's poems under the title *Songs of the Art Catholic* for strategic distribution to various influencers.

"The bonny maid said Gabriel Rossetti was here."

"Stupid, sluttish girl."

Christina pretended she hadn't heard.

The visitor nodded. "Ah. I see her mistake. You, sir, are the elder."

"The one much nearer death."

"As any of us may be."

"And you are?"

"William Bell Scott."

"Does Gabriel owe you money?"

"He sent me some poems and, being in London, I thought to satisfy my curiosity about him."

Papa, his peaked cap pulled low on his brow, had barely looked up from the large manuscript book opened on the table beside the high-backed, winged armchair he wasn't about to give up. Instead, with a limp gesture, he offered Mr. Bell Scott another, smaller and harder, seat too near the fire.

"What a welcoming blaze." Their visitor tried to appreciate.

Christina hoped her profile didn't reveal she struggled to ignore him. She sensed he was curious about her, too. The Christina of old would have returned his interest, at least asking where he was from and what he did. The young woman he encountered didn't have to for she had addressed those hopeful packages of Gabriel's poems, specifically one to Newcastle-Upon-Tyne and the principal of the government school of art there.

"Christina, do you know where your brother pretends to work?"

She immediately began shuffling through the desk drawer for a scrap of paper.

The Scotsman walked over to pick up her pen that had fallen to the floor, the brightness of his eyes begging her to smile. She didn't; she couldn't. "So, *Signore Rossetti*, who does your son paint with?"

"William Holman Hunt."

Mr. Bell Scott's hand was eager for the address Christina had written down. He squinted as he read *Cleveland Street. Number 47. Near Fitzroy Square, a dreary house to the south-west corner of Howland Street, just before the workhouse.* "How quickly you write. Yet neatly. Seems like you've been there. The studio, I mean."

She shook her head. Gabriel had described it to her.

"I thought you would've posed for the Art Catholic. He would be foolish not to use the perfection of your discontent."

If Mr. Bell Scott never spoke to her again, Christina would have been left in no doubt he was a friend for life.

"The man is superb," the next day Gabriel agreed with her impression. "He auspiciously entered our evening, gave us the pleasure of a few hours in his company, and, after he was gone, many more realizing how smitten we were." Returned to Charlotte Street for breakfast, Gabriel was disheveled and glassy-eyed, with a worrisome cough.

"Aren't you glad you wrote to him?"

"It was you who doubted I should. Certainly, not so 'gushingly.'

Well, Chrissy, it seems my gushing over his *The Year of the World* was exactly what his own doubts needed, a shameful amount of others' indifference corrected by how I read it in one sitting and was lit up by it."

"I wish you had been here, so his visit was less awkward."

"Yes. He mentioned he was sorry to have intruded upon you and Papa. He felt wished away as soon as he appeared, you were both so intent in your solitude."

"Oh, dear."

"You might have said you also read *The Year of the World*."

"But I haven't."

"I've told you enough about it. Oh, I know, you've grown out of little white lying. Then you should have shown him your *Verses*."

"Oh, no."

"Of course, Papa prevented any sociability — worse, any spontaneity. Well, Scott is in London a few more days, so I'll take him a copy."

Christina was about to say that, six months after its limited printing, there wasn't one to give him, but Gabriel correctly assumed Mama had put a few aside.

Nonno had printed enough of her little poetry volume for Christina to worry and hope who might receive them. Over a few weeks of preparation the previous summer, his visits to Charlotte Street increased, so he could help decide which pieces to include, and suggest adjustments to them, initiating her realization that editing was as tedious as mending socks. Once she started going through the notebooks Maria had kept up with, Christina was surprised how many poems she had written. And such a variety, from the simple cadence and sentimental reflections of the beginner to the influence and even imitation of what she was reading, to devotional reflections that pleased Mama, to the catharsis they offered when dark moods, illness, and unspeakable circumstances threatened to bury her.

Writing, which, eventually, even Dr. Hare prescribed, was the best medicine for her. She felt stronger seeing her poetry in print, even if *Nonno's* partiality and possession of a press made such an achievement possible. A clever way with words would never make her as useful as dutiful Maria and William, and, with deference to her dear mother, Christina must not let pride take precedence over humility. Yet even Mama wanted her to celebrate, especially as it was her own father who showed such belief and pride in her youngest.

As her maternal grandfather, I may be excused for desiring to retain these early spontaneous efforts in a permanent form, and for having silenced the objections urged by her modest diffidence, and persuaded her to allow me to print them for my own gratification ….

Years later, affection pristinely preserving a copy of her first *Verses*, Christina still found encouragement in her grandfather's prefix to the reader—and writer.

Her name might not have been Polidori, but her heart was owned by Tuscan warmth, austerity, and loyalty, by a man who always had time and counsel for a willful child, woeful girl, and watchful young woman. The courtship of her deepest desires and devotion was completed when a bouquet of roses and *canzonetta–Queste rose ch'io ti domo symbol sono nel diverso lo colore del tuo spirit e del tuo core*–marked the day her poetry went to press for the first time.

Christina accredited any praise to the courtesy of family and friends. They were all so kind and forgiving of her trembling attempts at sonnets, ballads, even hymns. Impartial critics wouldn't have overlooked her thievery from the Bible, stories of the saints, and folk tales, and her obsession with mimicking characters and circumstances from novelists like Maturin and Lady Georgina Fullerton. She could hardly trust the judgment, as Gabriel teased, "of those who have been too much honored by the gift" of her book.

She didn't think she wanted to publish for money, comparison and criticism the price she would pay. "Perfection is not possible, but improvement always is," was one of Mama's favorite sayings. It was sagacious advice Christina could never argue with, but often, especially in those early years, wasn't sure mattered when she wrote to shelter, not showcase, her musings.

The Rossetti sacrificial lamb, William, offered some wisdom of his own. "So here you are. Not sent off to be a governess but left behind to be a poet; surely a better way to make a few bob."

"It seems like trying to sell one's soul."

"Selling the chance for others to discover their own."

Christina thought it presumptuous to believe stringing words together could have such an effect. At the same time, being misplaced and miserable stirred ambition in her, enough to write with the passing thought of future publication in *Blackwell's, Macmillan's,* or *The Athenaeum.*

***

The summer of 1847 not only brought Christina's poetry out of safekeeping, but also her body out of London for another seaside holiday, this time to Herne Bay with her mother and father. There she was subjected to the company of girls nearly her own age. Anna Mary was a relative some twice or thrice removed, while Christina met the

Newton sisters at the local church. Unsociably but more significant was the rediscovery of how a sea and its sky could make her limitless, too. She often left her acquaintances to their promenading and pleasure-seeking in donkey or goat cart rides, gypsy fortunes, sticky buns, people-watching, and giggling spells. She did join them once to ride the wing-propelled Neptune's car to the far end of the wooden pier to see steamboats coming or going in the Thames Estuary. Otherwise, Christina spent hours by herself, not drawn inward and downcast as she was at home, but experiencing life freely, unquestionably, irrepressibly, like the sea winds, waves, and birds. Also magically, even mythically, poetically, as rosy shells grew wings and starfish sparkled with jewels, seaweed was made of satin and pebbles gold and ivory.

It's not the seaside you need, Gabriel wrote to her the following summer when Brighton was Christina's coastal destination to aid her recovery from bronchitis. *Not sea air or baptism by sea water. But, instead, to resort*—she enjoyed his play on words if not his having mostly his own interests in mind—*to the germ of an idea for a sister-and-brotherhood beyond what blood has given us.*

It was tempting to immediately leave rainy, boring, snobbish Brighton, although not Christina's decision to make and contrary to how desperate she had been to escape London and Papa who, this time, stayed behind to sit for a portrait Gabriel had been commissioned to do of him. There was something stirring in her eldest brother's circle, something William, when he came down for a weekend, only hinted at.

If *bouts-rimés* had occupied his thoughts as much as they filled the time he was there, he might have played more competently.

"Hardly fair," William lightly chided Christina winning contest after contest. "You feel, see, hear, and breathe poetry. This mere civil servant isn't even good at making a game of it."

Christina hated when William dismissed his abilities and ambitions, yet, like all the family, she relied on him doing so. William's devotion was more practical than passionate, ideal when a situation required a level head to lead the heart. In stark contrast, Gabriel loved with words and winks, flamboyant gestures and fantastic promises, smiles that blinded and genius that beguiled, everything, anything to keep others devoted to but not dependent on him.

"Can't you speak to your brother when you get back?" Mama asked of William. "I'll be here another week, at least, and Papa reports that Gabriel continues to procrastinate on the portrait. His godfather has been patient but is beginning to wonder if it will ever be done."

"I've tried, especially to the point that ten pounds was paid in advance to him. Gabriel merely says he has to go to Gravesend to see a friend, or here or there for this or that. He insists he will begin any day."

Mama read from Papa's latest letter, "Gabriel doing my portrait for Mr. Lyell is as certain as my traveling to the moon." She shook her head wearily. "Your papa won't confront him. He's afraid insults will come back."

William exchanged glances with Christina, so she assumed he was also thinking their brother's impossible behavior was of Papa's making. Who among family and friends couldn't own some of the blame for indulging and excusing Gabriel?

"Well, Mama, you may be the only one who can nudge his conscience and convince him of his obligation."

"And you, William, are the most like me in this family. So—oh, what's wrong, dear?"

It was a pain like no other, stabbing Christina's right cheek and eye. She didn't cry out, gurgling as she struggled to breathe, leaning her head to one side and supporting it with the flat of her hand. By the time Mama stroked her back and William helped her stand and move from the card table to the chintz sofa that was prettier than it was practical, whatever ailed her eased enough for there to be more discomfort in the fuss she had caused.

CHAPTER EIGHT

Charles Bagot Cayley was one of the few private students Papa received during the relentless decline of his eyesight and health. Christina wished she could remember the day, hour, moment Charles first arrived. Unlike Mr. Scott, he was expected, which was why she saw him from the end of the hallway or the top of the stairs and stayed out of the parlor until he was gone. The weather, time of day, and even year had slipped away because in the context of her life then it hadn't been notable.

She never thought of herself as young and foolish, but overlooking Charles, even once she recognized he was—borrowing William's impression—"a shy, unworldly intellectual with a cerebral sense of humor" much like herself, was proof she had been. Fortunately, providence kept him around while she succumbed to longings that fed her poetry better than her soul and tricked her heart.

At seventeen, it was Gabriel's influence, and not just in the titles and dispatch of two of her poems to *The Athenaeum,* that brought her confidence and confusion to Number Seven Cleveland Street.

It wasn't far from home, yet a world away from living soberly and safely. Walking a few blocks north on Charlotte Street, turning left on Howland Street, Christina and her mother, arm in arm tighter and tighter, found the house where and as Gabriel had warned they would. In a neighborhood sliding into sordid, degraded by pawnbrokers, penny barbers, rag and bone yards, and loitering figures they dare not acknowledge, they smelled sewage, acrid smoke, and dampened timber. They heard words that were vulgar and, worse, blasphemous. As promised, the Strand Union Workhouse was almost on the doorstep of the lodgings Gabriel shared with William Holman Hunt for his artist's life and livelihood.

They considered turning around.

"But Gabriel expects us, is counting on us." Christina was surprised and relieved that Mama changed her mind.

Gabriel had already worked on the drawing of the painting they were to sit for. The previous August, while still pretending to reside in his father's house, he had often stayed up from midnight to past dawn, using a crow-quill pen, lightly and heavily, to reveal his independent thought and style, and ability to appreciate ordinary details in an extraordinary way.

Those preliminary sketches didn't prepare his mother and youngest sister for the den of distempered maroon they stepped into a few months later. Barely lit stairs, mustiness more obvious as they climbed them, the second floor also creaking, and narrow, dark quarters beyond a half-open door hardly offered the welcome they expected.

They stood just inside the doorway, noticing Gabriel sprawled on a raggedy day bed under the room's only and east-facing window. Mama wondered out loud if they had the wrong time or even day. Christina was certain they hadn't.

"Gabriel, you have company," bellowed behind them. Christina jumped into a turn towards the pale-eyed and -skinned, chestnut-haired Mr. Hunt, whom she knew from his few visits to Charlotte Street.

"What?" Gabriel opened his eyes, winced, and swung an arm across them.

"He hasn't been drinking? It's like poison to him."

"Oh, no, Mrs. Rossetti. Burning the candle, for which you can blame me. Although he never refuses to stay up all night for one reason or other, usually working, or just to talk and smoke."

"Or a moonlit row on the river?" Christina couldn't resist revealing she was sometimes Gabriel's confidant.

"It wasn't the first for me and I doubt the last for him. Being a night owl is a rule of the brotherhood. Only waived for that meek little chap Collinson, who needs his beauty sleep."

"What are you muttering about, Hunt?" Gabriel was standing and swaying. "Make yourself useful. Stoke up the stove. Help me set the scene. My Saint Anne and Mary V are here, and I have a masterpiece to make."

It might have seemed little was accomplished that first visit, scenery, props, and people arranged and rearranged as if staging a play, which, after all was a great deal in bringing a story and themes, characters, their thoughts and emotions alive. Far from being impatient, Christina was exhilarated by helping to drape fabrics, string up curtains for framing and a backdrop, pile books, and situate chairs.

"I'm surprised you're not depicting Saint Anne teaching young Mary to read." Mama paused in her more and more frustrated attempt to tidy the flat.

Mr. Hunt successfully blocked her from interfering with his easel, small round table with pallet and paint box, and whatever else cluttered his working area.

"I know. That's how it's been done in the past by Ruebens, Murillo, Tiepolo, Jouvenet, and others, as I see it, symbolically. By instead portraying her instructing Mary in embroidery, I will create a more probable scene, and one less commonplace."

Christina waited almost breathlessly for Mama's response, knowing how much her approval meant to Gabriel, even once he had moved out from under her wing. "Truth in nature," Christina spoke before one or the other or both decided what to say. "So, I've heard, is the Brotherhood's objective."

"Yes, we're a league of sincerity." Gabriel's shoulders relaxed and his smile prompted his mother's.

How could Francis Polidori Rossetti be anything but pleased with his depiction of a mother guiding her daughter's stitchery for a divine purpose to come? How could she not be proud her storms were settling into a picture of calm to represent them more than any distress they ever experienced or caused?

"And what will the embroidery be? I couldn't tell from the drawing."

Christina had asked the same question of Gabriel. "What else, Mama, but the lily held by the child-angel."

"Of course. Such a lovely idea. Hopefully, not spoiled by my participation." Mama must have been happy; she was showing a playfulness rarely seen since Papa had been sick. "Feel free, Gabriel Charles, to be as kind to my appearance as time hasn't been."

"*Mia carissima mamma*, your grace is my inspiration."

Mama shook her head, then stepped closer, hooked his arm and stroked it. "I suppose I can settle for that."

Gabriel's sketching had already designed the setting and costumes. He was especially resolute in its colors of "earthy reds, greens, browns, and gold, with white for the lily, angel, and dove, pale blue for Saint Joachim reaching for a deeper splash of that color in the vine he was pruning, and fading gray for young Mary."

"Why not white for her, too? For her innocence."

"Because, Chrissy, her true purity is yet to come."

Mama sighed and crossed her hands over her heart, moving to sit on the daybed Gabriel had been sleeping on when they arrived.

"'Until the end be full, the Holy One abides without. She soon shall have achieved her perfect purity: yea, God the Lord shall soon vouchsafe His Son to be her Son.'"

"Mama hears the makings of her son's salvation." Christina took her place in the chair before the imaginary embroidery frame. "I, of a sonnet."

"From the artist who would be a poet."

"You can be—are—both."

"Which comes first, the chicken or the egg?"

"I think words suggest the pictures."

"Then I will have everyone else think the opposite. Promise you won't tell."

***

On the second visit, a few days later, Christina didn't notice the shadiness and shabbiness of the location and look of Gabriel's lodging and studio. Mama's hand held hers rather than the other way around. The ascent into a holy scene where Christina would inspire the painting of purity felt like the best thing she had ever done. The light from the east—why Gabriel wanted them there early in the morning— miraculously broke through the rain and fog intent on spoiling that October. This time everything was ready for Christina to pose at the needlework frame Gabriel had convinced Aunt Eliza to part with for a few days, which he counted over weeks. No sooner Christina had, as she thought, perfected her leaning, her brother decided he wanted his Mary to sit upright, "in duty circumspect," to the attention of her actual and pretend mother, who was stiffly seated adjacent to her.

Gabriel came over and delicately adjusted their hand positions to be close but not touching. "There must be no doubt you are pious, humble, devoted to, and yet distinct from, each other."

"There won't be, son, if you portray us as we are."

He had requested his sister wear a modest dress, no bright colors, not black or gray, and with very little lace or other adornment. Christina had one she thought would do: beige, like the beach where she had last worn it. The summer sun had faded it, and splashing algae had stained it, its removable collar no longer crisp or undoubtedly white. He loosened her hair and, after putting the pins in his pocket, pushed it behind her shoulders "so it might seem longer than it is." Fiddling with the folds of her skirt, he ordered her not to move from how he had "sculpted" her, asking the same of Mama, whose favorite shawl functioned as a wimple, while a large, musty blanket served as a mantle.

"Don't close your eyes, Mama," Gabriel gave yet another command.

"I thought it might be appropriate to pray."

"Not in the Art Catholic's church."

"May we blink?" Christina hoped she might ease the seriousness that overcame Gabriel once he was behind his easel. His refusal to humor her made her say rather harshly, "May we even breathe?"

He grunted and, when he dropped his brush, swore.

"At least until he makes you immortal," quipped Mr. Hunt from his own creative corner of the League of Sincerity.

"Keep still. And quiet. I don't want to make a muff of this."

Christina saw Mama's frown and wanted to scold Gabriel for disrespecting her. She was dissuaded by a pat on her arm.

"Not many of us are like Millais," Mr. Hunt ignored Gabriel's demand, "able to chat away while painting, hardly needing to concentrate, such technical brilliance, such confidence—"

"Arrogance," Gabriel mumbled.

Mr. Hunt put up his hands in surrender and within ten minutes thought of an excuse for going out.

Christina knew Gabriel bristled at Hunt mentioning Mr. Millais' skill because of lack of belief in his own, despite his outward bravado and calling his hand "cunning" as it drew and painted "delectable images from deep within."

Taking a cue from her mother, Christina decided it was worth putting up with Gabriel's irritability, along with the discomfort of sitting in one position for hours, her cramping stomach, parched mouth, heavy eyelids, and headaches that lasted for days. All was endured for the cause of encouraging Gabriel's enthusiasm for artistic truth, withholding nothing of his heart or vulnerability. Of course, she was also self-serving, staying as close to him as she could, living vicariously through him so she could explore her contradictions, unconventional urges, and the more audacious aspects of her own creative instincts.

She would never know for certain whether Gabriel was sincere or not but his suggestion that she be admitted into his secret society threw her into conflict between her need for self-expression and self-control. She never wanted to be entirely defined by her gender, yet, if only to realize Mama's relief, accepted she must act appropriately to it. As time went on, she rarely wondered about the what-ifs had she been male. At seventeen, she was bound to be teased by them.

Gabriel's artistic comrades objecting to her officially identifying herself with their challenge to the art and literary establishment—as, he assured, they would any woman—was a blessing only God in his corrective wisdom could bestow.

"I told them I never meant for you to attend meetings," Gabriel was unconvincing in his retraction. "Only that, at our get togethers, I would read your poetry out loud."

Those gatherings hadn't been altogether denied her, at least not in how they began when they were held in the dingy, damp back bedroom on the third floor of 50 Charlotte Street. A raucous entrance by artists Holman Hunt, John Millais, George Stephens, and sculptor Thomas Woolner was hardly quietened by Gabriel, who never doubted his family needed livening up. The fervent band of young men might look into the parlor, which seemed to please Papa, who would have followed them upstairs if Mama hadn't objected. Christina tried to balance herself between being glad to see Gabriel's friends and worrying they might do him more harm than good. She was largely ignored, possibly because they had rejected her inclusion in their association. Maria, if she was home, at most offered a nod before dropping her attention to her writing or book.

There was one more painter in the group who had little to say, or, if anything, softly, hesitantly. He was courteous but familiar to the Rossetti women, his attendance at Christ Church on Sundays, up until recently, a common occurrence. While the others quickly and noisily flew in and away, James Collinson perched himself on one leg and then the other, lingering long enough to make Christina wonder if he was more interesting than at first he appeared.

CHAPTER NINE

It would have to be a long engagement. Gabriel preferred it not be. "Think again, Chrissy. The bookseller's son is perfect for you. *Charity Boy's Debut* was exhibited at the R.A. well ahead of anything done by the rest of us. He's a painter of great promise. And, after all, already brethren to Will and me."

Gabriel knew the reason for Christina's initial refusal, the one she spoke about. "Anglo-Catholic, Roman-Catholic, Art-Catholic. What does it matter?"

During many sittings for *The Education of Mary Virgin*, Gabriel made a point of crediting James Collinson's poem *The Child Jesus* as its inspiration. Christina's path crossed again with this unlikely disciple of Gabriel's, as she suspected, by design, not accident, in the Cleveland Street studio. Gabriel invited Christina to help him decide on the right model for the child-angel. Mama only allowed her to return on a Saturday when William could accompany her. They stepped around half a dozen urchins in the second floor hallway, Mr. Hunt trying to keep them physically and behaviorally in line. He explained they had been brought over from the workhouse.

Mr. Collinson was lurking in a corner of the studio, so Christina could barely see him. Like Mr. Scott, she was curious about him because he was about her, but different from the Scotsman, she didn't expect to be for long. While the workhouse children were brought in, Christina sat in the center of the settee below the east window, spreading her skirt left and right, trying not to look towards the arguably handsome "dormouse" in the shadows. That she thought of the nickname given Mr. Collinson by one or other of the Brotherhood meant she was unsuccessful in ignoring him. She convinced herself it was because she knew dormice were nocturnal, which made the comparison of him to one ridiculous.

Even Gabriel grew frustrated by James Collinson's inability to stay awake when he and his cohorts loved to philosophize and prowl. "I sometimes wonder he's an artist. There's nothing impulsive or daring about him," he prefaced his telling of how, after a meeting at the Cleveland Street studio, the members decided it was a perfect night for a walk in the country, at least as Regent's Park imitated. "Collinson insisted he must go home to bed. I told him he'd had enough sleep, more than was beneficial to him. As if I had persuaded him, he said he just needed to change his boots. When we got to his house, we knocked and knocked until finally, because we were disturbing the neighbors, he showed himself at a second story window, which he opened to tell us we had gotten him out of bed and he was going back to it."

Christina was rarely out after dark and hardly dared consider what wandering the city beyond sunset, let alone midnight, was like.

One by one, the youngsters failed to be short, thin, patient, or angelic enough.

"Damn it, girl. Stand straight. And you're pigeon-toed, your hair a rat's nest."

Gabriel's face reddened and his eyes enlarged as he violently waved his arms and shouted insults at the not more than seven- or eight-year-old girl who had come into the studio at the end of his patience. She began to cry and look for somewhere safe.

"It's all right, darling." Christina embraced her and was reminded of frogs put out to dry and floating belly up. "My brother is wicked sometimes. As my dear *Nonno* advised, better you forget and smile than remember and be sad."

"*Nonno*?"

"My grandfather."

"I got no one, Miss."

It was as Christina was wiping the little girl's eyes and even letting her blow her nose on the soft hanky, one she had less than delicately embroidered with budding violets, that she realized Mr. Collinson was standing a few feet away.

"Maybe, Miss, I can do that."

"What's that, darling?"

"Not remember, not be sad."

"Oh, darling. I hope so."

"Damn," Gabriel's voice boomed.

"You're scaring her again." Collinson might have impressed Christina if he hadn't immediately lost his courage.

"Which proves she's not the child I need." Gabriel turned back to William and Mr. Hunt. "What a waste of an afternoon. I'll go with Wooler's niece after all. She's gawky, but, at least, has posed before, and more than once in a while washes her face and brushes her hair."

William saw what Christina knew, that the girl needed to get out of there as soon as possible. The only place she had to go was hardly where Christina wanted to take her, but she tightly held the girl's hand as they followed the line of other children William was leading across Cleveland Street to the workhouse. Collinson was at the very end of the procession.

"No, no, I'll see them in." Her brother insisted Christina and Collinson wait outside the prisonous building's grimy front walls. "I won't be long. They'll just want to know we haven't stolen any."

William couldn't smile at his own joke.

"Goodbye, Miss."

"I'll come visit you." Christina couldn't smile, either.

"No, you won't, Miss."

"How kind you are," Mr. Collinson said when it was just the two of them.

"Kind? Not kind. Useless."

"You don't realize—"

"What? What should I realize?" She immediately regretted her snarling.

He bowed his head and folded his hands, otherwise not moving.

"I'm sorry. Seeing a child swallowed up by this monster," she waved her hands high at each of the square-windowed wings of the workhouse, "leaves me wondering what good I can ever do."

The broken pavement in front of the workhouse gate presented a decent distance between them until Mr. Collinson crossed it. She saw him coming as, up until that moment, she hadn't. Suddenly, he was a speculator, or what some would call a suitor, a man of faith and not only in the religious sense as he trespassed into her likely brief life and assumed he was going to be welcome.

She was too shocked to refuse him before William appeared, but there had been time for the embarrassment of Collinson reaching for her hand which surprise allowed to tremble and fall into his. She heard what he said and didn't say, simultaneously feeling flattered and framed, his being "enticed" by her "loveliness" and "generous heart" and "devotional spirit" stealing her good sense and humility. Somehow, she allowed him to set her up as accessory to a crime, leading to a proposition that stirred excitement but, also, fear of the trouble it could bring.

"You can't let him think you're as much as engaged," William told her on the way home.

"I didn't say yes. I didn't say anything."

"Which means you didn't say no."

She didn't want to jump to any conclusion. She wasn't eighteen, not yet desperate to leave her family, seek a stranger's devotion, have her own home, children, or even, with a long engagement, to settle her future on such goals. At the same time, a courtship, especially if its culmination was a way off, might be distracting, even fun, although not if Mr. Collinson was as lachrymose as Mr. Hunt branded him.

Gabriel admitted James Collinson was more on the serious side than the rest of them. "Not without hope of conversion to a cheerier doctrine. At least, Chrissy, you might give him a reason to stay awake."

Her oldest brother made her blush, but also wonder what power a woman might have. Before that day at the Cleveland Street studio, hardly a nod, never a word had passed between Mr. Collinson and herself. The very idea that this godly, hesitant young man would, on the street, act on impulse, take advantage, and declare himself in love with her was almost impossible to believe.

Therefore, she might pretend it never happened.

***

"Look whom I've taken possession of. And convinced to pursue my most clever and comely little sister."

Having made his pronouncement, Gabriel escorted Mr. Collinson into the parlor, just behind Maria carrying Papa's supper tray of soup, beer, and a crusty heel of bread he would struggle to chew and swallow. Christina followed Mama's lead, politely welcoming their guest. Once it was ascertained he wasn't hungry but, with Gabriel's urging, would have coffee, Mama began to question him about his family and work, loud enough so her husband could participate in the gentle inquisition, even ask a question or two of his own. Inevitably, the subject of Mr. Collinson's disappearance from Christ Church came up, his explanation self-conscious but unapologetic.

"Ah, Moony," Gabriel greeted his older sister returning with a porcelain cup and proceeding to fill it from the pewter coffee pot brought in earlier for their father. "We may keep our friend's head up a while longer."

"We would hope this isn't a permanent defection."

"Well, Mrs. Rossetti, there—"

"I warned it would be a problem, Jimmy." Gabriel was standing behind where Mr. Collinson was sitting, playfully pulling up his shoulders.

Mr. Collinson didn't appear to appreciate Gabriel's humoring any more than his warning. Mentions of Bishop Nicolas Wiseman and Dr. John Henry Newman aligned, as far as the Rossetti Anglicans were concerned, with Papal aggression to Romanize the English church, didn't help his cause. As if determined to seal his fate, showing an obstinacy Christina almost admired, he added, "There are Catholics in your family."

Although he tried to stand, Papa only succeeded in raising his voice. "Like there are undercurrents in the sea, to suck one down into drowning."

"Christina, come here," Mama insisted, Christina obeying, and their guest rising at her approach. "What would you say to Mr. Collinson?"

Her legs weakening, her head throbbing, Christina just wanted to run away.

"I won't speak for you."

"I know, Mama."

"How you torture him."

"How you exaggerate, Gabriel Charles. But you do need to tell him, Christina."

"Not here." Christina waited for Mr. Collinson by the front door, which she opened to the chill of the late October evening. She stepped out onto the stoop before he did, glad it was too dark to see what he was hoping for or dreading. She could hear him breathing and thought his hand brushed her arm. "I'm sorry. So very sorry. But I cannot marry … a Catholic."

"Cannot or will not?"

"What does it matter if the outcome is the same?"

"My heart tells me it matters."

He wasn't about to convince her, but he was confusing her.

"It's cold. I must go in."

"Here. Take my coat."

"No. Thank you, Mr. Collin—"

"James. Please."

What was he pleading for? She was surprised what she hoped. "Hurry home before you catch a chill. Goodnight."

She went inside and closed the door, on his vanity if he was still on the other side facing it, on hers if he had given up that easily and was gone.

She turned and Gabriel was waiting with a fleeting frown, greasy curls falling over his eyes. He flung the paisley-patterned scarf around his neck back over one shoulder and waved her out of the way, ignoring her advice to put on a coat that was nowhere in sight, while muttering, "James is probably going to throw himself into the canal or the Thames and it will be a shame, a damned shame."

He left and Maria came down the hall. "More of a shame for you to marry because some pathetic fellow, whom you hardly know, and, worse still, Gabriel introduced you to, is, for the moment, infatuated with you."

The front door opened to William getting home from work, "What's up with Gabriel? He stormed past only saying he had to catch Collinson, who I take it has been here."

William hung his damp coat and hat on the rack Christina had to step aside from for him to do so. "I can guess why and needn't ask how it went. And not just because of Gabriel's behavior. You look far too righteous, Maria, and you, Christina, culpable, as if you just murdered someone."

CHAPTER TEN

Mr. Collinson didn't do anything more reckless than remove Christina's admitted objection to their engagement.

"How can he help himself?" William was the first she told of the second proposal. "You are by far his superior."

Christina wanted to be flattered when, soon after she rejected him, James decided to return to the Albany Street Christ Church fold and the perpetually penitent Reverend Dodsworth. Waiting outside after the service, his resolve was further tested, Mama, and, therefore, Maria and Christina, the last to leave the church.

He greeted them with a slow, slightly stuttered request to speak to Christina privately, looking startled that no one objected.

When he took Christina aside, Maria couldn't hold back entirely. "Just remember, my sister is a treasure others value."

"Of course."

"Moony—Maria—means well."

"As I do, Miss Rossetti, wanting to please you and be as you need."

Christina's embarrassment was as much due to doubt as humility. If only pure love was James' motive and could be hers. Even as young and inexperienced as she was, she suspected trickery in his sacrifice, nothing given up he wasn't all along thinking he might take back.

She agreed to marry him with a quick nod she hoped Mama and Maria didn't see or, if they did, thought was about something else. They would have to know soon, but William, a well-practiced go-between, would be more composed telling them. He might even draw them into a pact not to involve Papa until it was necessary to.

"Collinson did let slip," Gabriel revealed, "his hope you might yet become Catholic. I advised him to hope only to sell more pictures, so he could afford to marry before you change your mind."

***

To present Christina *in absentia* to James' mother and sister, William went to Mansfield with his future brother-in-law, as did a painting Collinson had miraculously completed of Christina, and a copy of *Verses*. Christina was certain William would do her justice and use her poetry to prove her intellect, wit, and artistry, while not sharing her foolish longings or morbidity. However, James' view of her as a slouching, shadowed, severely coiffed, pinched mouthed, puritanically dressed woman of ten years older than she was hardly recommended her as a desirable choice for a wife.

Gabriel had almost convinced her she was pleasant enough with wide-apart, oval-shaped, translucent eyes, a slightly upturned nose, well defined chin, and, as he described, "cupid's bow lips and a fairy princess contrast of pale complexion and dark hair." Christina usually knew when he was sketching her, annoyed with him tempting her vanity, but also forgiving if she saw herself helping him develop his craft.

She hadn't consciously posed for James. He claimed his piece was from memory.

"The stunner has missed the mark on this one," Gabriel said after mentioning he had seen Collinson's rough sketches that "promised a prettier Christina."

"I think he has deliberately made her plain and miserable," Maria added, "needing to dull her to deserve her."

Christina should have been insulted by the first impression James wanted his family to have of her. She made the mistake young women do when being chosen was more important than being choosy, and having a lover was a desperate, yielding ambition, because the chance might never come again. An older, wounded, hardened yet strengthened Christina wouldn't allow desperation to rule her choices like she did when James Collinson fooled her fledgling self. At the time, like a young bird struggling to fly, she needed to settle on something, so why not his branch, leafless and wavering as it was?

Maria accused Christina of agreeing to marry the first fellow who asked because of what youth, illness, and Papa might not excuse her from for much longer. "I can hardly blame you. If I hate being a governess, you would a hundred times more."

Christina concentrated on "first fellow," the implication that James Collinson might be just the beginning, not the end, of marital possibilities. "I think I could love him enough."

"Enough for what? A lifetime without poetry?"

Christina wondered if Maria was jealous, a tendency her sister had exhibited less than when they were children. As a girl, Christina had relished rattling Maria's halo and ruffling her wings. It was never Christina's intention to hurt her, merely to find vulnerability and love her more for it. In that respect, nothing had changed.

"It will be a long engagement," Christina assured. "One that's hardly noticed."

Maria shrugged.

"Who knows how it will end." Christina grasped her sister's arm before she could walk away. "Perhaps at my grave."

"Nonsense." Maria's mouth quivered. "You will not die for James.

Or any other man. You have better things to do."

It was too easy to believe Maria would never care as devotedly for anyone outside of family or anything but duty, scholarship, and worship. She was the surefooted and pragmatic one, immune to a human frailty like falling in love.

***

The postman came a day early and stole the pleasure of my hearing from you tomorrow. Christina began a letter on the twenty-third of November 1848 to William, relieved he was *securely housed* in Mansfield with James, his mother, and sister. Train journeys were unpredictable and seemingly interminable, especially for those waiting at one end or the other. She knew she was posing too many questions, relying on William's patience and pleasure in reporting, worrying needlessly and justifiably about every little thing left up to a brother's prejudice, her poetry, and a portrait. She hoped the mother and sister of her intended weren't alarming. *I have an impression of Miss Collinson—who I can't bring myself to call Mary—as too clever.* Also, that *the house at Pleasley Hill is too neat to be welcoming and its windows are kept open in winter.* She thought she could easily be friends with the Collinsons' bull terrier, hoping William, who had recently been dabbling in art, would send her *something in the way of a drawing* of the *hideous-enough* creature.

She asked William to remember her to James. She wasn't comfortable with writing to her intended; they weren't even at the point of the polite informality she enjoyed with Amelia Heimann. Not yet. If ever. They needed to see each other and talk more. The Rossetti parlor was a place of participation and openness that might provide relief to James' awkwardness and loneliness in London. He would dine with them, although not for the first time, Gabriel having, without warning, invited his partners in the art of words and pictures to Charlotte Street to eat "exotically and enthusiastically," as Millais put it. Everyone, except James, gave themselves fully to the occasion, his meager consumption of food and drink a kind of conceit. She hoped with only him as a guest, at last a significant one, he would allow himself to be as human as he was English.

I watched and waited with a steadfast will: and though the object seemed to flee away, that I so longed for, every day by day I watched and waited still.

Maria's implication that Christina had accepted James to avoid the dreaded governess alternative to marriage was well-founded. He was the least intimidating of the young men she knew. Mr. Hunt or Mr. Millais were more physically appealing, articulate, creative, and not apt to fall asleep in her company. She liked Gabriel to draw attention to her when they were around, if only so she might shyly scold him doing so. In truth, Mr. Millais was too bourgeois and unorthodox, and Mr. Hunt, although puritanical, was too distracted and unsettled. Due to their intense camaraderie with Gabriel, they were both like blood brothers to her.

She waited for James to return, was committed to not only marrying but discovering him. She envisaged how they would eventually enjoy each other, sharing controversial thoughts and glances, even whispered readings, discovering another's favorite authors and books as revealing as any confession. After a winter of becoming well acquainted, by spring or summer they would be ready to escape chaperoning ears, if only to walk one way and the other in front of the house. It would feel like they traveled far, away from singleness and endings, towards joint goals and accomplishments. The wind would be warm and sleepy, its latter attribute suiting James so well. He would admit he liked the glimmer of the stars more than the glare of the moon, while she would profess her pleasure with both.

And dreaming through the twilight that doth not rise or set, haply I may remember and haply forget.

Returning from Mansfield nearly a week before James, William had little more to say about his trip than he had written, although he offered hints that his weariness was more to do with an impossible task than travel. Despite the "delightful country walks" London could not offer him and the dull excise office routine it did, he proclaimed his relief at being home. For William, that meant sitting in the kitchen with Mama and Christina, eating leftover pasta, wanting to talk of anything but the Collinsons. He teased Betsey because he knew the young servant was a little in love with him. Grimalkin's fluffy kittens enjoyed scaling his legs and the PRB—those initials Gabriel had finally added to his *Mary Virgin* painting—was on his mind.

Christina didn't welcome James back as readily as she had intended to, taking her cue from his own restraint. Betsey let him in, Mama put down her sewing, Maria her pen, and Papa grunted. William wondered how his mother and sister were, which prompted a few words from James, a few more from William, and back and forth went their small talk. James didn't once glance in Christina's direction. Her cheeks burned, her thoughts were blasphemous, and the temptation to remind him of her existence harder and harder to resist.

"And if thou wilt, remember. And if thou wilt, forget," she sniped.

James reacted by threatening a repeat of his impulsive and uncharacteristically aggressive approach in front of the workhouse, this time with witnesses. He stopped short of joining Christina on the well-worn but singularly soft Chesterfield sofa.

"You are well?"

Christina nodded and put out her hand to him.

"How cold." He no sooner held it than let it go. "William says you often suffer the damp in winter."

"Yes."

"So, it was better you didn't come to Pleasley Hill."

"The rain soaked us more than once." William pulled the conversation out of its privacy.

"Christina is not as fragile as your portrait shows her to be." Mama's honesty was never misplaced. "I'm afraid your mother and sister think she will be a burden to you."

"No, no. They saw her sobriety and modesty and look forward to meeting her."

A roguish laugh meant Gabriel had arrived, snow sprinkling off him as he stamped into the parlor and headed for a warm by the fire. "If only you'd known her as a child. All laughter and tantrums and tears. Well, Jimmy, she'd have set you running for your life, mate."

"But you said she—"

"Was as prudent and pious as you?" Gabriel swung his arm around Collinson's shoulders, holding him up after causing him to lose his balance. "Unfortunately, she has become so."

"Not unfortunately for Mr. Collinson," Maria quipped.

"Ha." Gabriel plopped down cross-legged into a puff of dust from the mat in front of the hearth. "Betsey, oh, Betsey. A little beating is in order. Of this rug, I mean."

Papa grumbled something, but only those who already knew his vulgar opinion of the maid heard what he said and were embarrassed.

Christina posed straighter and smaller on the settee, James hesitating before sitting without a decent space between them.

"*Bravo!*" Gabriel was victorious.

***

William Bell Scott made his second visit to 50 Charlotte Street just before Christmas after stopping to see Gabriel in his studio. He was "startled but impressed" by the paintings-in-progress, "a fly as real as any picnic pestering one in Hunt's." If Christina heard right, Gabriel's *Mary Virgin* made him eager to see "that young woman who hadn't yet revealed the sound of her voice to him."

Mr. Scott returned without a doubt he would be welcomed, bear-hugging William, gentler with frail Papa, and kissing the hands of the women. The dispersion of holly sprigs from *Nonno's* garden for decorating the mantle, top of picture and door frames, and wherever they were out of the way of the kittens, was put on pause. Their visitor from the north filled the Rossetti and Polidori need for stimulating, amusing, unpretentious company, energetic conversation, and forgiving competitiveness. It was Mama's and Maria's first meeting with him, and Christina wasn't surprised their caution quickly turned to delight.

Christina realized a new pleasure, Mr. Scott's glances flirting with her independence, curiosity, and contradictions, his perception describing her "quietude" as "sacred and terrible at the same time."

"That's our Christina." Papa applauded.

"And so, mine."

Mr. Scott was such a contrast to James, who continued to skulk in and out of their lives. Christina was relieved he wasn't there that evening, for she might have cried out that she couldn't marry him. Instead, she only thought so, until their guest had her complete attention, and everyone's, even Papa's, as Mr. Scott exhibited knowledge and appreciation of "Gabriele Rossetti's infamy and influence, studies and writings."

Mr. Scott was Father Christmas come a week early, bringing the gifts of his good nature and intellect, and deliberate smile.

"Will you be in Edinburg for the holiday?" Mama took advantage of a lull in his conversation with her husband.

"Aye. The Athens of the North or Auld Reeky, depending on the day, will be a welcome break from Newcastle."

"I've read Christmas isn't celebrated in Scotland." Maria got his attention.

"Nay flagrantly. We Scots enjoy a bit o' subterfuge, though. So, we find our ways."

"Oh?" Mama looked as giddy as Christina felt.

"We keep the home fires burning, so to speak. Any excuse for feasting and bevvying." Mr. Scott leaned back and outstretched his long legs, Christina envisioning him permanently making himself at home. "And mistletoe. I see holly. Solid green and variegated. With and without berries. But where's that persuasive parasite, mistletoe?"

"Italians don't need that kind of persuasion."

"Neither do Scotsmen, *Professore Rossetti.*"

Mr. Scott offered to assist Christina in yuletide decorating, pricking his fingers and dropping more holly than he placed anywhere.

"It hasn't been officially announced: Christina is engaged." Mama informed their guest once he stepped out of the parlor to leave.

"Really? Well, Mrs. R, I'm not surprised. To some adoring artist or writer, I hope."

Christina didn't want to tell him, but her mother's raised eyebrows insisted she did. "He is an artist. Gabriel thinks a very good one."

"He belongs to the Brotherhood?"

"Reluctantly, awkwardly," William critiqued.

"Hmm."

Mama couldn't wait longer. "Mr. Collinson."

"James Collinson?" Mr. Scott looked at Christina as though she had changed into someone else.

"You know him?" William handed their guest his coat and hat.

"I haven't met him. Heard a little about him. And read of his early success exhibiting at the R.A."

"He gives them what they want. I was recently in Mansfield with him, to meet his mother and sister. They are a decent family. And approve of the match."

Mr. Scott's head tilted up, his eyes hardened, and he rubbed his chin. "Then it's all set. As so many things are. Before we are ready for them to be."

CHAPTER ELEVEN

Socializing was one of the obligations Christina liked least about growing up. When it took her from her own bed, it felt like punishment, even banishment.

As to my getting on—she wrote to William when, after endless bouts of melancholy, bronchitis, and wearing on everyone's nerves, she was exiled to Clapham—*so far, I have resisted riding off on one of the donkeys found on the Common.* Mrs. Marshall was welcoming and diplomatic, never mentioning why Christina was sent to stay with her for a while, although it was likely Mama had discussed the James Collinson situation with such a trusted and tactful friend.

Christina wondered why she couldn't go to the Polidoris.

"Precisely because you are too at home there."

Mama was right. Christina had to learn how to present herself outside family. The society beyond wasn't going to entertain her moods. Her sarcasm would be misunderstood, her quietness heard as arrogance, her talent for poetry judged unproven. Those others weren't going to forgive her no matter what. When she stepped out of Rossetti-Polidori territory, she was no longer in a place of belonging. In a less remarkable way, it was like her father leaving one country, culture, and future for another. He had talked about returning to Italy with his wife and children, wanting his sons and daughters "to take root, grow up, and branch out there." Christina had never heard Mama in favor or against the idea, but Maria claimed to know this dream of his was their mother's worst nightmare. As it turned out, Papa never actually had a plan and the only passage his illusions bought him were towards disappointment, infirmity, and vicariously through his progeny whose voyages would take his new life back to the old.

"Now that would be the perfect honeymoon for you and Jimmy."

Christina was never certain Gabriel was an earnest or a facetious matchmaker.

"Inspiration would abound for painting and writing, and, even for you two, *l'amore*, which the dead can't avoid *in Italia*."

There had been no conversations with James about their wedding. At best, they spoke of the weather, their health and families, and exchanged views on art and poetry. At worst, he would venture into the arena of religion and say something to worry her before she was once again left to wonder what he was about. She was glad to see him go, although it hardly seemed she was when she couldn't close herself up in her room soon enough to collapse on her bed and cry rather than curse him.

Mama might have sided with Christina if she had refused to go to Mansfield. Francis Polidori Rossetti was running out of patience with being in favor of Mr. Collinson. He was encouraged to call regularly, warmly received with food and refreshment, conversations centering on him with genuine interest in his wellbeing and work. Papa, who soon guessed what was going on, was, surprisingly, not inquisitive of his future son-on-law's financial prospects. He did want to know James' reading preferences, which gave him permission to talk about his own publications.

Mama allowed James to sit next to Christina on Sundays at Christ Church, and suggested he take her out during "the best seasons for strolling" or, because "Christina needed to experience the magnificence of Verdi," for an evening at the opera.

"As long as William is willing to go along to Regent's Park, and Maria or myself or both also attend Covent Garden, there can be no objection."

The walks only happened in poetry, because, as far as James was concerned, "the air was too damp in spring and flies ate him alive in summer." The opera was "not his thing" with its tendencies towards "violence and melodrama."

In William's opinion, James decided to spend time with his family in May to avoid the response to his *Italian Image Boys* at the 1849 Royal Academy Exhibition. When, in August, Christina heard he would rather paint landscapes on the Isle of Wight than be at Pleasley Hill when she was, Christina considered asking her mother if it would be better if she didn't go, even called off the engagement.

First, she ran those thoughts past William, only then learning James had asked her brother to accompany him to Ventnor. "He seems to prefer your company to mine."

"I don't think he knows how to be with women, even his own relations. He's also quite ill at ease with most men. It's just that I'm almost as dull as he is."

"You could never be." She realized she was also offering an opinion on James.

"Put it this way: he knows I won't make fun of him, not even his going to bed at nine o'clock."

"You're too kind and patient. Don't let him take advantage."

"And when you're married to him? Won't you? Won't you accommodate him?"

Accommodating James might mean the opposite of what it did with most other husbands. Gabriel, brimming with physicality, claimed he "chose Jimmy" for her "because he was priestlike."

Now all the cherished secrets of my heart, —Now all my hidden hopes are turned to sin.

Containment of behavior and expectation was necessary, but Christina must have her liberty. Her mind must wander, her wit keep its flair, her emotions roll on high and low, her creativity grow more daring, her heart not give up on its longings before she knew what they were. *Part of my life is dead, part sick, and part is all on fire within.*

***

As Mr. Scott had casually intimated, Christina wasn't ready for settling down. William's concern made her realize betrothal was as close to not being able to change her mind as she could get. She should feel committed to preparing herself in all the ways marriage required. Instead, her intention to was interrupted by resistance and a search, albeit a secret, silent, renounced one, of other possibilities. She found herself often thinking about Mr. Scott. She hoped Gabriel might say he had heard from him and, especially, that he was coming down to London again. Christina fretted he would visit while she was away. It didn't happen during her week in Clapham, but another at Pleasley Hill increased the odds.

If such timing was to be, she would have to hope for the consolation of hearing how disappointed Mr. William Bell Scott was, too.

***

Christina set off unprotected and unprepared for Nottinghamshire, certain she would never forgive James Collinson. She was going to be put on trial without counsel, presumed guilty of not being good enough, her innocence condemning her. As much as she didn't want to be as sick as she had been in January and June, an ailment in August on the verge of September would have given her an excuse not to travel.

Mama chose the clothes she packed and the reading she brought, which, "in case it was noticed, as it most certainly would be, could affect the Collinsons' opinion of you."

At the last moment, Mama ran into Christina's room with yet one more thing to bring. "Lace never ceases to please well brought up ladies. When you're sitting in their parlor of an afternoon or evening, you may work on this piece as though you heart is set on finishing it."

Mama and Maria went with Christina to Euston Station, her sister holding onto her hand through the compartment window, even as the train began to slowly move. Christina heard their mother gasp.

"Let go, Moony, let go," Christina felt sad saying, and relieved once she was freed, turning towards what was ahead.

Pulling up the window and sitting down, she was overwhelmed by fear and desperate to get off the shuddering, stranger-filled ride. She wanted to go back, further back than that morning, or the day, or even ten or more years before; back to a never-ending happy, indulgent childhood. Perhaps this was her punishment, at last, for willingly, willfully going missing at Holmer Green.

It wasn't until the train had fled Mama's "chimney-pot city," that she noticed who else was in the compartment: a woman only concerned with the girl crying beside her; the man in the seat across looking down at his hands who wouldn't have been identified as anything to do with that lady if it wasn't for a boy who hardly kept his balance between them, whining incoherently, ignoring orders to sit, tugging the man's jacket sleeve and the woman's skirt.

Christina realized no one would know her for most of the day. She could be anyone going anywhere. What could be more liberating than not having an identity? What could be more dangerous? Which was why Aunt Charlotte had provided the funds for first class and a few tips, some useful, others forgetting Christina had traveled before, just not such a distance all alone. *Dress quietly and unpretending, avoid unnecessary garniture, which I know you, like your sister and mother, usually do—being summer you will want the fabric on the lighter side, but, also, for maneuvering and drying quickly if you get caught in the rain or there is a spill. I recommend a travel corset, so that sitting so long is easier to endure. Don't remove your bonnet or gloves, for doing so opens you up to misinterpretation. Your carryon bag should be small and your purse inconspicuous, most of your money in a pocket sewn into your petticoat. Keep to yourself without being rude, yet don't seem desperately alone. No matter what, remain dignified. Have a porter help you with your trunk, but tip him discreetly, for a show of generosity may bring unsavory attention.*

No sooner the man, woman, and children disembarked than others climbed in, a gentleman, who very possibly wasn't, sending Christina back to the notebook she intended to fill with reflections of her trip. She hadn't even taken the pencil out of her purse yet. Before she could consider another strategy for ignoring him, a middle-aged woman asked him to lift her small carpetbag onto the rack on Christina's side of the compartment. It was only natural the lady should claim the seat below, her size and skirt sprawling, so, although the seat was designed for three, there was hardly room left for a toddler. One, drooling "Nanna," was soon plopped on the large lady's lap, the child's pretty if pale presumed-to-be mother sitting across from Christina. The barely whiskered father took his place next to her, which left the odd man out of any opportunity to be problematic again.

He got off the train soon after. The others, as Christina discovered not by asking a question but answering one, were also traveling to Mansfield. She surprised herself by settling into the journey, regretting countryside she had never seen before sliding by, wondering what she was missing of flora and fauna, insect and amphibian in the fields, hedgerows, hills, rivers, and woods. Peeking, steepled villages intrigued her, towns as spare junctions or distant scenery also rousing her curiosity. City stops meant more dark, smoky, echoing tunnels to pass through. Christina wrote a few lines and, leaning towards the window, bending her notebook's front cover up, made a clumsy sketch of the child. For a while, once again anticipating meeting the Collinson women, she felt nauseated and a headache coming on. The last hour was almost pleasant, lost to drowsiness and dreaming her journey would take her much further north than Mansfield.

"Wake up," she heard and felt a nudge of her arm, her compartment companions standing and gathering their things. "You're where you said you were going."

"Not quite." The man hung back to let Christina leave the train ahead of him. "I believe the shuttle to Pleasley goes from another platform. Check with the porter."

"Good luck," his wife said once they were all off the train.

What Christina heard was: *Your ticket is a return fare; go back to London now.* Instead, she followed the original plan and the porter with her trunk.

"From London, Miss? Quieter here. Pleasing … in its way." He wasn't wrong if he thought she would catch his play on her destination's name. "Enjoy your visit."

The two-car, classless train rattled and moved as slowly as, at a good pace, she could have walked, which obviously didn't amuse one young fellow she would have to tell William reminded her of Thackery's Hannibal Fitch when he was splendidly riled. It was a thought, like others and the green and pleasant valley scenery, to distract her from wondering how she would endure the week ahead.

As the train pulled into Pleasley Junction, Mary Collinson was immediately recognizable, small in stature and stylishly somber, her crinolined skirt giving her a shape her body could not. The ties on her bonnet warned of a stiff breeze, so Christina held onto hers as she stepped out of the carriage. Miss Collinson stood still on the platform except for putting up a gray-gloved hand and nudging her accompanying servant who rushed towards Christina.

"But … yer so … pretty."

"Thank you." Christina gave the young woman her carpetbag.

"She's so pretty," Miss Collinson was also told as her servant was sent on to make sure the porter put Miss Rossetti's possessions on the back of the trap.

Christina felt to blame for the insensitivity of the servant's words, Miss Collinson's good looks disfigured from an eruption during some past illness just as William had informed. It must be devastating to lose one's appearance, not slowly, almost imperceptibly, unsurprisingly through aging, but shockingly from one reflection in a mirror to the next.

"Christina, at last."

"Miss Collinson."

"Please, call me Mary. I hope it will not feel awkward for long."

CHAPTER TWELVE

Christina could hardly believe what she was reading. There had been no skirmishes, not even during various matches of whist or one of bagatelle, victory alternating between Mary and her, congratulations and commiserations lighthearted. They had gone out walking together, along footpaths with well-maintained gates and stiles, over the flattest and driest of pastures, and around arable fields hedged in by ripened blackberries that provided a juicy snack. Usually, they were pulled in one direction or other by a hideously handsome canine, the very one William had predicted Christina would want to steal away.

"What is it?" Maria caught Christina holding the letter as though she was about to tear it up.

"Oh, nothing. It hardly matters." She quickly folded it.

Christina's admitted affection for Sol, a boisterous bull terrier, couldn't have instigated the disappointing directive she received in the post that morning. It also was unlikely to be Christina's weariness with Mrs. Collinson's talk of beaus, as perpetual as at Amelia Heimann's. Mary didn't find such pedestrian conversation appealing, either. Christina thought a chivalrous flavor might be more to Mary's taste and had asked William to send her a particular poem, which she had read out loud to her.

> As I laye a-thynkynge, a-thynkynge, a-thynkynge,
> Merrie sang the Birde as she sat upon the boughe;
> lovely Mayde came by,
> And a gentil youth was nyghe,
> And he breathed many a syghe
> And a vowe;
> As I laye a-thynkynge, her heart was gladsome now.

Mary's expression refused to appreciate the sweetness in those last lines by Thomas Ingoldsby. If there was then or ever anyone Mary Collinson considered a way out of or dalliance from spinsterhood, she wasn't telling.

Christina expected, as their relationship grew sisterly, that Mary might reveal some hoped for or hopeless involvement. Until it was written that would never happen. Could a pretty poem be blamed? Had she misinterpreted what she thought was overall a pleasant and productive visit? Had she given herself too much credit for getting through it tolerantly, valiantly and, at times, enjoyably?

There hadn't been much idleness with Mrs. Collinson in charge. Although in her sixties with a slight limp from rheumatism, James' mother was otherwise strong and well, an active lady who expected plans to be made. Parlor time was only for the sickly, because of inclement weather, or for proper digestion after supper and before bed. Like Mary, Mrs. Collinson might've been nice-looking once. She was intimidating towards Christina.

"What mother wouldn't be, on sizing up a rival for her son's affections?" Maria offered her usual sensible perspective.

"Not Mama. She would feel more for the poor, uncertain girl than herself. She would want her to be at ease."

"Our mother is like no other."

"She's a saint."

Mrs. Collinson was a good woman, just not a remarkable one. Her daughter was attached to her, but not warmly. At first, Christina had thought her association with Mary would never progress beyond obligation, the first day—what was left of it by the time she arrived at the Collinson's terraced house less shabby than their neighbors'— tedious and unimaginative.

Christina made lace with an insistence her own family would have recognized as a sign of uneasiness, even bad temper.

"We heard of your delicate health this year, so we'll do nothing until we're assured you're rested." Mrs. Collinson's consideration had an undertone of inconvenience.

Her daughter stood up. "I thought tomorrow or the next day, Hardwick Old Hall. Required visiting for this area."

"Yes, Mary," again Mrs. Collinson sounded anything but agreeable. "Miss Rossetti should see it. On a warm, dry morning or afternoon, of course, considering her constitution."

Christina noticed James' portrait of her hung in a dimly lit corner where it would be mostly unobserved. "James made me look so sad and sickly," Christina finally admitted out loud, immediately realizing, by Mrs. Collinson's pursed mouth and raised eyebrows, she shouldn't have.

She returned to the subject of the Old Hall. "It must be 'the real live crumbling castle' William wrote to me about."

"James likes to paint there," Mary noted as she walked over to see what Christina was imperfectly creating with thread, bobbins, pins, and tiny pillow. "Looks complicated."

"My Aunt Eliza taught me. Well, tried to."

"Perhaps another visit, a longer visit, once you and James are … you can teach me."

So, she wondered, what had gone wrong? Two days later, sunny beginnings fooled them, but the hired phaeton excursion of a few miles to Derbyshire and Bess of Hardwick's stately ruins was better than hoped. A couple of quick showers and more threatening kept Mrs. Collinson huddled in one of the few sheltered areas of the roofless Elizabethan structure, so Mary and Christina could explore most of it without her. To Christina's surprise, Mary was talkative, mainly about the Hall's history and the much-married Bess. They went wing to wing, down long corridors, up mossy stairs, and into large and small dilapidated rooms, finishing with a revolving gaze up through floorless, roofless four stories into the sky.

"Such a pity it's overcast. The plaster friezes show up so much better in sunlight."

"No matter, Mary. The experience has been brilliant. Perhaps more atmospheric."

"Like the fortunate misfortune of the Old Hall being picked away at, stones and lead stolen, its majesty left to collapse."

"And to inspire."

"As perfection rarely does."

Christina had fought an impulse to touch the scarring on Mary's face. Instead, she hooked her arm, slightly squeezing it, at the time no reason to apologize. "Look. The sun peaks through. We shouldn't keep your mother waiting longer and explore the park before it rains again."

Once more, Mary proved she was knowledgeable, this time identifying trees, native and foreign, by their Latin and common names, the grounds graced with sprawling specimens that Bess herself, hundreds of years ago, had likely found shade and shelter under. The gardens, defined by walls and hedges, the rainbow palette of summer lingering and subtly changing to autumn's golden withering, gave Mary an opportunity to show off her botanical studies, as she explained, from books she had access to in her father's shop. She could even identify the fish swimming in the pond and was particularly detailed in the information she imparted about the kitchen garden's herbs and their uses, culinary and medicinal. Christina listened and looked with her instinctive interest in nature. From far away, she saw individual trees for their silhouettes, and close up for distinctive bark and roots. Their leaves were weaving frames for spiders and sustenance for caterpillars, like flowers were for bees, ladybirds, and butterflies. Thickets were bedtime and nesting refuges for songbirds. Grass was a treasure trove of slinky worms, slimy snails, and cool, sweet-eyed frogs that Mary shared Christina's fascination with.

"Another time, we'll tour the new hall," she promised as she climbed into the phaeton after her mother and Christina had.

It seemed Christina had made a good start with the Collinsons. Her first walk with Sol and Mary happened the following day and a second the next. Talk of Mr. and Mrs. Charles Collinson coming to Pleasley Hill ended with the announcement of a trip to Mansfield instead.

"Just you and Mary." Mrs. Collinson deprived herself of the excursion. "There's not room for three of us, as I believe Anne's sister is staying there already."

Christina had expected Mary to be happy at the prospect of days free from her mother's management. Instead, her sister-in-law-to-be was quiet, even sullen on the train into the city, and angry in the cab to her brother's residence above Collinson Booksellers in West Gate.

"Charles should have been at the station."

"Perhaps he had to attend the shop."

"Half day on Saturday." Mary's answers were curt, especially to anything Christina asked about Charles. Only the day before, she had prophesized Christina would be "a favorite with CC due to her unalterable self-possession."

Christina was impressed by Mary's understanding and flattered by Charles even before she knew whether he would like her. Once they did meet, it was a struggle not to be inflated by his comment on "how delightfully different Miss Rossetti was from that strange portrait." Christina didn't even try to subdue her own delight in Mrs. Charles Collinson, who, clear-eyed, personable, and only a few years into her twenties, was the most to Christina's taste of anyone she had met in Mansfield and Pleasley. Anne's welcome and hospitality were genuine, and she continued attentive while being full of fun but also willing to engage in serious conversation. Her sister Carrie was likeable.

In hindsight, Christina realized she should have been more concerned with Mary's moodiness and isolation from the camaraderie she, Anne, and Carrie shared. She had thought it was a good thing to get along so well with "CC's" wife and be at ease playing with their baby Maud. Although Mary had looked forward to showing Mansfield to Christina, when finally the chance came, she dragged along. Anne was the guide up and down the two main streets, in and out of her favorite shops, and, for a brief rest and contemplation, the Gothic church. The highpoint for Christina had been the marketplace near the Town Hall and its florid cross, which, as she was happy to believe, "marked the center of Sherwood Forest."

They had gone out one night to some friends of Charles and Anne, their host, Mr. Foster, wearing a coat more appropriate for breakfast than an evening *soirée*. He fell asleep while his daughter sang, Mary accompanying her proficiently on the piano and briefly emerged from her sullenness to harmonize on a couple of refrains.

Other evenings they stayed in, occupied with conversation, reading silently or out loud, Mary going to bed before everyone else.

Christina and Charles discovered they were evenly matched

playing chess, Anne getting away with applauding Christina's maneuvers more than her husband's because she did so playfully and prettily. Was Mary upset that Charles' wife was so easily loved and forgiven? Did she think Christina had turned her back on their budding friendship, even to the point of wondering if she would do the same with James if someone more entertaining and effusive came along? Christina knew, unfolding the letter again, she should have been more sensitive to Mary feeling left out. It was only on receipt and reading the first few lines of it that Christina considered how solitary it must have been for Mary during the first six years of her life without the company of siblings. Even once they came, her brothers were much younger, and she still had *no friend like a sister*.

"Who is it from?" Maria had returned to Christina's room.

"Mary Collinson."

"To thank you for the portfolio?"

"She barely acknowledged its delivery."

"How rude."

"I was presumptuously so to think she would want it. I might've done better to give her that silver friendship ring I saw in the jewelers on Newburg Street after all."

"But she doesn't wear jewelry."

"I know. Not even as little as her mother who sometimes displayed a cameo broach and still wears her wedding band."

Maria bit her lip but said what she was thinking. "We must purchase the ring today and get it in the post tomorrow."

"Oh, no. She wants our correspondence to cease."

Maria sat on the bed next to Christina. "I thought all had gone well between you."

"At first. We began as though we would be allies. We never quarreled. And then, I ... well, I may blame myself." Christina gave the letter to her sister's demanding hand.

"I'm sure you shouldn't." Maria, lifting it close to her eyes, wasn't silent for long. "Oh. I'm even more convinced you shouldn't. Did you read all of it?"

"I was afraid to."

"It isn't you, Chrissy. Except as she might like you too much."

"She wrote that?"

"No. It's implied. 'Despite my hopes, I can't help considering James' affairs unpromising and his return to Catholicism likely.'"

If anything, James' affections were slightly more active, and his religious loyalty not discussed and, so, not questioned. He exhibited more confidence in his work and its prospects, and he was obviously looking forward to marriage as evidenced by the painting of a mother and child he was doing.

Until the work's completion, Christina only saw his charcoal drawing of her on one of his visits to Charlotte Street. Gabriel reported his progress transposing it onto the plein-air background.

Collinson sublimely captured the location. I should know. I sat there for hours thinking and writing or doing nothing at all except enjoying the view of Culver Cliff, William wrote from the Isle of Wight, where he had extended his holiday in its temperate southwest.

When Christina finally saw the painting, it should have pleased her. It was more flattering than the portrait mercifully hidden in the shadows of Pleasley Hill. This one was skillfully executed, engaging, and enigmatic. A sketchy young woman posing in her parlor was reimagined into one fully colored in an idyllic pastoral scene. She was not obscured but defined by being plainly dressed, a poke-bonnet with ribbons untied, and center-parted dark hair framing her down-gazing face. A mahogany desk chair had become a rustic bench beside a stile. Walls, ceilings, and roof had been removed, allowing her fresh air and outlooks of land and sea. A great tree offered shade, and an object on her lap provided a narrative.

Others assumed James' expectancy had given Christina a child to call her own. Yet the young woman who might be her was more likely the girl's governess, her expression slightly bemused while the child didn't seem to need her for more than the holding of a bonnet she was stringing flowers for.

It wasn't long before Christina realized the little girl was drawn out of James' memory not anticipation, a cleaner, tidier, healthier, better dressed version of the one they had given back to workhouse wretchedness.

*****

"Now that Mary is off limits, I will write to Charles and Anne instead," Christina announced to almost everyone but James, waiting until he had gone home for the evening. "They were so convivial and even said they were glad James had found me. Of course, I didn't show my contempt of such a concept."

"I hope not," Mama spoke and sighed at the same time. "I'm sure they only meant to compliment you."

"I've already started a needlepoint I think Anne will like, perfect for the nursery. I must find some special toy I can send little Maud. Anne will be amused if I mention Charles will soon get tired of winning at chess. I might even ask if they've seen my portfolio."

Anne and Charles Collinson's answer was silence. Christina

wouldn't admit she was upset, although an overdue and longed for visit to Park Village tested her resolve, *Nonno* seeing through it. His parting embrace, as strong and reassuring as ever, left Christina in no doubt that he realized all wasn't well. Christina couldn't help dreading Amelia Heimann's interrogation, even knowing it would be well-meaning, motivated by natural inquisitiveness, friend to friend. Too many weeks since their last meeting and the Heimann's yet unseen house on Edward Street and Hampstead Road finally convinced Christina to brave Amelia's curiosity, a Thursday evening invitation also extended to Mama and Maria.

On arrival, Christina insisted on wandering all over the Heimann's comfortable new residence, including the kitchen and garrets, avoiding talk about anything else except reminisces of the happy hours Amelia and she had enjoyed in London on Liverpool, and George Streets, as well as at Brighton. There was a peek into the nursery, the Heimann's two boys asleep, so Christina's wish to offer them a story, a delightful one about three bears Mary had told her niece, would have to wait. By then it was time for cognac, cakes, and, finally, cards. Christina knew Amelia was too competitive, especially against her husband, to concern herself with anything else.

Before it was too late, their hostess lured Christina into Dr. Heimann's study, saying she needed advice on where to hang a certain drawing Gabriel had given her.

"He did? He never told me."

"He thought you might object."

Christina puffed with puzzlement. "Why ever should I?"

"It isn't a recent likeness."

"Of whom?"

Amelia's nervous smile answered

"Of me?"

"I told him I would like something of his for the new house. He insisted on choosing, saying he knew exactly the one. Although he warned you would object with that 'blas—,'" Amelia put a finger to her lip, "'humility you had grown into.'"

Christina hardly felt humble hoping the portrait her brother had given Amelia was flattering.

"I was a little deceptive." Amelia carefully unrolled a profile pencil sketch Gabriel had done of a pouty, pubescent Christina a few years earlier. "I haven't framed it yet. I was hoping you would sign it."

"I would never wear those ringlets now, although the combs—there was one matching on the other side—still have their uses."

Amelia went over to her husband's desk, flattening out the drawing, dipping a pen in a metallic-rimmed ink bottle.

"Not on the back?"

"No. I want to see your beautiful handwriting every time I look at it."

Christina was soon leaning over the drawing, even knowing whatever she wrote couldn't be corrected and wouldn't be hidden, not hesitating to write out:

My dear Mrs. Heimann
Yours affectionately,
Christina Rossetti

"Oh, thank you, my dear." Amelia's eyes moistened, but emotion didn't distract her from the other reason she wanted to be alone with Christina. "Maria told me."

"She shouldn't have."

"You should have."

"I would have."

"When? Once you suffered too long by yourself?"

Christina felt her legs and composure weakening, Amelia's arms around her holding her up and together.

"How could anyone want to 'cease correspondence' with you? Like not wanting the sun to ever come up again."

"You know," Christina thought of something she hadn't for a while. "I've never actually seen the sun rise."

CHAPTER THIRTEEN

When I awoke, the sun was at its height, and I wept ...

Christina's gloomy use of the rhymed words William had sent might cloud over the warm, sunny moments he was eking out at the seaside resort of Ventnor where he would spend the first days of his twenties.

It was his habit to be kind rather than altogether honest. By return post he admitted he *might prefer a merrier birthday present but couldn't complain about a Christina-at-her-melancholic-best one.*

William would edit, and Christina provide poems for, the new PRB literary journal. Like her grandfather's printing press, the whirring and clicking of Gabriel's schemes could legitimize her verses, the difference being that they, like the other contributions, would be anonymous.

On the verge of a tour of European art galleries with Mr. Hunt, Gabriel asked Christina to tell William not to hurry back to London. *The prospectus can wait. Mr. Stephens' offering is in a chaotic state at present. At least Mr. Hunt has done two etchings ...*

Christina owed Mr. Hunt an apology for rushing past him on the stairs at Charlotte Street without acknowledging him. It wasn't as though he was easy to ignore, with his golden-red beard, Middle Eastern robes, strong cigar smell, and hearty laugh.

Unintentionally, I broke the rules of my impossible politeness, she admitted to William without lingering on her regret. She finished the letter with Maria's excuse for not writing to him because everyone else was, Mama's pleasure when hearing from him, and Christina's own thoughts on a long poem of James' to be included in the brotherhood's upcoming magazine.

She could have been annoyed that James wrote poetry, very clever poetry, but there was that provocative part of her that welcomed sharing the arena of verbal maneuvering with him. Collaborative competition was a Rossetti tradition, more about bonding and improving than one-upmanship. As to whether it would work as well with someone from outside her sibling society, she need only look at how Gabriel and his creative cohorts frequently fell out, so far not irreparably, but what was there to hold them together when disagreements couldn't find compromise and jealousies festered over uneven successes and unwinnable women?

In Christina's experience, family ties could be strained, almost to the point of being broken, but not severed. She had seen the pride and pain in *Nonno's* eyes whenever anyone either didn't know or dared to defy the censure on any mention of his eldest son wantonly gone from the earth nearly a decade before Christina arrived.

Christina had another example of familial devotion threatened but not destroyed in her conflicted feelings for her father. He was the hero of her childhood. She was once his *vivace* Christina. According to him, she was born with ease, and so she would live. As early as sitting on his knee and clapping her hands together to accompany his Italian version of pat-a-cake, he encouraged her to dream of pretty things, of pleasure. He promised picture books and boxes of figs for good behavior, bestowing them as if without condition. His generosity was expected for what he called his children's "small greed," grinning mischievously when he brought them "what they wanted more than deserved." Christina still had a chest of drawers he had given her "because Maria had one," with a shiny key to secure whatever she put in it.

"As long as you don't lock your heart away from your Papa," he had said with a kiss on her hair, convincing his youngest *cucciola* he could do no wrong.

At almost nineteen, Christina knew she had been fooled by his once vigorous charm. She was reconciled to his failings and had grown out of believing him without question, caution preventing a repeat of his worst offence and circumstances taking her even further away from him. Mama was an awe-inspiring example of loyalty, reminding her brood that their father remained *patria potestas*, head of the family. She glared down Gabriel's "no more than a figurehead" muttering, even though her efforts, along with Maria's and William's, proved his contention. Still, she insisted on Papa's supremacy: age and infirmity weren't his fault, his inability to provide more difficult for him than for them, his irritability because he wasn't the man he once was.

As expected, Maria and William offered no argument. Gabriel still scoffed but was also a little tearful. Christina accepted that until she was married, she would continue to read to her father and copy out his scribbled, blotted writing, make sure he took his medicine, ate correctly for his ailments, and was cleanly attired, the last only if Mama or William assisted his dressing. Her heart was, at least, open to pitying him.

Sometimes it seemed that the best she could do for Papa was to let him win at chess.

Unlike his brother, James didn't know how to play. Christina thought that, after hearing about her serious matches with Charles Collinson, he might want to learn. Over a few autumn evenings, she relished the opportunity to teach him and initiate him into her family's enjoyment of contests.

About the same time, she decided she would take William up on his offer to pay for her to have art lessons. Becoming a bona fide artist was something to aspire to, but her main motive, at that point verging on desperation, was to turn a stiff and embarrassed courtship into a Collinson bond like her Rossetti-Polidori one of shared endeavors as well as affection.

James soon gave up on chess, He was impatient, not only with the intricacies of the game, but also with pleasing her. The signs were there, but didn't show her a way out.

Now the leaves are withering how should one love at all?

Another portrait to pose for offered an alternative, productive engagement; being the handmaid of the Lord a worthy occupation. William sitting for the Angel Gabriel completed a happy, if draughty, distraction of camaraderie and creation with her brothers.

At that time Gabriel worked on Newman Street above a hop-shop or dancing academy as its proprietor tried to improve it.

"Why is the painting tall and narrow?" Christina wondered with her first glance at the work in progress.

"It is one half of a diptych. Its companion will depict the Virgin's death."

"Will you have both finished by spring for the R.A.?" William slapped his arms around himself in an attempt to warm his sleeveless, sheeted body. "Anymore coal for the grate?"

"Doubt it." Gabriel urgently picked through the pile of brushes on the small pedestal table next to his easel.

Christina noticed they were all thin-handled and fine-bristled. "No wonder you take so long to finish anything." She also looked at his pallet, noticing he wasn't mixing colors, but using fresh daubs of unadulterated white, blue, and red paint.

"I hope you won't get bronchitis again." William repositioned the woolen shawl that had slipped off her shoulders.

"I haven't even caught a cold." Christina had resigned herself to shivering in her flimsy nightgown for the sake of Gabriel's vision and to prove as enduring as any of the other models who sat for him.

"Interesting." As he leaned forward, William put a hand on his brother's back. "Even with as little as you've done, I see the perspective of Giotto. Yet I also see Flemish primitive, what you and Hunt were so taken with in Bruges. Before you started, I noticed you had followed Van Eyck's practice of preparing the canvas with white ground."

Gabriel smiled. "I'm sure it will all seem a confused mess to those, like Ruskin, who think their opinions matter."

"A risk worth taking. But you must enter both panels together."

"I don't paint to exhibit."

"You must, Gabe, to make a name for yourself, a living. Your work must be seen. And critiqued."

"Says the would-be critic."

"Now I see why you want me contorted on a corner of that saggy cot." Christina though it wise to change the subject. "And all wrinkly and looking about to jump up and run away."

"I thank Collinson for your disquiet." Gabriel was still brooding over Mr. Hunt falling into arrears with the rent on Cleveland Street and defecting to James' studio in Brompton.

They had spoken of many things during the hours of posing and painting, breaking to eat and drink, and for Christina and William to wrap themselves in blankets long enough to feel their fingers and toes again. Not once, until that moment, had anyone mentioned the man Christina had, without good reason, agreed to marry. She was almost convinced the last year of his waxing and waning hadn't happened; that somewhere out there was *the face not seen, the voice not heard, the heart that not yet —*

Christina was jarred into the reality of James' ambiguity, and, more disturbing, her own. Why would she not want him mentioned? If she was truly in love, she would long to hear others connect them. Gabriel moved on to discussing *Thoughts Towards Nature* with William, who glanced at her a few times. She tried to listen, Gabriel on fire with his ambitions for the magazine; William, if not meaning to extinguish his brother's passion for the project, dosing out some common sense to cool it down a little.

***

Christina never liked reworking her poems, although she wasn't as spontaneous and casual about their composition as William wanted others to think. Observation usually planted the seed for one, reflection fed its germination, her mood nourishing or rotting its growth, more often the latter. Her contributions for the upcoming PRB venture were harvested by Gabriel out of a half dozen or so she thought might be ripe enough for the first art and wordsmithing feast Gabriel hoped to serve up by the beginning of January.

As the time approached to hand *Dreamland* and *An End* over to William's final proofing, Christina questioned everything about their "mournful cadences and disappointed desires," which was Gabriel's portrayal and satisfaction with them. She felt that, even in anonymity, she was about to reveal too much of her unrestrained, sorrowful, unholy self. She came close to withdrawing them, to telling William she wanted to before she saw Gabriel again and it was too late. Her oldest brother's tendency to procrastinate was well known. He usually found it hard to stay committed to a project, distracted by every opportunity to do something else, especially to play. He didn't pretend otherwise. "As soon as a thing feels like work, my interest in it is gone." He was about conception, not completion, his energy feeding off immediate gratification, which often sabotaged long-term goals. Finally, he was riding high and steady on a worthy ambition, making no secret of his happiness achieving it with his siblings on board. Christina couldn't let him down.

Too few chords and sad and low sing we so.

It was just before Christmas, nearly midnight, when William returned home from a gathering of the Brotherhood. Christina was in her room ready for but not yet in bed. She didn't want to wait until morning for news of the meeting and met William in the hall.

"Gabriel's not with you?" Since he had moved into a studio by himself, their brother spent more nights at home.

"No. Collinson and I were the first to leave. Your intended, not surprisingly, because he was mopey. While I have such a headache from so much arguing, pouting, and proselytizing, let alone the smoke from those damned cigars most everyone smokes."

"Not James?"

"No. He would rather choke on Catholic incense."

Christina's expression must have given away her thought of *What does William know that I don't.*

"Sorry. It's the headache speaking."

She convinced him to take some warm milk in the kitchen where Grimalkin and the couple of her kittens they had kept were waiting to do the same.

"Who was there?"

"Everyone, I think. All the official PRB set, as well as Madox Brown, Cave Thomas, Deverell swiveling his chair the entire evening, Hancock repeating '*Guardami ben, ben son Beatrice*' to goad Gabriel, and too much coffee drunk. At least they settled on a name."

"*Thoughts Towards Nature*?" Christina hoped. "I like its simplicity."

"No."

"Oh, dear. They didn't choose *The PRB Journal*?"

"No. And not *The Scroll, The Harbinger, The Seed, The Sower, First Thoughts, The Truth-Seeker,* or *The Acorn.*"

"What then?

"Guess."

She did, remembering Gabriel's preference; she liked it, almost as much as her first choice, after all, it being just an elaboration on it: *The Germ: Thoughts Towards Nature in Poetry, Literature, and Art.*

CHAPTER FOURTEEN

Ellen Alleyn appeared and disappeared through her words, warbling melodically and melancholically, a songbird heard but never seen except perched on a page, and then by so few. Her engagement in life was meant to be sweet and safe, a natural movement from branch to branch towards the inclination of nesting. Instead, she was senselessly shot down by naïve expectations, which the afterlife would relentlessly look back on as bad judgment.

It is an empty name I long for; to a name why should I give the peace of all the days I have to live.

It was a name Gabriel invented after the first printing of *The Germ*, so, when it was decided not to risk presenting further issues as the work of one, Christina, unlike the other six male contributors, could continue to conceal her identity. She should have argued she wasn't afraid of owning her poems, that it might be what she needed to do to grow stronger as a writer. From far away in wintry Wiltshire, where she was visiting Aunt Charlotte, a disagreement with Gabriel, via letters he was unlikely to answer, was unwinnable.

Christina was at home for the New Year's Eve delivery of fifty copies of the first issue to Charlotte Street by the printer, George Tupper. Throughout that last day of 1849, its artists and authors arrived. Papa was delighted with the complicated company, while Mama panicked at the lingering of so many hungry, thirsty men eager for a new decade and the wild ride of rebellion. She sent Betsey to the shops with the week's allowance for food, Gabriel convincing her that the success of the magazine would repay her hospitality and "make a little starvation worth it."

By the time the second issue was out, it was clear the Rossetti household budget would not be reimbursed for a while, if at all. The initial bill for printing was £18, under one hundred at a shilling each sold, far from enough to cover it. *This has been an expense that can't be repeated*, William warned. *Gabriel's enthusiasm has begun to wane, but there have been some encouraging responses and his ego isn't about to give up yet.*

Christina wanted to be back in the fray of the struggling, but not yet defeated, project, instead of *kept away in the grandeur of Longleat, shivering in a woolen shawl.*

"Enjoy the privilege my association with the Marchioness affords you," Aunt Charlotte advised. "And stay in rooms with a fire lit."

Christina couldn't fault Lady Bath's hospitality and Aunt Charlotte's attentiveness. Talk of a servants' ball gave her something besides returning home to look forward to. Such an informal affair might prove *Signore Parodi's* lessons hadn't been wasted, although she was long out of practice.

What was supposed to be a shared celebration with estate staff and gentry proved more awkward than amusing for both. Good intentions and all the trappings were there. Champagne, which Christina loathed, flowed, the best silver was laid out; royal cooks, waiters, and an orchestra from London were brought in. Longleat servants were waited on and entertained as though they were masters. Some may have enjoyed the pretense of equality for a few hours, but, because etiquette, reserved conversation, and knowledge of choreographed dances were required, their disadvantage was as evident as ever.

Word was, once the ball wound down around eleven, whether their employers gave permission or turned a blind eye, the servants took the party downstairs. The kitchen was rearranged, leftover food and drink from upstairs made a banquet, a couple of fiddlers and other Horningsham villagers, whether family or friends or sweethearts, smuggled in. At least, as she laid in her bed, that was how Christina imagined the missed part of the festivities.

She did appreciate the daily luxury of solitude at Longleat, a large residence echoing with silence and respectful of personal space. The high wind, not possible in the obstructed landscape of London, was another indulgence. She ranked its clear and present sound slightly less than that of the sea.

If it had been summer, the estate's *gravel lanes, rising lawns, majestic old trees, and meandering water—long leat*—would offer Christina an escape from pretentious interiors and persuade her to settle for a while, be grateful, and *pour out poetry*. Aunt Charlotte expected an end-of-January thaw, outdoor activities having to wait for her niece's congestion and cough to clear anyway. Until then, how could she not appreciate an apartment large enough for two sofas and four armchairs? She tried to, sampling all its furniture, especially the Regency rosewood desk positioned for gazing at the panoramically frosty view beyond the room's massive, mullioned window. Aunt Charlotte, proving her relation to Aunt Margaret, closed the heavy curtains to keep her "delicate niece" out of draughts. From the valance-tasseled, half-tester bed, Christina admired the Flemish tapestry warming an adjacent wall. She intended to mention it in a letter to Gabriel, along with being *impressed by one part of his soul sermon* included in *The Germ* and her sighting of *The Girlhood of Mary Virgin* hung too high in the Marchioness's sitting room. Instead, she told William, who always passed on essential information.

If our brother shows any interest in writing to me, please do not put him off, she added.

Too much of savory sauces and sweet puddings urged Christina to utilize her room for exercising times daily around it, except the hearth her aunt insisted was kept blazing stifled her breathing and made her want to sleep.

Her weariness also came from writing letters. They went out every or every other day to William and Amelia, and, at least, once a week to Mama and Maria, only a few to Gabriel and James.

She pined for her small, plain Charlotte Street room, and Grimalkin and her now adolescent offspring. There was nothing better than being at home, and, especially, in one's own private piece of home, surrounded with familiarity while alone with her thoughts. She needed an out of the way place for daydreaming and kneeling with a sense of nothing changing, leaving little space for wanting what wasn't needed.

***

James destroyed the potential pleasure of their reunion more than a week after Christina had returned from Wiltshire by announcing, "I think I shall soon be done with painting."

"I'm not far away," Mama whispered with a hand on Christina's shoulder once she convinced Papa to leave the parlor with her. William was at the Excise Office, Maria using the upstairs study.

"Don't put up with nonsense." Papa was less concerned than his wife that James could hear him.

With her parents gone, Christina and James sat together on the settee, her right hand straying towards his until it settled for him ignoring it. The conversation between them started and stopped a few times.

"But what of St. Elizabeth of Hungary?"

"It may well be my last."

"That would break Gabriel's heart."

"Plenty of others to mend it. And break it again, more emphatically than I ever could."

Christina wanted to ask James what he knew of those "others," specifically, one she had heard about, first from William describing *a lissome, rather plain, red-haired shopgirl.* He had also recounted Mr. Deverell boasting about his discovery in a Milliner's off Leicester Square and elevating his new model to a *staggeringly beautiful being, tall and slim with a delicate, perfected face for modelling.*

"I don't know if I can continue with the PRB. If my true faith will allow me to."

She only said: "Not this, not this," and clasped her hands against her heart.

"I had hoped … well, I have to accept you won't change." James wouldn't look at her, his arms hung over his knees. "Unless … no, you won't, will you?"

"What are you asking me?" *What is he telling me?*

"It won't happen at once, but … I've looked into applying to Stonyhurst in Lancaster."

"To study what, if not art?"

"It's a Jesuit Seminary."

Christina was afraid her legs wouldn't lift her. As she finally stood, she turned away from him but was the one rejected.

***

No one was surprised Christina suffered the end of winter, *icebound, hunger-pinched and dim,* for she often did. Fleeting sunshine gave no warmth, nests remained dark and empty, hasty buds were threatened by frost, and there were episodes of blinding sleet.

Do come, do not come, do come she repeated in her thoughts while confined to bed, her Longleat cough and some ugly blisters returned. She was kept medicated by her mother and sister and understood their frowns when she asked whether James had called or sent a note. If William or Gabriel looked in on her, they might tell her how *St. Elizabeth of Hungary* was progressing.

"It must be very beautiful." She hoped to prompt them to reveal more than "it's coming along" or "you know Collinson always produces decent work."

Instead, they offered news about *The Germ.* Gabriel was as relieved as William was anxious about passing on the proprietorship and editorship of it to the Tupper brothers, who intended to finance it from then on. A name change was also agreed upon, too much like an explanation, in Christina's opinion: *Art and Poetry, being Thoughts towards Nature, conducted principally by Artists.* Necessity overruled her responsible brother, but a few more months proved William's worries over failure and compounding debt justified.

Christina didn't want to add to his anxiety by revealing what James had told her, although it was likely that, after spending more time with him than she had, William had known of James' revised plans for a while. Gabriel had long since bowed out of the mess his matchmaking had made. Otherwise, there were clues that didn't need her to give them away, resulting in Maria thinking out loud that James was conspicuously and, therefore, unconscionably, neglectful of her sister, and Mama suggesting, in her gently brutal way, that it might be better he was.

Papa agreed. "That dull creature should never join the Rossettis."

Christina revived some affection for her father through the lack of convention in his remark. Proper thinking would maintain her betrothal to James was about whether she could become a Collinson—a Catholic Collinson, an aberration even in his own family.

By May of the new decade, when the PRB's printing enterprise was gasping for breath, Christina knew the survival of her engagement was also unlikely. At least the magazine's short life had been creative and exciting, drawn a few favorable notices, and sparked some controversy. Disappointment was not regret over believing in its possibilities, its failure not for lack of trying. There was nothing left of her awkward, aimless, dispassionate future with absent James but the ridiculous waiting for it to be called off.

According to William, Christina had Mr. Millais to thank and blame for James turning up again. *The Carpenter's Shop* depiction of the holy family had earned John Millais the distinction of pictorial blasphemy and convinced James that the PRB was jeopardizing his soul and salvation.

"The hardest thing is letting Gabriel know. I've written him a letter. Would you look it over?"

The hardest thing is letting Gabriel know? You're not engaged to him, she silently, momentarily raged before surrendering to what Mary Collinson called her desire to "do all from self-respect." Christina dared not take him into the parlor where she knew Papa might belittle him and, if not Mama, then Maria, would want to know why he had come. Ideally, Christina wished she could pretend to read his letter right there in the front hallway and send him on his way, but there wasn't enough light to fool him. She knew it was Betsey's night off, so she led him to the kitchen, dusting off the flour left on the table from the girl's sloppy baking and cleaning up. She hoped the room might infuse him with its heavy scent of garlic and basil, so his betrayal of the Rossettis would literally make him stink.

She called Grimalkin, hoping she would come and turn on him if he reached down to pet her.

"I just want Gabriel to understand my reasons. It's not personal or coming out of jealousy or meant to seem ungrateful."

She was unable to fathom what he wanted her to understand, how he expected her to react to the very first line of the letter, calling himself *a sincere Catholic,* following-up on his declaration that he was considering a Jesuit college. Did he think it would encourage her to read further? She did, to where he claimed he couldn't *as a Catholic, in good conscience, support spreading the artistic attitudes of those who were not.*

William had come in and uncomfortably raised his voice. "This is preposterous. I think you need to leave."

James agreed without hesitation, forgetting the letter falling out of Christina's hands. William picked it up and followed him beyond where she could see.

The woman knelt but did not pray, nor weep nor cry.

Christina's engagement to James had put her on trial to prove her innocence; his mother, brother, sister, and sister-in-law the first to give their verdict, as Amelia assured, not because of any crime Christina had committed.

I pressed forward to no goal, there was no prize I strove to win.

The Brotherhood bid him good riddance, or so her brothers assumed by "the lack of conversation about his departure." Gabriel at first proclaimed no hard feelings, while William, for once less inclined to be tactful, admitted he never really enjoyed James' company.

"You've been spared a lifetime of his righteousness, indecisiveness, cowardice, and narcolepsy."

Christina would, eventually, realize fortune came by way of misfortune. She accepted she had been tricked by girlish fancy and had avoided more serious consequences than a summer that didn't spare her the torment of wanting and not wanting to hear from James. Her mother thought she should formally release him, what he was expecting her to do. *Nonno* agreed, his opinion usually enough to sway her one way or other. "Although a coward, Mr. Collinson is a gentleman." Fortunately, her grandfather didn't press the issue while she was in Gloucestershire with him, *Nonna*, Aunt Eliza, and Uncle Philip for a few weeks of pleasant, pastoral leisure and excursions. A trip in August with Maria to Brighton was curative for her sister but triggered another Christina relapse into despondency. Maria especially enjoyed and benefited from sea bathing; an activity forbidden Christina by most of the doctors who had ever attended to her. It was a long, humdrum, humid, headachy month, one day much like another. Christina walked the strand with little interest in what the traveling tradespeople offered and patronized the shops on Western Street even less. There was, fortunately, only a little socializing scheduled, usually taking tea with dreary acquaintances of their mother. Christina was most content staying in the rooming house with the intention of writing, but she only accomplished two or three scraps of poems. Reading and needlework were also attempted, napping often the most successful choice she made.

She blamed a neuralgic migraine as the cause of her sending inquiries she shouldn't about James' whereabouts, work, and health to William's workplace.

I direct this to you at Somerset House because it would displease Mama so much. I trust you will not let her know of my weakening.

Mama found out by way of William's inability to lie to her and dictated the letter to break off the engagement. Even with her mother's help, Christina could barely compose it, her handwriting unrecognizable, not quick or neat as had impressed Mr. Bell Scott, or as beautiful as Amelia would wish to look at every day. As required by custom, Christina was obligated to return any correspondence she had received from James, and tokens of affection—the former a few brief missives, the latter nonexistent. James had mentioned a Collinson family ring, "now that my sister Mary has given up hope," but Christina had never received it.

"What about that book of hymns?" Maria mentioned.

To inspire your poetry to a higher purpose, James had inscribed in it. Christina also recalled the rare anticipation in his eyes as he handed it to her, the only time she feared he might kiss her.

"Must I?"

"Ye—." Mama stopped herself from being ruthless.

Christina was relieved once the letter was written and posted, but doubt returned when William confirmed James had received it.

"He turned quite pale, seemed to choke a little as he pulled it out of his pocket and, almost immediately, put it back."

I prayed for him; was my prayer sin?
I sacrificed, he never bought;
He nothing gave, he nothing took;
We never bartered look for look.

At last, James Collinson was freed for his spiritual calling and she for hers. That was how she initially endured the breakup, respecting his religious conviction that had tested and confirmed her own. Spiritual empathy didn't prevent her from feeling ashamed as a young woman with a failed engagement in her history. She hadn't been able to make a man unequivocally devoted to her and wondered, would it ever be possible?

She prayed to be loved in the gaze of God, but also, at some time, by a divine man who saw her heavenly on earth.

Was her prayer sin?

Envy was sin. A perverse part of her wished she could be like the models Gabriel and his art brothers used, desired, even loved. She rarely met them but would hear about their bountiful beauty, lack of inhibitions and hygiene, bold laughter, and unapologetic cursing. William also spoke of their misfortunes, not directly scolding Christina's discriminations but making her want to correct them with compassion.

She didn't succeed while she was still lost in the fog of feeling sorry

86

for herself. Rossettis and Polidoris rallied around her with the condition that she didn't mention James. She struggled but agreed to engage herself in the life she was left with, which included, and was soon dominated by, preparations for moving to the day school Mama had taken on.

"I will make my way there somehow," assured Charles Cayley, who was studying Italian with her father. "Walking is my usual mode of transport."

Both men welcomed Christina's presence in the parlor during the lessons. Papa found it helpful for her to engage with Mr. Cayley in instructional conversation. She found relief in discussing more books than she had yet—would probably ever—read.

She was also distracted by William's first visit to Mr. Bell Scott in Newcastle.

Christina was certain she was getting over James until, taking a break from packing for the move to Arlington Street, Mornington Crescent, walking through Regent's Park with Maria and William, she saw him. On a day too cold for flies, weak sunlight ineffective in drying the damp, he was by himself but untrue. It was a blow, and she went down, conscious long enough to wonder if he would respond to her fainting. Later she was told he walked on as if without noticing.

> *Therefore we parted as we met,*
> *She on her way, and I on mine;*
> *I think her tender heart was set*
> *On holier things and more Divine:—*
> *We parted thus and gave no sign.*

PART THREE

I looked for that which is not, nor can be,
And hope deferred made my heart sick in truth:
But years must pass before a hope of youth
Is resigned utterly.
~ from *A Pause of Thought* by Christina Rossetti

CHAPTER FIFTEEN

Along with a roomful of London ladies, Christina learned of Mr. Scott's imminent arrival at the beginning of the afternoon's art class. She knew one other student, Emily Rosalind, the daughter of a friend of Mama's, Elisa Andrews Orme, who was a patron of artists, emerging suffragette, and sister-in-law to the poet Coventry Patmore. It was obvious Emily was there to humor her mother more than herself and waste her father's money, which his successful brewery business allowed her to.

Christina utilized every moment William's hard-earned sixpence bought to improve her drawing skills.

Assuming none of the other students had ever met Mr. Scott, Christina was the only one expecting the government official from the National School of Design to be more beguiling than bureaucratic. Tall and rugged, diabolically handsome with thick hair and eyebrows and a piercing gaze, his syllabic speech mesmerizing and mischievous, he navigated the maze of aproned ladies, clutter of easels and tables holding casts, vases of blossoming branches, and bowls of tumbling fruit. Although he was there because of a professional interest in Ford Madox Brown's experimental school for artisans in Camden Town, he couldn't help being too personal, regarding more than artwork.

"You can't finish if you don't begin, Miss—"

"Orme." Emily Rosalind blushed as Christina was determined she wouldn't.

"My dear Miss Rossetti. Yet again, *mignon*, you don't disappoint. While others copy beautiful objects, or, like Miss Orme, daydream of doing so, you draw wood shavings picked up from a joiners' yard. The Millais effect?"

Christina nodded. She'd had months to adjust to what she shouldn't expect from Mr. Scott; disappointment eased by knowing his place in her family's affections allowed a safe haven for him to remain in hers. She would soon meet his wife Letitia, whose existence William discovered when he visited Newcastle the previous autumn, along with her being "amiable if scatterbrained, talkative even when no one was listening."

"I hope you will persevere."

"You sound like my brother William," Christina wanted to seem dispassionate, "who thinks playing with rhymes and being holed up in Mama's school aren't enough to occupy me."

"Are they?" Mr. Scott's hand went out to hers. She gave him her sketch.

"Almost no one wanting my poetry or lessons serves my basic laziness."

"I think Millais has the edge." He handed her drawing back but lifted it before she could take it. "There they are. Those richly-hazel eyes."

"How my brown ones envy them." Emily Rosalind stole Mr. Scott's attention again.

"They needn't."

Christina didn't see if Mr. Scott had satisfied her friend's vanity for she bowed away to withhold her irritation. Too late she realized the tone of her voice gave it away. "It's strange. I have no real interest in doing art. Perhaps, despite and because of my brethren, I've become bored with thinking about and looking at it."

"Is she not a loveable creature of the Almighty's making? Although she acts as if she doesn't know it."

"William Bell Scott," came a shout, which set everyone looking at them, or made Christina aware they already were.

"Sorry to tear you away." Mr. Madox Brown put an arm around Mr. Scott's shoulder. "There's so much else to show you. And Emma hopes you'll dine with us. Unlike Miss Rossetti, she doesn't hesitate to admit she's enchanted by you."

Mr. Brown was right. Christina would have denied it if there had been a chance before she was abandoned to wood shavings and being in an intriguing amoral world but not of it. She could shield and satisfy her bohemian tendencies in that stuffy room in the North London School of Drawing, where respectable women pursued a pastime rather than vocation.

Eventually, Mama had approved Christina's attendance, not without questioning William's willingness to pay the fee.

"I'm earning an extra £50 yearly from my art critiques in *The Spectator*. I can afford it."

"I suppose, as you're not married. But Henrietta waits, so it should be saved."

"I doubt she does, Mama."

"Well, my son, if you were a little more assertive—"

"I can go without," Christina didn't want to say. She liked Henrietta Rintoul and the idea she might one day call her sister, but, more urgently, Christina needed a distraction from housekeeping and teaching, having little tolerance or talent for either. The dreary, cramped house on Arlington Street felt more like a prison than school, let alone a home. The back garden with rose trellises scaling the scullery walls, a grassy patch, and even a scrappy crabapple tree was its only improvement on Charlotte Street. It offered Papa a chance, if one he rarely took, to get some exercise and soothe his complaints, a tapping cane his eyes, the women in his world, mainly Christina, also assisting him.

Even while helping her mother run the school, and although they had a new more capable servant, Christina was at her father's beck and call, witnessed by the few pupils enrolled, mostly shopkeepers' daughters just out of the nursery. They gathered in the front room for exercises such as counting imaginary geese, cats, and canaries. Their eyes and mouths opened wide when *Signore* Rossetti's voice loomed largely incoherent except for "Christina" and, too often for Mama's tolerance, "Damn," or an even more offensive word.

"If you must, *in intaliano*," Mama would scold him later, "so all my proper little English girls hear is an old man grumbling."

Everyone, even Gabriel sporadically for meals and sleep, resided at 38 Arlington Street. Maria had given up governessing to take on Mama's private students around London and was otherwise occupied by charitable causes, research, and writing. William, enduring a civil servant's long hours and slow ladder-climbing, and writing for *The Spectator*, continued to contribute the most towards household expenses.

Christina wasn't sorry William enjoyed Gabriel's company less.

"Have to be so careful not to put Gabe in a difficult spot because of Lizzie's moods. If we thought Collinson—" William paused to read Christina's reaction, his relief strengthening her resolve to accept and adjust, "didn't fit in with our family, this young woman's sarcastic, chaffy talk, as if she would rather turn off all conversation, makes her even less likely to."

Christina did and didn't want to meet Gabriel's first true love, "radiant with the tresses of Aurora," his obsession with women's hair often overlooking the unreliability of their virtue and intellect. She hoped Miss Siddall was a woman of moral repute, steady faith, and, despite William's assessment, interesting thoughts. Christina anticipated feeling dark and dumpy around her but was determined not to mind if Miss Siddall urged Gabriel into serious work and a settled life.

Christina didn't expect it to be years before she met Miss Siddall. William explained the long wait by "Sid's" talent for coyly refusing invitations and avoiding introductions, disappearing at the announcement of an intrusion, or, if caught off guard, escaping eye contact, a word, a nod, a smile at a kind greeting, even a compliment.

That other William, whose opinion Christina always welcomed, also confirmed Miss Siddall's behavior through firsthand experience. "In the romantic dusk of an apartment," Mr. Bell Scott found Gabriel and a lady he didn't know and could hardly see.

"I waited for Gabriel to introduce her. He didn't. She rose. I made a little bow. Without acknowledging my presence, let alone courtesy, she went into another room and never came out for the duration of my visit."

"How did you know who she was?"

"I guessed. But, according to Gabriel's silence, I might've imagined her."

Christina wondered why anyone would flee Mr. Scott and was tempted to say so.

"As I recall our first encounter, you were almost as rude—"

"Oh, I wasn't, was I?"

"Well, you made me feel quite the intruder. At least you didn't slink sulkily away."

"'The slight but serious girl endured my astonishing appearance and usual impertinence with disapproving interest,'" a new voice, in the conversation not the room, jarred Christina, mostly because, for once, it was worth listening to. "Will told me all about his first acquaintance with the 'remarkable Rossettis.'"

Christina had almost forgotten Mrs. Letitia Scott was there in the Arlington Street back parlor on this sweltering July evening. She sat on the two-seater with Maria, whose full figure pushed Letty, as Mrs. Scott liked to be called, into an upright posture that didn't hamper her chatter about every insignificant thing she could think of. Maria, with no arm maneuvering room to discreetly wipe her flushed, sweaty face with the handkerchief her right hand held ready, exhibited remarkable patience and cordiality with her couch-mate.

"And now I know why." Mrs. Scott's attention darted at Mama who, although trying to be available to all their guests, was leaning towards the young man standing in front of the unlit hearth between where she and Papa were seated. He was a paternal relative, born in Abruzzi, educated in Naples, and affiliated with Mazzini's *La Giovine Italia* and involvement in the 1848 uprising. His narrow escape to political exile in London was reminiscent of his uncle's, as was his desire for society in which his scholarship and soul would flourish. His arrival perked up Papa, enlivening the old man's reminisces of the beauty, history, and glory of their homeland as nothing had for a long while.

Along with her mother, father, and the two Williams, Christina was more interested in what her cousin Teodorico Pietrocola had to say than in Letty's gossipy babble. One story convinced even Mrs. Scott to be quiet long enough for its telling.

"There was a fellow student who was a priest, a few years my senior.

I went to his house so we might go to mass, one that he was going to offer. I found him feasting on ham and figs and drinking wine. 'Sit down, sit. I saved some for you.' I couldn't believe my eyes or ears. 'It's a mortal sin to eat before receiving the Lord,' I said. Yet he laughed while dribbling wine and wondering that I believed bread could be the body and wine the blood of anyone. 'Not anyone.' I felt such a fury. 'Jesus, our Savior.' He was undeterred in his blasphemy, if anything, more emboldened. 'My boy, if you accept all the mother church tells you, you will believe much that is untrue.'"

Mrs. Scott's immediately broke her silence. "Oh, and so I cannot be a Catholic. No, no, I can't."

"Well, you aren't, my dear. Not this month, anyway."

Christina eventually understood what prompted Mr. Scott's sarcasm. Getting to know his wife was observing what William described as her "dancing around piety while trying out almost every doctrinal camp."

"Obedience is the fruit of faith. Patience is the early blossom on the tree of faith," Christina offered as much to her poetic memory as to anyone listening.

"*Bellisima.*" Teodorico raised his hands together in prayer-like approval.

Maria nodded before turning to Mrs. Scott with a forgiving smile and pat on her arm. "Attend Christ Church with my mother, Chrissy, and me on Sunday."

Mrs. Scott flushed with excitement. "I will. Oh, but …." She looked for her husband who was leaning on a doorframe and examining some writing Teodorico had shared with him. "When are we leaving London, Will?"

Christina noticed Mr. Scott wince.

"Will," Mrs. Scott pleaded.

Teodorico moved quickly but tactfully to retrieve his notebook. "I never meant to monopolize your attention, sir." He bowed slightly towards Mrs. Scott, strands of his dark abundant hair, slightly reddish in candlelight, flopping over his eyes reminiscent of Gabriel's.

"What, dear?" Mr. Scott finally responded to his wife.

"Are we still in London on Sunday?"

"We catch the train midday."

"What time is the service, my dear Maria?" Mrs. Scott was generous but never artificial with her affection.

"Ten. There wouldn't be time."

"We must stay longer next visit, Will. For you to talk poetry and art, and me to go to Christ Church. And just for more time with our lovely friends."

Husband and wife, despite the emotional distance between them, smiled agreeably at each other.

"I, also, wish to attend your church," Teodorico said softly. "If that would be appropriate."

"You would be most welcome." Mama's eyes glistened as she extended a hand and her faith to him.

Teodorico had another request, not made that evening, but communicated a few days later through Gabriel who arrived as if everyone was waiting for him.

He wasn't wrong in that assumption.

"Cousin Teo wants to add Rossetti to his name. If Papa agrees."

During a bad week, their father had been confined to bed. Maria was unanimously designated to go up to his room to try to get an answer from him. It didn't take long, for, as she related, although Papa could hardly find the breath or words to speak, he immediately sat up and clapped his hands that only a few hours earlier couldn't hold a cup or a spoon.

"Is Will not home yet?" Gabriel wondered.

"He's at the Rintouls." Christina broke her promise not to tell.

"Ah. Courting. Or 'not really.'"

"And what about you, son?" Mama hurried to approach him. "Will you bring Miss Siddall to see us soon?"

"When it happens, Mama," he said while opening the front door, a cat running in. "For now, you have a visitor who has no doubt she is welcome."

CHAPTER SIXTEEN

Christina preferred not to read her work out loud. Instead, Mama or Maria were Papa's eyes. They were accurate and articulate, respectful of her rhythms and rhymes, delicate with her meanings, and obviously proud of her accomplishments. Yet there was often something—someone—missing. Christina suspected she wasn't the only one thinking of Gabriel who always insisted he "perform Chrissy's poems." He did so with pretentious preparation, as if about to portray Hamlet Act 5, Scene 1, standing with his legs apart, his right hand on his right hip, left one holding, instead of a skull, the open notebook too far away for his poor sight. He didn't miss a thespian beat, with a choreographed swing out and up of his arm, bringing it closer to his deep-set, dark-ringed gray eyes, which, despite their failings, eventually focused expectantly on his little sister's way with words. She worried he would be disappointed, especially as his high, rounded brow, which prompted Mr. Hunt to sometimes actually call him Shakespeare, furrowed.

Her apprehension was usually unwarranted. There might be suggestions, mostly for changes to titles and a word here and there, but, with few exceptions, Gabriel gave confidence and credibility to her writing. Observation, reflection, solitude, delight, and disappointment urged Christina to write poetry. Gabriel's interest and insistence made her a poet, if an absent, nameless, and pseudonymous one.

Her reliance on Gabriel's opinion didn't mean to discount the involvement of Mama, Maria, William, or, especially, *Nonno*. She knew in another family, a less exceptional one that wanted her married more than intellectually and creatively committed and waited predictably for a succession of pretty babies not words, she wouldn't have so naturally gone in whatever direction her muse took her.

I watched a rosebud very long brought on by dew and sun and shower, waiting to see the perfect flower. Then, when I thought it should be strong, it opened at the matin hour and fell at evensong.

Miss Siddall's monopoly of Gabriel and sensitivity to rivalry was, after all, just another inconvenience. After the breakup with Collinson, Christina learned to be more self-reliant, something a youngest and indulged child never thought she would have to be. Throughout a solemn and sickly adolescence, she struggled with the realization that life wasn't all about desire, expression, and fulfillment, but thought she would die before a longer view was required. Once it seemed she wouldn't, she attempted to navigate ups and downs by building strength, and, retaining faith, not lose her way.

"A penny for your thoughts," Mama would ask Christina when she was little and sulking longer than was tolerable. In another context, Christina opened a short story she had written with the same query, knowing secrecy was tricky to one who, without lying, didn't always wish to tell the truth.

Not everything Christina scribbled had been or was for sharing, not even with Gabriel. Slipped out of sight and sometimes into the fire, many poems and most of her prose didn't grow beyond infancy. She had hopes in their birthing but soon realized their weaknesses and accepted they were too sickly to survive scrutiny. Those that weren't incinerated but held on with shallow breath were hidden away to pretend they didn't exist, although once in a long while they were visited with hope they might yet improve.

Such was the case with a little tale she had written out in an exercise book entitled *Maude*, a familiarly pretty child grown into a pale girl and compulsive rhymester of whatever came into her head or stirred her emotions. Like Christina at fifteen, Maude Foster would rather be ignored, considered plain and unremarkable. So she told herself when it was brought to her attention that the right circumstances and company could light up her eyes, make her cheeks glow, lift her to full height, and animate her.

"To look more beautiful than you did as a child," Christina was certain Mama had whispered on, at least, one occasion, looking as beautiful as ever herself. Naturally, Christina incorporated it into the narrative, along with how she felt about hearing others consider her clever. She wasn't sure she relished or regretted any discussion over why and how so much of her verse was broken hearted, whether she wrote foolishly or affectedly about what she couldn't possibly understand, or out of some secret discontent.

Perhaps there was a degree of truth in all these opinions.

For a while, Christina convinced herself she wrote for diversion, even dissection. *Nonno's* pride and printing press and Gabriel's germinating gave her a taste of ambition's fruits both sweet and sour, but only as she was invisibly tempted and could give it up at any time.

"Yes, I continue to write now and then as the humor seizes me," she spoke in fact as well as fiction. Writing couldn't be seen as the pleasuring, punishing creative process Gabriel openly made the brilliancy and bane of his existence. Christina must remain restrained and humble and show only that she was occupied not preoccupied by any activity other than being a virtuous, useful woman.

I dare say she is very good … but that does not make her pleasing.

It would be extravagant to leave a candle burning and, therefore, useless to have paper and pencil at the ready, certainly affecting to tell anyone she lay awake at night thinking up verses and stories. Still, if there was some inkling of inspiration, she took advantage of the solitude and silence except for purring and, in the small house on Arlington Street, Maria's funny, wheezy snoring. Prayers were said at length before Christina's body slowly curled, her mind unwound, and there might be hope she would remember a theme, rhyme, or turn of phrase in the morning. Usually, weariness was a more urgent need to fulfill and only sleep wasn't lost.

For Maude, it was in her writing book she found the seed of a new piece, nourishment for one already sprouted, or a last attempt at a remedy for another grown to the point of withering. A combination of commonplace and scrapbook, album, and lockable diary, it contained writings and drawings before, if ever, they were meant for others to see.

Folding back its timeworn cover and leafing through its often-flattened pages, the words had been scratched out neater than the pictures. Like Christina, Maude felt her literary efforts showed more potential than her artistic ones. It was never reported whether Maude took any instruction to improve the latter, but Christina did let her occasionally share a developed poem or two with family, friends, and almost strangers.

Seated between Miss Savage and Sophia Mowbray, she was attacked on either hand with questions concerning her verses. A flood of ecstatic compliments followed ... she was so young, so much admired, poor thing, looked so delicate ... if only Miss Foster could be induced to publish.

"Why not send it to Tupper and Sons, a story for girls in the Miss Edgeworth mode?"

"I don't know, Will. I'm not sure it's good enough to publicly put my name on."

"Ellen Alleyn?"

"She died with *The Germ*."

"Did you show it to Her Highness, after all?"

Another summer stay at Longleat had given Christina the opportunity to taste greenhouse grown breadfruit, take carriage rides to church, read a journal kept by Aunt Charlotte when she was in Italy a decade before, and observe pet monkeys fastidiously grooming their whiskers and rattling the chains restricting them to their perches. Despite her aunt's and Lady Bath's best efforts and fine weather, there was much dull time, which either made Christina listless and homesick, or offered her the leisure and necessity for writing. It was then she added poetry to *Maude* and felt enough at ease with Lady Bath to ask her opinion on the story.

"She judged it lacking in 'elevation.'"

"Really? I think it highly moral and thoughtful."

"She objected to the commonplace conversations. I guess in her world there never are." Christina thought how tiresome it would be to always have to say something extraordinary. "The verse was more to her taste."

"Well, there are many commonplace girls who would enjoy reading it."

"Perhaps my nieces, if I ever have any." She waited for William to reply, wanting to stamp her foot when he didn't. "Not that they would be ordinary. When will you propose to Henrietta?"

"I think there is an understanding."

"'Don't let it become a misunderstanding,'" Christina quoted their mother. "Anyway, the manuscript is put to rest in a drawer, never to be revised. One day I hope to write something better."

"No doubt you will." William knew to qualify his reply. "That is the thinking the best writers have."

Christina didn't lie about her intention to leave *Maude in memoriam*, but within hours of her conversation with William a deliciously dark and wildly romantic idea had her impulsively resurrecting it. Flipping to the last pages and the character she was left with, Christina added to the actions Agnes, Maude's closest cousin, took to conceal what was *never intended to be seen. The locked book she never opened: but had it placed in Maude's coffin, with all its records of folly, sin, vanity … and true penitence also.*

It was a melodramatic stunt of mourning and weak writing before the story was finally buried with the assumption it wouldn't be brought up again.

***

Christina was soon working on another prose piece to prove she could do better, setting it *not a thousand miles from fairyland* and herself free from the fetters of realism. Influences of her childhood, like *Jack, the Giantkiller, Red Riding Hood, Perrault's Fairy Tales*, as well as those by the Brothers Grimm and Hans Christian Anderson, had already influenced her reading to the few children attending the Arlington Street school. She had no objection to reciting others' work, especially with an elfin audience so open to believing. She thought how playfully Gabriel would do it, one day his babies lucky to have a father who was an overgrown child himself. Christina hoped her eldest brother would grow old more like *Nonno* than Papa. Nearly ninety, grandfather Polidori wasn't a burden but a beacon, physically and mentally active, jovial, and generous with his time and heart, and always welcome into everyone else's.

Varying her voice and facial expressions, Christina was compelled to continue by the giggles and gasps of her audience following her through clever, consequential tales. Characters, places, and events came to life in her and, hopefully, the children, Christina reliving her own first experiences of literary enchantment, trickery, ruin, and redemption. It could get quite lively when she encouraged the little girls to perform their favorite scenes, just as she and her siblings had done. Similarly, squabbling over parts and props was usually conciliated, but when it escalated out of control, Mama was still capable of stepping in to call the play off.

She settled the girls down with a firm, yet gentle reminder that "learning how to avoid conflict by putting aside wants and wills to compromise was as important a lesson as reading, writing, or arithmetic."

Mama took Christina out of the room. "Dear, offer the gift of fantasy with caution. Even as it entertains, it must contain instruction. Yes, you want the girls to enjoy their schooling, but as a teacher you can't allow yourself to weaken in your moral and practical responsibility towards them."

She wondered if Mama had privately scolded Papa when the parlor was in an uproar with his young sons and daughters acting out whatever imaginative chaos he had instigated. He did sometimes tease them about justifying their mother's fear that they would "never be content with real life." Otherwise, Christina sensed her mother's struggle between loving her husband's and children's bonding, spontaneity, and creativity, and realizing she had to be a killjoy and insist on preparing them for serious living.

It was unlikely Gabriel's progeny would benefit from such a sobering, stabilizing influence, born of a woman more likely to be desired for her tumbling hair, pouting mouth, vacant eyes, and goddess poses.

If Christina's role as a teacher was rigidly defined, it was not so as a writer. She hardly knew where to begin. Except she had already, long since, for the challenge of rhyming and reproducing what she saw and felt in successions of words that fell into magical places much as drawing strokes did for the boy Gabriel.

Perhaps writing was the other reason she hadn't married Collinson, why she had begun to suspect she wouldn't marry anyone. Would it ever make her a living so she wouldn't be a burden on her family: enough income to keep her frugally clothed, contribute to the rent, and support her infrequent need to travel? Writing could give her the solitude she needed, but other than income and avoiding governessing and more romantic fiascos, she didn't know what its providential purpose was to be.

She might begin again by more consciously considering what she wanted it to be. Entertaining? Educational? Melodic? Melancholy? Bucolic? Urbane? Sensational? Sobering? Prayerful? Predictable?

Not predictable.

There were more than a few branches to her creative tree and who knew how many yet to emerge. Climbing along them, unsure which would hold her to the end, she felt the need to try them out, to risk. *Nick* took her as far away from herself as *Maude* kept her too close. She had found a narrative style suited to her imagination and message, the latter saved from over-moralizing by uncanny creatures and happenings fantasized by the former. She had to admit, for all its seriousness, *Nick* was a gratifying project: a fable with elements to amuse, amend, and, hopefully, meet Mama's approval. Christina thought it would, starting with its pretty pastoral backdrop of a stone cottage with flower, kitchen and vegetable gardens, a farm supply of *milk, eggs, mutton, butter, poultry, and cheese*, fields full of *hops and barley for beer, and wheat for bread*, and an *orchard with fruit*, reminiscent of holidays at Holmer Green. Mama would also be pleased with its illustration of how, when insecurity, envy, and anger control one's actions, wealth from possessions may create poverty of character. Mama would certainly applaud the redemptive ending, but would she, or anyone, recognize the self-admonishment of the author's own faults in it? Or consider how Christina's disillusionment influenced it?

CHAPTER SEVENTEEN

By the time Christina realized there was only one sheet of paper left, it was too late to keep her handwriting smaller and tighter. Instead, she condensed her thoughts to avoid crossing. William tolerated it. Mama and Maria didn't, only their eyesight complaining, which Christina couldn't disregard, even over one hundred miles away.

She had almost gotten used to heading her letter with another new address, but not that she was left there without any relatable company. Longleat was nearby, but Aunt Charlotte had gone to London, before Mama, to help Aunt Eliza care for their weakening mother. While the housekeeper, Mrs. Bryant, was chatty and regularly inquired if there was anything Christina needed, the cook and maid responded awkwardly to her wandering around the house. A young groundsman, whistling brightly at a distance, was silent and shy as Christina walked past him along one of the gravel paths that crossed the garden at the back of the tall, terraced house. She was on her way to check on two fig tree seedlings she had planted in a sheltered spot, intending their appearance and bounty to console her father's upcoming removal from London.

In the center of the yard was an apple tree, small but about to burst larger with blossoms she hoped wouldn't be rain-ravaged and sent too soon to the ground. Violets and blue-eyed speedwell were impatiently spreading through the grass. Christina confused the lad about to roll his reel mower over them, begging him not to.

"S'pose it can wait." He obliged her, at least for one afternoon.

Christina did consider Reverend Bennett an agreeable neighbor who might call or, more likely, she would meet in or around St. John the Baptist's. It was an imposing church, not unique because of its Norman, even Saxon, origins, or tower and spire, but due to its entrance that passed a holy well and *Via Crucis* with scenes from the Stations of the Cross sculpted from stone. Lady Bath supported Reverend Bennett's Tractarian views and considered his sermons the best she had ever heard. She was impressed by his "apostolic approach," no matter his controversial views and practices had caused riots and forced his resignation from a previous incumbency. Despite the doubt, even protest, that initially greeted his appointment—eggs thrown at Lady Bath the day of his induction—so far, he was popular with his Frome-Selwood parishioners and had nearly doubled the congregation for Sunday service.

It remained questionable whether the Rossettis would be able to claim the same turnaround in their fortunes running a school. There was a rush to organize the classroom, supplies, and schedules, and advertise for students in addition to the few the Dowager Marchioness and Dr. Bennett had secured. Classes had just begun when news of *Nonna* stole Mama's attention and, soon after, with night traveling, reassuring presence away.

28th April 1853. Brunswick Pl., Frome. My precious Mama. Thank God that dear Nonna didn't die in pain, and that you were there. I am pleased she thought of me, although she probably doubted my love.

The question of whether Christina would attend *Nonna* Polidori's funeral was left up to Mama. As much as Christina wanted friends and family in London to know she longed to see them, it was more important not to give the impression that she hoped to escape her management of the Frome house and school. She had efficiently handled the arrival by rail of a new bed from Heal and Sons, and some business of Aunt Charlotte's, taking the opportunity while in Frome to buy *a suitable counterpane* from Gilmore's. There were choices to be made about reupholstering a couch and, knowing Mama was *no miser*, Christina approved an additional two shillings, six pence for *extra stuffing, horsehair, and the best castors*. She was learning the uncertainty of students' attendance, such as little Sarah arriving at school to be *taken away an hour later* and Lucy Gough having *not appeared, rumored to have gone on a week's visit somewhere*. Mrs. Bryant had agreed *to perform her duties conscientiously* while Christina was away, with the condition that at least one of her daughters spend the nights with her. Reverend Bennett had allowed her to bring them to stay at the Vicarage, so how could Mama object?

If Christina did go to London, she wouldn't travel until Monday, giving time for Mama to issue her yay or nay by return-of-post. On Saturday morning, Christina finished up the school week, and in the afternoon made the rounds of parents, letting them know there wouldn't be classes for a fortnight. That left Sunday after church for packing. She wanted to travel light but had to include Mama's and her black silk dresses, jackets, and mantles, crape for trimming, and a couple of veiled bonnets suitable for mourning.

***

Christina silently, penitently, thanked her departed grandmama for the opportunity to be once again with *Nonno*, even in the chill winds and disturbing disintegration of Old St. Pancras' churchyard. They had walked together solemnly, not slowly, *Nonno's* long, sturdy legs insisting on a strong stride, through a propped-open iron gate and along broken, bulging pathways. Christina held his lower arm a little tighter at the sight of cluttered headstones, like an assembly of unsettled spirits, falling this way and that. She wondered why her grandmama was to be buried in such a troubled, neglected place, until they stood where a brilliant, betrayed son had waited in death longer than he had lived for his mother. Christina felt *Nonno* lean on her, not with his large still active body but the weight of his conflicted thoughts about Anna Maria Pierce of Middlesex and her genteel family. Respected for being honorable, avoided for being austere, her High Tory opinions and dedicated Anglicanism were not to be challenged. Once beautiful enough to catch Gaetano Polidori off guard, she had been a dutiful wife to the point of bearing eight children. Because of "an internal complaint," assumed but never admitted to being the struggle between shame and sorrow, she took to her bed long before it was necessary.

"She is with him now. I hope she forgives him at last," *Nonno* whispered but must have realized Christina heard, knowing she always hung on his every word.

"Have you?" Christina, despite the *don't mention Uncle John* rule, felt prompted to ask.

"Our sons, my sons … of all, he had the advantages for ambition. But also a quick temper, oversensitivity, and a tendency to melancholy. Like you, *mia cara.*" He squeezed Christina's hand, his ungloved one trembling but not cold. "Asked to be Byron's physician, he was warned it would do him no good. I had hopes for him again when he was dismissed, but he wandered aimlessly until he only headed for death. Don't ever be aimless, my treasure."

"Oh, *Nonno*, not enough to—"

"He was the pet of his sisters, especially your mama."

The hanging of the Gainsford 1816 portrait of Uncle John was always her mother's first order of business in making each new residence home. Christina had witnessed Mama reading his letters, what they revealed not shared. Her affection and never-ending grief were as obvious as her embarrassment when she was caught holding his haunting words against her heart.

Christina had also seen the pages in Mama's family album devoted to Uncle John, as had Maria, William, and Gabriel. The blue velvet scrapbook had soft black paper pages that tore easily and a handtied binding that often needed tightening. It was Mama's way of keeping her family in one place through drawings, poetry, pressed flowers, snips of hair, quotes and thoughts of her own, newspaper clippings, and, eventually, photographs.

"Like a star in the halo of the moon: invisible," Mama faintly read out loud what was inscribed on her brother's headstone.

Papa, suffering a bad cold along with his other ailments, had stayed home. Maria was standing between and comforting Aunt Eliza and, especially, Aunt Margaret, who was prone to nervous tremors that, in such a situation, might trigger hysteria. Aunt Charlotte, looking exhausted, was escorted by patiently attentive William, Henrietta Rintoul on his other arm. Uncle Henry was in charge of Uncle Philip and soon had to take him away because of an inappropriate outburst. There wasn't a sign of Gabriel, who hadn't made it to the service at Christ Church, hope fading that he would appear, even less likely he would bring Miss Siddall after he announced at the viewing, "It's too soon since the loss of her brother."

Always some excuse, Christina thought. *Does she really even exist?* William had met her; Mr. Scott had observed her avoid meeting him. Christina had seen Miss Siddall's luscious copper hair on her own head that had become Jesus' in Mr. Hunt's *The Light of the World*, for which they had both posed, the closest they had come to being in the same room together.

"Ah," she heard *Nonno* exhale. Gabriel was coming with Cousin Teo.

"Oh, bless you." Mama reached out for Teo's hand, passing her into Gabriel's arms that squeezed and convinced her even a goddess couldn't come between them.

Nonno stroked Gabriel's shoulder and leaned close to him.

It didn't seem like they were in the city, the birdsong unusually clear, smells not of smoke and sewage but moist earth and crumbling stone. The wind only met the resistance of wide-limbed trees and the structure of a historic church. As with many overused burial grounds, Old St. Pancras was layered with souls and soil, deepening its solemnity while elevating it above street level, building a *road from earth to sky*, a bridge to heaven.

Although at first Christina found the graveyard unsettling, she slowly opened poetically to its neglect, even brokenness, how it was unencumbered by civilization. She envied Granny Pierce coming to rest in such a quiet, lonely, ancient place. Simple prayers, silent tears, a lowering of expectations, the casting of dirt and violets and turning away of those left breathing was all it took for her to sink, *in sorry plight, out of sight.*

"*Grazie tante*," *Nonno* repeated as he acknowledged Amelia and Charles Heimann, Mrs. Orme and her daughters, Ford Madox Brown, and some Christina recognized as *Nonno's* neighbors from Park Village. A few others she couldn't in any way identify.

Aunt Charlotte's ability and inclination to be fiscally benevolent were responsible for the somber carriages to and from Christ Church and Old St. Pancras.

One had waited. Not, as it turned out, for *Nonno*. He insisted on walking, although his shoulders slumped and his knees struggled to bend. Christina held his arm, so he knew he was supported. She did most of the talking in response to his questions about Frome. "Some peaceful countryside around it. An abundance of gentle green hills and slight valleys, no boldness or grandeur, but a quaintness and quietness reminiscent of Holmer Green. The wildflowers are charming, begging me to paint them. I may try my hand at primroses. In watercolors, I think I might do them justice."

"Do so, for me, *mia cara*."

Don't wait for roses ... primroses blossom today. She felt some urgency. "I will, Grandpapa. As soon as I get back."

She told him she had planted figs in the garden for Papa. She also described the school and the few children who had so far enrolled, even some of their mothers. His smile disappeared when Christina was ruthless with herself. "Of course, who knows what they say about me. Perhaps the name of a Frome Inn—the Blue Boar—sums it up."

Back at 15 Park Village, a wreath of laurel and boxwood was hung on the front door and, like the bell knob, tied with black ribbon. Within, the clocks were stopped, the curtains drawn, mirrors and a painting of the deceased covered with black crape.

Nonno didn't go into the parlor to mingle with those who had come in respect and for refreshments. Christina discreetly, disappointedly, watched him flee out the back of the house, presumably to the solitude and solace of his shed.

"Let him go," Amelia advised with a steadying embrace. "You must do what he can't."

Christina tried to appreciate those who cared enough to spend another hour or so in consideration of her family's loss, more amiably than the women of that family did once most everyone, including Uncle Henry, William, Henrietta Rintoul, Teo, and Gabriel, left.

"It's hard to know how Papa is taking it," Aunt Eliza mentioned as she sipped more tea and ate another biscuit. "Mama made him a widower decades ago."

"No," Christina's mother argued. "He never saw himself that way but remained devoted to her. Hardly a day he didn't sit with her, tell her about his projects or news of the family, and read to her."

"Of course, Frances. I know that better than you," Eliza sniped. "But, also, how it upset him not to be able to go for a walk with her, to the opera or seaside, not even to share a meal at a table with her. How frustrating to have a wife so long in sickness."

"How could you know better? Hasn't my husband been unwell for years?" Mama bristled, looking apologetically towards Christina.

"We both have our crosses to bear," Aunt Eliza's tone wasn't conciliatory.

"Certainly, you both inherited our father's loyalty and tenacity." Aunt Charlotte's hope for a truce came too late to prevent Aunt Margaret overreacting to her sisters' argument, her breathless laughter quickly turning into weeping and choking.

Maria gave her a handkerchief while persuading her to sit down again.

"Christina." Uncle Philip grabbed his niece's hand to take her along on what seemed a willing escape the moment she entered the library. "I have a new book to show you."

He insisted she sit down before he gave it to her. It was a children's book, Uncle Philip's never-ending favorite genre. *The King of the Golden River* was by John Ruskin, a name she recognized with mixed feelings.

Mr. Ruskin was a significant critic, one who could make an artist successful or send him into oblivion. In response to his slight of Gabriel while offering praise or, at least, hope for almost every other official, and unofficial, member of the PRB, Christina might have rejected the book in her lap. Her curiosity wouldn't let her. She turned its pages that were most affecting to her: included a multitude of intricate surreal drawings by—she looked back to the title page—Richard Doyle, also the illustrator of her copy of *Grimms' Fairy Tales*.

"May I borrow it?"

Uncle Philip frowned. She was sure he was about to refuse her request. "You didn't understand."

"I know." Christina resigned herself to handing the book back to him. "Neither a borrower nor lender be. When it comes to books, a wise rule I break far too often."

"No." He pouted, his arms crossed. "From me to you."

***

May rain grayed the passing countryside and misted the train's windows. Mr. Ruskin's delightful fable of love and goodness overcoming evil provided entertainment for two Rossettis returning to Frome and a third on his way there for the first time. Christina intended to read silently, thinking her father would sleep most of the way, but Mama insisted, as they were the only ones in the carriage, she do so out loud.

Christina might yet overcome her reluctance for reciting in other more public and potentially critical circumstances. It was easier to practice on those who, if anything, were inclined to praise her too much.

"'In a secluded and mountainous part of Stiria there was in old time a valley of the most surprising and luxuriant fertility.' Can you hear me, Papa?"

"Like a clear echo across that valley, my girl."

Papa had been much more cheerful leaving London than expected.

There was a fine singing thrush repeating itself nearby. Every time Christina heard those feathered pan pipes leisurely filling time, reverberating clearly independent yet harmonious notes, she wondered if it was to send an alarm or just a cautious greeting.

She pointed the bird out to Maria before they saw it, slowing them down as they walked around the garden, insisting they stop once she had narrowed its location to the brick wall of a shed covered with berried ivy.

Three months earlier, Christina had found a young thrush struggling to get off the ground, likely fallen from its nest, which was never discovered.

"I took it home. Of course, my intention was to set it free once it was self-sufficient. But it wouldn't eat or drink. So the next day I put it in a field near the cover of a hedge, praying it would survive, that, if it couldn't by itself, an adult bird would care for it, and that neither a cat nor nasty lad would find it."

The song thrush was still there, peeking through the ivy, the berries too juicy to abandon, perhaps comfortable with their intrusion for the reason Christina hoped.

"Why don't you ask it?"

"What question would that be, Moony?"

"If it remembers you."

"If so, for being its torturer."

Maria shook her head, as she often did at Christina's gloomier perspective. She raised her plump arms, her dark eyes widening, her mouth curling to one side, her straw hat slipping back but not off because of the plaid ribbons knotted under her fleshy chin. The thrush was on the roof of the shed, its black-flecked cream chest expanded, and buffed-brown wings outstretched enough to show yellow underneath. Its head lifted alertly, its eyes like onyx buttons. Its throat rippled, and straight beak rigidly opened and closed to offer musical resonance and escape for its thoughts, which could only be interpreted as gratefulness for life.

"There. Although you didn't ask, it answers."

Maria was a strangely whimsical creature despite her intellectualism, sensibility, scrupulosity, and resolute religious practice.

Gabriel declared that Maria often set him right.

Christina envied her sister's uninhibited, unburdened piety. Mr. Scott, according to William, understood after only a few meetings that "she could make sunshine in a shady place."

There were many visitors that summer of 1853, including Polidoris and Cousin Teo, who was in need of a break from his struggle to find satisfying work in England. Mama and Aunt Margaret went to Longleat for a few days in June, Christina staying behind to keep school as she had been there enough times to be satisfied, even bored, with its magnificence. Aunt Eliza managed only a week away from London and *Nonno*, who was less well than it seemed he would always be. She enjoyed herself, especially a day in Bath with Mama, and went home looking refreshed. William also stayed too briefly, but long enough to join Christina and Mama on an excursion to Wells in a little carriage comfortable as intended with two inside and one in the box alongside the driver. It could still be described as a fine day, despite pouring rain on the way there that forced William to squeeze inside, the good humor and family fellowship that resulted, also in a tour of Wells Cathedral, compensating for any inconvenience. William, en route to Southampton to spend most of his holiday in France, was easily convinced to, before he crossed the channel, stop in Salisbury and explore its cathedral, which guidebooks claimed was almost the equal of York Minster.

Christina had hoped Gabriel would ease her exile with a visit and news of creative, even risqué, ventures. Instead, due to, as Mama regretted, a little quarrel with him, he was eventually lured away from Blackfriars and Lizzie to the Scots in Newcastle.

Christina met Maria at Frome station early afternoon on the 22nd of August, the gray gloom of the day brightening the moment Maria stepped into it, proving Mr. Scott's observation. Tripping on her skirt to hurry down the platform, her purse swinging out as she threw her arms open, Christina felt joy at her sister's appearance until she stepped back from Maria's comment on hers.

"Still in mourning?"

It wasn't as if Maria made much of a contrast, dressed predominantly in gray with purple braid on her cuffs and the front closure of her bodice, white lace peeking over her bare hands and edging her collar. Unlike Christina, there wasn't black crape pushed off her face or draped over her arms. Maria was wearing an everyday if out-of-date summer frock, her equally old bonnet trimmed and tied with purple taffeta ribbon. Even in the humidity of late summer, Christina had not yet given up the burden of silk and wool blended bombazine.

"I shouldn't be surprised, seeing as your letters are still black bordered. Glad I'm here, if for no other reason than to insist you chose fun over fatalism. As you know, to the surprise of anyone who hears and thinks I'm a saintly stick-in-the-mud, I always question the months and months, even years, of donning mourning. Why insist on being cheerless for so long?"

"I suppose our dear departed wouldn't want that."

"Well," Maria frowned with a glint in her eyes that prepared Christina for the droll humor coming, "Granny Polidori might."

They leaned into each other as they laughed, Christina, feeling calmed and cheered, rescued, and strengthened, wondering why she ever doubted her sister was her best friend.

Once they arrived at Brunswick Place, they joined Mama and Papa in the garden for the first time in days drenched with sunshine not rain, to take tea Mrs. Bryant had prepared. Christina noticed the shadows under Maria's eyes and the otherwise pallor of her face. Normally one to overindulge in the generous spread of egg salad and watercress sandwiches, scones split to be layered with jam and clotted cream, and a new Chinese black tea infused with bergamot oil Queen Victoria was said to favor, Maria nibbled and sipped.

"I have some new thoughts on Dante you might write down for me," Papa said to his oldest daughter from his wheelchair off to the side of their table.

"No." Christina's frustration with her father blocked what she expected would be her sister's compliance. "Moony's here to rest her eyes and brain, for country air and pleasant diversions, to bloom as she hardly is at present."

Maria's quick smile confirmed it was her hand patting Christina's under the small wrought-iron pedestal table. "And so, Sissy, what do you have in mind for my blooming holiday?"

Their plans began leisurely, taking pleasant walks in the vicinity of Frome, which was as much country as town, meandering through Millennium Green, a haven of cow parsley, tall trees, water falling, and birdsong. Some trails Christina had already scouted, others were newly discovered with Maria, who was a better walker than expected. It was a pity the idea of having a donkey and chaise hadn't yet been realized, mainly because somewhere affordable to shelter them hadn't been found. If they'd had one, Papa might have ventured beyond the small garden at Brunswick Place with his daughters and wife.

Drizzly or just cloudy-cool days made use of the gray alpaca waterproof cloaks from Swan and Edgar's Aunt Charlotte had given them. When the rain was too heavy or they gave in to Mama's concern for their health, they stayed in. Maria did some transcribing for Papa after all, her patience with his lapses of thought and civility exemplary. Her gentleness assisting his disabilities and feeble attempts of writing were encouraged by her "nostalgic appreciation of the devoted father and brilliant man he once was."

"Have I told you, Moony? You so remind me of my mama."

"Many times, Papa. Always, I'm flattered."

"Everyone thought I'd be disappointed my firstborn wasn't a son. But no. With your thick curly hair, dark complexion, plumpness, and strength, all I could think was 'Mama, Mama, I wish you could see this one, no doubt descended from you. *La mia piccolo luna.*'"

Maria later told Christina there were tears in his eyes. Christina tried to forgive him enough to believe it. Maria thought of what might help: a poem he had written, and she had preserved in a small box kept for such mementos.

"'Christina and Maria, my dear daughters, are fresh violets opened at dawn. They are roses nurtured by the earliest breezes. They are lovely turtle-doves in the nest of love.'"

"I don't remember him writing that."

"You were only four. Notice, he put your name first."

Maria didn't know why Christina was resistant to any talk of their father's affection. She never would.

"You were sitting on his lap when he shared it with us." Maria's eyes lowered with the recollection. "You giggled, hugged his neck, then, in all seriousness, insisted turtles and doves were not the same creatures."

"And now I know better."

Another indoor activity was, of course, reading, silently and to each other, either way interrupted for discussion. Lacking a good circulating library in Frome, Mama had joined a society for obtaining on-loan books from London. They came weekly: poetry and prose, the latter biographies, memoirs, philosophy, and essay collections. Some were engrossing, a few proved painful, one was agreed upon as a favorite. The second volume of *The Stones of Venice*, about the art and architecture in the title's city, had, for Christina, moved its author, John Ruskin, even closer towards vindication. Maria, although aware of his critical neglect of Gabriel's work, seemed to have no previous censure of him to overcome.

"Do you know that the woman in Millais' new Scotch picture is Mrs. Ruskin, a result of her husband inviting John to accompany them to the Highlands earlier this year?"

"I've heard so, Chrissy."

"William says the Ruskins' marriage is miserable."

"She is far too young for him."

"William also thinks Millais is quite smitten."

Maria shrugged. "I don't listen to gossip."

***

They began to doubt the weather would ever dry out long enough to make a healthy expedition further afield. Finally, a settled spell of days rather than hours convinced them to take the omnibus to Bath, as easily arranged as accomplished for it passed right by Brunswick Place. 2s/6d each way, it allowed six hours in the Roman city before the last one to bring them back the same day.

"For six hours, 'I allow Bath is pleasant enough.'" Christina wondered if Maria would catch the literary reference. "Longer and it might prove 'the most tiresome place in the world.'"

Maria hardly hesitated. "'Oh. Who can ever be tired of Bath?'"

"Jane Austen's heroine was more nimble-footed than we are."

"She probably traveled in more dignified fashion than a box on wheels with the risk of fleas in the straw lining the floor and little air to breathe or chance to glimpse any passing scenery."

Maria and Christina shared the affordable journey with eight passengers sitting and smelling like sardines in a tin where no more than six were planned for. Every bump in the road was a strong jolt that meant no one could relax; there was little space between one side and the other. Skirts were crumpled, and bonnets removed unless their owners were willing to suffer crooked necks for the sake of what was proper. Fortunately, male travelers usually preferred to ride the knifeboard on the roof, a reason to travel on a fine day. Not having to endure the dampness of straw under one's feet was another.

"I didn't think you read novels anymore." Christina upheld her supposition with a quote, "'They soften the intellect into resistance of real reading.'"

"I said that? Well, they do, with some exceptions. Still, when you mentioned we would visit Bath, I went to the library and, after investigating a few travel logs, remembered *Northanger Abbey* offered a literary preview."

"Not long now and we'll arrive 'in all its white glare.'" Christina realized by the empty faces of the other travelers that, although they must have heard Maria's and her exchange, they weren't listening. "*Persuasion*. Austen's best."

"I'd forgotten how much Bath figures into it."

Once disembarked on Dorchester Street, they put on their bonnets. Maria pulled a map out of her satchel and unfolded Mama's notes with it, handing them to Christina.

Maria hardly looked at the map she had likely memorized.

Christina was willing to let the two women she admired most lead the way. She expected her sister would insist on starting with the Pump Room, Roman Baths, and Abbey, the city's main attractions for her sister. They were all in the same vicinity and not far from where they stood.

Maria surprised with a different plan. "Let's do the long walking while we have the stamina." She leaned close to Christina while drawing a route on the map with her finger. "Saint James Parade to Westgate with a slight turn to Saw Close and another onto Beauford Road. Then through Queen's Square to Queen's Parade and Royal Avenue, which will take us to the Royal Gardens and Crescent, west along Brock Street, around the Circus, and to the Assembly Rooms, all of which Mama and Aunt Charlotte recommended and I know you, Chrissy, have been looking forward to. We'll complete our overload of Georgian sightseeing with a little shopping and refreshment. We must buy something frivolous at Jolly's and try the marzipan at Mollands. Which means we'll probably not have the energy, time, or funds to patronize Pulteney Bridge before you tolerantly if wearily allow me to indulge my obsession in the warm springs of antiquity."

"I'm sure I'll enjoy the baths as much as you."

"The Abbey will offer you easy escape and a hard seat if, as I'm sure will be the case, you don't."

Setting out arm in arm, before half a mile, they agreed it was too warm to stay so close. The day went as expected, bonding and differentiating them. Mutually exhilarating and exhausting, Christina's romantic responses to "such a fine city, situated on hills and in valleys, extensively elegant, golden-stoned and gracefully gardened" grew impatient with Maria's relentless academic perspective.

"The Gothic Revival came about as a backlash to Palladianism, while maintaining a coherency through the use of the same creamy limestone."

If Maria was ever irritated with Christina, she hid it in her seriousness and humor. "Horse droppings on the streets also offer continuity."

As if affected by the harmonic result of Bath's eclectic ancestry, their own contradictions embraced a camaraderie no one who knew them as children would have predicted. They walked side by side with the same main intention to stroll through the day and share their reflections on what they were seeing, thinking, and feeling.

Christina would later write to nine-year-old Charles Heimann about Bath having *a very nice park*, failing to mention it was named for and opened by Princess Victoria when she was only eleven. If Christina had been more confident of his interest, she might have added the magnificence of the gardens and arboretum first viewed from Queen's Parade through stone gate piers topped with lions. Gradually sloping up northwest, the grounds were landscaped with flowerbeds lushly crowded and vibrantly colored, at their best as such plantings usually were by mid-September. She would have described the towering trees, especially the deciduous ornamental and mature natives transitioning from summer to autumn with a flourish that hardly forecasted their imminent austerity.

Sending Charles a small pocketbook purchased in Bath, Christina mostly regretted not sharing some words about the obelisk, which, according to Maria, had a "tripartite base that swept beneath a band of Vitruvian scroll molding and was set within a circular balustrade." Otherwise, Christina knew only what Mama had put in her notes and she saw for herself: that it was a focal point of the park because of its position and dedication to the Queen verified by the delicately carved relief of the monarch's wreath-encircled profile. Like the Roman Baths Christina had briefly wrote to Charles about, the royal memorial had probably been part of his studies. Next time she visited Amelia, she would determine whether he wanted to hear more about historic landmarks in the Avon Valley city.

She thought there was a lesson in good conduct and empathy for the girls at the Fromefield school in the anecdotal story of a comment made, during the opening of the park in 1830, on the thickness of young Victoria's ankles. Repeated to the Princess by someone seemingly as unkind as its initiator, Victoria became so angry she had not yet, even as Queen, visited Bath again. It was reported she vowed she never would.

Maria overheard a tour guide sharing the rumor with a small group of fashionable ladies, some of whom couldn't help checking that their skirts covered any lower leg imperfections.

"Thick ankles, eh? Who would have thought I'd have something in common with Her Majesty."

Christina eventually made her front parlor students giggle at Maria's comment. At the time, she thought it wise to not be amused, and whisked her sister away. They didn't plan on going deeper into the park anyway, but moved on to the long row of curving, conjoined, columned town houses on the Royal Crescent, the backdrop to a walled, elevated lawn where a colorful hot-air balloon was being set up. They were lucky to claim an empty bench before a crowd gathered to watch one of its two riders remove the restraints holding its wickerwork car to the ground while the other controlled the flame that tilted and lifted the inflated conveyance into the sky.

Christina was impressed but not enticed.

Maria looked dazzled. "I think I might if I had the chance." Then devilish. "Although my thick ankles and other parts probably mean I wouldn't be allowed to."

"Thank goodness for your girth," Christina stood, because of the sun baking her, a little wobbly like the balloon, "if it saves your neck. We must get on."

"Six hours may not be enough. Why did we not think to stay overnight?"

"We can't afford it." Christina knew wasn't a convincing reason, as they might have found cheap accommodations off the main thoroughfares. "But, truly, Mama didn't want you to be more than a few hours away from Frome when she has 'to miss you so much already.'"

"And she needs you at school."

"That, too."

Maria, having struggled herself with governessing, understood Christina's glum expression and tone. "How long before you think she'll give up on Frome? She mentioned there might soon be the competition of a new boarding school there."

"Not while cholera is spreading in London. You should extend your stay, Moony. It's bad enough Gabriel is living on the river at Blackfriars, and William stays there sometimes. I heard the last time the plague was in England there were no cases, at most one, in Frome."

"I hope the Scotts will be all right."

"Oh, no." Christina gasped. "Are they in London?"

"Not since earlier in the summer. But William heard cholera is raging in Newcastle."

"God preserve Mr. ... and Mrs. Scott."

They walked while they talked, along Brock Street towards The Circus, which Mama noted its designer, John Woods, had described as 'The Great Canopy of Heaven.' They entered one of a trinity of entrances into Bath's version of the Colosseum: tall, segmented rows of superior residences, a trio of Royal Crescents, forming a circle centered by a railed formal flower garden and smooth, straight, still-summery plane trees.

Christina laughed. "Just like the old days. Mama wrote we're to take special note of how the façades are tiered with Doric, Ionic, and Corinthian columns."

"Did she mention some aspects were influenced as much by Stonehenge as the Colosseum?"

Christina skimmed over the relevant section of Mama's remarks. "No. How so?"

"Those gentlemen up there," Maria pointed to the balloon disappearing into the clouds beyond the southeast corner of the city, "could probably verify what's not obvious from our grounded viewpoint. Wood was fascinated with the druids and their stone circles. The Circus has the same diameter as nearby Stonehenge. Suggestive of the sun, it's positioned in a ley line to the Royal Crescent, obviously a representation of the moon."

No matter how much knowledge one had, Maria always knew more. As Papa had declared when they were children, his oldest, his favorite, was "gifted by nature with an uncommon intelligence." Christina was never satisfied with being 'the pretty one,' yet couldn't find the desire, let alone discipline, to dedicate herself to study like her sister did. Not measuring up intellectually and, especially, spiritually to Maria had once caused resentment and could still be frustrating. Increasingly, Christina was grateful for her sister's example and wished for more of her companionship. Far away Maria was in all ways distant, not much of a letter writer.

If the moon came from heaven, talking all the way, what could she have to tell us, and what could she say?

If the sun could tell us half that he hears and sees, sometimes he would make us laugh, sometimes make us cry.

They had dallied and discussed too much through the first part of their agenda and picked up the pace towards the Assembly Rooms Christina had already accepted she couldn't give the attention it deserved. There wasn't one gentleman with a visible pocket watch to ask the time, but, fortunately, a wall clock in the building's elegant foyer told them what they already knew, at least regarding that day. So much yet to explore together, they needed more time than they had.

CHAPTER NINETEEN

"Oh, no. Dear Grandpapa."

When Mrs. Bryant brought in the postman's delivery, Papa anticipated news of his absent wife. "Yet another night I'll sleep without her. You do everything to make me happy, Christina, but she is my soul and I need her to come back."

After hearing Christina cry out, he saw the letter crumpled in her hand. "*È morto*? My old friend Gaetano?"

Mama offered little hope. Christina felt her mother's anguish. Or was it her own? Why was it so difficult to distinguish?

"Well, is he?" Papa attempted to stand, Christina getting there just in time to ease his falling too hard back into the armchair.

At the time the letter had been sent, *Nonno* was in a coma from a stroke he had suffered shortly after Mama's arrival in London. She had gone the Monday after Christina's birthday, predicting she wouldn't be away for the whole of the Christmas season. The lease on the Arlington Street house had expired; Maria and William temporarily moved into weekly lodgings nearby above a chemist shop. Mama was needed to sort through the family's belongings to determine what was for storage and what should be sold or otherwise disposed of.

Her father looked extremely ill himself, his fear of what he thought Christina wouldn't confirm curling him forward with his arms hung over his knees. Everyone, including Papa, thought Gaetano would outlive him. Despite *Nonno's* great age, Christina had never seen her grandfather worse than a little tired, stoically arthritic, or ignoring a cold. Only a few weeks earlier she had sent him a poem, one Gabriel had criticized for its title and a few "old shop" lines. She needed *Nonno*, her muse's first and foremost champion, to approve it, not allowing herself to expect he also might find fault with it.

Christina hadn't heard back from him. Mama assured he would send his thoughts by way of her correspondence for lately he refused "to subject" anyone to his "old man's scrawl."

Once again, looking forward was spoiled by what would be missing. September and October had been busy and blissful, thanks to Maria's visit. As fleeting as they were, those last few hours in Bath accomplished a cherished memory of a sisterly stroll through the Austenian shapes, shades, and imagined sounds of the Assembly Rooms. Maria's brilliant memory also pulled out a quote from Dicken's *The Posthumous Papers of the Pickwick Club* describing the ballroom, long and octagonal rooms. *The hum of many voices, and the sound of many feet,* dresses, feathers, and jewels, *music low and gentle, but very pleasant to hear in a female voice, whether in Bath or elsewhere.*

They had tea and marzipan at Mollands. Gifts for family and friends, like Charlie's pocketbook, found them rushed and, therefore, impulsively shopping at Jolly's department store and the Guildhall Market. Although weary, they hurried to satisfy Maria's desire of following in the footsteps of richly draped Romans seeking relief from ailments, aging, and angering the gods, Sulis Minerva awaiting their pleas for mercy or revenge. Maria and Christina, encumbered by their purchases, agreed they felt more like the slaves that stumbled along behind their masters carrying toiletries, towels, and a change of toga. Their movement through the Bath House was mostly threatened with tripping or turning an ankle by centuries of crumbling, burying, excavation, and the trudging of visitors. Current restoration work hadn't yet repaired, had even exacerbated, areas of rough and broken pavement.

They didn't want to hurry through the maze of small pools, changing and warming rooms, or walking the entire pillared perimeter of the main rectangular bath, torches being lit as late afternoon turned to evening.

"Did you notice the signs for the caldarium, tepidarium, and frigidarium? The Romans thought there was great benefit to bathing hot, then warm, and finally cold," Maria instructed what Christina had already learned from Mama's notes while on the street level terrace before they descended into the steamy, sulfur-smelling, grimy, green abyss once the site of Roman riches and indulgence.

Christina couldn't wait to get out of there.

She couldn't fault Maria's decision that artifacts of jewels, coins, pottery, and household implements took precedence over the Pump Rooms that would have satisfied a longing for more tea. Across a half-shadowed, flagstone yard, the Abbey, looming grandiosely and perpendicularly gothic, was Christina's inconsolable regret of what had to be left largely unexplored. She did manage to escape the "absolute necessity" of Maria tasting spa water and questioning a guide, allowing herself to linger with others gazing up at the Abbey's west façade. Its elaborate carving depicted angels ascending the ladder on the left of the grand entrance and descending another on the right. Walking into the nave, Christina was mesmerized by its purity and light. She had just realized its soaring arches, fan-vaulted ceiling, vividly colored stained glass, and how fortunate she was to be there for the soothing strains of evensong, when Maria was behind her, tugging her bell-shaped sleeve.

The Abbey rang them off on their panicked way; it was a wonder they found the flexibility, energy, and breath, also for laughter, as they ran like schoolgirls to catch the last bus back to Fromefield.

"Whoa." Thankfully, the driver, who had already flicked the reins to move the horses, was sympathetic, if rather impudent. "Well, tha's put a blush in yer cheeks."

"'I shall never be in want of something to talk of again.'" As they found seats, Maria offered yet another Austen novel quote. "'I shall always be talking of Bath.'"

***

Fromefield's peaking autumnal colors offered some consolation after Maria returned to London. November was dreary but also restorative, an adjustment and relief after months of visitors and daytrips. Once a week or every other, Christina shopped in town. Nature walks were few and far between because of damp, chilly weather. As winter came before it officially did, Christina morphed into an interior creature, knowing it was time to hide away and exist on what was stored within. School was winding down for the Christmas holiday, which promised four weeks of aristocratic leisure. Teaching was almost rewarding at times, as she had never expected it would be, the few girls still at the school quite comfortable with each other and their teacher, Mama relinquishing that role more and more to Christina.

She finally had the opportunity to try out the new paint brushes William had sent along with Maria. Out of regret for complaining that two had split quills, she was determined to make good use of them—so far an inadequate portrait of Mama. Such a forgiving, if not forgetful, creature, William had given her a five-pound note for her birthday. She considered spending a few pounds on replacing worn items in her wardrobe, the remainder saved. When Mama returned, a trip to London might be considered good use of it, if after Boxing Day, at least to celebrate the New Year with her siblings. Another incentive was to show appreciation for Amelia's gift of a pretty collar and sleeves by wearing them in her friend's presence.

Christina intended them to complement a frock other than black or gray, her azure-blue conservatively contrasting the crisp white of the butterfly-themed guipure lace.

"I won't stay until the twenty-fifth. Papa doesn't want me to go at all, but there are things to be taken care of. Once they are, I'll be back, and you can be on your way," Mama said wearily while they waited on the platform for her train.

"I wish we could all live in London again."

"We will, dearest," Mama squeezed Christina's hand, "before too long."

How comforting it was to make plans in one's head; in one's heart, more foolish. A few days later Amelia's present had gone from being impatiently draped over Christina's vanity table mirror to storage in a deep drawer with a few other frivolous accessories.

In due time, they will allow me some vanity, almost two months later Christina wrote again to Amelia. *Nonno* had been gone as long, *ninety years a mere step that led to eternity.*

"When will she return? When will she?" Papa lamented what kept Christina from London at a time nothing should have prevented her being there.

You must stay with your papa. It is too hard for him to travel now, and even if you took on that challenge, there is nowhere in London for him to stay comfortably. Thirty-eight Arlington Street is no longer at our disposal, except for moving out our things. Maria and William have no room for an invalid, Gabriel is neither here nor there, my sisters, brothers, and I crammed into the Park Village house where the viewing is also taking place. Console yourself that none of us were able to properly say goodbye, although I imagine the pain added to your grief because you will not attend your grandpapa's burial.

"She doesn't write to me," was Papa's response to Christina revealing Mama's instructions without reading him the entire letter.

"I'm certain she wishes to. She has so much to attend to."

"There are others. Aren't there others?"

As Christina tried to console him, she wanted the same consideration to come back to her. He shook his head and slumped in his chair. He didn't refuse the meal Mrs. Bryant had prepared for his unpredictable appetite. Although Christina didn't eat or drink anything, she felt as if she was choking while sitting adjacent to her father at the dining room table. The dropped leaf on the opposite end to him was a stark reminder of Mama's absence that day and for a few weeks more. He continued to concentrate on missing her, while the emptiness of Christina's thoughts, the tightness of her throat, the stiffness of her limbs, and, especially, the rebellion in her heart were reactions to a loss simple patience couldn't reverse.

Remember me when I am gone away, gone far away into the silent land, when you can no longer hold me by the hand.

"I've hung your mourning clothes on the wardrobe," Mrs. Bryant alerted Christina after she agreed to stay overnight. "And I had just put them away."

"I should have got rid of them, instead of inviting bad luck for their use so soon again."

"Not many can afford to do so, Miss."

"Of course. I cannot."

Nonno had once claimed Christina "was always ready to be sad."

When his time came, she wasn't. Instead, she waited for his response to a poem, and for any delay to pass quickly until she saw his large smile, heard his hearty greeting in Italian or English, felt his burly arms around her, and they sat side by side to discuss her writing and so many other things.

She had to rationalize not attending his funeral, persuade her emotions she wasn't betraying him. She only needed to think of his body laid out, repeating, with much more to grieve, the bizarre, torturous viewing of her grandmother, of someone who wasn't there. Why would she want to see bold, brilliant, big-hearted Gaetano deprived of sight or breath, to spoil her remembrance of him as tall, strong, and active, suddenly his silence meaning he had nothing more to say? Why would she want to be one of many following his coffin and bowing their heads at the graveside, her sobs and prayers perfunctory rather than personal?

She wouldn't resign her distinction as his favorite and need to have known him as no one else did.

For if the darkness and corruption leave a vestige of the thoughts that once I had, better by far you should forget and smile than that you should remember and be sad.

Christina had not been given a choice but was finally convinced it was better she stayed away from funereal rites and the family uncertainty now the Polidori pillar was gone. She was glad Papa didn't want to talk about his "old friend Gaetano" and that Mrs. Bryant took on more of the time and tasks associated with her father's care.

Christina needed to manage her mourning like a dove on a solitary branch, composed out of remembering while trying to forget.

Underneath the growing grass, underneath the living flowers, deeper than the sound of showers ... there a very little girth can hold what once the earth seemed too narrow to contain.

***

Expecting the worst, Maria, William, and even Gabriel came, but Papa, who so wanted it to happen, was unaware all his family was around him again. Just a few weeks into the new year, a paralyzing seizure had rendered him senseless, his survival in doubt. Work, and in Gabriel's case, the gamble of love, demanded three of his children couldn't stay beyond knowing, as the doctor assured, there were signs Papa would recover enough to live a little longer, but without much functionality.

"Time to admit to the failure of the Fromefield enterprise," Mama announced before they left, handing William a list. "Here are a few houses for let, one on Albany Street, which is always ideal, being near to Christ Church. I wish I'd had time to look for more, but that is your mission now, son."

"Wherever we settle," Christina surprised herself as she teased William, feeling *Nonno* would have approved why she did, "please don't, under any circumstances, call our new home 'a crib,' such slang creeping into your vocabulary worrisome."

"Comes from the company an art critic keeps," Gabriel offered his own relief that his "sibs" could still have fun with each other.

Mama frustrated their banter, the darkness around her eyes a sign of worry as much as weariness. "Maria must inspect any real possibilities. I don't want us to have to move again for a long while."

Christina felt the same, for various reasons. Once a new refuge in London was chosen and school by the Rossettis recessed forever, she remembered why she hated moving, packing requiring *the giant Aegaeon's one hundred arms and as many legs as a centipede*. Writing to Amelia was a pleasant interlude in any day, an exercise for fostering friendship and excuse for rest and diversion, the latter also achieved by late February walks along the footpaths of Millennium Green—the Primrose Hill of Fromefield—and beyond. Through barely leafy woods there were early spring flowers to accidentally come upon and search for, and birds breaking the silence as if noting her intrusion. Squirrels didn't need prompting to squawk less musically while flying as ably from tree to tree. The way opening onto a field offered the sweetness of lambs and moist grass, *the earth was green, the sky was blue*; Christina *saw and heard a skylark hang between the two*. Shelley had written a longer and loftier poem inspired by that spritely bird that *singing still dost soar, and soaring ever singest*. As expected, there wasn't a poetry collection at Brunswick Place that included it and Mama's book borrowing society had faltered. If not in the Rossettis' library or Uncle Philip's, then hopefully a public one not too far from 45 Albany Street would bring Shelley's full rendition of *the sweetest songs that tell of the saddest thought* back to her.

CHAPTER TWENTY

One face looks out from all his canvases, one selfsame figure sits or walks or leans ....

Almost from the moment she was back in London, Gabriel nagged Christina to come to Chatham Place. As usual with Gabriel's habitats, it was creative chaos, dust in the light from windows and lamps, the smells of newly stretched canvas, linseed oil, varnish, a back-drafting chimney, and, whether or not any windows were open, the Fleet Ditch sewer stench. The largest easel was in use, others for display. On a couple of small trestle tables were cups with brushes, the majority fine tipped, and wet and dry porcelain pallets smeared with, as critics sometimes faulted, overused colors. Sketches were strewn about like litter; Christina worried they would be damaged or even discarded. Velvet draping half covered a bamboo screen near a small couch for models and napping. Most of the furniture was recognizable from Gabriel's previous studios, some of it stolen from the family and past, such as a large rocking chair once playfully jostled over by youngsters who eventually also shared a favorite book. The cabinet it may have been pulled out of was there, as was a table where those same siblings competed to share their drawings and rhymes. Mirrors, large and small, hung, propped, and freestanding were from the Rossetti collection. No one knew how or why they had accumulated, only that Mama was never fond of them and glad to let Gabriel satisfy his obsession for them.

We found her hidden just behind those screens, that mirror gave back all her loveliness.

Miss Siddall was sitting slightly hunched, her arms resting between her knees, her hands clasped just below. Her waist, like the wicker chair she perched on and Christina thought was one she had scolded a feline or two for clawing, was lost in the bunching of her skirt. Even with Lizzie's torso swallowed in billowing gray and her shoulders slumped, her height was evident, her stretched neck, uplifted chin, thick, mahogany hair loosely ballooned on the nape of her neck elongating her.

A queen in opal or in ruby dress, a nameless girl in freshest summer-greens, a saint, an angel—every canvas means the same one meaning, neither more or less.

Christina saw what Gabriel did. Even simply, somberly gowned in cotton and shawled in wool, this woman was fascinating, not as she was but meant to be.

As Christina entered fully into her view, Lizzie stood up and took a few sliding steps forward, greeting her visitor with kind if evasive gray-blue eyes. She extended her hand, warm in intention but cold in its flesh.

Oh, she is not well. I must be kind to her. I must ... not jump to conclusions about her. I must ... not mind Gabe loving her. Christina was afraid she acted as condescending as she felt, patting the other woman's hand.

Gabriel rushed towards them, his arm around Lizzie to move her away from Christina. Taken by surprise, Lizzie was a ragdoll in his control. Once she regained her will, she shrugged him off.

"Well, what do you think, Chrissy?" Gabriel blurted, immediately clarifying his question. "Of the Blackfriars crib? The way the rooms are built out over the river, windows on all sides, there's plenty of light and a magnificent view from the balcony of the Tower, Parliament, and Westminster Abbey."

"If only there wasn't such a stink from the river."

"I hardly notice anymore. During the day, it's busy and interesting. At night, there's the shimmering reflection of gas lamps on the bridge and wharf side."

"He notices. In words I won't repeat." William stood before an easel-supported canvas it was obvious, by its illuminated position and proximity to paints and brushes, Gabriel was currently working on. "You've made good progress."

"Which one is it?" Christina moved to have a look. "Oh, a watercolor." She tried not to sound disappointed.

"Beatrice Meets Dante at a Marriage Feast." William glanced between his brother and Miss Siddall.

"And denies him her salutation," Gabriel added, not brave enough to look at his "Sid" sitting and slumping again.

William leaned into the painting to examine it more closely. "He's captured you for eternity."

"Sitting for him certainly can seem an eternity." Christina thought she saw Lizzie struggle not to smile.

"You didn't refuse, even though Mama said you could. You begged to pose again."

"Well, Gabe, your memory fails you. But one thing doesn't." She stepped back from the painting, looking around at all the other evidence of Gabriel's vocation. "Having your muse constantly close."

"I don't live here," Lizzie finally spoke, softly but emphatically.

According to William, it was true. She went home every night.

He walked the short distance from his Somerset House office to regularly drop in on his brother after work, sometimes to stay the night. After all, it was his signature as co-owner and money that was keeping Gabriel at 14 Chatham Place. If Miss Siddall were still there, she would dine with them. Around nine or ten at the latest, one or the other of them would accompany her home about a mile and a half over the river to Old Kent Road, her father opening the door before she stepped up to it.

Gabriel and Lizzie were alone together at other times, their behavior left to the frailty of restraint. She had practically lived there once, albeit while Gabriel was traveling, furtively coming and going as a woman so slim, faint, and quiet naturally could. *While I'm away, Lizzy is staying at Blackfriars to paint and, probably, sleep, too.* Gabriel wrote to William from Newcastle, assuming, as he often mocked the Rossetti siblings' compulsion of "spilling the beans" to each other, Christina would soon know, too. *I've told her to not to let anyone in. My order for you is to discourage anyone from going there.*

Gabriel had included a caricature of himself thumbing his nose at his landlord.

Christina wondered what lie Lizzie told her family, obviously abetted by someone they trusted, regarding those nights her father didn't wait for her to return home.

There was something other than the ambiguity and unconventionality of Gabriel's relationship with Lizzie that, although it may have protected her honor, made Christina even more uneasy. It stemmed from his turning the Rossetti obsession with Dante Alighieri and his elusive Beatrice into a quest for an actualized perfect love: The Blessed Damozel. He thought he had found her, *lean'd out from the golden bar of heaven*, in a hat girl. Her grandfather was a Sheffield scissor-maker, her father a southeast London cutler, her distinctive tresses inherited from her mother and fondness for poetry beginning when she discovered Tennyson's on a piece of paper wrapping butter.

The legend of Lizzie was well underway.

Lizzie was a Celt for Hunt, and a chilled Ophelia for Millais. First, she was *Twelfth Night's* Viola for Deverell, poor handsome Deverell who found her "stupendously beautiful" but let her heart and good sense be stolen by Gabriel. Bad luck plagued Walter to the extreme, his life taken, too, that past February, by kidney failure at the age of twenty-three. Before Gabriel monopolized her, Lizzie posed and was paid to supplement what she made as a milliner's assistant, Mrs. Tozer allowing her time off from her normal hours at the shop.

Christina had been safeguarded by her sisterly relationship to the Brotherhood. Miss Siddall had no such protection from artists' licentiousness. How could her head not be turned by these handsome, or, at least, interesting, and imaginative men? How could she not be flattered by their impression of her?

It wasn't enough for Gabriel to pose and paint her into the story of another piece of his work. Or not take improper advantage of her interest in, even infatuation with him, which Christina commended him for. She didn't fault his effort to elevate Lizzie from a fairly poor, plain, pliable young woman whose hair color, like her inclination to be an artist's model, didn't define her character. His having her drop an L off the end of her family name was ridiculous. Creating *a saint, an angel* out of Miss Siddall or any woman was all right for art but not real love and life. There were only vain promises in his seeing her, not as she was but fulfilled his dream.

"Chrissy, come see the Sid's drawing and painting. I predict one day she'll better me. She might illustrate those poems of yours I've been talking to Allingham about publishing. I want you to look at some of hers, too."

"Oh, I don't know if they're ready for that," Lizzie limply objected.

Gabriel encouraging Lizzie to seriously pursue art and poetry was the hardest aspect of the relationship to accept. Christina hadn't forgotten how, just when she hoped to please him with her own artistic efforts, he instructed her not to say or do anything that seemed like she was rivaling Lizzie.

Christina followed him to what was obviously Lizzie's designated section of the studio off the main living room and was even more upset knowing she couldn't help but look disagreeable. Christina had always been his female protegee, looking up to his expectations, motivated by his praise, more so by his criticism, spurred on by him enjoying the possibility of stirring up her storm, forgiven whether he succeeded or not. It was, for so long, an honest, openly dependent love between them unafraid of being spoiled by anything or anyone.

Now, inevitably, his true love was someone else.

As Gabriel uncovered and unstacked paintings and flipped through sketches, Christina hoped for consolation in the mediocrity of Lizzie's work. Instead, she didn't doubt she had lost him.

"Oh, this one. William told me about it." Christina was drawn to a completed, or nearly so, pen and ink drawing on a tripod easel facing a simple slat-back chair in front of a floor-to-ceiling window view of Blackfriars Bridge. "What do you call it?"

"I, um—"

Gabriel stole Lizzie's chance. *"Lovers listening to Music."*

"Obviously."

"You know, Chrissy, how I like to be consulted on titles."

"How you like to impose them." Christina encouraged the return of a little affectionate banter with her brother.

"I see you and Gabriel in the couple's faces." William brought Lizzie back into the conversation.

"Hunt thinks it's you, Will."

"Well, if it is, dear brother, I posed in my sleep."

"If it is, I might have to kill you."

"It's a joke, Gabe. Like Hunt played on you at Jack Tupper's."

"Yes. And the Mad was lucky I didn't kill him."

"Instead, he lived, apologized, and you bonded again painting backgrounds in a deer park in Kent."

"What was Hunt's sin?" Christina really wasn't curious.

"He introduced Lizzie as his bride."

"You agreed with him doing so?" Christina reacted to Lizzie laughing softly.

"Didn't agree, but I didn't mind, either. Just a little fun."

Christina saw Gabriel's struggle, caught between devotion and defeat. She didn't like Lizzie playing with his dream of her, even though she thought it a foolish dream. She turned her body and confused intention back to Lizzie's drawing. "The young women look foreign." She refrained from saying, *like I do.* "The child is angelic. What is the stringed instrument? What was the inspiration for the piece? Some literary source?"

Christina expected Lizzie to shy away from saying anything about her art and wasn't surprised to hear Gabriel instead. "She drew the backdrop at Lover's Seaton, a cliff between Hastings and Fairlight."

"First, I wrote this." Lizzie made use of a long arm to offer Christina a small open notebook without having to move too close to her.

Christina didn't take it. What if Lizzie's poetry was as intriguing as her artwork? "You read it to me."

"Oh, no. I can't."

Or won't, Christina understood.

Gabriel swooped in, losing the page, gesturing Lizzie to find it, kissing her hand as she pulled it away, clearing his voice before he began. "'Love kept my heart in a song of joy; my pulses quivered to the tune; the coldest blasts of winter blew upon it like sweet airs in June.'"

The silence that followed was, at least for Christina, lonelier than if she had been without a friend in the world. *He feeds upon her face by day and night, and she with true kind eyes looks back on him, fair as the moon and joyful as the light: not wan with waiting, not with sorrow dim, not as she is, but when hope shone bright.*

The tour of the rest of the flat, only a corridor, small bedroom, and balcony, was William's idea. The end of the visit came soon after, sudden and necessary and only partially because he was invited to Henrietta Rintoul's for supper that evening.

***

Christina's heart should have ached less for a drawing she had seen at Chatham Place of Gabriel sitting for Lizzie, who leaned forward in a determined effort to capture him, and more for Papa taking his final breaths. After barely a month in one of the most pleasant houses on Albany Street, Mama, Maria, and Christina, returning from Easter Sunday service at Christ Church, were met by William's distress. Dr. Steward came down the stairs with a fatalistic shake of his head and suggested Dr. Hare be called. Despite a series of strokes, Papa had rallied for the move back to London and the prospect of having all his children around him again or, at least, in Gabriel's case, close by. In the weeks since, he had declined until he was as ill as he had ever been. Still, it was shocking that within a few hours he had gone from flirtatiously insisting Mama help him dress so he could have breakfast with "his favorite women" to becoming so weak he couldn't hold up his head as William talked and read to him in the parlor.

"Dr. Stewart came quickly and helped me get him to bed."

From the beginning, with twenty years' age difference between them, once she made it through childbirth, and he was diminished by aging and ailing, Mama must have prepared herself for life going on without Gabriele Rossetti. For the next few days, she was the most resilient amongst them, or seemed so. She might have tried to hide what she was dreading, but there was no mistaking her hope the moment she received word Papa was recognizing anyone or trying to speak. She rushed to his bedside, taking his hand, sometimes holding it up to her flushed cheek and even to her salted, swollen lips. In the last hours, she read him an Italian translation of the Liturgy, which, as Christina also witnessed, pleased him as much as it did those who ever doubted his faith.

Gabriel had returned from Hastings, leaving Lizzie there to benefit from the sea air. He sat with his failing father a few times and yet accepted a dinner invitation to Denmark Hill from the Ruskins. The niceties, awkwardness, and intrigues of his evening were interrupted by a summons home to join Mama, his siblings, Cousin Teo, and the Polidori Aunts for Papa's final moments.

They were anything but peaceful. Papa was agitated, insisting he saw his long-deceased mama and that General Guglielmo Pepe got into bed with him, before a last desperate plea:

"*Ah, Dio, ajuiami Tu!*"

There was someone else—a flesh and blood visitor—who came spontaneously, kindly, and memorably for the second time that day. Knowing there was little chance he would be admitted to the sickroom, Christina greeted him with an apologetic smile.

"There are still so many around him. Perhaps, if one of my aunts comes down—"

"No, no. Family should be with him."

Christina stretched her arms back to hide her hands behind her wide skirt. She didn't want him to know she was trembling. "I believe earlier he was told you were here."

"Well, that is something."

"In the last few hours, he has only recognized Mama and William. And some who have already passed. I don't think it will be long now."

"I must not keep you." Charles Cayley hadn't moved far from the front door. He turned to open it and then back to say, "I hope that somehow *Signore Rossetti* realized my deep gratitude for the lessons learned and friendships forged."

CHAPTER TWENTY-ONE

Mama had taught them to treasure books and now she had burnt some. Her behavior was distressing but understandable, as they were copies of Papa's five-volumed *Mistero dell'Amor Platonico*. She had always disliked the "gigantic, sacrilegious" work, but only to the point of expressing her relief that it was published on the continent, not in England, and complaining about the crate of copies he insisted went wherever he did.

No one expected Mama to try to erase a large part of her husband's literary accomplishments, certainly not so violently or so soon after his body was unceremoniously brought to Highgate Cemetery and lowered into a grave deep enough to eventually have most of his family near him again. She should have given the books away. The burning seemed impulsive yet was obviously organized: the volumes not hysterically torn apart and dangerously flung into a fireplace or the kitchen range, but neatly piled to make a little bonfire in the backyard, carefully lit and attended. The exorcism happened while William and Maria were at work and Christina was visiting Amelia. William was sleeping at Chatham place while Gabriel was back in Hastings with Lizzie. The sisters returned home within half an hour of each other to smoke still hanging in the air outside and Mama sitting in the kitchen with the empty crate at her feet. The maid shrugged when asked to tell what she knew, but looked as anguished as everyone who realized what had happened.

No one ever spoke to Mama about her extreme action, not even William when he finally found out. He always saw himself as the keeper of Rossetti matters, so not knowing what his mother had done until months later when he was looking for Papa's personal inventory of the book was a blow. Fortunately, he couldn't shout while he was gasping for breath.

Christina insisted he calm down and sit in her room until he did. "What is done is done."

No doubt he wanted to hear how some copies had been, if not rescued, than stored in a place Mama didn't know about.

"I don't think so. Except where they have gone as gifts. I always felt sorry for the poor souls who, just because they were polite enough to show interest in Papa's work, left carrying a great deal more than when they arrived." Christina saw she hadn't humored her brother.

"Bigotry," William murmured.

"What?"

"Mother and her bigotry."

"How can you say that?"

"Because of her intolerance for anything that doesn't suit her strict beliefs. In that regard, Chrissy, I fear you follow too closely in her steps."

"There is no one less prejudiced than Mama. Think of how she opened her home to all those strangers Papa was always gathering up. She might have insisted it stop, for Papa didn't like to cross her. Instead, she made sure they were always welcomed."

"Her destruction of Papa's books was out of character." It was as if William was arguing with himself. "But, no. I cannot condone her action."

Christina tried putting Mama's behavior in the perspective of Aunt Charlotte burning Uncle John Polidori's diary, not, she insisted when pressed to explain, to erase his legacy but protect it.

"And remember my fictional Maude asking her friend to burn her poems? And that her writing book be buried with her? She didn't want anything to cause unnecessary upset for those left behind."

"Papa never asked her to do it," William quickly injected. "He always had, and, I suspect, still has, the sort of self-opinion that involves self-applause."

Christina caught a hint of William alluding to existence after death. Perhaps their father's reply to Maria asking if he recognized his youngest son had turned William in the direction of faith, even if it hadn't moved him closer to it.

"I see him, I hear him. He is written on my heart."

Bury thy dead, heart-deep; take patience till the sun shall set; there are no tears for him to weep, no doubts to haunt him yet: take comfort—he will not forget.

***

Papa bequeathed all that was his to *Cara Francesca moglie mia*, which, not surprising, amounted to nothing. It had been years since he had contributed to the family's finances. Christina had little doubt Mama meant to destroy Papa's demons for them all and continued to act in their best interest by soon reverting to her predictable, practical self. Even through the appropriate mourning period, the gloom of Papa's failing disappeared with his grumblings, illnesses, and clothes. Life went on lighter and brighter without him. It was easier for Christina to be grateful she was the daughter of Gabriele Rossetti now she need only think of him as a hero to his native country and, without fear of exile, his wife and children.

It was a relief not to have to live awkwardly with him any longer.

Christina agreed with Mama—Maria and William not contradicting—that hungry, thirsty, miscellaneous Italian males who had sought out the company of *Professore Rossetti*, even when he was frail, confused, and churlish, weren't missed.

Women absent of husbands and, much of the time, sons and brothers, needed to be more discerning of who they allowed into their home.

Christina suspected her mother wanted what was left of the family to be more Pierce than Polidori or Rossetti. For the most part, they already favored her mother's side in their manners and speech, where they lived, what they ate, how they prayed, and the company they kept. To those who never witnessed her volatility, Christina easily seemed the quintessential English rose, whether her petals were sweetly opening or sadly withering. Not so for her sister. Papa and mirrors had long reminded Maria of her resemblance to *Nonna Rossetti* in her *fisonomia tutta Italiana*, along with her dark, course hair, a body as round as her face, and feet, she joked, so large a man could wear her boots. She exemplified Mama's adage: "If we cannot have what we like, we must like what we have." Maria may have appeared foreign in the land of her birth, but her generosity, good humor, tolerance, intelligence, resilience, and productive activity made her welcome there and wherever she went.

Maria was fortunate to have to rely on her character, education, and purpose rather than looks. William's hair was thinning, Gabriel's girth was widening, and Christina was beginning to realize the likely fate of her own exterior. Often said to have inherited Mama's pale blue gaze, clear skin, and softly shaped face, midway through her twenties, Christina suspected she would age with the same drooping eyes, darkening under them, and squaring of her jaw. She wanted to be above vanity, but it took a creature more selfless than she was to resist looking for white hairs and wrinkles and worry about the size of her waist. She hated herself for it, but she also couldn't help comparing herself to the forbidden women who dazzled her brothers and their brotherhood. Lizzie was a year older than Christina, but still kittenish, curling and stretching, pouting and purring, playing with Gabriel's infatuation as though she would always be young.

Christina began to understand why Mama disliked mirrors and let Gabriel take them away. A few were still available, hanging on a dresser, the reflection of Mama in middle age, or just the realization that the promises of youth would not be fulfilled.

All things that pass are woman's looking-glass; they show her how her bloom must fade, and she herself be laid with withered roses in the shade ....

Christina's expectation was for a cheerful visit with eleven-year-old Lucy Madox Brown. William had briefly mentioned observing her five years earlier at Ford Madox Brown's studio in Portland Place as quiet but surprisingly self-assured for a child. Christina's first glimpse of her arriving by train was pleasing and poignant: Lucy walking happily hand-in-hand with her father, who had gone to Gravesend, Kent, where she lived with her aunt, to accompany her to London. She looked every bit an artist's daughter in a limp, short-waisted cinnamon-brown dress with full sleeves, its neckline sagging with a broach too big and barbarian for a young girl, her thick auburn hair tied into side bunches with sage-green ribbon. All seemed well, even as introductions were made, Lucy smiling shyly, greeting each of the Rossetti sisters with a warm stare. Her silence seemed as agreeable, until her father dropped her hand.

"No. I want to stay with you."

Christina was reminded of her own childhood willfulness, except Lucy didn't turn red or stamp her foot.

"The Rossettis have been looking forward to your visit, my darling."

"But why can't I stay with you?"

"And disappoint Maria and Christina?"

"It's because of Emma and—"

"Emma? She is—"

"Not my mummy. And Cathy always acts as if I don't exist."

Lucy looked at her father with adoration one minute and suspicion the next, but Christina knew how that was possible. She put a hand, almost as a caress, on the girl's back. "It will be fun, Lucy. We can walk to the Zoological Gardens, view the city, have a picnic on Primrose Hill, and visit other favorite places from when Maria and I were your age."

"Like we did last time," Maria also reminded her sister of Lucy's stay at Arlington Street during the family's Frome separation. "Only now we have Christina to make triple the trouble."

Christina hugged her sister's arm. "I'll do my best—I mean, worst."

"Unless Papa takes me, I won't go to church."

"Well, Lucy," Maria refused to be shocked, "as long as you don't mind not going with our William." She re-tied one of Lucy's ribbons. "Did you note the double negative?"

Lucy's father saw his chance to get away. "Before you return to Kent, you can visit your sister Kate ... and her mother. And see what I'm working on."

"The day after tomorrow then," Maria decided for him. "I'll bring her around teatime." She took Lucy's hand. "Today we've invited

Charlie Heimann, who is only a year younger than you. Of course, like most boys, he will boast about himself. He likes to mention the prizes he wins at school."

Christina laughed. "He thought I was impressed when I suggested he would soon be attending university but knew differently when I found out he had no idea what being facetious meant."

Their attempt at amusing Lucy didn't prevent the tears she tried to hold in. A few finally rolled down her cheeks as her father walked away with one quick look back.

Teatime with Charlie and, as Christina had hoped, Amelia and Dr. Heimann, was pleasantly dull compared to a visit to Ford Madox Brown's studio and part-time residence on Newman Street. His second wife, Emma, another pregnancy not yet obvious, and their four-year-old daughter, Cathy, were also there. Although the Rossetti sisters and Lucy calling was arranged not spontaneous, he excused himself because he couldn't afford to let the paint on his pallet "dry and waste like Gabriel's so often does." Little plump, blonde Cathy went on playing chattily with a broken-legged doll. Emma apologized without reproach for her husband's inhospitality, as well as any messiness, including her own appearance, which was slightly disheveled.

Christina thought of Gabriel's accusation that Emma had been tempting 'the Sid' to carousing and inebriating.

In the soft spoken yet conspiring way she had, Emma countered her own girlish prettiness with the suspicion she looked as tired as she felt because she didn't have "help with the housekeeping like in the country."

By "the country," Emma didn't mean anywhere like Holmer Green, or Melliker Farm in Kent where Lucy had spent most of her remembered life, but northwest, newly suburban London. There had already been some discussion that Lucy might eventually live with her father's new family in the small house they leased at Church End, Finchley, that had a narrow, fenced in front yard with a gate the child Christina would have, like Cathy, defied orders not to swing on.

Maria's offer to tutor Lucy was eventually taken up, but without the welcome to reside full-time in the Ford Madox Brown world. £40 a year and the Rossettis' humble hospitality would provide Lucy with an education and a residence in London until Emma, two more babies later, saw her usefulness.

The July after Papa's death, Lucy returned to Melliker Farm in Kent. Whenever she had spoken about her "Eden," where she "chased after chickens, geese, and goats, took long walks to find the rarest wildflowers and best tasting blackberries, and jumped off a pier to swim with her cousins," she seemed to want to be happier there than she was.

After the girl's departure, Christina exiled herself, at least from summer, a string of rainy days keeping her in the house, familiar melancholy in her room. Her thoughts lingered on Lucy and her own changed circumstances. Lucy wanted nothing more than to be where her father was, to share in his moods, obsessions, successes, and failures, not yet realizing the risk of being ruled by them. She was still on the innocent side of her relationship with him. Christina understood Lucy's longing to be undeniably loved by a father unlike most others, to feel special to him but also because of him. She gave some consideration to the good and bad times she'd had with Gabriele Rossetti, but more to what she would do now he was gone: life, probably a spinster's life, possibly a poet's life, hopefully a purposeful life, ahead of her without the excuse of his care and the constant reminder of her ambiguous feelings towards him.

But first I tried, and then my care grew slack, till my heart dreamed, and maybe wandered, too …

Finally, she could move on to her adult life.

Still, she was afraid Papa's literary disappointments foreshadowed hers. Despite her brothers' best intentions in trying to find a publisher for her prose piece *Nick*, her fantasy about it being a breakthrough was long since disillusioned, the manuscript retrieved from Messrs. Cundall and Addey along with the sin of wishing for fame.

By day she woos me, soft, exceedingly fair: but all night as the moon so changeth she; loathsome and foul with hideous leprosy, and subtle serpents gliding in her hair.

Despite modest, false starts—publication in *The Athenaeum*, *The Germ*, and a few Italian *versi* in *The Bouquet*, a magazine started by some aristocratic young ladies who attended Christ Church—Christina might denounce but couldn't refuse ambition. Unlike marriage, she still considered its possibilities and allowed its pursuit impulsive behavior.

Christina asked herself a question: was a song unsung still a song? Perhaps, as an unconsidered breath was still a breath, but to sustain life, to make breathing worthwhile, there must be more. To have a voice, she needed to be heard. She had spent days going through her poems, choosing ones she thought were brave enough to face an editor who dreaded the receipt of a packet from *a nameless rhymester*, but had the recourse of the wastebasket. They had to be even more resilient in case of acceptance. Carefully, she copied out *Symbols, Something Like the Truth* or, as Gabriel wanted her to retitle, *Sleep at Sea, Easter Even, The Watchers*, and *Once*, and *Long Enough* he insisted should be *Dream-Love*.

She considered interrupting her use of black-bordered stationery for the cover letter, but, with shame, thought it might evoke enough sympathy and give an edge to her submission.

1st August 1854. To Professor Aytoun. She briefly thought how Gabriel would be furious, *Blackwood's Magazine* not a favorite of his for its attacks on Keats and Tennyson. *As an unknown and unpublished writer,* she began and knew she went on too long, should probably have never mentioned *egotism or foolish vanity,* or that her *productions* might be more worthy of attention than so many others the magazine received. Obviously, by his silence, Professor Aytoun didn't agree, and without the return of her poems, she assumed where they had ended up.

A few months later she would try once more to find a stage for singing on, this time submitting to *Fraser's* with William bargaining his sister's desire to be published with her not expecting payment.

Needless to say, not even able to give her poetry away was the ultimate rejection. Rather than contemplate that writing wasn't to be her vocation after all, she preferred to believe the timing wasn't right. *Heaven's chimes are slow, but sure to strike at last.* In the meantime, patience and another occupation were needed. She had the example of Mama, Maria, and even William adjusting their lives to what was possible and needed to be done, often selflessly, mostly without complaint. Then there were the muddles Gabriel's egotism, impulses, and fantasies got him into.

Mama always said there was never a lack of ways to serve Christ by appropriately maintaining themselves so they could assist others. Answering their church's call for volunteers, Christina began taking food and clothing to the poor on Robert Street, a short distance from her more fortunate dwelling on Albany Street and the affluency fronting the west boundary of Regent's Park. It was satisfying, if depressing, and, naively, whetted her appetite for more charitable work—more adventurously charitable work. There was a war in the Crimea, Christ Church a local center for organizing the patriotic fervor of its congregation to support, on the home and battle fronts, Englishmen heroically and bloodily engaged in it. A number of the parish's ladies applied to serve as part of a nursing corps in the Old Barrack Hospital, Scutari on the Asian shore of the Bosphorus. A few less were accepted, among them Elizabeth Polidori, who, like her youngest Rossetti niece, the decisiveness of death had recently relieved from family obligations. Aunt Eliza led the way, tempting Christina to follow.

She left the rosy morn,
She left the fields of corn,
For twilight cold and lorn
And water springs.
Through sleep, as through a veil,
She sees the sky look pale,
And hears the nightingale
That sadly sings.

PART FOUR

A windy shell singing upon the shore:
A lily budding in a desert place;
Blooming alone
With no companion
To praise its perfect perfume and its grace:
A rose crimson and blushing at the core,
Hedged in with thorns behind it and before:
~ from *To What Purpose is this Waste* by Christina Rossetti

CHAPTER TWENTY-TWO

We call then, on Christian women, who are not bound by their pecuniary circumstances to work for their own living ... and those who are mothers in heart, though not by God's gift on earth, will be able to bestow their maternal love on those who are more to be pitied than orphans, those most wretched moral orphans whose natural sweetness of filial love has been mingled with deadly poison.

"Sister Christina."

She stood at the entrance of a long and lofty laundry brightened by high windows; the only way of knowing it had once been stables was being told so. Less than a dozen young women, some still girls—at least in age—were capped and aproned in white, for most their pale blue gingham frocks too loose. They stood back to back at sinks along the right side and tables to the left, washing, ringing, ironing, and folding their own clothes separately from linens sent from the West End to raise needed funds for the institution. A rainy day meant it all was hung around the room rather than outside on the drying ground where lines radiated out from a center post to other poles and even tree branches.

The class seemed safe and sorry in steam, the smell of lye, and silence, not breaking the rules during muted hours as they turned and greeted Christina in unison also as required.

She thought back to her first visit to Park House. She had an uphill walk from the omnibus stop to a postern entrance in a wall set slightly back from the road. It was locked but, remembering the directions on the correspondence that had set the day and time of her interview, she knew to pull the short chord dangling from the gate's lintel. A distant bell rang with the impatience of her tugs until, finally, coming closer and closer, steps sounded on gravel and keys jangled. Christina announced herself, feeling colorful in dark blue and gray, greeted by a black costumed portress who led her along a deeply shaded path to the colonnaded entrance of Highgate Penitentiary. Christina met with the Warden, the Reverend John Oliver, little else in his room besides an oak library table, a few chairs, and a bookcase. Scripture excerpts were plainly painted above the doors and mantle in the center of which sat a simple wooden cross. He was said to be a man dedicated to social reform and charitable work. Christina wasn't immediately convinced he did so with true compassion if, as he explained, his mission was to teach its "fallen charges to hate what had been pleasant to them and love what they had despised."

We must not look at goblin men, we must not buy their fruits: who knows upon what soil they fed their hungry thirsty roots?

As a child Christina would have cried if told to refuse pleasure and love punishment. *Nonno* had assured her that she didn't have to be miserable to be good.

At thirty, she struggled to hear the sound of his voice.

"Ah, Sister Christina. There you are."

"I'm sorry I was a little late this morning. We received news from my brother—"

"I believe it's your day for Bible studies." Mrs. Oliver, the current Lady Principal, gave a wave for the laundry ladies to turn their attention back to their work.

"Which I prefer to pretending expertise in domestic activities."

Fortunately, there was little scholastic instruction expected of the few volunteer sisters whose time was concentrated on religion, moral fortitude, and training for domestic service. Despite the experience she'd had in Mama's schools and helping Maria tutor Lucy Madox Brown, Christina wasn't comfortable teaching academics, mainly because she didn't feel prepared to do so. If only she had learned her lessons better when she was the student. As a child, Christina found her mother encouraging intellectual excellence in her daughters as well as her sons tiresome rather than enlightened. Subsequently, she realized the folly and wisdom in Mama being less diligent in preparing her girls for what biology might fool them into thinking they were primarily made for.

Send such a woman to her piano, her books, her cross-stitch; she answers with despair! But send her on some mission of mercy ....

The Crimea wasn't Christina's next adventure after all, her application rejected because she was too young and inexperienced. She was consoled by admitting she wasn't heathy enough for lengthy foreign travel or serious nursing and through Aunt Eliza's frustration with *having gone so far to merely manage hospital supplies.*

Christina's *mission of mercy* kept her close to home. She took over Aunt Eliza's Christ Church duties and continued to visit the needy on Robert Street. For the last few years, she had regularly gone to north London and the St. Mary Magdalene home in a mansion at the top of Highgate Hill. Spacious and airy, run by strict rules but kind intentions, it was kept meticulously clean by volunteers and residents. At times it was a pleasant place, its girls and young women encouraged to embrace decency in their leisure as well as training and work. On fine late spring, summer, or early fall days, there might be an hour or two for them to walk the broad pathways around the grounds. They could also choose to read—what book or magazine monitored—in the shade of a mature chestnut tree or Portugal laurel. Croquet and tennis were played on clover-green lawns, games most didn't know when they arrived and would probably never participate in again after they left. If the weather or season kept them indoors, a fire was lit in the main parlor. Besides reading, respectable recreation was needlework, drawing, and painting, lessons or even a performance or two on the piano with or without singing, or a round of whist. There was also the option of board games, draughts the most popular, the Staunton boxwood chess set untouched until "humble Sister Christina" revealed she knew how to play.

Christina wasn't surprised by the aptitude some of the young women had for the game, having already experienced the quickness of their minds and cunning of their characters, and read the reports on their past lives.

'Come buy our fruits, come buy.' Must she then buy no more such dainty fruit? Must she no more that succous pasture find, gone deaf and blind?

The penitents weren't allowed to keep to their dormitories during the day unless they were ill, avoiding solitary situations that might tempt regressive thoughts or feelings. Yet it was impossible to prevent them from becoming attached to their personal partitioned spaces and unconscionable to discourage their enjoyment of even the most basic privacy and sense of possession. Having their own beds and linen, washstands, mirrors, walls also for hanging religious and other appropriate pictures was essential in developing their self-respect. Each Sister was assigned a particular group, usually according to age, who slept in the same dormitory, and took lessons and daily exercise together. Chapel services, mealtimes, and Sunday rest hours brought all the groups together, although, because of their varying degree of reformation, mingling was closely supervised. Christina was a floater, aiding other Sisters when and as needed, and even helping with administrative tasks, a position created for her in consideration of her desire to volunteer on a daytime basis. Her willingness to stay overnight once or twice a month and the lack of response to the Penitentiary's advertising for more help were enough to secure her a position.

Jessie Walker, the Principal Sister offered a teary-eyed welcome. "You will never experience such peace and happiness as you will here. A power is given to one of duty, especially such a holy duty. To cheerfully perform it is a great privilege. I only wish we could persuade more ladies to join us. They do not realize what joy would rouse their souls. And they need not sacrifice worldly ties by joining us. We are bound by no vow and can return to our own families at any time."

The nights each month Christina slept at Park House, she used the quarters of whichever Sister was on a few days leave. She preferred some rooms to others and one especially because it had a French bed hung with tasseled, rose-budded, dimity cotton and a cozy high-backed winged armchair upholstered with the same fabric. Otherwise, it was furnished like the other bedrooms with a sturdy dressing table that supplied a surface for correcting schoolwork and composing letters and more creative thoughts. Plainly framed prints of sacred scenes and a wooden cross similar to the one she had seen in the Warden's office interrupted the creamy wash of its inner walls. A square aperture into the area where her temporary charges slept meant she could keep an eye and ear on them.

Christina didn't like spying for disciplinary reasons but was curious about their whispering, and sometimes moved by soft sobbing. She was also concerned that their silence, if not because they were obeying the rules or soundly sleeping, might mean they were irrevocably lost to giving up.

One may lead a horse to water, twenty cannot make him drink. Though the goblins cuffed and caught her, coaxed and fought her, scratched her, pinched her black as ink, kicked and knocked her, mauled and mocked her, she uttered not a word.

Christina would rather believe that most of the captives of St. Mary Magdalene were quietly imagining hopeful futures. After all, now they were saved and safe, finishing preparation for good Christian lives, for maintaining themselves through respectable work, even for fulfillment as wives and mothers.

***

After the students left, Christina stayed in the last classroom on her rounds of Bible studies, the one part of the curriculum taught by her to all the groups on some of her day shifts. She had time left to go through letters written by the girls and women, making certain addressees, general content, and any affection expressed were appropriate. On the rare occasion the standard wasn't met, the Warden would speak to the offender. Christina felt it an uncomfortable assignment, an intrusion she wouldn't have liked, while realizing it was for the benefit of these less fortunate. At the same time, she wished it offered more intimacy with them, something frowned upon as the Penitentiary viewed her as their instructor, not confidant. Knowing the scrutiny their correspondences would be subjected to, the inmates revealed little more than their activities and health, with questions about the recipients'. Writer's curiosity a reflex to Christina, childhood games not so long ago they couldn't be replayed, it was impossible not to read between the lines or look for double meanings, even secret messages.

Christina's restraint was really tested when there was any attempt at poetry, which occurred more often than might be expected, usually in closing to express what otherwise they didn't dare to.

The letters were mainly to mothers, sisters, aunties, and cousins, now and then to brothers and fathers, some who undoubtedly cared for their sisters and daughters, others who needed convincing, which irritated Christina. She suspected they were culpable for the very transgressions they hesitated to forgive.

She sat by one of the open windows, the scents and sounds of May just beyond, *no time like Spring when life's alive in everything*, a good time to be married, if ever there was for Gabriel and Lizzie. A ten-year engagement had hardly made a difference to him, while Lizzie's heart and health had suffered for it. The twelfth of May, Gabriel's birthday, was supposed to be the day he gave into the commitment his illusions longed for and his behavior sabotaged. He made the announcement in mid-April when he returned to London from Hastings where he had, a few days earlier, left "desperately ill" Lizzie.

"I don't believe you'll do it," Maria couldn't hold back.

"It's why I need money for a special license, so my Guggums won't have to stand in a cold church."

"Who knows if that's what you'll use it for, but William will give it to you."

Whatever it benefited or was wasted on, his thirty-second birthday came and went without a wedding.

I wish we once were wedded – then I must be true; you should hold my will in yours to do or undo …

Christina only had one letter left to read. After so many with nothing to report, she was not prepared for it to be disturbing and not just because the Warden would have to insist on changes before it could be sent. That morning, the 24th of May 1860, just as Christina was leaving home for the penitentiary, the post delivered news that Miss Siddall had finally become Mrs. Rossetti at Hastings' St. Clement's Church. Gabriel and his new wife would travel to Boulogne and Paris to stay in France for the entire summer.

The letter by Helena—not her real name but one she was given at the reformatory—was brief, obviously in response to news of an approaching marriage. *I want my brother to be happy, but I also wish to never meet his wife. Without any reason, I am so prejudiced against her, I just am.*

Christina wanted to confidentially speak to Helena, to share something of her own similar situation and feelings. Instead, she complied with the limitations of her position and gave the offending correspondence to Reverend Oliver.

"Oh, dear."

"Please. Don't be severe with her. She thinks she's lost her brother, possibly someone who has understood her better than anyone else."

"Yes, yes. It might be. But I must show her that her words are cruel and unchristian, that if the world were to act so towards her, as she is a sinner, all doors of hope would be closed on her. I thank you for alerting me. Now I know I need to speak to her in a way that yields a more Christian temper."

Christina gathered her coat and satchel, ready to go home, knowing if she missed her usual omnibus she would have to wait an hour for the next. She took that chance, discreetly observing another Sister go to the Warden's office, leave, and return with a girl, no more than twenty if that, her hair and complexion ashen, her eyes red, her punishment already administered.

**

"Sorry I'm late. I had to speak with the Warden."

"Everything is all right, I hope." Mama gave Christina a look that still saw her as a child who might have done something she shouldn't. "It's been raining?"

"Just as I neared home."

Mama took her coat, wiping its shoulders and sleeves. "We've waited to have supper with you."

"I'll be down as soon as I've changed."

William admired Sister Christina's simple uniform as "elegant, even." She ritually, almost hypnotically, removed it, putting the soft, pure muslin cap with narrow lace edging on her dressing table, the string of black beads and silver chain and cross curled on top. The black dress with hanging sleeves, not vastly different from her usual day wear, was laid on her bed, Muff making herself comfortable on it. Christina was too weary to protest, even though gray-brown fur would take a good half hour to brush off. Instead, she added her own caressing hand to Muff's pleasure.

The only cats at the penitentiary were ones that strayed onto the grounds from wherever they were cared for or fended for themselves, some friendlier than others, just as the girls and women were more or less amiable to them. Beloved pets—cats, dogs, canaries, rabbits—were often mentioned in the letters Christina reviewed, subjects for some of the poetry and even quick sketches she could barely resist talking to their creators about. Once she did break protocol by sitting with an inmate in her cubicle, uncrumpling the news and the thin sobbing body beside her, their embrace happened upon by the young woman's group Sister who had, so far, kept the discovery to herself.

Who shall tell the lady's grief when her cat was past relief? Who shall say

146

the dark dismay which her dying caused that day?

Muff was one of Grimalkin's kittens, kept because she was most like her mother. She was still young and beautiful, but Christina, thinking of what was inevitable, felt the coldness of having already lost her.

Christina's morbid anticipation, which had slowed down her redressing, was interrupted by a knock on the door, soon after a man's voice answering Maria's. It didn't sound like William; it couldn't be unless he had forgotten his key. Christina feared it was John Brett, illogically, for it had been some time since he had been more persistent in pestering than painting her. She listened for the lilting liveliness of Mr. Bell Scott, her hope forgetting he wasn't due in London again until July. Maria's prospects for a caller were as bygone as Millais' friend Charley Collins and the platonic attentions of John Ruskin.

"William is staying at Blackfriars while Gabriel is away. Now for even longer with a trip to Paris."

"I just wanted to hand deliver the copies of my translation of *The Psalms in Meter* your mother ordered."

"How considerate, Charles," Mama greeted him. "You will take supper with us, won't you? We delayed it for Christina to return from her good work, and now, it seems, for you, too."

Christina felt flushed as she realized there was little more than a stairway and part of a hallway between Mr. Cayley and her half-dressed eavesdropping, quickly withdrawing into her bedroom to ready herself for supper and seeing him again.

CHAPTER TWENTY-THREE

Charles Cayley had slowly appealed to Christina, shyly coming and going over the years, a diligent student of her father's. Since Papa's death, Mama regarded him even more warmly. He was a scholarly discussion to Maria, who knew how to bring him out of his shell with certain topics. His "incurable intellectualism" bored Gabriel, his agnosticism found common ground with William, who thought him good-natured and well-read if "a rather anxious, shabby, old-beyond-his-years fellow."

"Not the sort of man who is attractive to the general run of women," William commented, having noticed what Christina thought she had concealed, "but such as one of exceptional order might genuinely admire."

Christina would only admit William was a better judge of character than Gabriel, who had wreaked the havoc of James Collinson upon her. A decade later, she didn't doubt infatuation was a poor substitute for a calmer connection between compatible minds and character. She had seen this in the happiness or not of friends and family. Although not yet completely immune to the charm and good looks of some men, who, especially in Gabriel's circle, believed no female could be, she found resistance in the reminder that heartbreak was hardly worth moments of flattery. As her sister-in-law discovered, being worshipped and enviable did not secure a woman's future. Christina was more convinced by her work at the penitentiary where there were too many tragic examples of vanity and desperation falling prey to fancy and false promises.

There was no danger of being wantonly wooed by Charles Cayley; Christina was amused by the mere thought of him trying. Who would, she wondered, understand her looking forward to the company of a bashful, balding, pink-cheeked man seven years her senior who wore an outdated tailcoat? No matter how disheveled he appeared, he carried himself with a quiet dignity Christina herself aspired to. Despite his linguistic expertise, Charles was clumsy at conversation, but, due to his serious intellect, he was compelling. Frequent absentmindedness added humor to him. He graciously took ribbing for it and didn't seem to mind the nickname of "Wombat," assigned by Gabriel, which sent Charles "on a mission to learn about the strange creature."

His reticence was respectful of Christina's. His modesty was true; his attention also sincere and unthreatening. Unlike James Collinson, Charles was easily welcomed as a friend of the family. Unlike John Brett, he never misused that privilege or gave reason for "No, thank you."

"You went to Brett's studio," Gabriel reminded accusingly.

Christina wasn't happy to defend herself but did. "With the Epps sisters, who were taking drawing lessons from him. He voluntarily did some sketches of me while we were there."

"You returned."

"Well, he decided to turn the sketches into a portrait and needed me there again for coloring. Letitia and Maria went, too."

"At least he wanted to make an honest woman of you."

Christina had learned long before that a proposal didn't a marriage make. At the time, Gabriel was reinforcing the lesson with Lizzie.

Christina had first met John Brett in late winter of fifty-seven at one of Mama's Thursday 'at-home' evenings, which attempted to repay the hospitality of friends like the Heimanns, Ormes, Patmores, and Scotts when they were in town. Mama also wanted to encourage her brood to bring home friends, associates, and potential spouses as probable as Henrietta Rintoul and as unlikely as John Ruskin. Aunt Charlotte's influence was evident, her career having been spent observing and even organizing social niceties and necessities. Christina suspected her mother agreed because she was missing the diversion of Papa's visitors after all.

If Christina had been in the same place as John Brett before, it hadn't been memorable. She hardly took notice of him that night, except for his flaxen hair, eyebrows, and beard, which made him appear to be peering through a shrub. She also decided he was opinionated, although she didn't go near enough to hear what about.

Over the next months, he turned up where Christina was, first at the independent show the PRB put on in hired rooms at Russell Place where Lizzie exhibited her artwork for the first time, during a visit Christina made with Mama and Maria to the Turners at Marlborough House, and at a few other social occasions given by mutual friends.

In July she, Maria, and Letitia Scott stayed with the Eppses at Warlington in Surrey, ten miles from where Mr. Brett was working near Mickleham on the background for an upcoming painting. When Christina went to his Box Hill lodgings, she noticed a copy of Mrs. Browning's epic masterpiece *Aurora Leigh,* a curious coincidence as it had influenced a new much less ambitious poem of her own reflecting on seduction and desertion, written long before she volunteered at the penitentiary.

I plucked pink blossoms from mine apple-tree and wore them all evening in my hair: then in due season when I went to see I found no apples there.

Christina thought of mentioning the coincidence but decided not to once she observed Mr. Brett's flirtatiousness with the Epps sisters. It wasn't surprising they didn't seem to mind, considering their father's habit of superfluous kissing the cheeks of all female visitors to his home. Christina and Maria barely, and not gracefully, avoided his "cracked" display of otherwise unexplained affection.

John Brett spontaneously sketching Christina didn't strike her as an indication of anything but the compulsive behavior she had seen in other artists. He was ambitious and vying for patronage, especially Mr. Ruskin's. Such a motive seemed obvious in his pursuit of a place in what was left of the PRB, which not only put him in Gabriel's and William's sphere of influence, but also Christina's society. In hindsight and considering he concentrated on landscapes and seascapes, his decision to do a portrait of her hinted at an objective she should have realized and immediately rebuffed. She only ever liked him enough *to strike hands as hearty friends, no more, no less*, his bright blue eyes appealing, his stocky build and bushy, broody face less so. His humor was sudden, often sarcastic and misconstrued, not unlike her own. His December birthday was only a few days after hers, his questions offering more details about himself. She wondered she was still naïve; at least, not on stricter guard for a man's notion that she was looking to be courted, not even when William offered the warning that on Mr. Brett's first sight of her, "he appeared to be smitten." Christina shrugged it off as brotherly bias, Gabriel and William not yet surrendering her to spinsterhood as they had Maria.

Maria almost upended their assumption about her marriage prospects a few years before John Brett entered the shrinking potential of Christina's. First, there was Charley Collins, brother of the writer Wilkie, a painter with High Church connections and PRB aspirations. Their relationship developed while Christina was in Frome, no doubt Maria a great comfort to Mr. Collins' newly widowed mother. Maria declared she only ever saw Mr. Collins as a friend and fellow aesthetic. It might have been she was already interested in another man—another John, more brilliant and stranger.

Maria encouraging Mr. Ruskin's polite attention was as unexpected as him extending it to her, even once his marriage was annulled, and the scandal of his child bride and Mr. Millais was fading into their fruitful future together. An invitation to dinner with Gabriel and Lizzie prompted the possibility of a prospect that would meet Maria's intellect and secure her financially.

It was logical but incorrect to assume that Mr. Ruskin's rejection of the young, vibrant, beautiful Effie Gray meant he might be drawn to Maria because of her modesty and loyalty, and, especially, her homeliness, which he probably mistook as the reason for her virtuousness. Maria would find approval with his mother, Margaret, who was devout, and, it was rumored, once wanted her son to become an Anglican bishop. Whether Mrs. Ruskin would consider Maria as potentially more than a pleasant dinner guest was doubtful.

If Mr. Ruskin had been a wiser man, he would have allowed Maria's warm heart to heal him. She always insisted she went to his Denmark Hill, South London residence because she was invited and curious. The fine house and grounds weren't far from the Chrystal Palace, "a cucumber frame between two chimneys" how, she reported, Mr. Ruskin described it.

"He begrudged it and other developments because they ruined the view from his study's window."

There was time before a summer sunset to tour the property's kitchen gardens, orchard, a little of its lime tree-fragrant woods, and what Mrs. Ruskin called their "small farm," a couple of young male employees herding chickens, goats, and pigs into shelter for the night.

"Then there was the ordeal of supper," confessed Maria, "during which Lizzie, already so thin, picked at her food. Which prompted Mr. Ruskin, his mother, and me, also, to make her the center of attention. Lizzie accounted her lack of appetite to a toothache, Mrs. Ruskin promising to give her 'a costly quantity of strengthening jelly made from ivory dust.'"

In Maria's opinion, given along with her detailed account of the occasion, Gabriel arriving late without an excusable reason was what put his sylph-like "Sid" in a less than amiable mood.

"My love. I knew you had the best escort possible in our Moony."

Gabriel could see only opportunity in encouraging a match between Maria and Mr. Ruskin: to keep the important art critic "on the Rossetti side" without losing Lizzie entirely to Mr. Ruskin's interest in her. Gabriel would rather sacrifice his elder sister than his Blessed Damozel to the necessity of this man who could be cruelly complicated. Christina was afraid John Ruskin would break Maria's heart, until, not for the first time, she witnessed her sister's sanguine acceptance of God's will through an unshakable faith that what was meant to would transpire, if not on earth, then in heaven. Maria rarely dwelled in disappointment, never in recriminations, always in resilience, an example for Christina to follow into and through the *selva oscura* of her thirties, if she, too, remained unmarried.

Was John Brett her last chance? He might have thought so, perhaps being one of those men often finding it difficult to believe there were women who refused to be saved by them. Many aging ladies were persuaded by desperation rather than sighs of relief. Christina wasn't one of them. Watching others do what she hadn't offered the benefit of objectively weighing the pros and cons, which, for her, focused on respect and commitment, shared values and interests, and enduring friendship as opposed to ephemeral passion.

Choose wisely, Aunt Charlotte had once written to Christina before James Collinson had tested her wisdom. *Good men are scarce, but fools are plenty.*

Which was John Brett? A good fellow in that he was honorable in what he proposed, but foolish in not heeding the hints she offered. How often she was told she didn't hide uneasiness well, annoyance even less. Yet he didn't notice he was wearying her with "do" and "pray" and every subsequent compliment she feared had an ulterior motive. It was no fault of Christina's that he assumed her interest in him was other than admiration for his art and polite association through friends and family. If he hadn't misunderstood her smiles and nods, their acquaintance might have continued with a few more escorted visits to his house in Camden Town, which he shared with a younger brother and older sister. Mama, Maria, and Christina first called on them for a preview of *The Stonebreaker*, the very painting Mr. Brett had begun the previous July in Kent. By early the next year, it was almost completed with hopes of it hanging prominently at the 1858 Royal Academy exhibition. Christina was glad of the chance to get to know his sister, who was also an artist, having liked her in briefer meetings when it was obvious Rosa's affection for John was as greedy as Christina's own for Gabriel.

There was interesting conversation, mostly between Maria and John, encouraged by *The Stonebreaker* and other paintings he showed them, including the miniature portrait he had begun of Christina, which Mama had heard about but not yet seen. That it still wasn't finished seemed to spoil the conviviality of the occasion, until Rosa intervened with the warmth of well-brewed tea and sweetness of iced sponge cake John persuaded her into admitting she had made.

"And miraculously didn't burn," finally spoke up their younger brother, who had hardly looked up from his reading, his legs flung over the arm of the best chair in the parlor until John pushed him out of it so Mama could sit.

"Please, Mrs. Rossetti."

"Thank you, John."

"Now and then I make the mistake of thinking I have time to sketch out an idea while I'm boiling or baking something," Rosa unapologetically explained.

She cut liberal slices for each of them, the consumption of which filled any awkward silences with nibbling and finger licking.

"That's why we don't let Christina cook." Mama smiled so everyone, including Christina, knew she was teasing. "She is much better at poetry."

"Can we see some of your art?"

Maria's question caused Rosa to immediately and nervously glance at her brother.

"You know which," John responded.

Christina knew what Maria didn't, because William was trusted and in turn confided to her that John had sold some of Rosa's work as his own.

"He claimed by accident, as she hadn't signed it. But I was there when a few of John's pupils arrived unexpectedly and the poor girl had to make a sudden escape so as not to be caught working on one of 'his' paintings."

Christina understood why Rosa let her brother pretend they were his, but didn't condone him taking advantage of their financial needs — easier to sell a painting by a male than female Brett — and the assumption that Rosa's ambitions should be subordinate to his. In a moment, what appeared a partnership that supported and encouraged a woman's talents became a manipulation of her generous love and expected submission.

No thank you, John.

"I think I will title it *The Hay Loft*."

After shyly, stingily showing her visitors only a few pages in a sketchbook, Rosa finally smiled, her eyes and dark ringleted hair glistening as she uncovered a small, completed canvas. It immediately pleased Christina in its depiction of a gray tabby cat curled on a broken bale of hay. Nearby was a woman's red peplumed vest, bright blue checked bandana, and straw hat, causing Christina to wonder if kitty was pretending sleep, on watch because of what was happening elsewhere in that barn's loft. She attributed the first possibility that came to her mind for the discarded clothing to the influence of her penitentiary work. The untold story of Rosa's lovely painting might have been just an innocent, solitary escape on a warm summer's day as the Rosas — and Christinas — of the world would be tempted by if they had the chance.

"John thinks I should submit it to the Academy."

"You must."

"Not under my name, of course."

"You won't let it go as one of your brother's?"

"Uh ... no." Rosa skewed her mouth. "I don't think it would pass as his. I'll use a pseudonym. As, I believe, you did."

"A few poems in *The Germ*. I haven't published much since."

"Oh. I hope you will soon." Rosa draped *The Hay Loft* out of sight again. "I thought Rosarius. Well, dear John thought of it."

Of course he had. Brothers thought of many things masked in concern for their sisters, convinced it was their duty to direct and dominate them. Although Rosa was older than Christina, she still valued John's judgement and ambition more than her own. Obviously, she hadn't yet learned the harsh lesson of losing him to another. It was just a matter of time, just a matter of whom he cast his bait out to and whether she could be fooled and hooked.

It wasn't to be Christina. He was the fish in the sea, not her, and she wasn't trying to catch any. Once John had shown off his work and himself, chided his brother and humored his sister, guzzled two cups of tea, and devoured a slice of cake, forced looks of interest slipped into boredom as the ladies conversed. All Christina saw, especially when he caught her watching him, was his desire for her to leave.

Rosa followed the Rossetti women to the door, so Christina expected she would be the one to open it when, leaving Mama and Maria at the omnibus stop, she ran back because she had forgotten her gloves.

"Oh." Mr. Brett was holding them against his chest before he gave them to her. "Do I still have an excuse to call on you?"

"You don't need one."

Until he turned up a few weeks later in the mid-afternoon, Christina was relieved he hadn't misunderstood her after all. She was alone; the maid had gone to the fishmonger. It was awkward to invite him in, but also not to, the doorstep hardly the place to make or refuse an offer of marriage, to hear him call her false and say she had no heart. Fortunately, it was too cold for open windows, but there were passersby. She let him come into the hallway, which made his eyes lift and brighten, so she felt she hadn't any choice but to reiterate her answer. Slumped against the wall, covering his face with his hands, she was glad she didn't love him and that he was gone before it was too late to conceal he had been there.

CHAPTER TWENTY-FOUR

Christina had never seen such misery. Looking prettier in despair and struggling to explain what she couldn't, Henrietta was sobbing, trembling, and thinner since she had last embraced her now not-to-be sister-in-law.

"You understand, Christina. I know you understand."

An hour's visit turned into an entire afternoon that tempted Christina's sympathy but won only her pity. How could Christina condone Henrietta's rejection of her brother's kindness and devotion, all the years he had given her the attention of his affections and also his intellect, especially as it appreciated hers?

"Will has been patient and faithful."

"Not quite, Christina. Then, what man is? Especially in the PRB circle."

"You're referring to him taking Annie Miller boating?" Christina noticed Henrietta stiffening. "Maria and I were angry with him when we heard about it. Well, my sister really found the most effective words, accusing him of being 'forgetful of Miss Rintoul.' It was like she had punched him. He was deeply sorry."

"As he was to me."

"Well, then, why?"

Everyone, including William, assumed the deaths of Henrietta's elderly parents within a year of each other would finally free her for marriage. One water excursion with a flighty artist's model shouldn't have overturned the engagement of a modestly handsome, principled bluestocking to a doe-eyed, attentive *Italianate* man of letters. Years of intellectual conversations and letter exchanges, chaperoned parlor visits and, at least once a year, cliff-walking holidays on the Isle of Wight, along with the unwavering consent of both families indicated the marriage would eventually happen. Unlike the passionate tussles between Gabriel and Lizzie, proving they couldn't live apart or together, William and Henrietta's protracted relationship was cool, quiet, and secure, almost invisible, which made it easy to be in the company of. Until its sudden severing, it was without crises, an enduring example of compatibility and constancy.

There was stunned disbelief after William's matter-of-fact announcement made as quickly as his escape from joining his sisters and mother for breakfast. He hadn't long returned from a tour of Italy, its ambitious and enviable itinerary taking him to Milan, Genoa, Florence, Bologna, Pisa, Siena, and even Bientina, the birthplace of

Nonno Polidori. Although excited to share his experiences, observations, and revelations with his family, William was most impatient to call upon Henrietta with hopes of a similar trip for their soon-to-be honeymoon.

Instead, he walked into the trap of heartbreak love too often sets.

No one saw if William was devastated the morning he fled his mother's and sisters' immediate reactions. The only other thing he ever said about the sad affair was that he "resolved to remain a bachelor." For the first time, Christina worried he might do something reckless, if not as bad as Gabriel at his wildest, then worse than William's sensitive nature and noble conscience could handle.

"Will would have been a considerate husband," Christina offered one last reason for Henrietta to at least regret her decision.

"Not considerate enough."

***

> *Wondering at each merchant man.*
> *One had a cat's face,*
> *One whisk'd a tail,*
> *One tramp'd at a rat's pace,*
> *One crawl'd like a snail,*
> *One like a wombat prowl'd obtuse and furry,*
> *One like a ratel tumbled hurry skurry.*
> *She heard a voice like voice of doves*
> *Cooing all together:*
> *They sounded kind and full of loves*
> *In the pleasant weather.*

Pleasant weather was always hoped for, an umbrella carried just in case. A long journey behind her and ahead, in between three weeks were spent in Newcastle Upon Tyne as a guest of the Scotts. It was Christina's turn to prove herself as worthy of their hospitality and society as each of her siblings had been. She expected to fall short, trying too hard to be sociable, losing her ability to converse, especially in the company of her hosts' friends, which Maria warned she would be often. Except for devotion to her family, as a woman Christina hadn't any accomplishments to boast of. She was afraid to be announced a poet to others who were and more often and successfully published. She expected her shyness would be mistaken for arrogance, her darkness would spoil the pleasures of the moment, and that she wouldn't be able to keep up with those older, even much older, in long uphill walks, overeating, drinking, and going late to bed.

As usual, Christina worked herself into a panic about being away

156

from home and family. It didn't help that the Scotts were late meeting her train at Central Station or the porter who carried her bags to a bench outside the nearest waiting room wondered if she was unwell. Irritation made her stomach burn, slightly eased by the sight of that same porter ushering a tall, red-faced, eccentrically attired middle-aged man with a feather in his hat down the platform. As always, the sight of Mr. Scott was engaging and embarrassing, especially the latter as he urgently lifted her into his arms.

"Unforgiveable. Unforgiveable," he murmured and let her go.

"Not at all." She reached for her traveler's possessions as if to prove the point.

His hand covered hers before it could escape. "I may be tardy, but ever yours."

She wondered why but wasn't sorry Mrs. Scott hadn't come, "the change of plans" a gift from providence. Also a curse, because Christina had no complaint about being alone with Mr. Scott for the fleeting time it took to reach his house. Their transport guaranteed prudent conversation, the driver behind and above controlling the trap door over their heads to take their fare and, when necessary, communicate with them. However, the cab that immersed them in shadows and left them no choice but to sit closely side by side provided Mr. Scott with another opportunity to capture her hand, this time the folds of her skirt and failing of her conscience giving the impression of consent.

"Oh, Chrissy. At last you're here."

"Dear Letty." By nearly squeezing the breath out of Mrs. Scott, Christina intended to emphasize the equality of her affection for both her hosts. Mr. Scott laughed and went on without them, carrying Christina's luggage into a half-timbered house with mullioned windows.

"I'm eying a terraced place in Saint Thomas Crescent," Mr. Scott later revealed after a tour of his residence, "which would be a step up, but not too high."

From the first evening, Christina was the least interesting of the Scotts' friends, people who obviously had gathered before. *From hand to hand they pushed the wine ... they sang, they jested and they laughed, for each was loved of each.* She relied on her listening skills, which allowed her to participate in conversations without stating she was the stranger in their midst.

They thought they knew her, being a Rossetti more hindrance than help, comparison and expectation not in her favor.

Even in June, Northumbria required rain gear, sturdy boots, woolen shawls, bonnets tied tightly as well as held onto, and never thinking how one's appearance held up. Christina couldn't help but imagine the warmth she would be enjoying if she had joined Amelia Heimann in the south of France. Christina's preference, if Newcastle could be called so, was determined by hopes for what she must not hope for.

She intended to be relieved when Mr. Scott's winks and smiles were directed elsewhere and disappointed when Mrs. Scott had others to chatter incessantly to.

If Christina had accepted Amelia's invitation, she would have had a cozier holiday but forfeited meeting the fascinating northern folk she did. She was soon willing to reconcile her shyness and curiosity to appreciate compelling company. The middle-aged marine painter, John Carmichael, told detailed, lively stories based on his first career seafaring between Spain and Portugal. Robert Bewick, son of wood engraver Thomas Bewick, proved himself entertaining, if less than proficient, on the Northumbrian pipes. The prize encounter for Christina was with slim, tall, serious Dora Greenwell from Durham, whose similar poetic style, Christian sensibilities, and kindness would continue their friendship through determined correspondence that defied geography.

Almost an entire day was allocated to cork-cutter Thomas Dixon, not yet twenty and an example of Mr. Scott's habit of befriending working class artists and writers. *From Newcastle to Sunderland upon a misty morn in June we took the train: on either hand grimed streets were changed for meadows soon.* And changed again, for Sunderland was as grimy as Newcastle. They carried a basket of tarts and sandwiches, jam, and oranges thankfully on such a damp day, not for outdoor consumption but to provide the hospitality Mr. Dixon couldn't afford to.

The longer but more comfortable and satisfying excursion to honey-colored Wallington Hall was undertaken to view artwork by Mr. Scott and meet Sir Walter and Lady Trevelyn, who had also commissioned a sculpture from Thomas Woolner and a watercolor, *Mary in the House of Saint John*, from Gabriel, which he was still working on.

"As promised, here she is." Mr. Scott nudged Christina to move her gently but insistently towards Lady Trevelyn. "The little sister of the PRB."

Christina minded his rakish mockery for only the few moments it took her to meet the small, brunette, sharp-eyed daughter of a clergyman and Huguenot woman. Christina wasn't surprised she had enchanted Mr. Scott, who claimed others like Mr. Ruskin, Mr. Swinburne, Mr. Millais, and the Brownings had fallen under her spell, too. Nothing Christina met in Lady Trevelyn contradicted accounts of her being direct yet warm, witty, unpretentious, effortlessly complimentary to others, appreciative of and knowledgeable about the arts and science. She was ready to be informed about anything, although one was more likely to learn from her. Everything about Pauline, as she insisted on being called when she could "get away with it," reflected pride in her humble but respectable beginnings and her altruism and pragmatism in using her rise in society to do as much good for others as herself.

Additionally, and unexpectedly, Pauline was an answer to gifts for Christina's mother, sister, aunts, and Amelia. The beautiful lace that capped and draped the plain arrangement of Lady Trevelyn's hair and edged the collar and cuffs of her elegantly simple dress alerted Christina to the lacemakers on the Trevelyn's other estate in Devon.

Pauline clapped her hands. "I have more samples to show you. You can order whatever you like and pay me once the pieces are in your hands."

Preceding lace and lunch was the viewing of the Central Hall and Mr. Scott's eight large canvases, which vibrantly depicted scenes from Northumberland history, prominently placed in the room's north and south arcades. Thomas Woolner's marble sculpture of a mother reading to her infant son was none the less outstanding on the west side.

"The courtyard was cold, dark, and dirty before it was enclosed. I wanted it to look and feel like an Italian *piazza* or French *cour intérieure*." Lady Trevelyn hooked Christina's arm for a slow stroll to circle the hall.

"And so it does," Christina said sincerely. "And reminds me that I turned down an invitation to *Aix-en-Provence*," she immediately wished she hadn't revealed.

Lady Trevelyn's pout was forgiving. "Rather than come to the land north of the Humber? So, a certain gentleman would have been disappointed? Intrigued by his praise and your poetry, I would have been, too."

A little dog named Peter followed Lady Trevelyn and Christina into a hallway and up a staircase, yelping at Christina's heels until she turned and sat on a step to have him on her lap, which quietened him but invited soggy licks on her face. Christina laughed and held Peter blameless, just as she did Mr. Scott's bulkier Olaf whenever he pawed and flattened her dress.

"Now we know what melts your reserve." Pauline waited on the landing above.

After at least an hour in the needlework room off the main bedroom, Christina deciding on more collars than she could afford, they were summoned to the spacious dining room. Like other parts of the house Christina had seen, its walls were a backdrop for well-spaced ancestral portraits and cases of china, the ceiling bordered with Italian *stuccatori*, fluted columns offering support and classical character. The floors were only partially covered with worn carpeting and the furniture, mainly eighteenth century and mahogany, was sparse and unpolished.

"I'm no homemaker," was Lady Trevelyn's explanation.

Sir Walter's notorious dislike of extravagance extended to food, going as far as subjecting guests to his personal, principled diet. Mr. Scott's warning that lunch would consist "of cauliflower and artichokes" was only slightly exaggerated. "And don't expect imbibements other than fruit punch and flowery tea, and possibly, if he takes pity on us, ginger beer," because, again according to Mr. Scott, "the contents of Wallington's ancestral wine cellar were long since wasted in a nearby lake whose fish didn't appreciate it." Christina had to admit—out of Mr. Scott's earshot—it was a meal that left her energetic enough to take a walk across the estate's rolling parkland, along the edge of its valley woods, around an ornamental lake, and through walled gardens.

Her rapport with Lady Trevelyn increased with their shared observations and enjoyment of nature.

"Walter thinks it might be time for some clean-up and restoration. As it turned out, he was right about the courtyard, but I question whether the grounds need any attention other than our enjoying them as they are."

"You must convince him." Christina stopped walking, turned, stepped in front of Lady Trevelyn, and grabbed her hands. "Certain destructions are irreparable and tragic." Immediately, she realized her indiscretion. "Madam. I'm so sorry."

Lady Trevelyn wouldn't let Christina pull away. "My poor dear. It seems I've stirred some troubling thought in you."

"You didn't mean to." Christina continued to struggle with a proper response to her eminent host. "Oh, Madam. How could you know? Some of my most pleasant memories are of a cottage in Buckinghamshire I frequented as a child. Lately, I've learned that a merciless steward has had nearby Penn Wood felled."

"The happy places of childhood are the most sacred of all. If we were lucky enough to have them." Lady Trevelyn saw her husband and the Scotts waiting for them before Christina did. "Now, before you leave us, let me show you the lilies, their buds swelling nicely. And my favorites: the sweet peas, how tall they climb, long their stalks, papery their petals, and sweet their scent."

The lily has an air ... and the sweet pea a way ...

The twenty-mile, five-plus hours with one break for refreshments and other necessities return to Newcastle was as stylish as the morning's journey to Wallington Hall had been, both due to the loan of the Trevelyn's barouche carriage. The ride back was also tolerably bumpy, if breezier, and dustier; fortunately the evening, like most of the day, warm and dry, with long lingering daylight. The sights they had taken in, the hospitality they had enjoyed, the dry quirkiness of its Lord and, especially, the vibrant beauty and interests of its Lady gave them much to think and, in the case of Letitia, to talk about.

"Pauline is a true woman, except without vanity," Mr. Scott interrupted his wife's gushing and, as he often did, ignored her presence for the chance of a straying flirtation. He leaned towards Christina who sat opposite, behind the driver's high box seat. "And very likely without the passion of love."

To meet worth living for … to meet worth parting for.

Christina was surprised but grateful that Letitia pulled him back, her voice straining for composure. "There are those of us who live very well without it."

***

Remembering Christina's wish to "encounter" the North Sea, the Scotts squeezed in an outing south of Newcastle to Marsden Bay and its famous arch carved from a limestone cliff by waves and weather. "'Where beyond the extreme sea-wall, and between the remote sea-gates, waste water washes, and tall ships founder, and deep death waits.'" Accompanying them were the words of Algernon Swinburne, vigorously recited by Mr. Scott as they had been by Lady Trevelyn when she heard where they were going. The Trevelyns regretted Christina had missed Mr. Swinburne by only weeks when he would arrive at his family's seat, Capheaton Hall, to spend the summer holidays and frequent neighboring Wallington. Gabriel had met the "diminutive, fluttering, crimson" young man at Oxford while painting murals in the Union Debating Hall, piquing Christina's curiosity about him.

The following day, she returned to London by herself and rail, for a few hours in the same car as a babbling baby and his equally pretty mother. Other passengers got on and off without much more to define them than their gender, age, quality of their clothes, and intention of keeping to themselves. Christina read, wrote, dozed, and woke to watch the miles grow between everything and nothing changing. For the second half of the journey, Christina faced a polite Prussian who she happened to meet in Regent's Park on a walk with Maria the following Sunday, glad that then he was able to see her with a face cleaned of travel's dust, sweat, strain, and unconscionable expectations.

CHAPTER TWENTY-FIVE

Gabriel laughed in that way of his that was insulting but, also, intriguing. *"A Peek at the Goblins*? Imitation is a form of flattery, but, perhaps, not what Mama's cousin's pixie tales deserve."

"I admit it." Christina was delighted to have his attention again. "I did think of ... well, borrowed ... okay, thieved the gist of the title of Mrs. Bray's book."

"Ah-ha," Gabriel said with a stern playfulness reminiscent of finding her in a childish game of hide n' seek.

She put out her hands, turning them wrists down. "And more than the title, I'm afraid."

Gabriel pretended to handcuff her and throw away the key.

"In my defense, as you know, I put my own twists and turns on it."

"And with the genius Mrs. Bray doesn't have." Waving his hands over hers, it felt as if magic released her to be who she was. "For you and me, originality can't be avoided no matter where inspiration comes from."

You and me. The phrase reunited them as Christina didn't think possible again and knew was temporary.

"Now *Cornhill* has rejected it and Ruskin is senselessly done with it," Gabriel scoffed, then schemed, "shall we see what Macmillan thinks of your tale of girls and goblins?"

Christina had already sent some shorter works to David Masson, editor of *Macmillan's Magazine*, although it seemed ridiculous that any of them might find a place where Tennyson's *Sea Dreams* had. *Does the road wind uphill all the way?* Not at that juncture, Mr. Masson quickly accepting the poem to which that question belonged, and Gabriel referred to as *Song of the Tomb*. Soon after, Mr. Macmillan requested a read of *the Goblin piece*.

"His judgment is as good as Masson's, with more boldness and imagination for taking risks than Ruskin. Less arrogance, too. And, of course, the influence to make things happen."

"He hasn't published anything of yours, Gabe."

"It's become complicated. Another reason not to have Ruskin involved. But it won't prevent Macmillan from considering your work, which I don't doubt he'll find unusually excellent. I have assured him there is a great deal of it."

Christina went from cautious hope that a poem or two might quietly appear in a significant periodical to the ambitious planning of a book of verses, second only to one her believing grandfather had compiled and printed more than a decade earlier. After publishing *Uphill, A Birthday,* and *An Apple Gathering* respectively in the February, April, and August issues of his magazine, Mr. Macmillan proposed a Christmas release for a small collection of her verse, *Goblin Market its main piece and influencing its design.* Gabriel would provide the frontispiece illustration: *a simple woodcut to fill, perhaps, half a page, with a grinning goblin and a sweet girl or something similar.*

"It's not meant for children," Christina insisted, worried the idea for a Christmas release meant they were its intended audience.

"No, it's not." Gabriel's eyes darkened. "When it only pretends to be a fairytale."

The previous December, his family finally had learned of its second expansion of the year, this one still pending and due to make himself or herself known in the spring.

The chance to finally welcome Mrs. Gabriel Rossetti came at Christmas, on the day itself.

Gabriel fretted over Lizzie's pregnancy, to the point of not wanting to talk about it beyond the announcement. She seemed healthier, almost bonny, and ordinary. She had, of course, put on weight, yet exhibited a lightness in being the thinner, gaunter, goddess Lizzie never did.

According to William, she had been extremely nauseous the first few months. She claimed that pregnancy had cured all her ills. "So, I must have many babies."

"It may be only your health that can afford to." Gabriel's grumpiness didn't prevent him moving towards her.

Lizzie had effortlessly reached up to take down the mistletoe ball Christina had needed a stepladder to tack to the top of the doorframe. Its red velvet ribbon looped on the fingers of her right hand, the newest Mrs. Rossetti held it just above her head, her beautifully blank face turned towards the notice of her husband, her silence rebuking and enticing him.

Gabriel kissed her as would have been bad luck and out-of-character for him not to. "Isn't it strange that ladies will stand beneath the mistletoe and when they're kissed declare they didn't know it was there?"

"I'm sure Fanny Cornforth knew what she was posing for. But then, she is no lady."

Christina had seen a certain painting and heard the talk. Despite her daring words, Lizzie walked timidly into the Rossettis' main parlor to meet the anticipation of Mama and Maria, and the curiosity of Cousin Henrietta, who had just returned from America.

Christina hooked Lizzie's arm as though they were best friends, with the vague thought that they might yet be when a baby made her a doting aunt and useful sister-in-law. Mama was also ready to forgive Gabriel's bride for keeping him away from his family, for at last she returned him with the promise of a grandchild.

William took his brother aside to distract him from the women insisting a flushed Lizzie discuss baby names. Gabriel would not be left out when the conversation turned to the enlargement of the flat at Chatham Place.

"Brilliance by Gug to ask if the Landlord would rent us the flat next door and put in a connecting door."

"So now there is enough room for us to live where Gabriel works." Lizzie seemed to find her nerve if it meant keeping Gabriel in line. "I don't have to wonder what ...," her eyes met his and she faltered a little, "when he will be home."

"If only we'd gotten that place near the Heath with its glorious old-world garden to provide backgrounds for painting. This year I spent over two hundred pounds on traveling to various locations, besides paying rent on Spring Cottage and Chatham Place."

The distance between their living quarters and Gabriel's studio cost him in other ways, too, mainly the trust of his *Queen of Hearts*. It was easier to be his sister than *inamorata*, although Christina shared Lizzie's worries of not knowing where he was, who he was with, or what he was doing. She also understood Lizzie's need to forgive him. That Christmas Day, Gabriel was as irreproachable as ever. His darkly circled eyes engaged everyone, his restlessness taking them all where he wanted to go. His deep, melodic voice, so reminiscent of Papa's, boasted that he had hung many of Lizzie's paintings in their new drawing room along with a birdcage for her beloved bullfinches. Attending the housewarming with William a few weeks later, Christina would see for herself the not-quite new drapery and carpeting and the shabbiness of the furniture the Gabriel Rossettis already had or could afford disguised with yards of richly dyed fabric her brother constantly bought "to dress" his models, further burdening his finances. The doors and wainscotting had been painted "summer green" and Gabriel was still talking about putting up wallpaper. "A stunning design of fruit trees with red and yellow oranges, and yellow stars" was his first contribution to a decorative arts company being organized by a "daily" friend of his, William Morris.

Lizzie shared her husband's obsession for blue-willow china, which was displayed wherever there was space on a surface, even specific shelving put up for it. The dingy fireplace was brightened by genuine Dutch delf tiles.

She accredited the transformation of their lodgings to Gabriel's time and effort. "I have been too tired to think of, let alone take part in, such drastic rearranging and decorating."

"Gabriel Charles wrote that was the case." Mama forced a silent admission from her oldest son. "I hope my suggestion of a curtain-maker was helpful."

"Oh, yes," William saved his sister-in-law from answering. "The window dressings are well done and make the place warm and cozy, especially on these long winter evenings."

"Of course, Blackfriars is temporary." It was inevitable that Gabriel was already looking elsewhere. "Need a suburban location. We might rent a house with the Burne-Joneses, so Guggums and Georgie can also share having first babies."

It was tempting to think that, confined within wedlock, Lizzie was luckier than the women at the penitentiary who had given birth without giving life except as noted in their records and, as Christina liked to believe, imagined in their prayers. *Their mother-hearts beset with fears, their lives bound up in tender lives.* Whether due to her own resistance or Gabriel's caution, Lizzie had avoided such shame for more than a decade under his spell, even her own sister Lydia expecting before her wedding.

Lizzie had long survived inconstant adoration like a tall, thin tree withstanding a windstorm intact, broken pieces of sturdier specimens strewn all around. There were more original metaphors to evoke her delicate determination. *White and golden Lizzie stood, like a lily in a flood, — like a rock of blue-veined stone lashed by tides obstreperously, — like a beacon left alone in a hoary roaring sea …* As a single light, most alluring at a distance and more necessary when she was absent, she repeatedly pulled Gabriel back from the blank sea his heart drifted upon.

Still, it wasn't certain marriage was meant for them.

Christina didn't doubt Gabriel's claim that this vision of the perfect woman had, on first sight, defined his destiny. Or that Lizzie's fortune and misfortune came from being painted thus.

From the beginning, it was too late to warn Lizzie not to *loiter in the glen in the haunts of goblin men.* She was captured long before she was caught, the lure of being loved overriding the sense of being free.

Christina's encounters with the women of Highgate Penitentiary moved her to explore the revelation that temptation and faith had much in common. Both persuaded through promises, needed questioning, caused uncertainty and anxiety, and sought a reassurance that might never come.

On the grounds of Park House, along one of the footpaths, there were large old apple trees, every September yielding a bumper crop. At Christina's interview and a few other times, too, the Warden made a point of mentioning the annoyance they caused him when he first took up his post.

"A stumbling block to getting the inmates to do right. They were offered punishment if they took any apples, even those on the ground, rather than satisfaction in themselves if they didn't. I knew we must convince them to count the most tempting pleasures as having far less value than honor."

The Warden walked into the classroom, interrupting the lesson Christina was in charge of until he did. The students immediately stood.

"This class is not long back from taking exercise, is it, Sister?"

"Not half an hour, Reverend Oliver."

He was holding something in his hand which he brought down for exhibit on the desk she stepped aside from.

"What is the problem with this apple?" he asked them.

The girls at the front must have seen. No one answered.

"Sister Christina, you tell them."

"A piece is bitten out of it, Reverend."

"And what is the problem with that?"

"Apple pilfering causes you distress, Reverend."

"Why is that?"

"It breaks a rule, Reverend."

"Not a rule, Sister, a profound trust."

He waited for a confession more confidently than Christina did.

"Oh, Warden. I did it." One of the prettiest and most intelligent women in the class stepped forward. "Oh, why for such a nasty apple? I knew I wouldn't care for it. But it looked so rosy … until I lifted it to my mouth and saw its bruises. For some reason they made me want to taste it all the more."

***

My heart is like an apple tree whose boughs are bent with thickset fruit.

It was a girl. It would have been. Christina should have had her future blessed with a sweet niece, a daughter of Gabriel, but suddenly the forever nameless child stopped moving towards her entrance into the world. Dr. Hutchinson and Dr. Babington, the head physician of Lying-in Hospital, could do nothing but offer a warning weeks before every little bit of hope was lost. On May 2, 1861, there was a birth as still as Lizzie's labor wouldn't let her already frail, laudanum and death poisoned body be. Gabriel reported the mother-to-be-and-not-to-be carried her grief with "too much courage to be downcast." Christina doubted that any woman, even those who never bore any heartbeat but their own, would believe him.

Finally, Paris wasn't just a destination for others to satisfy any curiosity Christina had about it. William's suspicion that she or their mother or both let him make plans without a commitment to go was proven wrong. By June, Mama was well recovered from the bronchitis that troubled her earlier in the year, and Christina could think of more reasons for than against her first trip to the Continent.

She had been to Folkestone a few times for her health and pleasure, never before to go beyond a view of the Channel and the lie that on a clear day, if she found a high enough vantage point, she could see France. The blue-skied but blustery steamboat ride to Boulogne made her nauseous, William and Mama fussing over her more than they should, if as much as she liked. During the train time to Paris, her stomach slowly settled, and, unlike her mother and brother, she stayed awake to witness the lush, bucolic scenery hypnotically sliding past. Paris offered them comfort, which Christina preferred to luxury, due to the hospitality of Mama's cousin Sarah, who resided there. During their week in *La Ville Lumière*, they humored William's interest in ecclesiastical architecture, hoping his atheistic obsession would be satisfied and not dominate the rest of their holiday. Instead, at every opportunity on their return route through Rouen to Caen and the Cherbourg peninsula, he gluttonized his hunger for exploring and making notes of every cathedral, church, or even chapel in the vicinity of their itinerary.

For the sake of Christina, for whom Normandy was newly discovered, and because William was good enough not to leave her and their mother to sightsee on their own, he interrupted his preoccupation with God's houses. They explored medieval walls, moated chateaus, narrow lanes of half-timbered buildings, and enjoyed the aromas and tastes from *les boulangeries*, and summer flowers flourishing in the market square where Joan d'Arc met her fiery fate. Not far from Avranches, they witnessed a blossoming effect of sunlight following a fierce thunderstorm. In a hotel where they took a meal, they were entertained by a portly cat who, obviously practiced in begging milk from well-chosen diners, joined the family's travel story characters as *la Chat of St. Lô*.

Other than blistered feet and overly gratified digestion, the holiday was a healthy one. It almost succeeded in being an escape from the injustice of death, except along the way they learned that, in Florence, on June 29th, Elisabeth Barrett Browning had breathed her last. It was one of Christina's great regrets that she never met her, the chance not given or taken when the Brownings were rarely in London. Hopefully for no other reason than oversight, the Rossetti women's company was never requested, not even to experience the "delightfully unliterary" Mrs. Browning apart from where Robert, Gabriel, William, and, on one most enviable "night of the gods," Mr. Tennyson also read his latest work and "discussed the universe."

"I would have had her stay, read her poems, speak her conscience, and even be combative." Gabriel revealed sketchy details, also, in a drawing of Mr. Tennyson reading his poem *Maud*, sitting casually with his right hand holding up the book he hardly needed to refer to, the other his left ankle. "But she abandoned us to attend to some 'dull ladies'—her words not mine—who had unexpectedly called and were waiting in another 'safer' room. Obviously, not my mother and sisters who wouldn't accompany Will and me there without a formal invitation."

Christina wanted to believe they wouldn't have been turned away, but also considered what would have been the lasting impression their assumption of being welcomed unsolicited would have made on the woman who might have been Poet Laureate but for Tennyson's prevailing credential of being male. They couldn't defend just dropping in with the excuse of simply expecting to drink tea and make small talk with her. Although Mrs. Browning forwent poetry reading and heady conversations with a Poet Laureate, Pre-Raphaelite blood brothers, and her beloved Robert to obey society's rule that women should withdraw from acknowledging their talents and passions outside of domesticity, Christina didn't believe that was how she wished to be remembered.

> She had lived, we'll say,
> A harmless life, she called a
> virtuous life,
> A quiet life, which was not life at all
> (But that she had not lived enough to know)

At the news, Mama said a prayer and lit a candle in the next church William led them to. Christina imagined that, at home, Maria also prayed for Mrs. Browning's soul but didn't cry, once again comforted by her belief that what didn't happen in this world was meant to in the next.

"You know, Chrissy, you are her natural successor." William frightened and pleased her.

***

Stepping out of the train at Waterloo Station, Christina didn't expect to see Charles Cayley at all, let alone running and waving a closed umbrella. After two long days traveling back from France through Jersey, Weymouth, and Southampton via ferry, steamboat, and train, enduring heat, dust, rain, more tea than food, strained patience, and little sleep, she would rather go unnoticed until she had been home to wash and rest. If any man should see her at her worse, she supposed Charles posed the least risk of her minding he did.

He was, as usual, untidy and outdated, hatless, comical tufts of hair around his ears, his beard and mustache in need of a trim. His waistcoat was missing buttons, his shirt rumpled and collarless, a dark, dingy cravat wrapped around his neck instead. His trousers were too short, the sleeves of his worn-out tailed jacket too long.

"How did you know?" she addressed the surprise of his being there.

He pulled something out of his breast pocket: the postcard from Rouen she had sent him. *Back on the 13th*.

"Yes, but I didn't say which train."

"I looked at the timetables. Have been waiting hours. There were numerous possibilities."

"Ah, dear Charles," Mama interrupted. "Have you been traveling?"

Christina hooked her mother's arm. "Only to meet ... us."

"I thought I might help with your bags," Charles further explained. "They always grow heavier on holiday."

"William is guarding them while we decide how to get home."

"I will go see, Mrs. Rossetti, if there are any cabs."

"Thank you, Mr. Cayley," Mama appreciated his formality with a teasing tone. "The best will be on the rank outside the platform."

Charles returned in less than ten minutes, having secured one and solved the problem of there not being enough room for all of them in it. "Of course, I will take the omnibus."

"I will, too."

Christina had ridden one alone among strangers many times, just as she had the train. After years of slipping, first studiously, then sociably into her family's view and affections, the safety of Charles' company could not be doubted. She noticed William possibly making those points to Mama.

"Thank you, Charlie, for your help. As you can see, our luggage is taken care of."

They all followed the porter pushing a loaded cart to where the cab was waiting. Christina, alongside Charles, watched her family depart, so they had to run to catch the next bus from Camberwell Gate. Its route over Waterloo Bridge onto the Strand, Regents Street towards Regent's Park would drop them a short walk from 45 Albany Street.

At first, surprisingly, especially as it was a Saturday, they had the lower level to themselves. Charles waited to see which side Christina settled on, the jolt of the bus almost foiling his plan—as Christina guessed it—to sit opposite.

"I wish I could have fetched you by carriage."

Charles could less afford one, even to hire for a few hours, than the Rossettis, his finances not recovered from a disastrous speculation.

Christina thought to console him. "I remember reading a book, *Saunterings In and About London*, the omnibus described as 'one of the necessities of life,' only ranked lower than 'air, tea, and flannel.'"

His hesitation to reply was predictable, absentmindedness always about him, patience needed to converse with him. "I suppose." He waved away a fly as though it was a much larger irritation. "If a necessity of someone else's life."

"Well, certainly not convenient for the expanding frocks of ladies' fashion," she said just to humor him and once more see his smile, which irritated Gabriel with its 'stinginess,' which, to her, proved Charles' sensitivity. "Have you ever ridden on the roof? Unless it's raining or snowing or just cold enough to, most men seem to like to."

"I ... I ... well ... try to avoid it. The weather may start out fine but not stay so."

"An umbrella is not much use up there."

"Quite. And it can seem perilous. I'm afraid I'm not very brave."

"That makes two of us."

Once across the Thames, the bus came to a shuddering stop, the driver directing those waiting to board, "Ladies, there is room inside. Able-bodied men, no more than four each side of the knife."

Christina stood, turned, her hands under the sides of her skirt, and sat next to Charles so they weren't separated as the car filled with an adolescent girl, a middle-aged woman, two young children who might have been twins, and an old man.

Christina leaned towards Charles as the journey resumed. "There was a time I was considered wild."

Charles scratched the tip of his nose, a habit she recognized as his struggle between prudence and curiosity. "Really?"

"As a little girl, I wanted to impress my brothers."

"Of course."

"As I imagine your sisters did you and Arthur."

"Perhaps Arthur."

"You're too humble, like my William. I must admit Gabe was the bad influence, and, therefore, the most exciting. Nothing has changed."

Charles used his eyes to remind her of the potential eavesdroppers around them.

She spoke softer and closer to his reddening ear. "Like when Gabe used his pocket money to take me on a bus, forbidden without Mama or Papa accompanying us. 'They are targets for pickpockets and even kidnappers, you know.' He promised an adventure, and delivered, especially when he persuaded the driver to let us sit beside him. I wouldn't have been more excited if granted an audience with the Queen. He lifted me up as if in a country dance and followed as agilely. You would never guess now, but Gabe was slim and sprightly as a lad. The horse looked so strong from that view, tail flicking, back gleaming, neck long and muscular, ears pricked, nose held high. I wasn't so happy when the driver brandished a whip. I even cried until he showed me how he stroked the mare with it, because after many years she knew what he wanted and he only 'used it to chat with her.'"

"Although disobedient, it all sounds harmless enough."

"Not quite. My brother realized if we went the whole length of the tuppence ride we would be late for tea and found out. When the driver kindly made an unplanned stop for us, Gabe got down first and reached for me, but, impulsively, contrarily, I jumped. And fell on my rump in the—shall I say, quite unpleasant—street."

The old man sitting across from them laughed, possibly as much at Charles' pained reaction as the visualization of Christina as a willful child in a pretty frock, ribboned curls, and white stockings until she was sitting in a puddle of mud and manure.

Avrà più spirit che tutti.

"It was okay." Christina also noticed how distraught Charles looked. "Nothing broken. Not even my spirit. Not yet. Gabe picked me up and we ran home as fast as we could and snuck in the back door. Our wayward Irish maid helped me strip, clean up, and dress again before Mama called; she only wondered whether we wanted marmalade or strawberry jam."

The bus stopped again, a clamor of boots coming down and going up, all but Charles, Christina, and the old man exiting the cabin, no reason the latter needed to say where he was going until he did.

"I'm on my way to Park Village." He finally lifted his shoulders and showed his full face, which was a handsome one despite its age spots and wrinkles. "Do you know it?"

His hair was white and thin, his eyebrows still dark and heavy, his eyes sunken but not yet lost, their gaze intense but kind.

"Yes ... yes, I do." Christina folded her hands in her lap. "My grandparents Polidori lived at Number Fifteen East."

"Printing press Polidori."

"Yes." Christina could hardly breathe.

"There were others beside him and his sickly wife."

"My aunts and uncles. They live separately now."

"I knew they would once—"

Charles lightly tapped her arm. "I was just thinking. Did you hear about Mrs. Browning?"

"Oh … yes, of course. The terrible news reached us in France."

Charles lifted his left hand. She thought he was going to touch her face, at least push back a straying strand of her hair.

Only his breath moved it. "Please, take care of yourself."

Her embarrassment realized a legitimate deflection. "It's coming up. The end of the line, where we get off."

"So it is."

Slowly, stiffly, his large physique no longer an ally, the old man stood and started walking to disembark.

"Sir, is someone meeting you? Charles could accompany you to your destination."

"I … I could. But, perhaps, he—"

"Come on, you lot," the driver shouted back. "I've a timetable to keep to."

Once off the bus, Christina made one more plea as the man slowly crossed the road away from her. "Sir. Sir. Will you be all right?"

"Don't worry about that bloke. He's ridden this route before. Foreigner, I think. Didn't you notice the accent?"

Finally home, Christina was overcome with exhaustion, excusing herself from socializing further with Charles who was, as always, understanding.

Maria wouldn't let him leave, hooking his arm. "For a month, I've been starved of good conversation. William has already gone to see Gabriel and Lizzy. Chrissy, like Mama, knows I will question her ears off, so she's fled like an antisocial cat to her room. Fortunately, you, Mr. Cayley, are here to share supper, projects, and whatever else offers itself for discussion and companionship and I will not refuse you."

Charles usually enjoyed Maria's company, enough linguistic interests and translations between them to avoid any clashes of piety and agnosticism. Or, if they did venture in that direction, Maria was secure enough in her faith to find his resistance to it more confirming than contentious. Once collapsed on her bed, Christina didn't think about him or even the foreign trip that left her exhausted. She wasn't concerned that she might have missed William Bell Scott—and Letitia—who usually visited London in July, or whether the reasonably priced *carte de visite* photographs taken of her before she set off for France would offer one suitable for the possible publication of *Goblin Market* and other poems. Instead, Elisabeth Barrett Browning and an old man were on her mind. She had heard of Mrs. Browning's involvement in seances and had wondered what they were like, but, so far, had resisted even skeptically curious participation. Christina's disapproval was because of opposition by her church along with suspicion of potential fraudulence, not a refusal to believe the dead could be called on to remember the living. *Come back to me in dreams, that I may give pulse for pulse, breath for breath ....* After all, the longing for reunion had slipped off her pen and even her lips more than once, safer in imagery, in private, in prayer.

CHAPTER TWENTY-SEVEN

Well begun is half done, the English proverb says. The Italians claim *il più duro è quello della soglia*: the hardest step is at the threshold. Also, as *Nonno* was fond of saying so Christina was fond of recalling, *cosa fatta capo ha*: that which is done has a beginning.

Christina didn't want to interrupt her work on the *Goblin Market* project, not even for a few weeks and a worthy cause. The process towards publication might have slowed, almost to a standstill, but she felt compelled to concentrate on the collection currently in Macmillan's hands as if a Christmas release were still possible. If not, she would have even more time to put the poems to rights—if ever she would be satisfied with them. When asked to reside at the penitentiary while another sister took a fortnight's leave, Christina struck a bargain to the satisfaction of both her muse and conscience and, as a bonus, bodily comfort. Highgate's management offered her enough 'leisure' time for her literary endeavors and her favorite tasseled, rose-budded, wing-chaired bedroom at Park House to spend it in.

The truth was, when she began her hiatus from family for the fallen of Highgate, Mr. Macmillan hadn't yet seen the entire manuscript of what could be her first and last hope for something other than sister or spinster attached to her name. Gabriel was supposed to send it to him, but, as with the frontispiece woodcut and most everything the assistance and talents of her oldest brother promised, procrastination and interruptions overruled his best intention.

His remorse promised two woodblock designs instead of one, which pleased author and publisher enough to believe he would come through. Mr. Macmillan confirmed the decision to publish Christina's collection using Gabriel as a go-between. He was in Yorkshire working on a portrait and stained-glass panel commissioned by John Aldam Heaton, yet another connection through Mr. Ruskin and Mr. Morris' Arts and Craft Movement. He sent the formal agreement, first proof, and samples of cloths for the binding to Albany Street, which William forwarded to Christina at Highgate.

Her excitement while unwrapping the parcel invited interest from a few of the women in the dormitory assigned to her.

"I like the gold."

"No, the gray-blue. The color of your eyes."

"The violet."

"Yes, the violet or puce," Christina agreed, then thought again. "Or the red. Especially if the book comes out for Christmas."

More of her charges joined those first to get involved, all their favorite fabrics fluctuating as much as Christina's did. They urged her to sign the agreement while they were there, but she needed to read it first. Her desire to do so in private wasn't because she thought the contract would present anything unacceptable, or that she minded the other women's interest. They encouraged her ambitions and indicated an elevation of their own.

She wanted to be alone with the moment when she authorized the two hundred pages of her rhythms and rhymes, music and lyrics, observations and insights, loves and losses, faith and doubts. When at last Christina had practiced her signature at least a dozen times and questioned whether she was ready to deal with the celebrity she didn't want any more than criticism, the ink flowed from her pen without a blot or smudge. It seemed she didn't have a choice.

She was a poet who needed to be published, to be read, to be heard, to be understood and misunderstood, to be remembered and forgotten beyond her grandfather's adoring partiality, and her brothers' need to fill a few pages in a doomed periodical. She might have been forever content with the objective acceptance and relative obscurity of her work in magazines if the persuasive and perilous prospect of a book exclusively for her poems hadn't appeared the opportunity she was waiting for.

She wasn't comfortable with ambition but wasn't immune to it, either. In her youth, she had played with it, like she would a doll, imagining its possibilities without needing more than the recreation of wondering. Later, she deferred considering it, like she did with love and marriage, especially once she had moved past expectations of an early death and the debacle of her engagement to James Collinson. All she had to do was steady her impulses while holding on to her hopes, have patience, and see disappointment as protection rather than punishment, to be grateful for a future predictable yet unknown.

She remembered that God's plan was the one she needed to follow and have faith in.

Into her *selva oscura*, Christina had discovered how time flies and possibilities fall away. *Hope deferred maketh the heart sick: but when the desire cometh it is a tree of life.*

***

"Will you come with me to Chatham Place?" There was resignation in Mama's voice. She refolded a letter received another day. The post had not yet arrived that morning, which was the first since Christina had returned from her stay at Highgate.

"But no one is there, Gabriel still in Yorkshire and Lizzie—"

"Has run away. From the Morrises this time."

"According to Gabriel, she loves the Red House and while there last summer seemed on the way to recovery."

"Janey is pregnant again. Lizzie was reminded more than she could bear. Poor thing. Even her own sister has a baby now."

"And Georgina Burnes-Jones has one, too."

Christina didn't want to see Lizzie or feel the guilt of not wanting to. She hadn't been in her sister-in-law's company for almost a year. Before the trip to Normandy, Gabriel had recommended no one visit her … *I mean, of course, except yourselves,* which, along with Mama and Maria, Christina determined meant they should stay away. Instead, they heard reports, as likely true as exaggerated, of Lizzie silently staring without sight, refusing to eat, needing more and more laudanum to sleep, and not emerging from her room where she often rocked the empty cradle she wouldn't let anyone remove.

A few weeks after their daughter's stillbirth, Gabriel persuaded Lizzie to stay with the Madox Browns. Besides needing a break from his wife's convalescence to get work done and generate income, he thought Emma, having suffered the death of a ten-month-old son and a miscarriage, might provide hope as well as empathy. The Brown household had become a happier one for the sake of eleven-year-old Catherine and first son Oliver, almost seven. Gabriel's plan turned out to be miscalculated, just because the Browns were so focused on their children. Even Lizzie's friendship with Emma and their shared drinking habits couldn't console her. After only two days, Lizzie left without warning.

"Before the cock crowed." Lucy Madox Brown's bucolic childhood revealed itself. She was living with her father, stepmother, and half-siblings, and arrived at Albany Street a couple of days after "the Normandy nomads" returned.

"Lizzie might claim no one saw her, but I did, concerned it wasn't a good time for her to be out alone on the streets. I asked where she was going. She told me 'home, to my … child.'"

Half a year later, on a chilly but dry December day at a decent hour, Mama and Christina were grateful William insisted they take a cab to Chatham Place. He also contributed the money a distantly worried Gabriel asked them to personally deliver to his wife.

Christina had sent a note announcing their planned visit, but without a response couldn't be sure they would be welcome.

Before they knocked, Christina and her mother heard laughter. Once they made their arrival known, it seemed Lizzie had been waiting to open the door. Noticeably thinner despite being shapelessly clothed, it was hard to judge her complexion as paler, her eyes naturally deep and heavily lidded. There wasn't any doubt that she was still effortlessly enchanting, especially as her mass of deep-red hair was partly, haphazardly, pinned back, a few Medusa-like strands around her face, lengthy neck, and drooped shoulders. Looking down, struggling to subdue what had amused her, she invited them in by standing aside.

Mama hadn't yet seen the enlarged apartment. For Christina, it was more cluttered and darker since she had. There wasn't additional furniture or objects, its draperies, curtains, rugs, and walls of artwork still colorful, an abundance of light through its many windows. Christina couldn't avoid thinking of its promise turned to pain. *A burden saddens every song: while time lags who should be flying, we live who would be dying.* When she had last been there, it was possible to believe its inhabitants would finally make a real life out of their love. That possibility wasn't altogether gone, but experience was its nemesis.

As laughter suggested and high-voiced recitation proved, Christina and her mother weren't the only company Lizzie had that day. Something unsavory might have been suspected if Christina hadn't thought of Gabriel's concern for Lizzie being left alone. Other than William, the only male he would approve as caretaker of and companion to his Blessed Damozel was Algernon Swinburne. "His decadence is more fabrication than reality, mainly because of his own bragging. He's that desperate to create a persona to be noticed. The red bush that causes his head to appear even larger and his body even smaller, his incessant fidgeting and babbling, along with the metrical virtuosity of his poetry, which, especially when drinking, he's never too shy to recite, guarantees he's noticed and unforgettable."

Once in the parlor, Christina and her mother had to decide for themselves where to sit and whether to sooner or later mention the mission that had brought them there. Mr. Swinburne solved the second part of their dilemma by standing suddenly, as though just realizing their arrival.

"Dear ladies, what a delight. We were acting out Fletcher's comic play *The Spanish Curate*. Do you know it?"

"I don't believe I do," Mama replied and kept her eyes on the younger Mrs. Rossetti, who hovered near the door that, if Christina remembered correctly, led to the bedroom.

"Uncle Philip had it in his library," Christina recalled. "It is quite good in its dialogue, humor, and maneuvering."

"It's Jacobian and doesn't get performed much anymore. The last time in London was decades ago at Convent Garden. There's word of another revival next year. Lizzie and I already plan to make it a date." Mr. Swinburne skipped over to her and hooked her arm. One tall, one short, they otherwise resembled each other: both faint and fiery, half-starved but rarely hungry, lazy and restless, clever and childlike, an aristocratic air about them yet vagabondish, too. William, the chief observer of goings on at Chatham Place, where for some time Mr. Swinburne had been a frequent visitor, was right. "Algie" was more of a brother to Lizzie than he ever would be to a fragmented band of rogue artists. They were siblings in hair and need and naiveté. "He brightens her considerably. But enables her more dangerous inclinations."

Christina thought how the same was once said of Gabriel's effect on her. Discipline—and cowardice—eventually had more influence.

"Come here, my dear."

Mama's request didn't move Lizzie until Mr. Swinburne gave her a little push. As she approached, Frances Polidori Rossetti brought a pretty pocket-shaped purse out from the folds of her skirt.

"Lovely needlework." Lizzie reached out to barely touch its *petit point* roses, leaves, and stems. "Did you do it?"

"Yes, dear. Take it."

Lizzie did.

"Open it."

"Oh." Lizzie slipped out three pound notes folded as Christine recognized was William's fastidious way with paper money. "So much."

"From Gabriel. He has generous patrons in Yorkshire," Christina said what she hoped rather than knew.

To Lizzie's credit, she was embarrassed and grateful. As Gabriel guessed, she had little food for herself let alone to offer, only some flat ale and overly used tea leaves, no hot water for the latter without any coal to burn in the fireplace.

"I hated to ask him. Instead, with the rent soon due, I started to consider what I could pawn he wouldn't miss."

"I said I would loan you the rent." Mr. Swinburne had sat down again, his hands drumming his knees. "And more."

"Yes, you did." Lizzie hung her head. "Now, not necessary."

"Who needs so many mirrors?" Mama shivered.

"Gabriel would sell me first."

Christina realized Lizzie was joking and that Mama wasn't sure.

"You know he wants a larger place," Lizzie was almost talkative, "for more mirrors and furniture and blue willow and who knows what else."

"Does he still obsess over wombats?" *The wombat is a joy, a triumph, a delight, a madness,* Christina remembered her brother saying longer ago than it seemed.

"He talks about owning one. He wants a menagerie of critters, I think. Which, I suppose, would amuse the children."

Christina heard her mother sigh and her poetry whisper in hopes of being heard.

Cat-like and rat-like,
Ratel-and wombat-like,
Snail-paced in a hurry,
Parrot-voiced and whistler,
Helter skelter, hurry skurry,
Chattering like magpies,
Fluttering like pigeons,
Gliding like fishes …

"I'm glad we didn't plan on staying longer," Mama said as she climbed into the cab, which her discomfort may have manifested to arrive ten minutes before the time it was ordered for. "I try to like her. I really do. I must find it in myself to. She is with child again. I am certain of it."

"It's a good thing Georgina didn't take the baby clothes Lizzie wanted to give her. Gabe pleaded with her not to."

"Wait." Lizzie's voice sounded desperate. "The purse. You forgot your lovely purse."

"The purse, Mama."

"Didn't I tell you, Christina? I meant for her to keep it."

"Oh." Lizzie's face flushed as Christina had never seen it do before. "Please … tell her thank you. And William for the money I will make sure Gabe pays back."

***

One little word. How she suddenly hated that one little word. Of course, she couldn't always avoid its use, but this time it was easily and effectively left out. Mama first noticed the mistake in the November 30th *Times* advertisement for Christina's little book. Another promotion was coming up on December 7th, so Christina immediately wrote a to-the-point letter with a mention of Gabriel's charming designs to soften it. She wondered if she should also send William to Mr. Macmillan's offices or even go herself.

What a relief that 'the' was removed from *Goblin Market's* identity. Mr. Macmillan was apologetic, especially that he hadn't caught the mistake. The second ad was perfect, and Christina thought she could finally fret less about the book's finishing for publication. Less than a week later she received a copy from Bradbury and Evans, well-established printers of *Punch*, Dickens and Thackery, and out jumped three errors she was sure had been corrected in the proof, one serious enough to break her heart if there wasn't time to correct it.

Soon she would realize there were worse things that might happen, mistakes that hadn't any chance of being fixed. In the immediate panic caused by a mangling of her musings, it didn't seem so. She worried about everything regarding the release of her goblins, even the American Civil War, in case English involvement or just the conflict itself threatened Macmillan's sales across the Atlantic. Gabriel's promise of the woodcuts being done sooner rather than later was dependent on the inexperience and disorganization of the newly formed Morris, Marshall, Faulkner & Co. As a partner, Gabriel insisted on using them; as a temperamentally talented artist among others, he empathized and, therefore, too easily forgave them.

As a result, the woodcuts weren't ready for the tight publishing schedule needed to bring *Goblin Market* and its accompanying verses out for Christmas.

"Don't worry. I'm certain Macmillan won't mind putting off its release until February, allowing just enough time for everything to turn out well."

Christina had a suspicion the delay was more her brother's doing than his or others' not doing. His own labor of love, a "full and truthful" translation of *The Early Italian Poets* was finally to be published before the end of the year by Smith & Elder. She might not like the devious way Gabriel delayed her launch so it wouldn't compete with his but could hardly begrudge him the culmination of a project he had worked on since he was twenty-one.

Gabriel and Christina were both past the deadline of an Italian proverb Papa had often quoted, especially when frustrated by his oldest son's sluggish ambition: *If you don't do it by thirty, you never will do.*

There was another their father left unspoken but had spent his life hoping: *Meglio tardi che mai.* Better late than never.

The death of Prince Albert mid-December meant Gabriel's book made its first public appearance under the cloud of national mourning. It also didn't help that his own loss lingered or that, once again, Lizzie was spending most of her days in bed, although he did get her to sit for preliminary sketches of Princess Sabra and Dante Alighieri's Beatrice.

He could not persuade her to spend Christmas with his family, warning them in a note sent on its eve.

New Year's didn't bring Gabriel to Albany Street, either. What finally did, on his own more than a month later, was his inability to go on living at Chatham Place.

He would never again need to convince the woman of his dreams to endure the trials of his reality. In the span of an evening, a cab took them to dine at the Sablonnier Hotel in Leicester Square, another back to

Blackfriars in time for Gabriel to set out to teach at the Working Men's College. He returned to find an emptied laudanum phial on the table beside the bed where Lizzie may or may not have meant to end her earthly journey so soon and unnecessarily when a little more waiting might have yielded her a life worth living for.

> *Indeed, when they shall meet again,*
> *Except some day in Paradise:*
> *For this they wait, one waits in pain.*
> *Beyond the sea of death love lies*
> *For ever, yesterday, to-day;*
> *Angels shall ask them, 'Is it well?'*
> *And they shall answer, 'Yea.'*

PART FIVE

Gazing thro' her chamber window
Sits my soul's dear soul;
Looking northward, looking southward,
Looking to the goal,
Looking back without control. —
~ from *Reflection* by Christina Rossetti

CHAPTER TWENTY-EIGHT

Christina never tired of the view towards the Firth of Clyde and the floating mountain, Alisa Craig. The protruding rock, ranging from navy to purplish blue, reminded her of the first and second edition covers of *Goblin Market*, while magenta sunsets that ignited the island defined the color she would have preferred. At the pleasant beginning of summer and her first Penkill holiday, there was no evidence of the sea-borne gales that gave the accommodation she moved up to a nickname of "The Windy Room." She was grateful for Miss Boyd's offer of the laird's chamber like *the best at Tutor House and much larger*, enough to chide William that he wouldn't find anywhere as fine in Naples. However, once introduced to the vistas from the third floor of the castle's sixteenth century tower, she begged to make its small bower her own for the duration of her visit.

Besides looking out beyond Penwhapple Glen to the sea and, at times, even to the mountains of Arran, Christina often gazed down, her elbows propped on cool masonry, her hands fanned out to support her chin. Below was a garden of moss-covered paths and benches, shaped by bushes and shaded by trees, scented by arched, rose-laden lattices. A clovery green terrace with a sundial was run wild with rabbits until, alerted by the sense of being seen, they stood as still as stone.

That morning, as the bunnies scurried away, she saw the reason she was up earlier than would be good for her energy later in the day. He came into the sunlight, no less magnetic than Alisa Craig. Still in a tasseled, tartan nightcap and long red and gold dressing gown, he was an artist in observance and a poet in thought.

Not for the first time, a clear dawn had distracted and drawn him out from his usual search in the library for a book to take back to bed.

It was the jackdaws that made William Bell Scott—or Scotus as Gabriel had convinced almost everyone to call him—look up. They were noisy and active where they gathered and nested in nearby treetops. Christina dared not open and lean out of the window, instead imagining them lifting and looping over the castle, their "chyak-chyaking" joined by the screeching of fledglings hungry for worms and flies.

"The window exactly framed you," Scotus revealed he had noticed.

At breakfast and other meals, he was positioned at one end of the table and Miss Boyd, mistress of it, the other. Christina sat across from Letitia who put down her fork and continued to be uncharacteristically quiet. Christina smiled at the crisply aproned and capped maid who placed a plate of scrambled eggs in front of her, and immediately took a mouthful to disguise the reason for her own silence.

***

Christina often wondered how she would survive without the expression of written words. If it weren't for letters, she would struggle to maintain friendships and conduct whatever little business she did. Receiving them acknowledged her existence in the safest way. Unfolding news, reflections, witticisms, and opinions from her mother, sister, and brothers felt as intimate as spending an evening in the parlor with them. An exchange of *bout-rimés* was a reminder of the clever camaraderie they shared. An affectionate salutation was as reassuring as a hand clasp or a kiss on each cheek.

It was the writing that had no purpose other than being created that saved Christina from uselessness. There was prose, for storytelling and proselytizing, which she stumbled along in, hoping to one day find her stride. There was poetry, the only dance she was any good at, especially when she partnered with nature and love, hope and pain, and God.

It had been years since *Goblin Market*, its accompanying verses and woodcut designs, had been published just over a month after Lizzie's death. Gabriel, having fled their tragic love nest, stayed a few months at Albany Street, pretending to seek comfort in family and occupation.

"The inactive moments are the most unbearable."

Need of distraction pushed him to finally complete the drawing for the *Golden Head by Golden Head* sleeping sisters frontispiece. Not every action he took to appease his pain had such a productive conclusion.

"Oh, no. He didn't. He can't have."

Tragedies upon tragedies: a child, wife, another child, and a gray-calf notebook all gone into disintegrating depths of earth.

"Madox Brown begged me to stop him."

"As I would have, Will."

"And my answer would have been the same, Chrissy. I felt the gesture did Gabriel honor and, after all, they were his poems to do as he liked with."

"But their publication was already announced in his *Early Italian Poets*. Tell me there are copies."

"There would be no sacrifice if there were," Maria joined the conversation.

"Gabriel would not be Gabriel if there were," William said. "Swinburne thought it 'quite lovely the way the book nestled in her hair.'"

The only reference Gabriel made to the deed was that he would never write poetry again. He wouldn't endorse or rebuke the rumor regarding Lizzie's last words pinned to her nightgown. Christina dreamed that, instead, the note had been left in the small needlework clutch-bag Mama had given her daughter-in-law, Gabriel burning it with some letters.

"See if the purse is there," Christina instructed William who, after the funeral, took their mother to Chatham Place to fetch Lizzie's bullfinches.

It was never found. Mama didn't need to explain how troubling it was to go through everything in the apartment, especially Lizzie's clothes and possessions. "Her easel held a sketch just begun to be colored, her life as sacred a work-in-progress. It's hard to believe she thought it was finished."

The inquest forced Gabriel to speak of Lizzie's dependence on laudanum, adamant she took it to calm not harm herself. Her doctor, sister, housekeeper's daughter, Mr. Swinburne, and, inevitably, the jury concluded she "accidentally, casually, and by misfortune came to her death."

Anything was possible with so much uncertainty, secrecy, and sadness, but Christina was inclined to agree that Lizzie intended to escape the struggle of living, not life itself.

"Gabe won't sleep at Chatham Place one night more," William explained his brother's unscheduled arrival at his family's house with a small satchel containing his clothes, a larger one for art supplies. "I told him he'd have to share my room, as there wasn't a spare now Aunt Margaret was living with us. Looking and sounding like the spirited brother I thought I'd never meet again, he proclaimed he would 'find somewhere spacious and splendid enough for us all.'"

The hope that Gabriel could so quickly get over the loss of his wife was like expecting Lizzie's bullfinches to sing as though they weren't missing the heart of their audience. Moving them from room to room, uncovering their cage, offering a new cuttlebone and millet-cake, even sweetly talking Lizzie gibberish to them, couldn't truly console them. It didn't help that the black border on letterhead, mourning clothes, and what wasn't spoken of weighed heavy on the household. The family reunion couldn't be a satisfying one because it wasn't a willing one. Also, reflecting Gabriel's worst trait, it was an inconstant one. He spent most days at Mr. Brown's studio in nearby Kentish Town, returning to Albany Street at unpredictable times during the evening, rarely late.

"Damn what is customary if it means I'm not allowed to do anything but be miserable."

Usually Gabriel didn't want supper, claiming he had already eaten. Most evenings he avoided the parlor, and, contradicting his reputation as a night-owl, went straight upstairs to sleep fitfully until he didn't stir before mid-morning or even midday. Christina should have left it to William to make sure their brother didn't do anything irrevocably foolish. Yet, if she woke in the night, she couldn't always resist the urge to check on him, even going so far as to bend over him and hold her breath until she felt his on her cheek. She resisted a stroke of his hair but not a prayer on her knees.

If William was aware of her ritual, he never said. Not even when Gabriel spoke of "angelic visitations" in his sleep.

And she is hence who once was here ... in the held breath of the day's decline her very face seemed pressed to mine.

"I swear, I heard her scold me for burying my poems."

***

What never changed was the two Rossetti storms stirring each other to paint and write more; to show, to sell, to publish, to risk and rival more. Finally, after four years of Gabriel insisting Christina put together a second poetry collection, *The Prince's Progress* came to Penkill, momentarily a pleasing addition to a holiday breakfast.

String untied, paper unwrapped, Christina flipped through its pages. "Oh, no."

"What is it, my dear?" Letitia put her hand out to Christina's arm.

"I recognize that pain," Scotus empathized through a mouthful of potato scone, realizing his cup was empty of tea to wash it down.

Alice stopped Letitia from filling his need, instead summoning the maid who was standing by the sideboard. "Is it bad?"

"The worst of the misprints left uncorrected. Which means there are probably others. At least, the woodcuts in my laggard book look nice. Once again, Gabriel held things up and, once more, he is forgiven."

"As he always must be," Scotus responded with a theatrical shiver as Christina pulled a folded paper from the book. "Ah, the dreaded errata."

"Alas, needed."

"We work towards perfection until it is out of our hands."

Christina knew Scotus wasn't referring to divine intervention. His Sunday morning escapes to the beach for walking and reading with Alice while she and Letitia attended Girvan's earthen-floored Church of St. Cuthbert further depleted any hope that this agnostic William, like another, might yet find his way to faith. Alice chose as he did, not only to forego attending church but to openly direct her worship in another, less glorious, more immediately satisfying direction.

If there be anyone who can take my place ... I do commend you to that nobler grace, Christina thought in poetry before she returned to her

188

exchange with Scotus. "I might suppose you were alluding to my creed exactly if I didn't know better. Or, should I say, worse?"

"You should say what you like. When you finally find your tongue, you usually do."

"A little prickly, my dear." Letitia turned to Christina and, therefore, Alice, too. "Did you know Lady Trevelyn refers to my husband as Mr. Porcupine?"

"In good fun, I'm sure." Alice lured Letitia's agreement.

"Actually, Christina and I fight like cats. It's our natures."

"More like cat and mouse," Letitia remarked. "It just varies who is which."

Christina was afraid she blushed as Scotus nodded in her direction.

"Agreeing to holiday with three ladies, I expected ailments and religion would form a large portion of the conversation."

Christina slowly considered a reply, her anger realizing an opportunity to impress a man she should never need to. She sipped tea, put her cup too deliberately on its saucer, and dabbed a slight spill on the tablecloth with her napkin, allowing time for someone else to react. Finally, she couldn't wait longer. "Well, you aren't listening if you conclude that is all we ever talk about."

"The hazard of being a man, an obstinate Scottish one," Alice calmly, succinctly, and irresistibly made the case for loving him.

***

"*Quel che piace giova.*" Italian once again offered the perfect proverb.

"Tell us what it means." Letitia hooked Christina's arm as they began the regular after-dinner walk down the glen.

"What one likes is good for one." Christina didn't appreciate being held back from keeping up with Miss Boyd and Scotus.

"Miss Rossetti," Scotus shouted back. "I know irony when I hear it."

"I know a doubtful compliment when I hear one," Christina hissed in return.

Letitia petted her arm. "Well, you must like it here, Christina, for you look very well, better than you do in London. But not at all fat as someone claims, the very fellow who sees you as the slim and winsome Lady Jane poor King James could only dream of."

"Thank you, Letty. But I'm under no illusions that is a likeness of me. An artist sees pieces of a model, not the whole. They use what they want to: the color of her hair and eyes, shape of her face, length of her neck. They maneuver her to find the necessary position of her head, droop of her shoulders, or outstretch of her hand. They imagine what they want to, such as turning the discomfort, even pain, of staying in one position for so long into a pining for love."

***

"'And she with true kind eyes looks back on him, Fair as the moon and joyful as the light: Not wan with waiting, not with sorrow dim; Not as she is, but was when hope shone bright; Not as she is, but as she fills his dream.'"

Scotus used Christina's own words against her attempt to seem unaffected by hours of his concentration on her. She prided herself on a modest, practical approach to posing, agreeing to it for collaborative rather than personal reasons, chaperoned, usually by her mother or youngest brother, even when sitting for Gabriel if he was sharing a studio. Religiously determined to dismiss the vanity it encouraged, she participated in the charade for art's sake not her own and never saw herself as a model for anyone's vision.

James Collinson drew on the tedium of their engagement, as evidenced in his portrait of her, as dreary as had ever been done of anyone. For *The Light of the World* she was the lost face that looked out from Mr. Hunt's canvas, consumed by the extraordinary fire and flow of Lizzie's hair. It had been a mistake to let John Brett sketch and paint her, not merely because she never saw the finished painting, but due to the annoying consequences of not understanding his motive until it was too late to prevent him misunderstanding hers.

Gabriel was the only artist who saw any usefulness left in her. Or so she thought. When she arrived at Penkill, Scotus was beginning to design murals for the castle's new circular staircase, part of renovations, including an entirely new east wing. The 13th Laird had begun it before his death, and the 14th, his sister Alice, was committed to its completion. During Christina's first evening, at supper in the hearth-and-tapestry-warmed dining room, Scotus announced he would require some of her time.

Christina looked at Letitia and Alice for shared surprise. They were amused by hers.

"To help bring the Scottish Solomon's poem, *The King's Quair*, to life."

Alice nodded with a warning that wasn't Christina's first concern. "Now remember, Will, you promised not to monopolize her. We have so many lovely outing possibilities, especially if the weather stays fine."

In between drives to Girvan, along the coast to Glendoune, visits to Old Killochan, the castle at Ardmillan, and two overnight stays at Alton Albany, Christina put herself at the mercy of Scotus' artfulness. Unable to resist the call of peacocks and the strong scent of spruce trees,

Christina arrived at sun-streaked stone steps that were a tiered placement for potted geraniums.

On the threshold of a test she might not pass, she opened the door of the stable block into an artist's studio.

CHAPTER TWENTY-NINE

While working, Scotus kept his distance and never smiled, only speaking when he needed Christina to adjust her pose. Thinking she was there to settle for anonymity because of the PRB penchant for seeing all women as one, she was prepared to be sketchily studied, but not subjected to deeper examination. *You construed me … for what might or might not be—nay, weights and measures do us both a wrong.*

The less circumspect cat and mouse nature of their association resumed at a circular white wicker table. Christina imagined Scotus took breaks and refreshment there with Alice, who was also an artist.

Christina drank lemonade from a recipe her hostess had "first enjoyed in Paris," while Scotus swilled and sipped whiskey, which may have encouraged him to finally speak of love.

"I've heard it rumored that Cayley is mustering the courage to propose."

"Really? To whom?"

"Your ignorance isn't convincing, Chrissy."

"He is a bachelor to his core."

"As I am. But certain women have a way of convincing us otherwise."

Or of convincing themselves. She knew he wanted her to say what she was thinking so they might spar a little. Instead, she finished her lemonade and silently considered Charles' rumored intentions.

"Ah. Have I made m'lady blush? Because of another man? I should be jealous."

Christina should be. Except she could never take the place of his other woman.

"We were surprised you came to Penkill. Alice would have been disappointed but understanding of your reservations."

"Why should I have any?" She didn't ask for him to answer. "Except it meant passing on Miss Cameron's invitation to the Isle of Wight."

"Julia Cameron, eh? Such is your growing fame."

She shrugged. "Even without the opportunity to come to Penkill, I wouldn't have accepted, Freshwater and its crowd too formidable for me."

"Hmm. Unlike a castle."

"Tennyson was going to be there."

"He's merely the Poet Laureate who has more hair on his head than I do," Scotus broke his own rule of not mentioning his balding.

"And face."

"He always bettered me on that. And, I suppose, poetry as well."

"Well, that makes two of us—for me, his poetry, not beard."

Scotus reached across the table. "Nothing should ever conceal the incomparable contour of your chin." His fingers brushed her cheeks.

Christina's heart was beating as it only ever had in fear or anger, neither what she was feeling in those moments she thought he was going to kiss her.

I heard the songs of paradise: each bird sat singing in its place.

The rustling feathers and panicked vocals of the peacock outside the studio sent Scotus back to his easel as though it was hours since he left it. Alice soon stood in the open doorway, her simply clothed and coiffed shape silhouetted, her intrusion decorous but deliberate, a basket hooked over her arm. Its contents were revealed at the table Christina had risen but not yet walked away from.

"Just bread and butter. I've brought a honeypot if you would like to sweeten it."

"As you do everything, my dear."

Christina had already noticed that Alice wasn't prone to blush or in any way respond to flattery, at least not socially.

"You've bothered Christina enough today, Will. I think we must take a drive somewhere."

"Christina needs some bothering."

"Sit down with me, dear." Alice took out a small china plate, placed a slice of buttered bread on it and the honey next to it. "Do you like modeling? I don't especially."

"I hate being noticed at all, let alone looked at for hours."

"I'd rather be on the other side of the easel. Also prefer to recreate scenes not people, so it is a pleasantly solitary endeavor. Perhaps I should have been a writer."

"Writing is, initially, essentially, quite solitary, but, if one pursues publication, it becomes crowded and complicated with others' opinions and ambitions."

"And by being a woman?"

"Of course. What in our lives isn't affected by that? Although I'm luckier than some, with a family that encouraged me to do the one thing I'm fairly good at. And long before I could claim any income from it."

"Yes, be glad you were born a Rossetti." Alice laughed almost without a sound. "At least, most of the time."

"For there have been hostilities amongst the clan," Scotus interjected. "Like when a largely favorable review seemed insulting, its comparison irritating, stirring a temper and causing a reaction that inspired a sarcastic mind and hand."

"What are you talking about, my love?"

"Christina Rossetti ... in a tantrum."

"I can't imagine such a thing."

"A caricature Gabriel did after an article last year in the *Times*."

"Caricatures are meant to be exaggeration."

"Well, maybe, Alice. But I hear our guest was quite the firebrand as a child. Reformed or just well disguised now?"

"How did you see the drawing?" Christina finally spoke up. "My brother gave it to me."

"He said he had, certain you would destroy it. Going through one of his notebooks at Tutor House, I saw a rough sketch."

Christina had meant to cast it into the very hearth depicted in the drawing, but the longer she had hesitated the more she had seen a brother's love not criticism for her fighting spirit, which, despite its suppression, he obviously believed was still ready for battle.

Scotus searched through his pencils, then put them all down. "Gabriel warned me not to mention it."

Alice was by his side, leaning on him, nodding, and smiling at what she saw on his easel. "Therefore, you did."

"Of course, my perfect friend." Scotus fit his arm around her waist.

Christina used weariness as an excuse to leave further posing and a drive for another day. As she left the studio, its shaded surroundings were noticeably more humid at two in the afternoon than ten in the morning, which made the midges inescapably angrier.

***

Christina still berated herself for seeing the worst in that *Times* piece reviewing modern poets, straying wildly from her initial delight at being included. Her expectation of what was to follow the acknowledgment of her *poetical art* put her off guard for the trick in a comparison that set her *simpler, firmer, deeper* efforts against the *full and bright* work of another poet who, in the review's critical confusion, was *wanting in form and decision of touch*. If only she hadn't jumped to a conclusion before she realized the intent of the article in calling her work more finished than Jean Ingelow's and, what Christina mistook as insult to injury, *difficult to mend*.

She never let go of her irritation at not being as *ambitious in her choice of subject* as Miss Ingelow, a *child of promise, of great promise, of the future*, who was ten years older than Christina.

Both Amelia and Gabriel sent clippings of the article, the former with the kindest intentions, the latter with older-brotherly impudence and hyperbole. Christina had herself to blame after expressing the slightest hint that she was envious and humiliated by eight editions over two years of Miss Ingelow's *Poems*, while *Goblin Market* languished for three before it achieved enough sales to merit a second printing.

The Times vexation occurred while Christina was once again in Hastings to convalesce, not as the doctor ordered but agreed with Mama's proposal. *Perhaps there is no pleasanter watering-place in England* .... It wasn't a summer retreat this time, but a winter-into-spring one. The Sussex town's mild air and low but prime position sheltered from north and northeast winds meant less fog and rainfall than other places along the southern coast. She arrived with headaches and coughing persistent and painful enough, even blood spotting a hanky, to cause worry of the worst her sickness might be. Correspondence from Cousin Teodorico, who had returned to Italy as the work of grace had moved him, was fraught with fear she wouldn't survive. He meant well with his recipes for easing her passage, but sea air, rest, and a seaweed, sugar, and lemon juice jelly that soothed the aggravation in her chest overruled his own homeopathic suggestions.

Mama and William left after brief stays. Uncle Henry and Henrietta were her Christmas companions, her "Polydore" cousin unquestionably suffering from consumption. Christina's affliction was probably another *tussis nervosa*, like she had suffered after the initial release of *Goblin Market*, which garnered good reviews but hardly secured her presence in the publishing world. Mr. Macmillan and Mr. Masson never asked for more poems for the magazine, so she assumed they didn't want any. Regarding a second book, which they also hadn't expressed interest in, she would rather it happen by accident than design.

For a while, Christina considered never publishing another collection, *Goblin Market and Other Poems* the laurels she would rest on if Cousin Teodorico's fatal prediction proved true. If not, she might settle for an unambitious middle age.

Eventually, Macmillan decided to risk getting more fruit from the little monster merchant-men. Christina needed the healing of Hastings because once again she was heading towards reviews, articles, comparisons, and the stress from expectations of success, failure, or the fear of being ignored. She was too used to shy and stay-at-home habits. She hadn't made the most of opportunities to engage with clever, concerned, creative, similarly challenged middle-class women like Barbara Leigh Smith Bodichon, Bessie Parks, Emily Faithful, and even Jean Ingelow. They had been meeting as the Portfolio Society at 19 Langham Place, which was the editing headquarters for *The English Women's Journal*. A pleasant location and building with reading and luncheon rooms, Christina was enticed there a few times, but, like other courtships in her life, the Langham circle never completely won her over. She hadn't forgotten them, just rarely attended meetings, and considered herself a corresponding member, submitting poems to whatever themes were announced for issues of the journal, often finding something suitable among her old compositions.

Such a practice wasn't allowed until Christina took it up, her apology also accepted.

She was experienced at petitioning forgiveness, especially in regard to declining invitations outside her usual activities and society, most necessary when she accepted knowing she would change her mind. Christina's appreciative agreement gave Mrs. Bodichon little hint of what was coming when teaching Sunday school offered an alibi for reneging on an excursion to Scaglands, the Leigh-Smith estate in Sussex. Even Mrs. Bodichon's gift of a painting she had done didn't moderate Christina's panic as the appointment approached.

I do not deserve your gracious forgiveness for my awkward apology but expected it, knowing you are cordial and understanding.

Unintended encounters with strangers, or those almost so, were tolerated politely as Christina required of herself, but felt dishonest when she could hardly wait to escape them. She had no idea Jean Ingelow was in Hastings until they couldn't avoid each other on the High Street a few steps from where Henrietta watched from a second story window. Christina wouldn't have recognized Miss Ingelow if she had only seen the photo circulated in advertisements and not met her briefly months before in similar circumstances, except they were in London. There had been someone they both were already acquainted with to introduce them and navigate their inhibitions—the only admitted competition between them until the *Times* article was published a few weeks later.

Miss Ingelow spoke first after their hesitant hellos. "I'm sorry to hear you've been ill."

Christina wondered how she knew, who had told her, and why it came up in conversation she wasn't present for. She saw the other woman more clearly. During their first chaperoned meeting, Christina had been concerned with the impression she herself was making. It might have been the different light that Hastings offered because of its open shoreline, a scattering of thin clouds headed towards Boulogne leaving the sun to reflect the cold but bright and rising intensity of the winter sea. Despite her plain looks and retiring manner, Miss Ingelow had moved into the spotlight to become someone Christina might like to know better.

"I'm on the mend, perhaps ready to go home. I miss my family so. Then I remember miserable winters I've spent in London and am almost grateful I'm here."

"Yes. I know what you mean." Miss Ingelow went on to wonder

what time it was and wish Christina a full recovery. She didn't mention the endeavors they had in common—neither did Christina—and never said where she was staying or why she was in Hastings, leaving Christina to silently guess that Mrs. Bodichon's influence coupled with a summons to nearby Scaglands were the reasons.

***

Christina never hesitated to accept invitations from the Scots. They had been friends for more than a decade and were an extension of family. Like sister and brother to the Rossetti siblings, so they seemed to each other. Scotus, especially persuaded by Gabriel, was a restless bird, who needed the commitment cage left open, not only to fly off, but also to return. The difference was Scotus' destiny with Letitia Norquoy wasn't a bewitching one. Christina had vaguely heard about the circumstances of their engagement: Letitia's offer to release him when she contracted an illness that left her unfit to fully be a wife, and his honor in marrying her anyway. Christina had also heard him say the decision was "the most imprudent" of his life.

Traveling to Penkill with Letitia hadn't prepared Christina for the extent of Alice Boyd's involvement in the Scots' lives. Letty's chatter was, as usual, entertaining, exhausting, and trivial. Once they arrived, her quietness alerted Christina to what might have already gone beyond her tolerance of Scotus' relationship with their lovely hostess. It also thrust Christina into a dilemma she had long managed to dismiss.

Three sang of love together: one with lips crimson, with cheeks and bosom in a glow … One shamed herself in love; one temperately grew gross in soulless love, a sluggish wife ….

Romance was everywhere at Penkill, its chivalrous past still seen in a coat of arms and suit of armor. Its layers of rooms, timbered, framed, and furnished in oak, were warmed with stone hearths and hanging tapestries, and adorned with scenery and stories reimagined on canvases and murals. Stairwells and secret spaces were enticing, towering views of the lush grounds and the sloping expanse of Glenwapple's concealing canopy enchanting. Raised up on that Ayrshire pedestal, serenaded by the somehow harmonious music of the wind, jackdaws, and peacocks, looking towards cloud-capped mountains or a sea waiting for sunsets, there was the temptation to believe in happily-ever-after.

Christina had taken a few walks with Letitia along the stream that meandered the glen east of the castle. They had picnicked on a rustic bench set back from its bank, as Letty explained, originally constructed by Scotus for a Penkill housemaid to sit for his painting of a woman with a lute. The immortalized, auburn-haired girl was surrounded, not by the wild brambles Letitia and Christina encountered, but the type of roses found tamely trellised in a carefully designed garden. One afternoon near the end of her stay, after dinner, Christina decided to repeat such an adventure, minus Letitia and the picnic basket. Scotus and Alice had been in the studio all morning and, as far as Christina knew, had lunched and were still at work there.

Christina wasn't empty handed, bringing along a hairnet, small glass bowl, and a scheme stolen from Alice telling tales of her girlhood, specifically of catching small fish for the castle's drawing room aquarium. Christina was reminded of the one Gabriel had eventually found for the shells and seaweed she had collected at Folkestone, now "a pond in the parlor" at Tutor House.

Due to heavy rain overnight, the air was humid and buggy, the stream had a strong current, and any clearing along its sloping, rocky bank was slippery. Christina had learned the hard way to wear her sturdiest boots, limpest petticoat, narrowest sleeves, and hair tightly coiffed, the fashions of a proper 1860s London lady not helpful for rambling through Scottish woods.

It was necessary to stop short of her objective because of voices that were more intimate than they should have been.

What thing unto mine ear wouldst thou convey—what secret thing, O wandering water ever whispering?

Christina didn't catch anything that afternoon but a glimpse of two artists, their futures, like their easels, side by side. The colors on their canvases were muted, the composition also comparable, their easy conversation confirming the agreement of their observations.

Wan water, wandering water weltering, this hidden tide of tears.

For some contrast, Scotus stood while Alice sat, her skirt covering what must have been a stool she was settled on. His hat fallen or discarded on the ground beside him, he put down his brush and bent over to touch the cheek of the much younger and more handsome Alice Boyd. She lifted her mouth to his and then her entire being into his embrace.

CHAPTER THIRTY

Christina was glad of any excuse to visit the wonderland that was Tutor House, the rabbit hole she might have fallen into if she had ended up putting the return address of 16 Cheyne Walk on her correspondence. Gabriel's original intention was "to have the companionship of family by rescuing its female members from Albany Street." The inconvenience of Chelsea to Maria's tutoring locations was one reason to decline, the style and associations of Gabriel's life another; nonetheless, mother, sisters, and even Aunt Margaret were willing to move in with him.

Suddenly, he squashed the scheme.

His new residence was a change from Gabriel's usual dilapidated dwellings. Christina wasn't alone in thinking it was the most beautiful house in Chelsea, others attached but not its equal. It gave the impression that once it had stood alone.

£225 for the lease, £100 yearly to the landowner, Lord Cadogan, and Gabriel was the tenant of a place he had "long had an itch for."

His rise out of insolvency and sorrow was evident in the arching, scrolled wrought-iron gate, flagstone forecourt, and five wide steps up to the paneled mahogany front door with a dragon-shaped brass knocker. His intention to live well, even without Lizzie, was asserted by triple stories of various shades of brown brick, the first and second each with three center windows of seven forming whitewashed splayed bays that promised to let the sunshine in at every angle.

Although Gabriel meant to upgrade his quarters, he hadn't turned his back on bohemian ways. In Chelsea, the comings and goings of a quirky artist and poet wasn't an anomaly. Pleasure gardens added noise and color to the area with restaurants, music, dancing, balloon ascents, and an American bowling saloon. Sometimes, after dark, there were fireworks over the Thames, and, every night, due to an abundance of roving gentlemen, the potential for discovering a new model.

When Gabriel, along with William on a part-time basis, Mr. Swinburne, and Mr. Meredith first occupied Tutor House, the embankment had not yet reached Chelsea. A narrow road separated the house's tall, gated entrance from the water, which was full of leisure boaters and longshore business. A few times, Christina stayed late enough to experience moonlight on the river reminiscent of the effect of the Blackfriars Bridge gaslights that poor Lizzie had been so fond of.

The house's interior and backyard belied its calm façade. Gabriel couldn't inhabit anywhere without his obsessions making it cluttered, fascinating, odd, and annoying. Soon it became apparent the neighbors didn't appreciate a zoo among their conventional gardens.

Mr. Dodgson had taken his time strolling the avenue of specimen lime trees which led to a sizable grassy area left to grow, wither, and die. If he had ventured into one of the field's far corners, he would have seen several cage-like outbuildings housing some of Gabriel's menagerie. One of its residents, a racoon Gabriel said had the face and teeth of the devil, was soon to be returned to the Liverpool animal importer it had been purchased from. Others, including a kangaroo and an armadillo, wandered the walled-in property, but not without the consequences of escape when neighbors realized mounds of dirt dug up and plants strewn about or, at the very least, chomped on. The chance of a few fallow deer couldn't be passed up, for what better creatures to grace the grounds of Gabriel's fantasies? *And the deer live safe in the breezy brake.* Unfortunately, because of one of them, the peacock did not, a stag's annoyance with the bird matching that of the humans subjected to its screams. While the neighbors worked on getting a no peacocks clause into the leases of Lord Cadogan's properties, the deer stalked the bird, stomping on its tail feathers and eventually pulling out most of them.

Christina first met Mr. Dodgson where his photography possessions had been set down near the steps from the garden into the house. She was relieved he sensed her shyness and spoke first.

"I th-th-thought the w-w-women were c-c-coming tomorrow."

His obvious anxiety motivated her to make it easier for them both. "Yes. My mother and sister are. Unlike them, except for the whim of writing, I'm unemployed. So today I tagged along with William."

"Yes, of course." His stammer disappeared as was said it did with children. "Since you are here, I may as well take one or two shots of you alone."

"Oh, I didn't dress for—"

"You are perfectly presented." He hardly looked at her. "Tuesdays are my lucky days. So I have confidence it won't rain, and the light will be ideal."

He talked to himself as he unpacked and set up a large box camera and tripod, and a tent filled with lenses, glass slides, chemicals, funnels, beakers, trays, dishes, scales, and a pail. Christina was amused by Mr. Dodgson's mutterings to the point of him noticing and obviously not minding her observance. His self-absorption softened into a generous smile. "I find it a capital plan to talk things over with myself. One can explain things so clearly to oneself. And is so patient with oneself. One never gets irritated with one's own stupidity."

Tall when he stood stiffly straight, appropriately reverential in a black woolen frock coat, matching waistcoat, starched upright collar, and gray bow tie that might have been silk, she found Mr. Dodgson delicate, defenseless. His head was small, his side-parted brown hair slickened, as if from a mother's tongue-moistened fingertips, and flowing in waves over his ears and neck. His face was pale and clean shaven, his mouth prettily shaped.

Compared to sitting for an artist, photographers were too busily burdened by the paraphernalia and processes of their trade to indulge in fostering relationships with their sitters. After a little bashful artistry, in few words Mr. Dodgson positioned Christina and, as soon as possible, escaped to concentrate on focusing the shot before he disappeared into his portable darkroom to prepare the plate. Ten or fifteen minutes of model patience was required for the time it took until he appeared rushed, holding his work away from the flaps of the tent, his cuffs, and anything else he might brush or bump it against. He did a final check with the darkening cloth over him and his magical machine, shut the lens, slid in the plate holder, pulled something up, and stood to the side.

"You may blink but don't otherwise move." After removing the lens cap, Mr. Dodgson counted slowly to ten, and put it back.

He hurried into the tent to confirm that Christina had been caught, as William described, first with "an intellectual profile" and then "a bantering air."

"I'm ready for whoever is next," Mr. Dodgson announced.

"Le Gros and Cayley are here." Gabriel stood at the stop of the house steps. "They said I might go first."

"Now I know why you wanted to come today."

Christina didn't contradict William's reasoning that her pleasure in Charles Cayley's company went further than acknowledgment of their friend's admiration for *Professore Rossetti's* writings, loyalty to Papa's frail, moody tutorage, and persistence in paying respect to his last breaths. Charles had secured a regular place in her family. Mama, Maria, and even William found Charles' eccentricities endearing, his politeness refreshing, and conversation sporadically thought-provoking. Maria was always eager for his evening visits, Christina content to watch them put their brilliant heads and obsessions together. She half-listened to what they talked about, for it was the unassuming manner of his presence and soft seriousness of his voice that held her interest. She didn't mind her sister realizing how acceptant Charles was of thinking, talented, inquisitive, even opinionated women.

In unexpected ways, Charles was conventional, stubbornly attached to at least one old-fashioned custom. His routine of paying morning calls on ladies to acknowledge a death, wedding, or birth, or leaving his card for no apparent reason, was puzzling. When it made its way into gossip, it was ridiculed. After all, as Mama asserted, he could make no claim to social climbing and, as Christina could attest, he had no charms for formal courtship.

Charles pretended not to notice the scorn of strangers and mockery of colleagues, but Christina's sarcasm couldn't be ignored.

"So, which lady's breakfast did you intrude upon today?"

"I … I never call before eleven."

"Why do so at all?"

"Oh, Christina, I never will again if … if you order me not to."

Christina felt ashamed. "Of course I won't order you."

"Well, Dodgson, are you ready?" Gabriel's shout brought Christina forward in time, if not to a clearer understanding of her situation with Mr. Cayley. Her older brother carefully folded the fabric of her skirt out of the way as he stepped around where she sat on the back stairs deciding whether she should go inside to greet a forgiving friend or be witness to Gabriel's performance for posterity.

There wasn't any contest. In the thick of the PRB and, especially, Lizzie years, Christina had been denied Gabriel's company too often. Written communication, even in pursuance of better poetry and its publication, wasn't a substitute for hearing his voice, or wondering if the mood in his eyes would correspond to or contradict the constant pout of his lower lip. She needed to be present to how he moved and dressed, be party to his spontaneous displays of affection and arrogance. Christina would have been foolish enough to move into Tutor House just to spend more time with him, any visit motivated the same, no matter who else was there.

She hoped Mr. Dodgson would capture Gabriel without restraining him. She helped to straighten and smooth out the dingy fabric hung from the staircase railing as a backdrop to the small side-chair Gabriel sat on. Stretching around him, she expected some of the playfulness that had once been common between them. She wasn't disappointed. Gabriel tickled and hugged her waist with a taunting comment on her lack of experience with draperies.

"Thirty years later, my li'l sister's face isn't red from bawling but embarrassment," he teased her more, before turning back to his self-regard. "How's this, Mr. Photographer?"

Mr. Dodgson, no doubt keeping in mind that his subject knew as much about posing as he did, offered no direction on how Gabriel should present himself. Crossing his legs to the right, the chair slightly tilted, Gabriel removed his hat and held it upside down on his lap. The lapels and body of his oversized coat were pushed back, his trouser-matching waistcoat buttoned high and pinched out to make him look farcically proud. His small beard and mustache were messy, receded waves of hair more lately combed. No matter how he stiffened his broad forehead, his eyebrow shadowed eyes looked down. Eventually, Mr. Dodgson did speak to urge patience while the slide was prepared and the focus was adjusted, stillness while the lens cap was removed.

Charles Cayley's attention turned from examining the camera when Christina came out of the tent, where, along with both of her brothers, she had been invited to witness the development of Gabriel into a leaner, more conflicted man since the loss of Lizzie. She made her escape at Gabriel's declaration that he wasn't happy with the picture and insisted they "have another go." Mr. Dodgson allowed they might "once Mr. LeGros and Mr. Cayley were taken care of." Christina prematurely put in an order for a print of the latter.

"He is a dear friend of the family."

"As Mama says, except for his financial and religious difficulties, he is perfect—"

Christina could guess what William didn't quite say.

Mr. Dodgson picked up on the situation and made a clever greeting of it. "Ah. Good day, Mr. Cayley. Your ears must be burning."

"Oh, no, I am quite well."

Christina couldn't hold back a quick laugh, covering her mouth, hopefully, before her impulse was noticed.

"An idiom, Charlie." Gabriel took out his frustration on the humblest target, before escaping into his Cheyne Walk refuge.

Charles lowered his eyes. "Oh, of course. Quite."

"*Allez*, Alphonse," Gabriel could be heard urging.

"Who is next?" Mr. Dodgson alerted them all to Mr. LeGros's youthful, handsome, and otherwise agreeable emergence from the house and, if Gabriel and William had any influence, onto the London art scene.

"*C'est bonne chance … I here … pour la photographie. Alors, Monsieur,* I have … *patience.*"

"*Non s'il vous plaît, Monsieur,*" Charles waved his hands in one direction, stepping in the other towards Christina. "I am content to wait, Mr. Dodgson."

"*Bien sûr, avec une si charmant compagnon.*" Mr. LeGros, doe-eyed in the direction of Christina, seemed confident he would be understood.

She thought Charles looked well, distinguished, his sideburns and mustache neatly shaped, shirt and collar well-starched, no buttons missing from his waistcoat, and his worsted-wool dress coat, one she hadn't seen before, a good fit and, most importantly, without tails. Then Alphonse LeGros, revolutionary in a single-tailed, double-breasted, brass-buttoned *habit dégagé,* filled her view and the role even Gabriel and Scotus had outgrown of an attractive, avant-guard, up-and-coming talent.

Christina was glad Charles was content to watch Mr. LeGros's photograph session, which was set up similarly to Gabriel's but proved a more affectionate courtship with the camera. Charles stood by her side, close enough for their shoulders to brush when she swayed a little, too long on her feet in uncomfortable shoes.

"Are you done, Alphy? Let me show you how I annoy the neighbors." Gabriel reclaimed the company of Mr. LeGros.

Christina expected Charles C. and Charles D. to stumble over each other's reticence. Instead, she watched the decent, potentially devoted man she was left with work well with Mr. Dodgson. There was an almost immediate recognition between them of another who was inclined to hide away yet curious enough to risk discovery. Mr. Cayley's interest in the instruments and methods of photography urged him out of his reserve and convinced Mr. Dodgson to talk eagerly to someone besides himself.

Perhaps, because of his age, Charles C. had the appearance of a deacon more than Charles D., who had earned the title but wouldn't let piety thwart his imagination and sense of fun. It remained to be seen whether Mr. Dodgson's magic would transform Mr. Cayley into an adventurer or prove him irrevocably *a dotard grim and gray, who wasted childhood's happy day in work more profitless than play*.

***

"Photographs always make me feel embarrassed, as if I'm eavesdropping."

"But it's lovely to have them, isn't it?" Christina was sitting opposite her mother at the card table where Mr. Dodgson's photographs were fanned out. "They did turn out well. Except for the group of five."

"The one I wanted most."

"I know, Mama. Pity it was spoiled, as though splashed with ink. I thought it was the rain. William said it was the accident of some chemical on the negative."

"At least a good vignette of Moony was made of it."

Maria stood behind her sister. "I was told not to acknowledge the camera."

Christina turned to tug her sleeve. "Well, of course, Moony, you did anyway."

"It was staring at me, so I stared back. Gabriel was as guilty. Of glaring, actually." Maria put her hand into the mix. "Here. Look at his conceit."

"All of us but you. Why weren't you in it?"

"The table and board are missing, too." Christina offered a clue.

"Because I beat Mama at chess in the first one."

"No, Maria, the game was in progress," Mama pretended to object. "That was how Mr. Dodgson set it up."

"But, dearest Mama, I would have beaten you."

"Of course. I practice needlework more." Mama's interest shifted to another photo. "Oh, I'd forgotten this one. Of dear Charles. I'm surprised, Christina, he hasn't called since you returned from Penkill."

"I'm sure he is busy, no sooner finishing his translation of the *Illiad* then beginning work on *Prometheus Bound*, a long-time goal of his."

"Bravo." Maria threw her arms around Christina's shoulders. "Must discuss it with him. Should we invite him to dinner?"

"No. I need some rest from dinners, from being amiable, from society." Christina alluded to the last leg of her Scottish holiday that had been spent in Edinburg at the invitation of Letitia's aunt. It had been exhausting, not least because she was ready to be home with only routine plans and expectations and more time for solitude and sleep. Letty was her lively self again and wanted to visit every museum and monument, attend as many concerts and church services as were possible in a week, and shop more extravagantly and spitefully than Girvan could offer.

"Charles is hardly society," only Mama could manage to say without mockery. "William can let Charles know that Maria and I will be going to Eastbourne next month and that you, Christina, will be glad of company."

"Once I'm rested, I will engage with the penitentiary again, which will take up my time."

"Ah, look what has been brought out." William arrived home early enough to be expected to make an appearance in the parlor. "Photographs. Irrefutable evidence of the sun." He picked up the group of four. "Well, Maria, I hope you won't give up chess like our Chrissy."

"Have you seen Charles recently?" Mama wouldn't be sidetracked.

"Dodgson?"

"No."

"Oh, Cayley." William side-glanced at Christina. "He has been missing ...."

"These need to go into an album," Christina advised as she had before and proved as delinquent at the task as everyone else. She returned the photos to a mahogany keepsake box and noticed the invoice in Mr. Dodgson's clear cursive handwriting. It reflected the order she had sent to him, noteworthy because Alphonse LeGros had merited two prints, Charles Cayley only one.

CHAPTER THIRTY-ONE

All Switzerland behind us on the ascent, all Italy below us, we plunged down St. Gotthard, garden of forget-me-nots ....

Pictures of the Italy Christina finally encountered weren't formed with a wooden box, glass slides, and chemicals, but by words as William used them for chronicling and critiquing, and in her own less constant scribbling. Despite the grueling travel and sightseeing, her younger brother kept up his diary, which he didn't mind sharing. By evening, Christina was often preoccupied with sore feet, headaches, or indigestion, and wondering what she might avoid on the next day's itinerary. Her imagination was helpful in the creation of excuses. Making sure Mama was settled as comfortably as possible was easily established for they usually shared a room. In any case, Frances Polidori Rossetti rarely complained.

William was obviously mindful of their mother's age and Christina's health only a few months after her Hastings convalescence. He limited the trip to northern Italy where transport was easier for tourists and the climate cooler than in the south, foregoing any visits to husband's, father's, and grandfather's birthplaces, and avoiding surviving Rossetti or Polidori relations. For William, it meant his longing to reach Naples was unfulfilled for another year.

"Maybe it would be better for the lovely scheme to fall through."

"You don't mean that, Chrissy."

"No, Will, I don't. But I can't help thinking what you will be giving up."

"Please, don't."

Christina wondered how Henrietta Rintoul had refused the kindness in William's eyes, then she knew a woman's reasons were often perplexing to others.

"I will think of it as my *fata morgana* of 1865. Every year should have one, and usually does."

Although Christina had been organizing what to pack for weeks, the day before they set out, she sat to be drawn by Gabriel as if nothing out of the ordinary was about to happen. She only referenced her impending tour of Switzerland and Italy to tease him that perhaps he wanted "a last portrait in case I am lost in the channel, an avalanche, or to an Italian more charming than you are."

"None likely," he replied. "But you may be unrecognizable after five weeks of Will exploring every cathedral, church, and museum along the way. At least we will have proof of your once-good looks."

She remembered France and knew the journey ahead would be challenging. Gabriel taunted her because he would never take his sister and mother on such an extensive holiday. The idea might reach the point of impulse, but, like moving them into Tutor House, would never become reality.

If Gabriel hadn't seemed so fragile, Christina might have defended her other brother as an excellent travel planner and a solid and dependable escort. William often sensed and surrendered to what others preferred for the sake of harmony, except for his agnosticism, which no one, however loved by him, could sway. Even to strangers, religious houses and representations obviously fed his worship of architecture and art rather than God.

William was a flexible companion, easy to spend hours with on the road, for he could be social or solitary, and content with both conversation and contemplation. It was reassuring to be with him in foreign places, his attention to detail committed to the comfort and safety of those in his charge, and his few impulses considered before acted on, and rarely irresponsible.

William never explained to anyone why he was traveling with his mother and sister, revealing their relation to him when appropriate, never with embarrassment. Gabriel might not hesitate to announce and gush about his family, but also not hold back his irritation with having to think about them more than himself. He would have soon grown bored with them as he did with most everyone and everything. At least William was tactful, escaping the limitations of a sixty-five-year-old mother and often ailing sister when they were early to bed, content to take tea in the hotel lobby, or wait in the shade of a European Larch or the cool, restful nave of a cathedral.

If William strayed from the platonic purpose of the trip, he did so discreetly, most likely in thought not action, certainly not in any way that spoiled the trust Christina and Mama had in him.

Christina already suspected William's bachelorhood was temptable before she read his journal mention of *a beautiful young woman at Faido's Airolo Hotel* where they dined on the way to Bellinzona. In between, around the summit of St. Gotthard, they saw red pigs, goats, small black and white sheep, and alpine roses reminiscent of rhododendrons that the carriage driver informed bloomed for a month only. After tea, around six, they explored the streets of the southern Swiss town, dimly lit by the few shops still open. Swooping bats tested Mama's nerve but delighted Christina and hardly distracted William, unlike what lie ahead. They came upon a group of women stripping vine branches and singing solemnly, then louder and livelier, ending with *"Viva le Fidelta"* repeated in a chantlike fashion. At first, all seemed oblivious to their audience positioned on the east side of twilight. Eventually, a few lanterns were held up to reveal several young females who were, going by William's mesmerized expression, as handsome as that girl at Faido.

He made no attempt to speak to them. He could have navigated their dialect but not their naturalness.

He hooked his sister's arm and they walked on. "Did you notice the appearance of the inhabitants markedly improved as soon as we passed from the German to the Italian side of the mountains?"

"A country half our own."

"Do you not wonder, Chrissy, what would we be like, our lives would be like, if it was all our own?"

"Wherefore art thou strange, and not my mother?"

"A new poem?"

"Thou hast stolen my heart and broken it: would that I might call thy sons 'My brother,' call thy daughters 'Sister sweet': lying in thy lap, not in another, dying at thy feet."

"I had hoped the trip, finally coming to Italy, would bring you joy."

"Oh, William." Christina pulled him closer, so if anyone saw them, if any of those young women saw them, they might think they were lovers. "You know me. Melancholy helps me find my joy."

Mountains of melancholy awaited her. The Alps first became real from a room at Lucerne where Mama and Christina had a view across the green, glassy lake to still distant snowy peaks. Christina was more insistently captivated by the loudness of a cricket somewhere on the balcony competing with the steamy sound of cicalas rising from the chestnut trees at the front of the hotel. The next day was assigned an ascent by water and land. They took a paddle-steamer through the bends, curving arms, rock-faced-and-forested mountain walls of Lake Lucerne to Flüelen. William was pleased to hire a carriage for just the three of them at a reasonable fare of 120 francs.

Wherein lies the saddening influence of mountain scenery? For I suppose many besides myself have felt depressed when approaching the 'everlasting hills.'

Even after a visit to Scotland, Christina had never experienced any landscape like the enormity and elevation of the Alps. Only death would have her look higher. It might not be far off, for she had never felt such danger while traveling. Their bargain carriage rumbled and swayed on its serpentine way through the Urseren Valley, unsettling even a light midday meal, indigestion owing as much to bulging rock faces rising steeply on one side, sheer drops on the other.

"I feel lured into wishing there was no way out," William said to break the silence that was explained by Mama's gloveless, bloodless fingers holding onto the seat's front edge each side of her skirt.

Christina's might have surpassed her mother's terror because sitting next to the window made it possible to look over the edge.

The few stops were for appreciation of the Reuss rushing relentlessly or snowmelt streaming down. When warm sunshine broke through, Christina and her mother were glad they dressed for the season to come rather than the one passed but still in view.

"Myth has it that the locals outsmarted the devil," William anticipated their crossing the Schöllenen Gorge and its *Teufelsbrücke*. "Initially a wooden bridge, it was such a difficult undertaking, a Swiss herdsman wished the devil would build it. Well, the fiend offered to, but only on condition that he could claim the first soul to cross. Once it was built, the villagers sent a goat over it."

"Surely, the devil didn't give up that easy."

"Of course he sought revenge, Mama," Christina jumped in with what else she already knew. "He intended to smash the bridge with a large stone. But on the way to do so, he met an old woman who was wearing a cross. He dropped the stone and ran away."

"The power of faith. And a little trickery," Mama took the opportunity for a lesson and mischief.

As expected, William didn't reveal whether he minded Christina finishing the story. "Ah, I see you've been reading up on it."

"A pamphlet at the hotel in Lucerne. While you were exploring the cathedral yet again."

"One of many such legends for old European Devil's Bridges, symbols of transition into another world, another life."

William did surprise her with such a mystical take on it, although immediately he insisted it was, for him, not belief but curiosity.

They reached the village of Andermatt in early evening. Before supper, after checking into a private house that provided lodging in two small, connected rooms, they strolled out of the village along the same road the carriage had brought them into it. By then it was dusk, with a sliver of a moon and stars increasing with the darkness.

Well, saddened and probably weary, I ended one delightful day's journey in Switzerland; and passed indoors, losing sight for a moment of the mountains.

Then from a window I faced them again. And, lo! the evening flush had turned snow to rose, and sadness and sorrow fled away.

***

"So far, William, you have tolerated Christina and me well. I know you are used to traveling with vigorous male friends or by yourself. I fear, at times, we are a burden."

Christina looked up from opening her leather writing wallet. "One he carries better than any man I know would."

"I have not always made the adjustment as unselfishly as you both deserve. After all, it was my idea that you should make this trip, finally step onto Italian soil, feel the Italian sun, and taste the food grown under it, and, especially, recognize yourselves in the lovely faces and figures and voices."

William's compliment and poetics almost caused Christina to forget what she was thinking, not to record in a letter to Maria or Amelia, but for a time when certain recollections, like traversing the pass between Andermatt and Airolo, might otherwise elude her.

At a certain point of the ascent Mount St. Gotthard bloomed into an actual garden of forget-me-nots. Unforgotten and never to be forgotten that lovely lavish efflorescence which made earth cerulean as the sky.

Thus I remember the mountain. But without the flower of memory could I have forgotten it?

"It seemed my mission to bring you 'home' to a unified Italy as Papa always wanted to."

"*Sì, sì.* So, you have, dear son." It was also a miracle Mama acknowledged her emotions publicly, albeit modestly, using the corner of a serviette to dab at her eyes.

We Englishwomen, trim, correct, all minted in the self-same mold, warm-hearted but of semblance cold, all-courteous out of self-respect.

They had broken the journey from Bellinzona with lunch in Lugano. Fortunately, William found the Cathedral there "of no particular interest," which made him even more eager to explore *il Duomo di Como*, and his mother and sister happy to be on the way to its Lombardy location sooner rather than later. Even before Christina saw beyond their hotel nobly positioned at the head of glacially glistening Lake Como, she questioned why they were to stay only one night.

William had the many attractions and four upcoming days of Milan on his mind and the itinerary to satisfy his interests and detail in his journal. Como, despite its *Cattedrale di Santa Maria Assunta, Basilica di Sant'Abbondio*, museums, art galleries, theaters, parks, and palaces was an overnight stop on their way to the great metropolis of Milan, the consolation William deserved for foregoing Naples that trip. Christina didn't regret the lack of time to trudge around Como's urban treasures. She preferred nature's creations to manmade ones. Lake Como, mere moments in the extent of her life and eternity, wasn't just an evening boat ride beyond the pier out onto sparkling, river-wide water embraced by flourishing flowers and trees, sunlight and shadows on the surrounding hills reflecting the moods of the sky. It was a romance she couldn't refuse, at least to remember with words reserved for true love.

So chanced it once at Como on the Lake:

But all things, then, waxed musical; each star
Sang on its course, each breeze sang on its car,
All harmonies sang to senses wide awake.

William hardly noticed her rapture or, if he did, attributed it to the good-looking Italian handling their lantern-lit, gondola-like vessel. Soon it was obvious the young fellow was more impassioned by Garibaldi routing 3000 of the 11,000 Austrians on a hill not far from where the boat slid through the lake's rippled mirror than the presence of a middle-aged English spinster.

Hark! that's the nightingale, telling the selfsame tale.

Eventually, even politics couldn't distract him or William from nearly nocturnal birdsong. Enthusiastic, repetitive, and complex crescendos of whistling, tweeting, trilling, gurgling, and sighing were strung together by silences punctuated by crows clamoring to roost, an outlying owl, and what Christina guessed was a sparrow lingering past dusk in the reeds around the edges of the lake.

"*Ah, Bellissima.*" The boatman lifted one hand from the paddle to lay on his heart, his dark eyes meeting Christina's observation.

***

So many changes opening up the streets, William wrote in his journal, *I'm afraid Milan is losing its charm of very narrow lanes and tall houses, and the relief of their shadows as an escape from the intense sun.*

They traveled by omnibus to Camerlata where they caught a train to Milan's Central Station. The premature departure of transport to the *Hôtel di Milano* meant they put up at the *Hôtel Cavour* instead, not far from the *Giardini Pubblici*, which the omnibus conductor claimed contained lions and tigers.

"Is the park open this evening?" Christina urged William to ask him.

"I intend to walk down to *il Duomo* after dinner."

"Please forgive my abstention, my dear. Tiredness has gotten the better of me."

"Of course, Mama." William looked relieved. "And you, Chrissy?"

"I might find the energy for a walk through a park, but not another cathedral."

"You don't mind if I go?"

"Do I ever?"

"Not as you have told me."

The truth was, Christina wished William had more interest in beasts than buildings, even just to humor her. Gabriel would have effortlessly indulged her as he pleased himself, prioritizing the sight of wild creatures over statues, gables, pinnacles, and stained glass. The next day, deluges of rain with intermittent lightning and thunder not only spoiled the parade of the National Guard, Cavalry, and Artillery down the *Corso Vittorio Emmanuele* but also the promise of time to discover landscaping and a zoo in the style of Regent's Park. The *Museo Civico* kept them dry, but its displays of stuffed animals for anatomical study were no substitute for living ones.

A wander through the *Giardini Pubblici* was eventually fulfilled, lions and tigers never seen, but there were deer warily clustered, also aviaries and enclosures for monkeys and even giraffes. Cathedral climbing came first, Christina expecting she would suffer the five hundred stairs to its roof during execution and recovery.

"Worth it. Not just for the bird's eye experience of Milan, but to appreciate the architectural grandeur of the cathedral." William went even higher, claiming that *Monte Rosa, Monte Blanc,* and Saint Gotthard were visible.

A carriage ride to see the illuminations was not all it could be because of heavy rain up until nightfall, when at least they were able to enjoy a street lit with Chinese lanterns. The next day, William hired a cab to take them to the Palace of the Archbishops, the Basilicas of *Sant'Ambrogio, San Vittore,* and *San Lorenzo,* the Ambrosian Library, and churches *Santa Maria delle Grazie* and *San Maurizio.* An after-dinner stroll up and down grand boulevards with double rows of chestnut trees further distressed Christina's feet to the point of her needing to rest at the hotel for a day and a half until they left for Pavia.

The last morning in Milan, once again Mama proved more resilient than her thirty years younger daughter. She walked to the *Palazzo Reale* so William, who said he wouldn't go without her, didn't miss seeing Luini's frescoes, especially "the grace of purity" of *Women Bathing,* and Canova's bust of Napolean.

Although Pavia offered yet another cathedral, more churches, and a pleasant position on the Ticino River near its convergence with the Po, it was disappointing in its condition and accommodations. William's main impression of the city was "decadence and neglect," typified by the shabby *Croce Bianca* with doors that didn't shut, windows that didn't open, blinds colored by dust, filthy floors and walls, and beds that were too small. Mama and Christina literally prayed they weren't also bug-ridden.

"Fortunately, the hotel is acceptable in other ways." William's grievances found compensation in the hotel's supper of risotto, veal cutlets, and local red wine. Always ready for a political discussion, he was indulged by the head waiter who spontaneously initiated one that, as far as Christina could translate, involved Napoleon arranging for the Italians to take Rome, then Venice, and a word from Garibaldi to raise

2,000 men against the Austrians.

More notable than Pavia's claim to the tomb of St. Augustine, and reminiscent of *la Chat of St. Lô* who begged for milk in a Normandy hotel, was a black lamb, white atop his head and at the tip of his tail, who wandered around the *Croce Bianca's* dining room taking sugar from any hand that offered it.

Next stop was Brescia, after a pleasing journey with fertile foregrounds and backdrops of mountains not recognized as part of the Alps. A welcome contrast to Pavia, its city center was uncluttered, busy, and bright, its cathedral impressive at twilight, and the *Albergo d'Italia* clean and comfortable. Before they turned homewards, the way to Verona offered splendid sightings of Lake Garda and a nervous delay at Peschiera where William was suspected an *emigrate Veneto* by an official until he showed his passport and proclaimed himself a *native Inglese, figlio d'un Napoletan*.

Bergamo to Lecco headed them back towards Switzerland, last chance for memories of Lake Como and *land of love, sister-land of Paradise* that was Christina's re-birthplace.

To come back from the sweet South to the North, where I was born, bred, look to die ....

"You are very quiet, my dear. Are you still feeling unwell?"

"Yes, Mama. But as long as I don't have to walk much, I'll be all right."

William hired a Fly to drive them north along the eastern side of Lake Como and beyond to Chiavenna on the right bank of the River Mera. Since Milan, Christina had felt constantly frail. Yet she was glad of the journey that had worn her down and almost crippled her. It meant she had finally met Italy like a long-lost cousin who reminded her of herself distantly removed, embraced her as a stranger who could have been a native, and allowed her to record that *with mine own feet I have trodden thee, have seen with mine own eyes.*

They returned to Paris by way of Coire towards Schaffhausen, Dachsen, and Strasbourg, although William preferred the Gotthard, Lucerne route.

"Tour guides often suggest going back a different way than one has come," he explained and argued with himself. "Yet, if it pleases, why not repeat the pleasure rather than risk the unknown?"

Christina was saddened, not by mountains this time but Italy behind her like the warmth and spontaneity of her childhood. She had been entertained by the expressive expatriates who crowded her young life, at times to the point of unashamedly weeping over missing the country of their birth. Later, in a less than contented time herself, Christina wondered why her father, almost blind, hardly able to walk or work, still believed he might return to Italy, and *Nonno*, as happily settled as he always seemed, still spoke of it as home.

Finally, Christina understood the regrets of exile, and its necessity and finality, too.

To see no more the country half my own, nor hear that half familiar speech, Amen, I say: I turn to the bleak North whence I came forth — the South lies out of reach.

***

"It's a pity you didn't get to Florence."

"And Naples." Mama reached out to the hand of her youngest son who stood next to her chair.

"I'm sure you will next time."

"Well, Mr. Browning, I will never go again."

Amazing as it was that Christina could finally hold Italy in her thoughts and heart as she remembered it, Robert Browning sitting in the parlor at 166 Albany Street because he wished to meet her was as incredible.

"'When Venice and Rome keep their new jubilee, when your flag takes all heaven for its white, green, and red, when you have your country from mountain to sea ...,'" Mr. Browning's recitation trailed off.

"Ah, Elizabeth's valiant Republican sympathies." William did his best to console him.

"Liberation was always a theme in her life."

So as not to dwell in disappointment or relief, Christina had dismissed the rumor that on his return to England after his wife's death, Mr. Browning, having become Gabriel's and William's close friend and received a copy of *Goblin Market*, hoped to make her acquaintance. It was surprising that years later he was still determined enough to employ the element of surprise.

A ring of the doorbell, William's hesitant welcome of, "Robert, come in, come in. Yes, Christina is at home. She almost always is in the evening," caused a delightful disruption to a dull evening.

Mama and Maria rose from their reading and Christina from her corner and disbelief.

She knew what to expect by how her brothers had described Mr. Browning and yet was astonished that "the impression of physical charm" they rightly attributed to him was cast in a full white beard and graying hair, sagging brow, dark-circled eyes, and weighted shoulders. He was shorter than she had imagined. His voice was strident for a poet, and she assumed the emphatic motion of his hands while he spoke was

214

acquired during years lived in the country where he had also left his heart.

... its truest tenderest part. Dear land, take my tears.

Mr. Browning used that residency and the freshness of three of his hosts' recent journey as the basis for conversation, which Christina barely participated in. When he brought up the historical poem concerning an Italian *cause célèbre* that he was writing, her interest as a fellow poet wanted to engage with him. She hesitated until he turned to William to inquire about the routes and methods of transportation taken to and from Italy.

"If it is possible for anyone to leave it behind."

CHAPTER THIRTY-TWO

Christina promised Henrietta she wouldn't be long fetching what she needed from the guest room in her cousin's Gloucester terraced house. She wanted to immediately reply to the letter delivered that morning from William without delaying a walk on the first fine day since she had arrived for a two-month stay with the Polydores. She might get it into the post before noon. With pencil in hand and her lacquered leather notepad supporting her scribbling, she wrote and walked along Oxford Street, dependent upon Henrietta to save her from stumbling, bumping into anything or anyone, or being run over.

"Well, it seems you don't love Charles enough."

"I'm fond of him, Ettie, but … I just hope he still likes to see me."

For a time, Christina didn't expect Charles Bagot Cayley would ever propose to disrupt their longtime, now and then, friendship. *The blindest buzzard that I know does not wear wings to spread and stir … he sports a tail indeed, but then it's to a coat; he's man with men; his quill is cut to a pen.* If anything, flirting with his affection had only continued his platonic pursuit of hers.

Ten years ago, five years ago, one year ago, even then you had arrived in time, though somewhat slow; then you had known her living face, which now you cannot know …

The longer Charles hesitated, aging and probability meant Christina wouldn't marry anyone and he would remain a bachelor. As she told Cousin Henrietta, she didn't want to lose his attention altogether. He would always be welcome to come and go, call and write, share books, interests, opinions, and even sentiments, just not to take away her independence. When William suggested he ask Charles to accompany them to Italy, Mama thought it was "a kind gesture," while Christina panicked at the prospect of Charles' pedantic presence for weeks, days and nights, on the road, in hotels, eating almost every meal together, and having to impress him with her grace, wonder, and endurance, all of which, as her family expected and Charles had yet to endure, were erratic.

"Where did he intend you live?" Henrietta, looking consumptively older than twenty, rose from the bench just outside the post office once Christina had sent off her letter. "I can't imagine his lodging is suitable."

"In Blackheath, with his mother and sisters. The little I've spent in their company, I like them."

"But you like your own family better."

"How could I not? I don't want to live anywhere without Mama,

Maria, and William; Gabriel at least close by. That's how it's always been. Even as we travel, are apart, and find others of interest, we always come back together. We cannot be separated."

"If you were fond enough of Charles, William was willing to keep it so."

"With an intruder in our midst." Christina heard how horrible she sounded.

"Poor Charles. It must have taken all his nerve."

Her cousin's consideration reminded Christina of her own response to another Henrietta, her brother William's Henrietta, whose heart had waited longer than it could remember why.

***

Charles had called before Mama and Maria left for Eastbourne. His reason, although he hardly needed one, was wanting a signed copy of *The Prince's Progress and Other Poems* promised to his sisters. His usual stuttering conversation about books he was reading, translations he was doing, exhibitions at the Botanical Gardens, and his brother Arthur's latest mathematical achievements gave no indication of the disruption his next visit would initiate.

It began well enough. Before Charles stepped into the house, he wondered if William was at home.

"He is." Christina tugged Charles' sleeve a little to invite him in. "Making a slow start to this summer Saturday."

William wouldn't stay overnight at Tutor House while Mama and Maria were away, but he had spent the previous evening there, or somewhere with Gabriel, and returned to Albany Street well after midnight. Christina wasn't worried that her brother was still upstairs, or that Aunt Margaret, while cackling in one of her crazy spells at the maid, wasn't much of a chaperone, either.

Christina ushered Charles into the parlor, offered Mama's armchair for his comfort, and the newest feline resident, named Princess, for his lap.

"An outcast from Gabriel."

"At least … not … a wombat."

"Oh, I wouldn't mind. Others here might."

Charles stroked the cat, who bristled a little, because, like Christina, she sensed his intention.

"Owls, a raven, rabbits, and tiny waxbills were hardly the company she should be keeping."

His laugh was more like a deep breath.

"She was exiled when one of the owls was found headless."

"How gruesome."

Christina sensed Charles was about to drop Princess to the floor and scooped her out of his arms, kissed and rocked her. "Gabriel has since admitted the raven did it."

"Oh, good. I mean ... not for the owl ... but, at least ...." Charles stood, walked around the width of Christina's skirt, went to the front window, and separated the panels of its lace sheers to look out.

"I know what you want to ask me, Charles."

His shoulders relaxed. "You do?" He turned from the window.

***

William had hoped money was the obstacle so he could come up with a solution. Christina's religious requirement was out of his control and sympathy, so she didn't mention it in her hurried, barely legible reply. Instead, she emphasized her happiness on being loved more than she deserved, while, as subtly as she could, noting she could not give such a gift in return.

She imagined William's frustration at receiving her letter and, as was its object, having to accept he couldn't prevent her being stranded in spinsterhood.

She had tried to stop Charles before he put such finality on her future. She coaxed him to sit in Mama's chair again, settling herself on the settee with Princess and questions about his own mother and sisters and work. They'd already had discussions prompted by Christina's religious practice, so it was unnecessary to interrogate him further. If a Christian, he was an extremely doubtful one who she had to conclude didn't, would never, share her beliefs. At least, unlike James Collinson, Charles never gave any indication that in courting her mind and heart he might yet align himself with her soul.

When she ran out of diverting inquiries, he stood again, she assumed to escape the awkwardness between them. Instead, he added to it, surprising Princess more than her new mistress as he tripped towards them, dropped to a knee, held Christina's hands, and declared his devotion.

She nervously laughed and wiggled her fingers free, quickly hiding them behind her back.

***

Bird of roses and pain, bird of love, happy and unhappy: is that song laughter or weeping? True to the untrue, in a cold land you guard your nest of thorns.

218

Everyone thought Charles had asked and Christina said no. She could thank Aunt Margaret for preventing a second attempt, or, more so, William. He managed to stop their aunt going into the parlor but not her thoughtless laughter, which to Charles must have seemed an echo of Christina's.

"Charles, please, get up. We'll talk about this. Just not now."

He slowly complied, not for the first time looking old and defeated. "It need never be mentioned again."

To Charles' credit, it never was. To Christina's, she had avoided refusing him outright, if not herself the guilt of doing so. *None know the choice I made; I make it still. None know the choice I made and broke my heart* .... There had been no return to easy feelings at the time, Charles excusing himself and barely greeting William as he departed, even ignoring Aunt Margaret's almost lucid request for him to come to the kitchen for one of the scones she had baked.

"I hope under Mrs. Stevens' supervision." William referred to their cook who was around the same age as Aunt Margaret but of sounder mind.

"Well, sir, did you smell anything burning?"

William hesitated to say what obviously came quickly to his mind. "Only the bridges to a happier ending."

I used to labour, used to strive
For pleasure with a restless will:
Now if I save my soul alive
All else what matters, good or ill?
I used to dream alone, to plan
Unspoken hopes and days to come: —
Of all my past this is the sum —
I will not lean on child of man.

PART SIX

*Nature and art combine to keep time for us: and
yet we wander out of time!
We misappropriate time, we lose time, we waste
time, we kill time.
We do anything and everything with time, except
redeem the time.
Yet time is short and swift and never returns. Time flies*
~ from *Time flies: A Reading Diary* by Christina Rossetti

CHAPTER THIRTY-THREE

As a child, Christina was fond of mirrors. She had loved to make faces and strike poses in the many around the house, as did her brothers, especially Gabriel. Maria had always hated them, her dark complexion and plumpness portraying her plain and foreign, her aversion to seeing herself likely not, as she claimed, to avoid vanity but because of it.

Christina didn't have her sister's complaint. She grew paler and slimmer, her hair sleeker, her eyes more clearly blue, as English as she was anything. While Maria found her stride in being realistic about her appearance and ambitions, Christina was impeded by hers, wishing no one had ever thought her pretty or predicted she would become "a stunner." *While roses are so red, while lilies are so white, shall a woman exalt her face because it gives delight?* Nothing was accomplished by her looks being pleasant enough to stir passing fancies and flirtations, except reckless proposals, which seemed more about vanquishing than admiring her.

Another courtship, the last, faltered in every way but friendship, and, therefore, hadn't failed, neither age nor illness able to spoil what was true.

The mirror she held up with the intention of finally accepting what she saw was the same plain walnut-wood one that more than once had caused panic and pain. At last, her reflection was a relief, some might think because her hair had stopped falling out, her eyes bulged less, the blotches on her face had faded, and the goiter was smaller and almost unnoticeable if she wore one of her higher collars or wound a scarf around her neck Gabriel-style. Christina was glad she was less of a wreck than what Grave's disease had, at its worse, made her, but that wasn't the improvement that would make the most difference to her.

Youth gone, and beauty gone if ever there dwelt beauty in so poor a face as this ....

At first, there had been no easy way to realize her appearance drastically altered, especially as she was unrecognizable in the reactions of others, even those who saw her daily.

Neither her spells of depression and other ailing, doubts over discouraging Charles, the death of Aunt Margaret, Gabriel's worsening eyesight, or a grave exhumation had prepared Christina for what her fourth decade would bring. In the final stretch of her thirties, her health was better. Charles had not disappeared. Aunt Charlotte and Aunt Eliza had moved, along with their sister, Rossetti nieces and youngest nephew, to Euston Square. Gabriel's eyes had improved, so he was painting again, and, despite years in Lizzie's grave, his poetry was salvageable. Christina's writing had been noticed in North America, Roberts Brothers of Boston interested in publishing a collection of her prose. Increasingly, she received letters of praise and requests for autographs, and, although barely managing the confusion of longing for both recognition and privacy, she replied to each one.

There were always frustrations, especially when dealing with publishers, her brothers taking care of most of the negotiations, often at cross purposes. William wanted her to stay with Macmillan, who found *Sing-Song* of "high merit" but "perplexing." He initially offered meager terms due to doubts that it would suit English readers, and he wanted to delay a combined volume of her first two publications because there were copies left of *Goblin Market's* second edition. Unable to resist Gabriel's urging, Christina turned to Frederick Startridge Ellis, a Covent Garden bookseller who had ventured into publishing and was open to the idea of creating *a little circle of compatible writers* like Gabriel, Scotus, Mr. Morris, Mr. Swinburne, and herself. She sent *Sing-Song* by book post and hoped Mr. Ellis would also consider a collection of short stories she was just finishing the title piece for.

"Mr. Ellis doesn't want it called *Commonplace*. I couldn't think of anything else. Maria suggested *Births, Deaths, and Marriages.*"

Gabriel groaned. "Sounds like a church registry. It may not be your best work, Sis, not dangerously exciting to the nervous system. I rather like *Hero*. But you stray too far from your true occupation of poetry. Still, nothing you write is ever common."

"Aw, Gabe. I accept when I fall short, usually in prose. Anyway, I don't need to always be extraordinary like you."

"Well, I hope you are done with Mac."

"He won't give up his hold on the goblins and prince. Will thinks he will soon make a better offer to tempt me back."

Christina wasn't convinced she should completely turn away from Mr. Macmillan. Mr. Ellis was only willing to do a small run of *Commonplace and Other Short Stories*, although he did exhibit enthusiasm by the urgency with which he did so—or inexperience. Bad timing meant her book was upstaged by the slightly sooner and more sensational release of Gabriel's resurrected *Poems*. A month after the first thousand copies were issued, a second printing of the same amount was needed. Christina hardly minded the triumphant culmination of her brother's long-tortured efforts to be recognized as a poet as well as a painter. Mama's palpable pleasure in his achievement, which resulted in an invitation for Mr. Ellis to come to tea, was all the consolation Christina needed.

"Such a fine-looking Englishman," Mama declared.

It didn't hurt that Mr. Ellis paid well and in advance.

***

The expectation was that Euston Square would be an improvement over Albany Street, reports not encouraging about the declining character of their former neighborhood. A community consisting of lawyers, stockbrokers, a schoolmistress, an archaeologist, and a philologist, with the British Museum close by, should better suit the *Assistant Secretary—Excise Branch—of the Internal Revenue*, a *Teacher of Languages and Authoress of Educational and Other Works*, an *Authoress of Books— Chiefly Poems*, a *Salaried Companion to a Lady of Title*, and *Ladies with Income from Dividends*. Other than William's account of himself, which was official, the other descriptions he gave to the Census enumerator were not only amusing but indicated the high regard he had for the women in his household.

The residence at 56 Euston Square promised a safer, more suitable and spacious environment, with a whole upper floor for Aunt Eliza, who, unlike Aunt Charlotte, was a continuous resident. William took over the library in the evening to do his writing or just escape the crowd of ladies, Christina often doing the same during the day. Pleasant drawing and dining rooms were useful for making a proper impression on guests such as Mr. Ellis, Mrs. Julia Cameron, who came with a portfolio of photographs and yet another invitation to Freshwater, and Mr. Browning. A cozy parlor provided comfort for themselves or with other family like Henrietta Polydore, her father, and her mother when she visited from America. There was always welcome for close friends like the Heimanns, the Scots and Alice Boyd, and, as constant as a jilted man shouldn't be, Charles Cayley.

He had taken lodgings a few blocks away on Hunter Street, with the excuse of wanting to be near the British Museum, a desired destination for Christina, too, gratified mainly on fair-weather Saturdays when she might walk there with Maria. The expressed hope was that they would come upon the assistant Librarian, Edmund Gosse, in the Central Court's blue, cream, and gold domed Reading Room. He was a young, aspiring poet, his first published collection noticed in the PRB circle. Once Mama heard about him, he was soon in receipt of dinner invitations to Euston Square.

If Charles was at the museum, he could usually be found in the same vicinity as Mr. Gosse.

During the week, Christina might go by omnibus. She missed the freedom and purpose of traveling alone to and from the penitentiary, an activity age and increasing incidents of ill-health decided wasn't in her best interest. She continued some involvement through monetary contributions.

Maria made no secret of her suspicion that Christina's meetings with Charles at the museum weren't by chance. "He was seen greeting you on the steps."

"He arrived just as I did."

"Why deny it? Everyone knows he is your third brother."

Remember, if I claim too much of you, I claim it of my brother and my friend....

Charles' continued care of Christina and her family only deepened her affection for him. At least he was one male who didn't insist on managing her. As her association with Mr. Ellis faltered, she could hardly hide her frustration with blood-brotherly interference, less so with William, who had her creative and financial interests in mind, than Gabriel satisfying his impulses and agendas.

She was ready to take charge, writing to Mr. Ellis: *I apologize for my little book of nursery rhymes being bothersome to you.* She requested the manuscript be returned, giving him a way out and herself a chance that another British press and Boston's Roberts Brothers would take it on. Whether Mr. Ellis was hesitant to let it go or due to poor management, it was six months before *Sing-Song* was back in her hands, twenty-two poems missing from the manuscript. While asking him to recover them, calmer in her words than digestion, she took the opportunity to return his generous, unnecessary, and irritating compensation of £35.

The missing verses were only a brief obstruction to a fair copy of *Sing-Song* being reassembled for possible simultaneous publication in Britain and the United States. Roberts Brothers was still interested, engravers Thomas and Edward Daziel newly so and eager to work with George Routledge, who was about to publish Scotus' *Gems of Modern Belgium Art* and heeded his recommendation of Christina's work. Arthur Hughes was talked about for the illustrations and when he accepted the commission, she believed nothing could go wrong amidst so much promise.

Her middle-aged mind, heart, and soul were ready for success: stronger, stabler, especially as they were spiritually guided. Unfortunately, as had happened before, if never so radically, her body let her down. In her thirty-nineth summer, she was constantly out-of-sorts and lazy, as much symptoms of her nature as health, so hardly alarming. Trips to Folkestone with Mama and Maria did her good, although her constant weariness persisted. Christina had slightly more stamina through that autumn, enough to visit Charles' mother and sisters in Blackheath. She was cautiously cheerful at Christmas, only going out to fulfill a few more long-standing invitations, and to worship at Christ Church, where there was the new ornamentation of a large crimson cross positioned on the chancel arch. Rarely disappointed to stay home or avoid large parties, Christina was insistent that nothing cause her to miss joining family and friends at Tutor House on New Year's Day. Finally, she was witness to one of Gabriel's excessive dinners, set up in what he designated as the drawing room. It spanned the width of the house, its seven windows looking south and brightening the afternoon that might otherwise be shadowed by the opposite wall exhibiting Lizzie's artwork. Knowing the festivities would end beyond Christina's curfew for going out in the frigid night air, she stayed over in one of ten bedrooms on the third floor, next to William's usual one. Mama and Maria could have done the same, but they took a cab home without more explanation than that they hadn't brought their night things, an excuse they had made sure Christina didn't have. In respect to her reputation and health, Christina could only experience from on high the boisterous boyish behavior that went on into the early hours of the second day of 1871. According to William, such evening recreation was normal. After a late dinner, Gabriel was more in the habit of lounging in his museum-like sitting room than working in his poorly lit studio. Housemates Mr. Meredith and Mr. Swinburne and other male friends joined him until at least three or four in the morning, whether they wanted to or couldn't escape Gabriel's will. William complained that, between the resident parrot's mimicking, wood owl's hooting, and night owls talking, laughing, and arguing, "it was impossible to engage in anything productive, including sleep."

Once Christina went to bed, only one woman's voice was heard. Her cockney accent grated on Christina's nerves and her lack of shame was discomforting. Mama had let it be known that she would never have a housekeeper so free with her remarks and movement. Maria agreed but also with Gabriel, who thought the woman's East End malapropisms were amusing. In front of his mother and sisters, William was careful not to interact with the golden-haired, sturdy, insolent beauty more than was necessary. When he did, he was painfully polite. In contrast, Gabriel kept her at his beck and call, grabbed at her, and addressed her as "dear Elephant" so he might incite her indignation and return retort of "well, Rhino, you should talk." Scotus wanted everyone to believe she first attracted Gabriel's attention by cracking nuts with her teeth and spitting the shells at him. Fanny's version evolved from an accidental collision, so the pins fell out of her hair and it went down, Gabriel's that he "no sooner saw than approached her and loosened her locks to confirm their thickness and length." *I look at the crisp golden-threaded hair whereof, to thrall my heart, love twists a net ....*

"Ah 'tended 'is studio next day, where an' when 'e put me 'ead against the wall an' drew it for the calf picture."

Christina should have been grateful for Fanny Cornforth, who took better care of Gabriel than he did of himself and wasn't afraid to confront his destructive behaviors, such as mixing chloral with whiskey. She wasn't much of a housekeeper, horrible at handling a budget, and more likely to irritate the real staff than organize them, but she kept some semblance of a home for Gabriel. Tolerant of his boarders and guests, she was fond of his animal hoard, even willing to deal with its maintenance, the hens being her specialty. She made Gabriel laugh, emptied his mind and stirred his blood, and provided a muse that fleshed out his art without troubling his reality.

No one would ever describe Fanny as elusive. Unlike Lizzie and Jane Morris, frail, needy, effectively unavailable women whom Gabriel idealized, she was never hard to read. She made no secret of her enduring pursuit of Gabriel, not even when she wedded a Mr. Hughes, the brevity of their union corresponding to that of Gabriel's marriage. Fanny was ready and willing to move into Tutor House as soon as he did. So far, she had survived his moods, ever-increasing obsessions, and strange behaviors, ranging from the macabre in the retrieval of his poetry buried with Lizzie and seances to contact her to the comical in his consumption of half-a-dozen eggs and kidneys at breakfast, while a llama with a parrot on his back walked around the dining table upon which a wombat slept.

Although William reported raised voices, crashing utensils, and slamming doors followed by grudging silence, the necessity of Gabriel in Fanny's life had forgiven his scratching away her face from *Lady Lilith* and replacing it with the more refined one of would-be actress, Alice, also known as Alexa, Wilding.

***

Christina knew how it felt to have her appearance altered, in an even harsher way than had happened to Fanny, who would look out appealingly from more canvases yet. Mirrors would never again return loveliness to Christina.

"I see no difference in you." Charles either lied, which up until then she hadn't thought him capable of, or was blinded by a devotion that perplexed but still pleased her.

At times, Christina felt frantic, the curtain closing too soon. She wouldn't accept she was performing her final scene with so much left undone, unseen, unsaid, and, especially, unwritten, before her nursery rhymes were in print—in America, too—and she could surprise Charles with their dedication to his baby nephew. Having lived beyond her youth, survived the interruptions of love and other sicknesses, matured into measured accomplishment, and made it through the dark forest with a little income and integrity, growing old was an ending to look forward to.

She envisioned Maria and herself like Mama, Aunt Eliza, and Aunt Charlotte, living long, comfortable and content, sustained by their abilities, hard work, piety, frugality, income from dividends, and, not least, the benevolence of dear William. When he began thinking of his annual summer holiday, he insisted he wouldn't go if Christina was still so ill. Throughout the late winter and spring, besides neuralgia, migraines, nausea, abscesses, trembling, difficulty swallowing, speaking, even breathing, never-ending exhaustion, and disfiguring changes in her appearance, she also struggled with the guilt of preventing William from furthering his love affair with the Continent.

It was no good thinking Gabriel might step into his brother's dutiful shoes.

"He wasn't made to attend the sickroom," Christina quickly squashed the suggestion. "In any case, this summer will keep him away from London, in a pretty Gloucester manor with its even prettier mistress."

Christina was relieved William didn't bring up his last generous, ineffective effort to secure her an alternative to being a spinster sister.

She suspected Charles was relieved he hadn't married her. His lengthy bachelorhood hadn't prepared him to nurse her through long stretches in bed or, when Dr, Jenner told her to avoid stairs, lying endlessly on the drawing room sofa. The sacrifice to Charles' routine and work would probably have turned him from her as romantic rejection hadn't. Better that her intimate care was left to family and doctors and Charles attend her with books, ideas, and patience for when she might venture to the British Museum or the Botanical Gardens again.

She preferred his visits to exchanging letters with him while her hand trembled like an old woman's. Her once obsessively neat handwriting was hideous, almost a worse manifestation of whatever was wrong with her than her swelling neck, thinning hair, skin discoloration, and protruding eyes.

If only her heart was racing for Charles, for Scotus, for anyone, for any reason other than Dr. Jenner pronouncing she was gravely ill.

I have not sought Thee, I have not found Thee,
I have not thirsted for Thee:
And now cold billows of death surround me,
Buffeting billows of death astound me,-
Wilt Thou look upon, wilt Thou see

***

"The Italians want Papa's remains," William summarized what he read in a letter from Cousin Teo in Florence. "He thinks we should agree to have them exhumed and moved to Vasto."

"At last, Italy remembers him."

"No, no, Christina." Mama couldn't hide the panic in her voice. "I will not let them take him from me."

"Although I don't think the disinterment should take place," Christina hoped to calm her mother, "we should take pride in the proposal."

"Well, they can build a statue instead."

"Of course, Mama." William folded the letter.

A bath chair had also arrived that morning, a precious one with a slightly reclined, buttoned seat, the same dark blue leather used for its leg-stretch and footrest, its pivoting front wheel, like its two larger side ones and steering handle, painted red and outlined in gold. On loan from Longleat, it made Christina more embarrassed than she already was not to be able to walk. Unfashionable, weary, and damaged, she was an affront to its elegance. Disheveled, disappointed Charles, arriving in time to accompany her, only emphasized the anomaly of her rolling through Euston Square in such a pretentious way. Despite it being June, the weather as warm and sunny as Dr. Jenner recommended for her first venture outside in months, Charles tightly tucked Christina in with the Penkill tartan wool blanket Mama had suggested "just in case."

"Especially, to protect your neck and ears."

They didn't go far that afternoon, which was wise, considering Christina's frailty but, also, Charles', at least in pushing the chair she had no idea how to steer. Euston Square's public gardens were just across the road, enclosed by iron fencing, and cooled by damp grass and tall, broad-leafed plane trees, proving Charles had been wise to wrap Christina up.

"Please stop a moment." She closed her eyes to the touch of sunlight seeping through.

"Oh, dear. You're feeling unwell?"

"No. I'm imaging Regent's Park, where I'm sure the sun is strong and the flower beds flourishing."

Charles surprised her with a laugh. "Between my pitiful pushing and your precarious steering, we won't be finding out today."

Her own laughter was a little breathless yet relieving. "Yes. We are a pathetic pair at getting anywhere, aren't we?"

And sometimes I remember days of old when fellowship seemed not far to seek ....

Christina wanted to believe she was turning a corner with her health. She was encouraged by that companionable excursion a few steps from home, followed by a fortnight with Mama and the bath chair in Hampstead Heath. Most of August was for occasionally walking a little way to and on the sands at Folkestone. Until, just in time for William stopping there on his return from Europe, she was blinded by headaches, her throat swelled enormously, and a painful abscess formed in her mouth so she could barely eat and speak. She wore a full-head cap at all times to conceal her thinning hair from him.

Eventually, being at the coast only benefited her through a window, when she had the strength or, at least, assistance to get out of bed.

I'd rather look at the sea than myself.

She returned to London in early October. Dr. Jenner was at Balmoral in attendance to the Queen, so Dr. Fox prescribed digitalis for Christina's "poor circulation" and claimed "spasmodic nervous action" was the cause of her swollen neck, raspy voice, and difficulty breathing—sometimes to the point of passing out. The wine and brandy mixture he suggested her to sip all day only prolonged the migraines that, even among so many other discomforts, couldn't spoil her pleasure at the publication of *Sing-Song*, especially the illustrations Arthur Hughes had done for it.

She was also glad to be well enough to attend a dinner party at the Scots, until she was greeted by Scotus' silent shock, explained out loud by Gabriel who declared her "grown ten years older in a summer."

Gabriel has hurt me, himself even more. Christina was haunted by Lizzie's reasoning to never stop forgiving him.

"You must not get up." Maria lifted her sister's legs back onto the bed and under the covers.

Christina couldn't resist, for she was exhausted by her ongoing illness finally identified as *exophthalmic bronchocele* or Grave's disease, a thyroid disorder.

My life and youth and hope all run to waste. Is this my body cold and stiff and stark ...?

"And William sick, too?"

"I fear he will be if Gabriel is lost." Maria finished rewrapping the covering around Christina's throat, kissed her forehead, and, although it was after nine p.m., went out. The fly William had hired to let his family know Gabriel was in a coma was waiting to take his mother and older sister back with him to Roehampton.

Left under the care of Aunt Eliza, Christina asked for nothing but warm milk, for Princess, too, and prayers for Gabriel to remain on earth. She thought of the light in his eyes, the velvety resonance of his voice, his lounging walk, and the largeness of his embrace. He never minded if she tousled his hair, even to reveal it was receding, or stroked his beard up to his ears, and his moustache to feel the breath from his lips and nostrils. She saw him as she feared she never would again, negligently theatrical with his waistcoat buttoned up and sack-coat hanging to his knees. Sofa-posing with his head down and feet up, he was as easily elegant in corpulence as when he had been slim and agile.

There's blood between us, love, my love, there's father's blood, there's brother's blood, and blood's a bar I cannot pass.

His influence was never far from her. Whether she resisted or succumbed, she couldn't let go of its importance. Never before had it seemed so possible there would be no future to it.

For all night long I dreamed of you; I woke and prayed against my will, then slept to dream of you again. At length I rose and knelt and prayed.

"Oh, my dear." At daybreak Aunt Eliza found Christina lying on the floor, Princess stretched over her.

"Any word? No. Don't tell me." Instead, Christina said it herself, "He is gone."

"What? How do you know?"

"I don't. But expect the worst."

Aunt Eliza tried pulling Christina up, managing only to shift her to sitting.

"My legs are jelly," Christina explained her futile attempt to climb back into bed, wondering if she had permanently become an invalid like Mrs. Browning.

"Oh, goodness. Why didn't you ring for me, Miss Polidori?" The housekeeper, Mrs. Stevens, rushed into the room, shooed Princess away, squatted, sinched her arms around Christina's waist, and hoisted her onto the bed in herculean motion. "So very sorry, Miss Rossetti."

"Oh, no," Christina cried. "What have you heard?"

"Not that, Miss Rossetti."

"Thank you, Grace. Please get your girl to bring my niece some toast, jam, and tea." Aunt Eliza tactfully sent Mrs. Stephens away.

"I can't eat or drink anything, Auntie. I just want to know."

"You … we … will in the Good Lord's time." Aunt Eliza couldn't hide her tears either as she adjusted Christina's pillows and smoothed out her covers.

It was a day of failure. Failure to be where Mama, William, and Maria were. Failure to receive any news. Failure to have patience and faith. *To-day, while it is called to-day, kneel, wrestle, knock, do violence, pray; to-day is short, to-morrow nigh: why will you die? Why will you die?* Christina might have been asking herself, sensing Gabriel once more irresistibly reaching out to lead her where he chose to go. Such was the biggest failure of all her days, for, despite physical frailty, she should have had the spiritual strength to resist his influence and even guide him, if not back to life, then towards salvation.

The lantern may be placed so as to hide its light; such withholding amounts not to neutrality but to evil influence: the lantern which does not cast light casts shadow.

"Look who is here," was the interruption to Christina sitting up in bed silently bargaining with God.

"My dear mother and sister," she assumed, then, as her aunt shook her head, guessed, felt relieved. "Amelia."

"No. Miss Lucy Madox Brown."

Christina wasn't prepared to receive a visitor, a pewter brush long unused and left with her cap on a side table, her fresh nightgown and the sheet covering her sweaty. Aunt Eliza had only given into opening the room's window "a sliver."

Lucy must have tiptoed up the stairs, as was more compulsorily considerate than natural for her. She also kept her voice soft, was calm and conventional as she expressed her concern for Gabriel and explained that her father had gone to Roehampton.

"He is one to have around in a crisis. He will strengthen William, who must be so upset."

Lucy insisted on having the brush once Aunt Eliza had picked it up again.

"You must be gentle, Miss Brown. Christina's hair is no longer abundant like yours. Illness has made it as fragile as the rest of her."

"Of course, Miss Polidori. I know how to control my brushstrokes."

A glance indicated Aunt Eliza didn't approve Lucy's cleverness. "Make sure Christina puts her cap on, my dear."

"It's June, very warm, and you don't need it," Lucy muttered the moment she thought Aunt Eliza was out of earshot, compounding her disobedience by opening the window more. "When my lungs act up, a stuffy room makes me feel worse."

Christina had to admit that Lucy's attention to her breathing and, especially, hair was welcome. "Could you coil it like yours? It might prevent it from tangling."

Lucy rummaged the dressing table for pins. "How is poor Henrietta?"

It wasn't a question Christina expected from her. "Why do you ask?"

"I heard your cousin was quite ill."

"Oh … you mean Polydore."

"Who did you—ah. Rintoul." Lucy literally bit her bottom lip. "I prefer not to think about her."

"I remain Miss Rintoul's friend, she mine. As far as my dear cousin, she is consumptive, hopelessly so. Now Gabe is also at death's door, as I have been several times. Once I was convinced I would be the first Rossetti or Polidori of my generation to die."

"Let's not make it a race to that finish line." Having arranged Christina's hair, Lucy changed her mind about the cap, finding more pins to keep it in place. "Of course, like William, I believe the rewards to strive for are in life, not death."

Lucy mentioning William at any opportunity, especially as her concern and agnostic ally, supported what Aunt Eliza had speculated behind closed doors at Euston Square. Public gossip put the young poet John Payne in pursuit of attractive, artistic Lucy with her abundant auburn tresses, beaded jewelry, and bohemian clothes, despite what her stepsister Cathy described as her "bad temper because of an exacting will." Surely Mr. Payne was more of a contender than a heartbroken bachelor fourteen years Lucy's senior, who, although in appearance, character, accomplishments, and prospects was one of the best men Christina had ever known, was already devotedly—inescapably—responsible for a family with ever-increasing troubles.

"I will visit again tomorrow, if Mrs. Rossetti and Maria haven't returned yet," Lucy told Aunt Eliza on the landing outside Christina's bedroom.

"No need, my dear. I have help from my housekeeper and her girl, and my sister Charlotte is on her way from Longleat. Like your father, she will fortify us for whatever happens."

A few hours after Lucy left, Charles called and revealed that while at the museum, Edmond Gosse had informed him that Gabriel had suffered a serious apoplexy.

"My immediate thought was how distressed you must be," he spoke to Christina from her room's doorway.

"Did Mr. Gosse say whether my brother had gained consciousness at all?"

"He approached me hoping I might know more."

Aunt Eliza must have urged Charles into the hallway, for there was an emptiness where he had stood, and their brief conversation was barely audible.

"He agreed to go to Dr. Hake's," her aunt confirmed what Christina thought she had heard. "I gave him the cab fare, also enough for his return. At least there are hours of daylight left."

Those hours didn't bring Charles back, and, in the darkness of her nature and the night, Christina assumed it was because the news was, at best, not hopeful. Charles knew he wouldn't be able to console her. His cowardice when it came to emotions was one of the confidential considerations that had dissuaded Christina from marrying him. She had seen and avoided the possibility of being wedded to dispassion like Effie Gray.

Even Mama, for all her coolness and pragmatism, had given feelings precedence over sense in her choice of husband. "*Cara Francesca moglie mia,*" was Papa's greeting when Mama had been away or just out for the day teaching. His endearments made her smile and welcome his kiss, even on her lips, and now, Christina suspected, sometimes, in remembering, were the reason for her tears.

Charles didn't think to sweeten Christina in a lover's way, only to shyly call on a friend and engage her mind and a little of her time. In that way, he was more constant than it was likely a husband would be.

In my experience, such a virtuous man is rare, William had once written in his attempt to convince Christina that Charles wasn't merely her last chance to escape spinsterhood but her best. She might have had an argument with Charles' irreligiosity, but not with his character or, even inhibited as its expression was, his heart. The problem was with hers.

Perhaps she had witnessed too much wantonness, untouched by Pre-Raphaelite libertarianism but not unaffected. It awakened her passions, wooed her *to the outer air, ripe fruits, sweet flowers, and full satiety* … and proved the danger of them: *pushing horns and clawed and clutching hands.* It showed her who she was and yet could never be.

***

> *So be it, O my God, Thou God of truth:*
> *Better than beauty and than youth*
> *Are Saints and Angels, a glad company;*
> *And Thou, O Lord, our Rest and Ease,*
> *Art better far than these.*
> *Why should we shrink from our full harvest?*

The second night of losing Gabriel was less about despair than accepting God's will. Christina prayed as she fell asleep and each time she woke until, window-light splashing across her bed to the notebook on the side table, she was tired of sleeping.

Mrs. Stephens brought her breakfast and the information that "Miss Polidori" had gone to church, which also told Christina that it was Sunday. While Aunt Eliza was out, Charles arrived with a written message from William, which was full of reassurances, not based on an improvement in Gabriel's condition but, as Christina understood, a refusal to give their brother up to a life unwisely and unluckily spent.

Or was there a worst consequence than Gabriel's death, what William referred to as *a fearful alternative*?

"What do you think he means?"

Without Aunt Eliza to take over the delivery, Charles had entered Christina's room and handed her William's note, immediately backing up to a respectful distance from her bed.

"Ah ... perhaps ... some disability?" His downcast eyes suggested he knew more than he would say.

"Physical or mental?"

"Well. Possibly both."

"Will you wait and take my reply? I'll be quick. My hand is steadier, or was before these last few days."

"Of course. Mrs. Stephens has offered me lunch. That will allow the time you need."

"As long as you chew well, and drink at least two cups of tea," Christina jested, to her own surprise, let alone Charles'.

Shortly after Aunt Eliza returned from church, Aunt Charlotte arrived in a carriage borrowed from Longleat. As was also usual, she filled the house with her positivity, reinforced by Mr. Madox Brown, who had promised Christina's mother and sister he would call at 56 Euston Square.

"Inhalation of ammonia succeeded in making Gabriel vomit, strong coffee and massage stimulated his circulation."

"Is that normal treatment for a stroke, Mr. Brown?"

"Dr. Hake … thought to try it."

"But is Gabe now conscious?"

"Not yet to speak or open his eyes, but this morning he did squeeze your mother's hand."

***

Christina had guessed before Maria told her what she wasn't supposed to know, and Mama must never. If it had been questioned whether Lizzie accidentally took an overdose of laudanum, there was no doubt Gabriel had deliberately swallowed an entire bottle of the tincture.

"At least you could go to him."

"Oh, Chrissy. Despite the reason why, you are fortunate you could not."

Christina not only heard Maria's weariness but saw it in the puffiness of her face and bent of her upper spine. Mama had gone straight to her room, having also not slept for over two days.

"How fortunate he was at Dr. Hake's. But why was he?"

"Concern for his delusional state, especially as Gabe thought Tutor House, everything and everyone in it, was turning on him. As a doctor and friend, Thomas thought he would be safer away from it. He couldn't stay here in such a disturbed state."

"If only I wasn't ill, he could have." Christina knew it would have been insanity. "He had laudanum. Since it killed Lizzie, he never used it."

"Until he wished to follow her. He must have hidden it on himself." Marie hesitated. "Or …."

"What?"

"No. I must not make accusations."

"Fanny?"

"William said she was alone with Gabe briefly before they took him to Dr. Hake's, supposedly to help convince him to go."

"She wouldn't have given it to him. She hates his use of chloral." Christina remembered an argument she had witnessed, Fanny alleging that he was killing himself. "No matter how he got it, why did he take it?"

"Mr. Buchanan's attack on his poems, and Gabe thinking—irrationally—Mr. Browning agreed with the criticism. Also, his remorse over disturbing Lizzie's grave, and his obsession with getting in touch with her."

Shall I meet other wayfarers at night? Those who have gone before.

"Seances."

"Yes."

"In them, Fanny is culpable." Christina could feel her face flush. "She claims to be clairvoyant."

"Too many around Gabe have humored him with them. Even our William."

"Too much chance for imposture, evil choices, and, not least, they … are … opposed by the church."

"Calm yourself." Maria caressed her sister's shoulders to persuade her to lie back. "You know I agree with you. But, be assured, William is merely entertained, not influenced, by them."

"One good consequence of his skepticism."

"How different our brothers are." Maria moved towards the door. "At least I know one will always be there for Mama and you."

CHAPTER THIRTY-FIVE

Moving along in a punt ably and amiably managed by Dr. Hake's son, George, Christina couldn't help but drift back to holidays at Holmer Green. She felt healed and hopeful gliding slowly past the golden-green banks, lacey weeds, and leaning trees that lined the Isis, how locals identified their piece of the River Thames just a few miles from its source. Mama, her face shaded and shaped by a green-ribboned straw hat Jane Morris had left behind, may have been reminiscing similarly.

Christina pointed out swans in the bullrushes her mother hadn't noticed, and, as if on cue, an adult pair glided into the open water followed by an almost orderly cluster of cygnets.

Not for the first time, Christina reflected on her mother's endurance that made her a saint but, as her reaction to Gabriel's crisis had revealed, also desperately human. Mama wanted him sent to an asylum. Maria and William, for the reason they thought their mother didn't know of, agreed. Christina was feverishly opposed to the idea.

Fortunately, Lucy's faith in her father was proven. Mr. Madox Brown calmly intervened by putting aside his own affairs and watching over Gabriel day and night, first at Cheyne Walk and then at a patron's house in Perthshire until Scotus arrived to oversee Gabriel's recovery and relapses. Even then Mr. Brown wasn't relieved of the situation, for William had been a physical and emotional wreck since nearly losing his brother and needed help managing Gabriel's finances before it was too late to ward off creditors. In those dark days, as in others, despite the recklessness of Gabriel's actions and restlessness of his loyalties, a few true friends navigated his moods, and forgave his most offensive behavior, because, as Christina knew too well, it was impossible to fall out of love with him.

Sitting in that pretty boat with nothing to do but slip through sparkling water, watch George live up to Gabriel's praise that the young man "kept everything going," and lose all sense of time, especially as it was a thief, Christina could finally enjoy going nowhere. Mr. Morris was right; Kelmscott was heaven on earth. It offered serenity, an oasis outside of the world, and immortality in the rhythms of its nature. It belonged to those who had eyes for its beauty and faith in its purpose. It required a willingness for transition. For Christina, it meant emerging from the self-absorption of severe sickness to enjoy simple pleasures again.

She and her mother had been on many journeys together, but one to a remote corner of south-west Oxfordshire rivaled the significance of all, except Italy, which was as necessary but much less leisurely. They were as close as they had ever been, in spirit and heart and a small boat, their feet side by side in opposite directions, their silence filled with water lapping and the song of swallows.

Eventually, the punt passed beyond a long stretch of willows weeping. *Have you no purpose but to shadow me beside this rippled spring?* George brought the ride to a stop where the riverbank met a meadow of hay-harvesters choreographed for toil, mostly women looking lovely in their plain cotton dresses and bonnets. Mama insisted George share in the basketed snack of buttered bread, strawberries, and cider. As was true for most of the outing, there was more observation than conversation, and it was well rewarded.

A singing lark rose toward the sky,
Circling he sang amain;
He sang, a speck scarce visible sky-high,
And then he sank again.

Back at the landing, George respectfully guided first Mama then Christina out of the boat. Leaving him to return the punt to the boathouse, mother and daughter, arm in arm, walked a wildly hedged foot-and-cart path past a farmyard with thatched barns, stabling, and a dovecot to reach a many-gabled house. Like the wall and other structures surrounding, it had been long ago constructed from local rubble-stone shaded gray with suggestions of sunlight in its veins.

The gate they approached was opened by Gabriel wearing a brown work shirt overhanging moleskin trousers. He held a bouquet of yellow Calendula or *the marigold, that goes to bed wi'th' sun, and with him rises, weeping.*

"I would give them to you, dear Mama, but it will be hard to get away with picking more. I believe old Philip counts them daily."

Mama slipped the basket off Christina's arm, unable to disguise what her hand had really been reaching for.

"Now the marsh ones are finished, and the painting isn't, these will have to substitute," he answered what hadn't been questioned.

"As his niece is posing, he might forgive you."

"No, Chrissy. I believe he thinks more of a marigold's bloom than of little Annie's." Gabriel turned and walked towards the house with the long-term limp caused, if not by a stroke, his lying stiffly on one hip while being in a coma nearly a year before.

"But would you dare to pick any of these?" Christina referred to the standard roses redolently cascading in white, pinks, and reds along both sides of the cobbled walkway to Kelmscott Manor's front entrance.

"Not if I value my life."

Barking was an immediate distraction from Gabriel's insensitivity. A black and tan terrier bounded out of the vegetable garden, physically and vocally pursued by an almost-grown girl clad in easy clothing to match her manner.

She caught the dog and pulled some greenery out of his mouth. "Bad boy, Dizzy. Now I must lie about who dug up cook's carrots."

"Blame Turvey." George came through the gate. "He'll get away with it, being the master's mutt. Now let's find Bess before we have to get Turvey in more trouble."

"Bess is Georgy's newest, a collie mix from Scotland." Gabriel realized his mother and sister were wondering. "She's a little wild, so he keeps her out of the house, why you haven't met her yet." He snapped his fingers and Dizzy was at his side. "Good thing Morris isn't here. He hates dogs."

"And Janey?" Christina knew she shouldn't ask.

"It would be a very good thing if she were here." Gabriel turned from saying more. "Come on, little Annie. This bouquet is drooping, and I want this painting finished. In a few days, Miss Wilding is coming for some serious work."

***

Annie Cunley from Kelmscott Village had been hired to help Mary, the cook and housekeeper Jane Morris had, like a hat, left behind. Annie was also employed as Gabriel's latest muse, at least since mid-May when he had sent apple blossoms to Euston Square and mentioned her in the accompanying letter.

He claimed Annie wasn't hesitant to pose for him and had no one to insist she should be, not even her uncle. In those parts, concerns for young ladies focused on hay lofts, woodland walks, and servants' attic rooms, not artists' studios.

Gabriel seemed to relish repeating the girl's bold reasoning that he was "too old n' cranky" for her to worry about.

"Since you bin here, Miss R, you do keep a good eye on him."

Christina had already spent a few afternoons in Gabriel's studio set up in the Tapestry Room through a bedroom and up three stairs on the second floor of the north wing. Blaming heavy, faded Flemish wall hangings woven with the grim story of Samson, and insisting all windows and doors were kept closed, Gabriel called the space claustrophobic. Admitting only that he didn't want to deny his still convalescing sister the tonic of country air, he allowed her to pull the thick curtains aside and push the creamy mullioned windows open to midsummer, so Christina experienced it as one of the largest, airiest spaces in the house.

George offered his observation that Gabriel shut himself indoors more often when Janey and the girls weren't there.

He also gets more done, Christina assumed. It was no secret Mrs. Morris was inspiring, but without her the obsessed artist was more likely to transform visions into masterpieces. Christina was encouraged by the stack of blank canvases, the also new — to her — painting case and easel, and the piles of old drawings he meant to rework, finally finish, and offer for sale.

Sometimes Gabriel was in the mood to talk, even to ask Christina's opinion about his art or poetry. She hoped he would, rather than wonder what was going on with her writing, nothing more to report than a request for *Uphill* to be reprinted in an anthology put out for English readers on the Continent. She was happy just to be with him, even if meant quietly sitting on a buttoned chaise lounge that served as a bed for the little sleep he managed.

Christina didn't intend to chaperone Annie modeling for a painting Gabriel wavered between titling "Spring Marybuds" or "The Bower Maiden," until she suspected both subject and artist needed to be watched. Annie's scowling might also be because Gabriel made her wear an oversized wool hood and stand in a reaching position for an hour, sometimes longer, without a break. He hadn't sketched the painting first, but depended on direct depiction "from nature," or, in other words, poor Annie looking as if, despite the sweat stain under her lifted arm, she was frozen in the time it took to place a jar of golden flowers onto a fireplace mantel.

"Is that Princess?" On closer inspection of the painting, Christina saw it included a cat playing with a ball of yarn.

"It is if you recognize her."

"No. That's old Tom from the farm —"

"Done for today, little Annie." Gabriel also dismissed her with a wave of his hand.

"Good. I'm suffocating under this thing." The girl pulled off the head covering, her loose hair abundant, long, and copper-colored like Lizzie's. Then so was Fanny's and Alexa Wilding's, Jane's darkly dramatic mane, well represented around the room, the exception.

Christina moved quickly to pick up the hood from the floor and return to her brother who was grumbling incoherently at the work on his easel. "You have made good progress," she remarked in hopes he wouldn't need more of Annie to finish it.

***

Miss Wilding arrived just as the rain did, steadily at first, on and off for the next few days. Christina needed somewhere besides Gabriel's studio for remaining indoors and joined her mother in the austere parlor Mr. Morris had personally painted sage green, information the housekeeper, Mary, thought everyone should know. Mama liked to read, write letters, or do embroidery when there was enough natural light. She chose the bird-patterned armchair rather than the "punishment" of a 17th century cushionless oak chair with a book box it was said Mrs. Morris favored.

Mama's catnaps persuaded Christina to indulge in her own on the daybed, so they were both refreshed enough to dine at eight in the Old Hall with Gabriel, George, and Miss Wilding.

Through the years, Christina had become acquainted with the dressmaker and aspiring actress through Gabriel's revisited *Regina Cordium, The Bower Meadow, Venus Verticordia, The Beloved,* and *Dante's Dream,* and from what was said about her, flattering when it came to her decency, nature, and physical attributes, if not her intellect. Even Gabriel, who was fond of her, admitted she wasn't bright.

"That makes her an ideal model."

Miss Wilding had come to Kelmscott to be a garlanded woman, *La Ghirlandata,* a new painting that besides flowers involved a harp and child angels. Gabriel hoped May Morris would sit for it later in the summer. He reassured his sister and mother that Miss Wilding was suitable company for them.

"Is that why you haven't invited Fanny to Kelmscott?" Christina really didn't need to ask.

"Quite impossible to."

Christina was relieved.

"Don't expect to be excited by Miss Wilding. I've never had a real conversation with her. She waits to be questioned and vaguely replies. I've never known anyone with such a lack of curiosity. Perhaps that's why she is so patient."

Gabriel captured Miss Wilding in vibrant colors, with flawless features and ethereal possibilities. As with other women he idealized, in person she was recognizably imperfect. Her hair was more brown than red, low on her forehead just as Gabriel illustrated it. Her neck was long when stretched, a move only for posing and on stage, but too thick to be graceful. Her nose nicely divided the symmetry of her face, her ears were a little large, her chin shorter and squarer than expected, her mouth not resembling cupid's bow but a childish pout more delicate than Gabriel's. Her crystal blue eyes were as hypnotizing as in the paintings and would inspire anyone to see her as more beautiful than she was.

Christina chided herself for critiquing Miss Wilding's looks, even if just to herself. Mama, who usually disapproved Gabriel's "off-the-street women," didn't doubt this one's respectability. She seemed most reassured by reports and finally her own experience of Miss Wilding's normality.

"If she bores Gabriel, at least she doesn't drive him mad."

Alexa, as she wished to be addressed, suited Christina's and Mama's holiday in Kelmscott, her quiescence accommodating its goals of rest, recuperation, and, belying her ambitions, lack of drama. Gabriel sleeping all morning and George "keeping things going" allowed the ladies uncomplicated, unhurried breakfasting. When it wasn't raining, Alexa joined Mama and Christina for walks in the gardens, which, along with the house, were sheltered all around by tall elms and walls that backed hollyhocks and held up ornamental grape vines, honeysuckle, and roses. Hedged sections took them along stone paths between herbs and vegetables, under a wisteria-laden pergola, across lawns for Mary's daisies, clover, croquette, and taking tea outside. They might also venture into orchards of forming apples and plums, and through a medieval meadow of seeding grasses, poppies, cornflowers, scabious, and dianthus.

… in the midst of the garden a lawn of very fine grass, so green it seemed nearly black, coloured with perhaps a thousand kind of flowers ….

Christina's favorite spot was dominated by an ancient Mulberry tree, its crown dense and sprawling, dangling clusters of berries beginning to blacken, its largest branch, which children had probably climbed and swung on, sturdily propped. Two rustic chairs offered a chance for rest. Christina insisted Mama and Alexa take advantage of them, while she leaned back against the tree's short gray ridged trunk and listened to the life in it.

"Oh." She was startled by something falling onto the letter she had begun to unfold.

"Not bad news?" Mama was too ready to assume.

"Look." Christina carefully picked the tiny, woolly, wiggling eavesdropper off the paper to show her mother and Alexa before placing it on a branch she could reach.

> "Brown and furry
> "Caterpillar in a hurry,
> "Take your walk
> "To the shady leaf, or stalk,
> "Or what not,
> "Which may be the chosen spot."

"A message from your muse," Mama sighingly spoke, "to write more like *Sing-Song*."

"Yes." Alexa surprised them with understanding the reference. "Gabriel gave me a copy," she explained.

"And the rhymes all my own." Christina was glad to make her mother smile and Alexa confused.

"Dear caterpillar ...
"No toad spy you,
"Hovering bird of prey pass by you;
"Spin and die,
"To live again a butterfly."

Alexa clapped as if imitating wings floating into the sky.

Mama didn't seem to notice. "So is William ... and his party ... back?"

"Since the sixth. He is—"

"Not ill?" Mama turned to Alexa. "He has worried so about Christina and been quite unwell over Gabriel's ... issues."

"No. On the contrary, he's," Christina paused, immediately suspicious of how William had described himself, "blissfully happy."

"He does enjoy his travels on the Continent." Mama knew that was not the full explanation. "Lucy."

Christina had read far enough to agree with a nod. *A week ago, at Basle, I proclaimed my feelings to her. She returns them and, despite our substantial age difference, accepts my proposal with her father's approval. I am only just now letting you know, after his reply was finally delivered yesterday. Lucy and I are engaged.*

"Of course," Mama folded the letter immediately she finished reading it. "It was Mr. Madox Brown's plan all along. Why he wanted Lucy to go on holiday with William."

"Also, with the Scotts and Alice Boyd," Christina explained to Alexa.

"Will you write to Lucy? When we return to London, I will have the Browns to dine with us."

"Yes, of course, Mama. Is there anything you would like me to tell her?"

"Only that she made the right decision. Our William will be a devoted husband to her."

"I wish I wasn't a dozen years her senior. Still, I can be her dear sister and friend."

Mama slowly rose from the garden seat, a hand pressed high on her chest as though she was having trouble breathing.

"Mrs. Rossetti, are you all right?" Alexa stood and reached out.

Mama stepped towards the consolation of her youngest daughter, instead. "We have lost him. We have lost our best benefactor."

"Our guardian angel." Christina huddled her mother, believing more than ever she couldn't be without her.

CHAPTER THIRTY-SIX

Life, and the world, and mine own self, are changed.

Maria had made the sacrifice of living in the world for many years. The Anglican Sisters of All Saints wasn't a surprising step for her as William Rossetti's household outgrew space for a widow and spinsters.

William's proposal to Lucy gave his eldest sister permission to finally wed Christ. Maria made no secret of feeling her existence for the good of her family would be redundant once another woman took custody of the house in Euston Square and the man who leased it. In terms of scholarship, Maria's contribution to the Rossetti obsession, *A Shadow of Dante*, had been completed and published. She was more than ready to confine her intellect, heart, soul, and sense of belonging to holy service.

A shadow may win the gaze of some who never looked upon the substance.

Since before she was twenty, Maria had been drawn to becoming a nun. Flirtations with Charles Collins and John Ruskin were but fleeting distractions along her path towards a single destination of spiritual devotion. Although at times unbearably bereft of Moony's companionship, Christina was sympathetic, in awe, even envious of her sister's certainty of divine vocation.

Maria agreed to Lucy sketching her as a Novitiate, her habit hiding the scaly red patches from the erysipelas she suffered on and off, but not the rotund cheeriness of her cheeks, the blackness of her eyes, and bossiness of her nature more diplomatic than it once was.

"Now, my dear, not wishing to frustrate your artistic inclinations, you may show my white hood, cap strings, and collar, but no cross on my breast. I'm only allowed a large, plain, black one hanging from my girdle, too low to be seen in your drawing."

The drawing was never developed beyond simple penciled lines and shadowing. Maria was unable to display it in her convent room, yet there was hardly a moment for Lucy to wonder what to do with it, Mama wanting it as soon as she saw it.

Writing from Kelmscott, Gabriel was the last in the family to learn of Maria's decision *to wear a coal-shuttle and umbrella for the rest of her life,* his flippant remarks leading to more serious ones that belied his being in her company no more than twice a year. *How can we bear such a loss? Along with Mama's, Maria has the healthiest thinking in our family. William's is close behind while Christina's and mine are all over the place and so nowhere. But our Moony will still appear at Christmas, won't she?*

After a last supper before Maria's induction, it wasn't until New

Year's Day that she appeared at Euston Square again. The All Saints Rule allowed one personal outing each week, so, from then on, she tried to come for lunch on Saturdays. She claimed she would never have entered the Order if doing so meant a total separation from family. Christina was glad of Maria's fairly regular visits yet distressed by them. There had been many partings over the years for holidays, finances, and convalescing, but never the bidding goodbye over and over to a shared life as they would never know it again.

> *My name begins with W.*
> *And hers begins with L.,-*
> *With details I'll not trouble you,*
> *But I love her pretty well.*

Lucy put off the wedding for nine months, but not the changes her in-laws were expected to naturally accept. Aunts Eliza and Charlotte fared better than their sister and niece, no question whether they should find somewhere else to live, for immediately on the engagement, 56 Euston Square's third floor was designated as private living quarters for Mr. and Mrs. Rossetti-to-be.

"Lucy knows I won't hear of other than my mother and sisters remaining in the house and under my care. Of course, my dear, sweet wife must have a room for a studio."

Lucy may have echoed William's insistence, but Christina couldn't shake the nagging doubt that such an arrangement would overcome differences of age, disposition, interests, sociability, and those yet to be discovered, let alone the argument William's side of spiritual skepticism would finally have feminine support for.

Even before the experiment was legalized in St. Pancras Register Office it faltered, and not because of religion.

"My coughing in the back parlor has never been an issue before."

It was one thing to have a home to hide in, quite another to have to hide in one's home. Christina thought Lucy knew the ongoing circumstances of her health that improved but relapsed, too, regardless of whether a dinner party was planned.

"It seems I shouldn't have been anywhere near the dining room."

"It's a trifle, Chrissy. Lucy had never heard you cough like that before."

"And claims it upset her—your—guests. At least, they were spared the worst noise I might make."

Christina could tell William struggled not to smile and show his sense of irreverence in a way she could appreciate. "I realize she isn't used to our sedate life. From what I've heard, Fitzroy Square is often bubbling over with people." She hesitated to ask why Lucy, not yet officially the angel of William's house, didn't have parties at her father's. "So there's bound to be some unpleasant sounds."

"Perhaps if you slept with Mama in the first floor parlor."

Christina temper was hardly soothed by William forgetting the difficulty she had going up stairs during a recurrence of her heart condition and throat swelling.

There was a better remedy, which, because of her nerves and other weaknesses, Christina decided to explain in a letter, no stamp necessary. She didn't want to offend William's continued and commendable concern for her and their mother but had to accept that Lucy must take precedence as his "love paramount." *Mama also thinks we should move out. We have sufficient income between us for, as you know, we don't require luxury. We will share a house with Mama's dear sisters, so we will have cheerful, considerate company. Let us know what you judge best.*

Only after the letter was sent did Christina realize she had offered William the option of deciding. A man who valued his reputation as one of his word and loyalty, he wouldn't willingly displace his mother and sisters. Yet, inadvertently, he had done so the moment he had declared his love with the appropriate intention of ending his bachelorhood. As the wedding grew closer, Lucy found fault with William's residence and its other occupants. Unlike Christina, she wasn't amused by Aunt Eliza answering her complaint about the drains being slow and smelly with "in my day, such things were left up to the Almighty." Lucy either didn't realize or care that her assessment of the furniture, curtains, and rugs as dingy was insulting. She didn't hold back her obvious irritation with the colorless clothing, pious practices, lethargic days, and quiet evenings—except for coughing and other sickly, senescent sounds—of her future female housemates, further evidence of the folly of William's well-meaning. Lucy threatened to replace Mrs. Stevens with a "real" cook after the honeymoon, and wanted more than two servants, wondering why the house-wide bell system for summoning them wasn't fully utilized. Anticipating post nuptial consequences Christina might look forward to, Lucy wondered how she would manage two flights of stairs to her and William's private rooms when she was pregnant.

"Adjustments will once more be made," she said with a certainty that whatever she wanted she would get.

After receiving Christina's letter and again insisting she and their mother remain at Euston Square, William decided diplomacy was having nothing more to say on the matter.

Mama wasn't surprised. "Even the most honorable man is cowardly, which is why women must use their own minds and be prepared."

The house was soon topsy-turvy, invaded by plasterers and painters, new carpets laid, and curtains hung in the most visible rooms, in others cleaned, as were all the chimneys. Furniture, where it would affect its new resident, was rearranged according to Lucy's instructions. The drains were improved by intervention of the landlord, and, although William and his bride-to-be wouldn't admit it, a much greater Master. For the newlyweds' third floor apartment, Gabriel offered furniture from Cheyne Walk they might need or merely liked. He was also generous in his offer to paint Lucy's portrait when she had time to sit for it, perhaps to make up for not attending the wedding eve festivities at Fitzroy Square.

"After these two years of being mostly away from London, I'm not up to every bore I know swooping down on me."

"You can take refuge in my—"

"Wish not to be there either?"

What once would have been a pleasant understanding to amuse him and Christina, weighed heavily on his shoulders. "Really, Chrissy. I mainly don't want to meet up with Swinburne, and you will not avoid him. I'm the one going to hell and yet you tolerate his abominable ways."

"He's on his best behavior with me."

"In your unofficial cloister. William claims you paste strips of paper over the offensive bits of Algie's poems."

Gabriel also skipped the register office and was worried guests at the wedding breakfast wouldn't smile on him. Christina and Mama assured he would be among family and true friends glad to see him after his illness and distance. They weren't certain their persuasion had succeeded until he arrived, gently greeted by Uncle Henry and Cousin Henrietta, the Heimanns, Letitia Scott, Alice Boyd, and Charles Cayley, more robustly by Scotus and the triumphant father of the bride. Lucy's half-sister Cathy, now Mrs. Hueffer, was cordial to Gabriel, while her half-brother Nolly seemed to avoid him. Finally, the Morrises showed up and it was as if Jane, in costume, colors, complexion, slenderness, and dark billowing hair, stepped out of a Gabriel painting she had posed for. *This is her picture as she was: it seems a thing to wonder on, as though mine image in the glass should tarry when myself am gone.*

She did smile on Gabriel, but he couldn't hold onto pleasure for long.

Neither could Jane, her husband's grouchy grumblings indicating he didn't want to be there. Maria had taken that day as the week's home visit and like Mr. Morris hung back, although to be discreet not sulky.

He must not have recognized her or just discounted her draped in white and gray, so little of her face visible.

Last to arrive, the Morrises were the first to leave, so Maria could tattle like she had on Gabriel and Christina when they were children.

"'I don't care for either WMR or LMB and they don't care for me,'" she tried to imitate Mr. Morris' gruff voice. "'I refuse to throw away hours of my life grinning at others grinning at those two,'" she hesitated and made the sign of the cross, "'boobies.'"

"It seems the author of *The Earthly Paradise* does not belong there."

"Poor Janey slapped his arm, Gabe." Maria continued to disclose, "But I think he was actually pleased when he realized who had overheard."

Gabriel chuckled. "Maybe he assumed you'd taken a vow of silence."

"It need go no further." Maria tucked her hands in opposite sleeves.

"Oh, Will. You won't tell Lucy what he said."

"Well, Chrissy, we promised to tell each other everything."

"Now that's where a vow of silence should figure in." Gabriel threw his arm around his brother's shoulder. "Oh, how can so old a bloke be so naïve?"

William hung onto Gabriel's embrace. "Maybe … I'll leave off … 'boobies.'"

Everyone but Maria laughed, her cheeks rising and reddening. Looking around at her siblings, Christina wanted to believe they all realized how little they had changed when it came to their bond of blood and destiny. The storms and the calms were in the same vicinity again, making for an interesting sky that brought the past into view before it disappeared into the future. They could have as easily played *bout rimés* or chess or acted out Shakespeare as remember it was William's wedding day.

"Without God's blessing." Mama was further distressed as she waited with her sisters for a cab to take them to live elsewhere.

"Earlier, Will, I was thinking you and Lucy looked cool as cucumbers. But it's obvious the heat is on." Gabriel was the first to notice his sister-in-law, who had already changed from bride to wife, standing apart from a family reunion that, according to her frown, appeared impenetrable.

Christina, remorseful after feeling glad for Lucy's discomfort, nudged William to go to her. *What are brief? Today and tomorrow. What are frail? Spring blossoms and youth.*

"My darling wife. You must be tired." William pulled Lucy clumsily into his arms. "Off to the Continent tomorrow. No one will mind if you go upstairs to rest. We have a long journey ahead of us."

O Lord Jesus Christ, the Bridegroom, I entreat Thee, give us all grace to hear Thy Voice; that married persons may love Thee in each other, and each other in Thee; and that the unmarried, keeping themselves from sin, may love Thee without let or hindrance throughout time and through eternity.

Annus Domini, the earthly years left for the Lord: the result of loss, recovery, and the threat of relapse, of looking into the soul and scripture for inspiration. Vanity was no longer viable, ambition exhausting, family fragmented, no one place to call home except for the ultimate destination of heaven. *This world is not my orchard for fruit or my garden for flowers. It is however my only field whence to raise a harvest.* The doctors diagnosed Christina's heart weakened and said she shouldn't overexert herself. Her faith insisted it had been strengthened and she must use it to its full. *I take my heart in my hand. I shall not die, but live. All that I have I bring. All that I am I give.*

Maria was the example she followed as far as she could without leaving life alongside her mother. Christina wore the habit of writing more religiously than ever, risking the opinion of those who wanted her to be a clever, capricious, even controversial Rossetti rather than a contemplative one. Lucy would have preferred her to be so.

Wandering without somewhere settling to return to was likely causing Mama's colds and bloody noses and aggravating Christina's own health issues.

Eastbourne was helpful for holidays and a healing stay at All Saints Hospital, where they were when Dr. Heimann died suddenly, and Lucy miscarried her honeymoon baby. Back in London, Bloomsbury Square was for escaping to and remembering how harmonious a household with aunts Eliza and Charlotte had been—and might be again.

Gabriel invited Mama and Christina for a second time to Kelmscott Manor, a trip planned, put on hold, and never to be because he dismissed all the servants, verbally attacked some local fishermen, and abruptly left heaven on earth forever.

An abundant supply of black-bordered stationary was needed for other departures. Cousin Henrietta finally succumbed to consumption; although anticipated, a difficult bereavement for Christina. *Darling little Cousin, with your thoughtful look … Tender, happy spirit, innocent and pure.* Lucy, not yet recovered from mourning the unborn, lost her nineteen-year-old half-brother Nolly to blood poisoning. *Upon the landscape of his coming life, a youth high—gifted gazed, and found it fair: the heights of work, the floods of praise, were there.*

At least, Christina's creative fire didn't die, the bellows of Mr. Macmillan's renewed interest blowing few and far between sparks into bursts that might flame steadily again. He considered reprinting her two previous poetry collections as one and, eventually, took a small volume of prose pieces, even more in the style of Lewis Carroll's *Alice* with Arthur Hughes' illustrations, from *Nowhere* to somewhere more pointedly named.

Dear Mr. Macmillan. The second choice must be the title, instigated by your remark — to one in my circle and approved by the rest — that my young heroines constantly meet "speaking likenesses" of themselves.

Only heirs to Gabriele Rossetti's temperament could understand the joy Christina found in sibling sparring over her book's title, especially with Gabriel, who regained his sanity long enough to out-argue her, helped by Maria, whose worldly-wise opinion could still be tempted.

CHAPTER THIRTY-SEVEN

"You must return for Christmas." While waiting for the train to take Christina and Mama back to London, Gabriel persisted with his preoccupation from the night before. "And bring the dear aunties. And convince Moony to come."

"I doubt she will—"

"Now she's parted with her gray hair?"

Christina hoped her facial expression didn't acknowledge his sarcasm. "Now she is fully professed."

"But what of family affections?"

Mama wasn't silent although she didn't speak—she couldn't. While she struggled with the lack of faith in her son, after ten blustery days on the Sussex coast, she also contended with a persistent cough.

Before Christina stepped up into the train car, she turned back to Gabriel and lifted herself to kiss his cheek. "Don't forget to feed the garden birds."

"I'll make sure," he removed her hand from his shoulder as though irritated, "that George sees to the feathered tribe."

The last three months of the year were hardly the ideal time to be at the seaside. Gabriel expected his insistence would bring visitors to property he had rented on the outskirts of Bognor Regis. Aldwick Lodge was near the beach, as he liked to emphasize, only seven miles from the train station following a lane west of the town, and large and unremarkable enough to "accommodate an uncomplicated crowd." He had fled the landlord's inspection of Tutor House and possibly being called as a witness in a libel case against Mr. Swinburne. As always, he left Fanny behind, but brought George and the dogs, paints, canvases, easels, props, notebooks, and other less obvious necessities.

Answering his own question on "family affections," when new parents William and Lucy decided to go to Aldwick at the same time as Mama and Christina, Gabriel declared there wasn't room for baby Olivia and her nurse. Christina, although delighted to be an aunt, was relieved whenever and wherever she didn't have to pretend to get along with her sister-in-law. So, other than the stormy weather uprooting the tall specimen elm on the front lawn, its fall just missing the lodge, and Mama catching a nasty cold that required a doctor's attention, it was an agreeable visit, especially—as was becoming essential to Christina's middle-age—to look back on.

Little time was spent outdoors, mud everywhere, sunshine in short supply, the wind rarely resting, and the beach one of the roughest in the area. November fog often shrouded what might have been an inviting view. Gabriel had never been particularly enamored of the sea; by his own admission, crossing the channel a reason he didn't travel to the Continent as often as William. Yet, according to George, Gabriel would, "on a sulky impulse, take violent walks, resolute and quick, over shingles, boulders, and ruins of wooden groynes, just to watch Dizzy shaking seaweed and barking at incoming waves."

In-between Mama's and Christina's first and second visits, Jane Morris arrived at Aldwick to pose for a chalk drawing of the head of *Astarte Syrica*.

> *Mystery: lo! betwixt the sun and moon*
> *Astarte of the Syrians: Venus Queen*
> *Ere Aphrodite was. In silver sheen …*

Christina strongly suspected Jane was the reason Gabriel was miserable when she and Mama returned to Aldwick with aunts Charlotte and Eliza, joined on the journey by George's father and two brothers. The lodge was large and accommodating enough for all, bedrooms on either side of the gallery, still spry aunties climbing the stairs to their beds. Another sleeping area was makeshift for Christina and Mama, screened off in the ground floor library. A separate wing was used by Gabriel as a studio where he could generally keep out of the way of his guests' hopes for a pleasant visit. At times, he showed signs of the paranoia and remedying that had almost killed him a few years before, Dr. Hake, out of friendship as much as expertise, challenging his continued use of chloral. Christina knew Gabriel wasn't happy with her because *The Lowest Room*, "barely fit for lavatory paper," had been included in Macmillan's new edition of her poems. As much as she wanted to be important to him, she didn't believe he was indiscriminately disagreeable because he doubted her devotion.

It might have been he hoped Maria would come after all, a letter delivered on Christmas Eve not convincing him that she willingly stayed away. Christina was glad he gave it to her to read and never asked for it back, so she could keep it from the threat of being torn up.

"For the most part, even I have turned up for Yuletides." Gabriel overlooked the drama he often brought to them. "How lonely she will be without us."

"She hasn't joined us for a few years," Christina inwardly regretted. "I know it's hard for you to understand, but self-denial is her spiritual joy."

Soon it was apparent Gabriel was intent on finding fault with everyone except Mama, and everything. It didn't seem to matter that he was to blame for the flys to Christmas morning service not being ordered. Christina had given him written notice well in advance with the assurance that she, their mother, and aunts would share the cost. It was fortunate one of George's brothers was there to borrow and drive a neighbor's four-seater trap. George himself was the target of more than his share of Gabriel's petty hostility, derided for sitting four women in "the best chairs" on one side of the table, four men opposite "grimly" facing them with Gabriel at the top "looking as if presiding over a funeral rather than a feast." The food was downgraded along with the cook and other servants: the carving slow, vegetables and sauces cold by the time they were brought out, no second helpings, and the plum pudding poorly made and drowning in curdled custard.

***

Gabriel stayed away from Maria's New Year's visit to 12 Bloomsbury Square, where Mama's and Christina's return to London took them as though it was home. Effectively, it was, whether they were staying there with Mama's younger sisters or on Euston Street that, after almost two years and a new arrival, was unquestionably under Lucy's rule. There was nothing of the finally freed prisoner about Maria, although her All Saints habit presented her even darker and more modest than unfashionable clothes once had. Her intellect was still eager for conversation and the brightness of her spirit wasn't diminished. Neither was her appetite for the turkey dinner that surpassed the fiasco at Aldwick, and equaled, as Maria revealed, an excellent Christmas meal at her 'Home' on Margaret Street.

William dropped by, for pudding and to be himself, adding to the satisfaction of the afternoon. He didn't intend to stay long as he was traveling to Newcastle the following day to give a lecture on the poet Shelley.

"My dear Lucy is already nervous without me at home, particularly in the evenings. It is so generous of her to urge me on with any endeavor that takes me away from her and Olivia for several of them."

Maria wouldn't let him go before he practiced the speech he had prepared, heeded her suggestions, and was drawn into other discussions.

He was pleased to hear Maria was "using her brain" in an English translation of her order's *Monastic Diurnal* and teaching Bible Studies to the Young Women's Friendly Society.

"My declining health prevents me from nursing duties, the Rules from reading academically or for personal pleasure, but the spiritual education of the poor fills my time and is gratifying."

The mention that she was unwell wasn't a sudden revelation. While still a novice, Maria had spent time at All Saints convalescent hospital in Eastbourne for erysipelas and general exhaustion.

"Will you put your names to this?" Christina delayed William and Maria's departure a little longer by producing an anti-vivisection petition. "Here are some flyers if you would give or send them out. There has been progress towards Parliament passing a Cruelty to Animals Act, but we mustn't assume it will be done or go far enough to end this horror of horrors."

William signed it for himself and Lucy, Christina reciting as he did so, "'Hurt no living thing: ladybird, nor butterfly, nor moth with dusty wing, nor cricket chirping cheerily, or grasshopper so light of leap, nor danging gnat, nor beetle, nor harmless worms that creep.'"

"My spirit signs it, dear Chrissy. But I can't actually do so."

For the first time, at least as Christina witnessed, the nun Maria looked frustrated with the restrictions put on her. Christina knew in that moment why she herself had faltered on the convent threshold, having entertained the romantic notion of giving up earthly relations, possessions, and purposes, but never convinced she should do so. *My lily feet are soiled with mud, with scarlet mud which tells a tale of hope that was, of guilt that was, of love that shall not yet avail …*

"I will pray for this wrong to be righted," Maria soon thought of a way to absolve herself, "and ask my fellow Sisters to."

"I can't get used to being one of many," Christina finally said out loud.

Maria replied with a loose embrace, whispering, "I will take a few flyers."

"Oh. Good." Christina gave her what was left from those William had accepted.

"Our Moony still shines now and then." he said as he noticed, a glance between him and Christina enjoying Maria's mischievous smile.

"I must leave now if I'm to catch the next omnibus. I rather not walk."

"You don't need to do either," Mama wouldn't let Maria get away without a tight, lingering hug, "if your aunties and I pay for a cab. There's usually one to be had in the square."

"No." William proved not everything had changed about him either. "I will get one to take me home … with a little detour."

***

For that winter into spring, Christina was occupied with her feeble involvement in the campaigns against vivisection and hunting. She also made scrapbooks for sick children, and played whist at Bloomsbury Square with her mother, aunties, and, often, Charles, who, having moved again, lived nearby. Unfortunately, Euston Square was still her and Mama's official residence. Whenever they returned, much effort went into avoiding confrontations which inevitably brought them to the conclusion Christina had initially jumped to, that William's new life could never concur with his old.

The search for lodgings suitable for Mama, her sisters, and Christina had begun, although it wasn't expected they would relocate until autumn.

Also in April, Maria was sent to the All Saints Mission Home in Clifton, near Bristol, Christina and Mama looking forward to a summer reunion with her there. Mid-July, Maria let them know she was unwell and accomplishing little more than attending Vespers, her transfer to the Order's hospital at Eastbourne imminent.

Christina and her mother were concerned, but unprepared for anything worse about Maria's condition than leisure, loving care, and air more bracing at Eastbourne than Clifton couldn't improve.

Their fears were focused on Gabriel's unsettled, irrational, and self-destructive behavior. No sooner he returned to London he was away again with George to Broadlands in Hampshire on the invitation of the Right Honorable William Cowper-Temple, who had purchased *Beata Beatrix.* William claimed his brother was only going to avoid the upheaval of alterations to his studio, walls doubled and wadding added to block out noise from the adjoining neighbors who were musicians. Christina was soon sorry she begged an invitation for her and Mama to Tutor House before he made his escape, not because they found him suffering leg pain and insomnia but due to his obsession with death. He was reading *The Letters of Benjamin Robert Haydon*, an artist Dickens declared had *utterly mistaken his vocation* and who, because of debt and disappointment, committed suicide, a knife to his throat succeeding as a bullet had not.

"Stretch me no longer on this rough world," Gabriel read the words Mr. Haydon had left to account for his final actions.

Christina felt most upset for Mama as her oldest son announced that if he "died suddenly, at any moment," he wished to be cremated rather than buried at Highgate, no cast made of his head, and all his letters burned. He hinted his Will would soon be drawn up, William named as an executor and probably Dr. Hake, too.

For a long time, Christina felt every departure from Gabriel could be the last, although there was equally every chance his behavior was more performance than prediction. She and Mama were eager to be off to holiday with Maria, even to a hospital, one they had stayed in before near Beachy Head, with clean, comfortable accommodations in spacious grounds overlooking the South Downs and English Channel. Journeys were getting harder for Mama in her mid-seventies, but, with a few adjustments, she persevered as she always had.

They didn't doubt Maria would welcome their company as she recovered from whatever infirmity had brought her there. They found her uncomplaining but extremely ill and unable to reassure them that she would return to her role as the example of health in the family.

For all the winds go sighing, for sweet things dying.

Quite a few days were for remaining indoors. There was no one other than themselves to engage with and little to do until Christina took up painting leafy designs on the corners of stationary to sell for one penny a sheet to raise money for the hospital. When it was fine, although usually breezy and cool, Christina and Mama sat outdoors on campstools near the hospital's gate.

The one thing Christina intended to do was delayed by the anxiety of acknowledging what Lucy had probably already heard: a new London residence for her in-laws had been decided upon. Christina wanted her letter to Lucy, the first and the last since she had been in Eastbourne, to be an olive branch of hoping separate roofs might repair their relationship.

Please, please believe I will do better, Christina wrote in response to Maria's urging for a reconciliation that would please William and their mother.

"And, most importantly, our Heavenly Father." Maria's voice was strange but her heart and soul recognizable.

***

'I marked a falcon swooping
At the break of day;
And for your love, my sister dove,
I 'frayed the thief away.' —

Christina responded quickly to put an arm around Mama's waist when they were told Maria was to return home, meaning the Convent on Margaret Street, with her All Saints Mother. While in Eastbourne, the only thing that had become clear about Maria's illness was that the first-rate medical advice London could provide was needed. It had been discussed, if not yet with anyone from the Order, that she might be allowed to stay at 12 Bloomsbury Square during the time it took to diagnose what was ailing her, and for treatment and convalescence. It was obvious Maria was in no condition to work, participate in the Sisterhood rituals or follow its rules, so why shouldn't she know comfort and care, physically and spiritually, from, her blood mother and sister?

"It is best if you and Miss Rossetti travel separately, on a different day altogether. Sister Maria is in good hands. In ours, humbly; in our Lord's, blessedly, eternally."

The next day, an ambulance took Maria, her Reverend Mother, and a nursing Sister to Eastbourne's train Station. The following one, the last Saturday in August, a cab came for two women who wouldn't be left behind for long.

The next months took Mama and Christina back and forth to Margaret Street and a toll on the strength of their bodies and hearts. Maria continued very ill, with little rallying except for her positive, patient nature whenever she was aware of anyone in the room. Eventually, her pain increased beyond her ability to hide it and so did doses of opium. A nonspecific lymphatic malady was suspected. Her inability to eat without vomiting precipitated exploration under chloroform, a uterine tumor found and further surgery—tapping—to insert a trocar to drain fluid from her swollen abdomen was undertaken.

Although Maria's demise happened quickly, the time spent at her bedside was long and slow, especially once it was advised she be kept quiet and spoken to for comfort not conversation. She was mostly too weak to talk even when she rarely wanted to, but, as Christina experienced once, and was told happened more, especially in the middle of the night, Maria's Italian spirit would suddenly rise to summon the young nurse who regularly attended to her.

"Oh, Annie, my Annie, come to me!"

Despite her own suffering, in a moment of realizing she was running out of opportunities, she found the strength to touch Christina's arm and advise her to be less melancholy.

Hope is like a harebell trembling from its birth ....

William visited at least twice a week, always uncomfortably, especially when, repeatedly, Maria mentioned that one of the principal reasons she had become a nun was to pray effectively for her brothers' conversions.

"Gabe is more likely to feel the pull of your prayers, Moony."

Faith is like a lily lifted high and white ....

Finally, Gabriel came, calm, coherent, and tender as he leaned close to Maria and held her hand without reaction to how thin and old she had become. He stayed two hours and brought her religious photographs from a *Book of Hours*, making his promise to be a better Christian more believable, although he soon diverted the reason for the gleam in his big sister's eyes to how much better he felt after his stay at Broadlands.

"You'll be glad to know I've greatly reduced my use of chloral."

He was tactful enough to not mention that he had tried and found some success with mesmerism to rid himself of leg pain and help him sleep.

He shared a fly with Christina to her new address at 30 Torrington Square where Mama and their aunts were waiting to welcome him for the first time since they had moved in. He stayed for supper and approved of the dining and drawing rooms, and Mama's idea of filling the latter with portraits of every family member.

"As it can never be filled with memories."

"I shall visit our dear Maria tomorrow," Aunt Eliza broke into the silence. "You mentioned, Chrissy, that the opium makes her lips and throat very dry, so I thought pomegranates or oranges to moisten them. Lady Bath was so good to send us some with Charlotte."

"Yes, Auntie E. It is worth a try."

***

Every effort was made to ease Maria's departure or, as days into weeks into months confused the outcome, effect her recovery and remaining on earth where so many preferred she stay even if she was more heavenly-minded. Her abdomen tapped a second time, sustained relief might be possible, and everyone held their breath until it was apparent it wasn't. Opium kept her comfortable but resulted in too many days when she was drowsy and unable to speak. Visits could be almost cheerful when she rallied.

Occasionally, Maria improved in unexpected ways. Like the afternoon she requested a mutton chop to suck on so it seemed she'd had a meal. On the recommendation of Dr. Fox, she tried barely cooked, finely minced beef enclosed in two slices of bread soaked with gravy. Even when she was too weak for solid food, she took noticeable pleasure in sipping lemonade with seltzer water.

The convent only allowed family members for visits. Christina, glad her own health held up, was there nearly every day, whether keeping vigil at Maria's bedside or praying in the dim light and, once her eyes adjusted, vivid colors and patterns of the mosaics in All Saints Church. Afternoons were reserved for Mama and, a few times a week, aunts Eliza or Charlotte. William would spend an hour or two some mornings when Maria was most likely to be awake.

A third draining was discussed but Dr. Fox feared it would only bring Maria more suffering towards not surviving. By early November, her body was undeniably reduced and, more significantly, so was her will to recover. Lamb chops and minced beef were no longer asked for or offered, although still welcome were lemons to moisten her mouth. Sweeter than sad moments were fewer and farther between. It was devastating when Mama could only bear to stay long enough to kiss her firstborn's cheek and mention there was a letter, especially if it was from Gabriel. It would be left in case Sister Eliza, who had volunteered to care for Maria and was trusted with the intimacy of her family bonds, found a better time to read it to her.

When Maria could communicate, wanting help to sip a drink or assure she was in very little pain, she did so with a quietness not just in her voice. There was less and less kindness in desperately wanting to hold onto keeping her alive, of going against the conclusion her body was giving itself up to that her faith had long been ready for.

She waited for Gabriel to recover from a cold, sore throat, and "the threat" of a stye to return to her. And to God? He realized he had waited too long but did seem to find comfort in knowing she believed it wasn't too late.

After William spent his last moments with Maria, he seemed to admit more than witnessing her talking to angels. One of the Sisters revealed that the night before, Maria had seen Christ and as clearly called him beautiful. After a morning of distress through gasping, her mind wandering, by about one p.m. she was silent until her last request, "Come along." Christina felt it was meant for her brothers but knew it would direct the rest of her life.

> *She clung about her sister,*
> *Kissed and kissed and kissed her:*
> *Tears once again*
> *Refreshed her shrunken eyes,*
> *Dropping like rain*
> *After long sultry drouth;*
> *Shaking with anguish, fear, and pain ….*

***

Mama and Christina returned to Margaret Street expecting to gaze on the face of their Moony one last time. They were refused entry to the mortuary. The Order managed the funeral, which was for family only in the private chapel behind the convent houses after the nuns took Holy Communion. There was no plan for mourning coaches to and from Brompton Cemetery or objection to flys being hired. Gabriel was encouraged to attend the chapel service, which he did and noticed *Maria Francesca, Sister of the Poor* engraved on the casket, 'Rossetti' omitted "as she had requested."

"She has left us as if she has never been one of us."

Christina agreed that Gabriel shouldn't go to the burial made even more conspicuous by a part-congregation of nuns, a test of his composure he likely wouldn't pass. Once there, she acutely regretted his missing the surprising serenity of Maria's sendoff as *loving mourners followed her, hymns were sung at her grave, the November day brightened, and the sun made a miniature rainbow* ....

CHAPTER THIRTY-EIGHT

Finally, they made it to Birchington-on-sea, a resort on the north coast of Kent that normally offered a change of air and hope for restoration. Not so in 1882, barely beyond winter and the colds and coughs that had prevented Mama and Christina from traveling a month earlier with Gabriel. Paralyzed in his left arm and leg from a mild stroke the previous December, he needed company for the journey. After George Hake's resignation and a few replacements in between, Hall Caine, an architect's clerk, aspiring writer and critic who had wooed Gabriel with a lecture exalting *Poems*, took on the position of his secretary and companion. Along with Mr. Caine's thirteen-year-old sister Lily, and Mrs. Abrey, a hired nurse, he escorted his employer to the newly built Birchington bungalow, offered rent-free by the owner on the suggestion of its architect, an old friend of Gabriel's.

Only fields separated it from the high headland and sea. It was also positioned near the railway station, so the bath chair Gabriel had bought, almost identical to the one that ferried Mama short distances in London, was as useful in bringing her to Westcliff.

Young Lily skipped out, distracted by the lad who had cheerlessly pulled the chair and, once its passenger had disembarked into the care of her daughter, had to go back to the depot for their luggage.

"When we arrived, Mr. Rossetti thought it didn't look like a house," Lily revealed what was already known to those who corresponded with Gabriel.

Christina, whose attention had been focused on Mama steadying her legs and smoothing her skirt, looked up and ahead, not seeing anything wonderful or wrong about the sprawling one-story wooden building with an asphalt roof. In different circumstances, she might have looked forward to taking tea on its veranda, anticipated the warm rooms and freshly baked bread its smoking chimneys suggested, and expected to enjoy its proximity to the sea. Instead, she feared the reason Gabriel found neither beauty nor comfort in the place.

Lily had more to say. "Before he even went inside, Mr. Rossetti wanted to go straight back to London. Tommy had to—"

"Who?"

"My brother. I still call him by his true first name, as he likes me to."

"You're the youngest?" Christina guessed, knowing Hall Caine was almost thirty.

"I am, Miss Rossetti. And he is the oldest, many siblings between us. But we are close in ways that matter more."

No one had expected that five years after Maria passed into eternal life, Gabriel would still be wavering at its door. He was a mess of uncertainties and contradictions, which, unlike Christina with her own, he never attempted to clean up. He complained no one came to see him and also when they did. Gabriel missed William's company but couldn't endure his brother "burdened by fatherhood." Yet Christina remembered Gabriel grieving his lost baby while observing the growing up of other people's daughters, even seriously wondering if he could adopt May Morris. According to Mr. Caine, he was charming and playful with Lily on the train from London to Birchington and, once he settled on staying at Westcliff for a while, was never contrary or gloomy with her. Christina had witnessed him taking an interest in Lily reading the *Arabian Nights* and relishing her amusement as he recited his favorite passages.

***

Gabriel continued to suggest Mama and Christina move into Tutor House. Mr. Caine revealed he overheard Gabriel assuring Fanny he never did or would.

"He told me to draw up his Will leaving everything to Miss Cornforth, or should I say Mrs. Schott? Of course, I refused. Then he wrote her out of his life."

Gabriel continued as a successful artist and self-saboteur, obtaining patrons and orders despite refusing to exhibit. He had money coming in, if not the sense to save it or himself.

He was as ill as he had ever been more times than most men could have survived or, at least, would have changed the habits that otherwise eventually would kill them.

He was determined to torture himself and others. In retrospect and contrast to Gabriel's high drama and continual crises, Christina believed Maria had timed her withdrawal from blood to spiritual family to gently prepare them for her physical absence and burden them as little as possible. After all, she was among the saints, in life and death, inspiring Christina to venerate those called to be in a new devotional collection. *How beautiful are the arms which have embraced Christ, the hands which have touched Christ, the eyes which have gazed upon Christ, the lips which have spoken with Christ, the feet which have followed Christ.*

Gabriel continued to weigh in on Christina's writing. *A Pageant and Other Poems* was a major work published before half-blindness, apoplexy, and addiction to cures worse than any disease affected his ability, not desire, to. He wrote poetry even when his penmanship wasn't pretty, often, with Christina's help, sending gifts of sonnets to

Mama as compensation for how much he would soon take away.

A Sonnet is a moment's monument, memorial from the Soul's eternity ....

"When Caine told me he'd sent for you two, I knew I was a goner."

Christina's first sight of Gabriel since January wasn't as shocking as expected. She was heartened he was reading books by Dickens, Wilkie Collins, and others, and able to talk about them. Turning the pages with his trembling right hand, whatever volume slipping to the side of or down his lap, it was obvious his left arm and hand were useless. He welcomed Christina but, especially, Mama helping him, his tender, tearful dependence meeting hers as it had fifty-three years before.

Two days after arriving at Westcliff, Christina entered the drawing room at one end and the entire width of the long bungalow. Two paintings, *Proserpine* and *Joan of Arc*, were propped on chairs either side of a gray-lighted window, contradicting William's prediction they never would be finished.

Differing opinions had long grappled with whether Gabriel's physical disorders were completely real or, at least partly, delusional, never more distressing than when he was convinced he could no longer draw or paint. His response ranged from anger to crying to resignation. Until he found motivation in the most mischievous of company and a mere mention of Scotus' hair loss.

"I've seen him without his wig." Gabriel accepted the challenge of the sketchpad put in his hands. In no time, his wicked humor and still viable talent made a good likeness of "Scottie's bald skull."

Christina claimed and destroyed the drawing, not wanting Mr. Scott, who mercifully hadn't been present at the mockery, to ever see it. She wasn't sorry it proved Gabriel hadn't lost his skill and encouraged him further to do, also in chalk, profile drawings of Mama and her, one of each, another of both, side-by-side looking like sisters. All three portraits hung in the house in Torrington Square, contributing to Mama's efforts, in sentiment, at least, to gather her family all around her again.

It was doubtful Gabriel attempted any artwork beyond February. Mr. Caine assumed the last shaky sketches he did were of his father on the request of Cousin Teo, who wanted to erect a statue of Gabriele Rossetti in his native town of Vasto.

Mr. Caine reported that during his first days at Birchington, Gabriel had taken short walks outside, the weather mild considering it was winter. By the time Christina and their mother were there, Gabriel refused to go out, even in the bath chair, remaining in bed most of the time. He sat up some evenings, although not for long once he began to experience discomfort in his "good" foot. Mrs. Abrey diagnosed gout, which was confirmed by the local physician. A uric purgative and lying down with his foot on a pillow eventually offered some relief, so with assistance he made it to the sitting room a few more times.

Christina and Mama were grateful for any signs of improvement, especially the clearness and composure of Gabriel's mind that brought him back to them even as they prepared to let him go. Mrs. Abrey warned he might seem better before, even right up to, the worst. They tried not to think so while he was cheerful, and conversant about painting and publishing, asked for the newspaper so he "might be part of the world again" while laughing at Christina who wondered when he ever had been.

He declared she and their mother were the lasting loves of his life. He granted Lily the distinction of being the last new one.

"Another nail in my coffin," he grumbled when Mr. Caine decided it was time to take his sister back to Liverpool.

Gabriel was obviously wasting away, food and tonics not strengthening his body, small doses of morphine and some surrendering to his whiskey cravings easing and exacerbating what Mrs. Abrey described as "mischief happening in his liver."

"The last I will ever get into."

"Oh, you never know." Mrs. Abrey finished giving Gabriel an injection, adjusted, almost caressed, his pillow and blankets, then turned away to reflect Christina's tearful smile.

Christina waited for the nurse to leave the room before she resumed reading out loud from Wilke Collins' *The Moonstone*.

"'Your tears come easy, when you're young—'"

"Remember when, as Papa said, you could fill bottles with yours?"

"Yes." She felt happiness come and go. "Hard to believe I was so effusive."

"Go on," Gabriel's voice was softer, his few words slurred.

"'Your tears come easy, when you're young, and beginning the world,'" she read again, and continued as suddenly she didn't want to. "'Your tears come easy, when you're old, and leaving it.'"

***

Not quite a year after Maria's death, Henriette Heimann Foote, Amelia's eldest daughter, died from an overdose of chloral hydrate.

However you can, you must get Gabriel to stop using it, her longest and dearest friend had added to the correspondence that constantly connected them. *Or you will have yet another hole in your heart.*

Christina already knew such wounds were inevitable, especially when thoroughly loving someone didn't mean they would care as much for themselves.

On April 1st, William arrived in Birchington, having not seen Gabriel for months. *Do not doubt our brother's illnesses*, Christina had tried to prepare him. *Do not be influenced to think they aren't real.* He found Gabriel hardly able to see or walk but talking reasonably about whatever topic came up, including Christina's ambiguous stance on women's suffrage. She stirred Gabriel's own confliction over a cause William normally wouldn't have withheld his thoughts about, especially since they were married to Lucy's.

The next day, before William left for London, Gabriel complained of difficulty breathing. The doctor was sent for and blamed abuse of chloral for a softening of Gabriel's brain that effected many of his other complaints, making them delusional and truly sickening and crippling him.

"I recommend Gabriel leave the dull seclusion of Birchington for somewhere more socially and medically sophisticated. Malvern, for instance."

"Not an option, Doctor."

William promised to return by Good Friday. In between were long days and nights that shortened the chances of his brother's recovery, the doctor checking in every and, eventually, twice a day. Christina became accustomed to reading to Gabriel until midnight or, when Mama did, she took the more silent, sorrowful overnight shift. The patient usually stirred by six, disorientated as the morphine wore off, which woke Christina. Otherwise, Mrs. Abrey did with a nudge.

William was back at the time he planned but not place he hoped to find his brother's health in. Gabriel's sudden, urgent request to see the Rector was alarming to those who didn't have faith and relief to those who did. Reverend Alcott obliged on Good Friday evening and prayed with him. Mama and Christina did, too.

Gabriel hated to be warm in bed. When he began to heavily perspire, an awning was put up, so the one large window in his room didn't need to be closed to keep the heat out. To the contrary, also on Saturday, because of a sudden diagnosis of uremia, Dr. Harris ordered him wrapped in a steaming sheet with the intent of making him sweat. Within hours there were signs of success, his complexion less flushed, his breathing less labored, his eyes more aware of Christina and Mama sitting by him and Mrs. Abrey and William in and out of the room.

With a burst of strength, he sat up and leaned forward, Christina taking her cue to rub his back in a circular motion.

"Yesterday I wanted to die." His voice was hoarse. "Not today."

"You shouldn't want to." William cleared his throat. "Instead, continue to work and produce finer things than ever. Such as *Proserpine* and *Joan* are. Janey will model for you again."

"She was wise to marry Topsy." Gabriel noticed Mr. Caine standing behind William. "Have you heard anything of Fanny?"

"Nothing at all."

"Would you tell me if you had?"

"If you asked me."

"Oh, my poor Fan."

Christina's hand slipped away from him.

"Please, Chrissy. Don't stop. Don't ever stop."

She didn't obey him when it came to his Last Will and Testament, signed, and witnessed that evening once revocation of an earlier one made before Lizzie's death was. The new version left everything to his brother and surviving sister, except Christina insisted Mama's name replace hers. She only allowed herself a small memento of her choosing, probably one of his drawings.

The Rector called again and wanted to read from *Ecclesiastes*. Somehow, he knew its story had impressed Gabriel in his youth.

"Perhaps later."

Aunt Charlotte had come from London with William and was Mama's companion for church on Easter morning, since, after her usual overnight vigil in Gabriel's room, Christina was too tired to go. In any case, she needed to stay close by him, exasperating Mrs. Abrey who wanted to relieve her.

It wasn't for Gabriel's sake Christina didn't want to leave, for others would attend to him with more composure than she could. Finally, she gave in to Mrs. Abrey, had some tea with a biscuit, and got some air watching William and Mr. Caine on the roof fixing the flapping tarpaulin that provided the makeshift awning over the sickroom window.

Having seemed slightly better after the first purge of poison, Gabriel was too distressed to receive any benefit from the second, especially with the addition of a tortuous linseed-and-mustard poultice applied to his privates.

"I'm sure I'll die tonight."

Reverend Alcott came once more and asked to pray with Gabriel alone.

Christina felt the painful joy, as no doubt Mama did, when he revealed Gabriel had affirmed a simple trust in God and the Savior.

Stop—and there's an end, and matters mend.

"Thank you, Rector. I fear we will be needing you again." Mama followed him down the long hall, their quiet conversation not one Christina wanted to overhear anyway.

"Take supper with me, Chrissy," William proposed before she went back into Gabriel's room. "Then you should rest as I will. Mama said she would sit until ten when I will have my turn. Yours will begin at two."

"I'm not hungry. When Mama gets back, I'll lie down, although I'm afraid to."

William nodded and solemnly walked away from her inclination to embrace him. Out of reach, he stopped and turned. "Lucy is coming, all the way from Manchester where she was visiting her father. She should be here by nine thirty or ten o'clock."

Gabriel was either falling asleep or trying to stay awake, his eyelids quivering to open or close. Noticing the evening light was withdrawing even sooner because of the awning, Christina went to the window to close the curtains, but was otherwise engaged when she saw the white-robed, ochre-haloed sun going down beyond Minnis Bay, sinking into the promise of a beautiful day to come.

The sun had stooped to earth though once so high;
Had stooped to earth, in slow
Warm dying loveliness brought near and low.

"Oh, Gabe. I must get you up to see this sunset." It was a ridiculous notion she didn't even try to carry out.

"Come here." Gabriel already sounded like a ghost, although his left hand lived again, long enough to move towards hers and clasp it. "I'm sure it is beautiful."

***

"I'm glad I lived," he saved to say to their mother.

After a lifetime of spontaneous living, it seemed he was prepared to die.

"Go on, Christina. It's my shift." Mama wasn't convincingly calm. 'Mrs. Abrey will soon be back. She went to find Mr. Caine to help apply a fresh poultice."

"Oh, I wish they wouldn't."

A few hours later, having slept on and off, there was a knock on her door, Hall Caine insisting, "Miss Rossetti. You need to come now."

Back at Gabriel's bedside, Christina wished she had never left. William supported their mother until Aunt Charlotte took hold of her, Mrs. Abrey leaning over Gabriel. Christina looked around her to see his head drooped right, his eyes nearly closed, and mouth fully open.

The hallway clock struck half past nine as Gabriel drew hard breaths until there was an uncanny stillness about him. Dr. Harris thought he was still alive but a stethoscope and those who prayed for his soul knew differently.

"Oh, no. Am I too late?"

"My darling wife."

William turned, as did Mama and Christina, to acknowledge Lucy, who had come just in time to embrace his loss and leave his mother and sister to the consolation of each other.

***

The service in Birchington's Medieval flint church on *a lowly hill* overlooking *a flat, half sea, half country side* had been simple, with under twenty mourners. During the burial, Mama was supported by Christina on one side and William on the other. It was a lovely spring day, the churchyard brightened by a blue sky, irises, and wallflowers, and soothingly scented by a lilac tree near where they stood.

Back at the bungalow, Christina slipped out of the after-funeral repass to find woodspurge and forget-me-nots in the grounds around Westcliff.

That evening, Mama in the bath chair, Christina, Aunt Charlotte, William, and Lucy returned to All Saints churchyard. Aided again by her surviving daughter and son, Frances Mary Lavinia managed to slowly walk to Gabriel's grave. It was already filled in, wreaths and other flowery tributes, including a cross of primroses, all around. Lucy wondered if they should move them onto it.

Mama cried, "No."

> *She groans not for a passing breath —*
> *This is forget-me-not and love.*

William, who, it seemed, was gone to his wife, rejoined his mother and sister holding onto each other. He helped Mama kneel, Christina handing her the poetic posy to lay all by itself on the mound of glistening turf.

> *From perfect grief there need not be*
> *Wisdom or even memory:*
> *One thing then learnt remains to me, —*
> *The woodspurge has a cup of three.*

EPILOGUE

Christina had been back in London a few days when she decided to visit the Scotts in Chelsea with the excuse of checking on Scotus' leg injury, the reason he had given for not attending Gabriel's funeral. At Bellevue House she was met with his absence—Letitia and Alice not there either—and the explanation that he had gone to South Kensington for the day.

When Christina returned to Torrington Square, Mama greeted her with the news that Charles Cayley had called to offer his condolences. "He was visibly upset assuming how heartbroken we must be."

"And disappointed you weren't here." Aunt Eliza always had to scold a little.

"He might have waited."

"We are not the best company right now," Mama bowed her head, not really to continue the mending in her lap.

"He'll call again," Christina told her conscience.

A few days later, Scotus sent her a copy of his newly published *A Poet's Harvest Home*. He noted no reference to them missing each other but did boast of his accomplishment at seventy.

My old admiration before I was twenty
is predilect still, now promoted to se'entry.

When, in the difficult months after Maria's death, Charles had sent her a pickled, prickly sea-creature, properly known as *Aphrodite aculeata*, Christina saw it as a symbol of the friendship they had preserved. *A Venus seems my mouse ... a darling mouse it is ... Venus-cum-Iris Mouse —* although it looked more like a worm or caterpillar—*in no mere bottle, in my heart.*

On Christina's fifty-third birthday, too soon after burying one brother, Charles Cayley fell asleep for a night into eternity. Not unexpected, it was planned for along with her leaving him the remainder of her estate after any debts were paid. If he breathed his last first, she would inherit the copyright of his works, a ring that once she had refused, and his writing desk.

His heart had failed him before, because hers had an irregular beat. She hid a bundle of her unpublished Italian poems in the desk, admissions of regret that didn't mean she would have done anything differently.

I loved you first: but afterwards your love
Outsoaring mine, sang such a loftier song
As drowned the friendly cooings of my dove.

AFTERWORD

In the years after Gabriel's and Charles Cayley's deaths, Christina continued to reside in the large and dreary house at 30 Torrington Square with her elderly mother and aunts Charlotte and Eliza. In 1886 Christina's *heart's quiet home*, Frances Mary Lavina Polidori Rossetti, had a bad fall and passed away a few months later. Left with the care, more so than companionship, of her two aunts, Christina considered moving them all to a smaller, cheerier house, possibly out of London. She soon realized relocation was impractical with two aged, ailing women, and might deprive her of regular visits from her brother William and her nieces and nephews.

Christina continued to write poetry and, more than ever, devotional prose. *Letter and Spirit: Notes on the Commandments* was published in 1883, *Time Flies: A Reading Diary* in 1885, *Poems* in 1890, *The Face of the Deep: A Devotional Commentary of the Apocalypse* in 1892, and *Verses*, a compilation of religious poetry, in 1893. William claimed Christina wasn't politically minded, but she did continue some involvement in a few causes. She organized petitions for the rights of minors and anti-vivisection, and in support of the Criminal Law Amendment Act, which included raising the age of consent for girls to sixteen.

Her valued if small world of family and friends continued to shrink. Aunt Charlotte died in 1890 as did William Bell Scott; her sister-in-law Lucy was stricken with consumption to which she succumbed while abroad in the spring of 1894. Aunt Eliza lingered frail and senile until 1893, her care shared between her niece and a servant Harriet Reed. Early in 1892 Christina was diagnosed with cancer and underwent a mastectomy, the surgery pronounced enough of a success for speculation, after Tennyson's death the same year, that she would be appointed Poet Laureate. However, her cancer returned, this time an operation not thought to be beneficial. Confined to bed, she was devotedly nursed by Harriet Reed and, likely, comforted by a beloved cat. After months of pain, physical and spiritual, the latter because she was weighed down by doubts that she was worthy to meet her Creator, she died on December 29, 1894, a few weeks beyond her sixty-fourth birthday.

> *The curtains were half drawn, the floor was swept*
> *And strewn with rushes, rosemary and may*
> *Lay thick upon the bed on which I lay,*
> *Where through the lattice ivy-shadows crept.*
> From *After Death* by Christina Rossetti

NOTES: QUOTED POETRY AND PROSE

DEDICATION PAGE

1) From *What are Heavy* by Christina Rossetti.
   What are brief? Today and tomorrow …

PART ONE

Chapter One

1) From *Hodge Podge*: issue No. 2 RF May 27, 1843.
   Magazine created by Frances Mary Lavinia Rossetti for her children.
   If we cannot do all that we would, let us do what we can.

Chapter Three

1) *To My Mother* by Christina Rossetti.
   To-days's your natal day;
   Sweet flowers I bring:
   Mother, accept, I pray
   My offering.
   And may you happy live,
   And long us bless;
   Receiving as you give
   Great happiness.

2) From *Jenny* by Dante Gabriel Rossetti.
   Lazy laughing languid Jenny …

Chapter Four

1) From *Love and Hope* by Christina Rossetti.
   Love reigneth, and reigneth low, and reigneth everywhere.

Chapter Five

1) From a poem included in a letter from Christina Rossetti to Bessie
Read
   … one hundred humble servants … their livery of red and black …
   Gravity and gladness mixed …

Thought here, smiles there; perfection lies betwixt.

Chapter Six

1) From *A Portrait* by Christina Rossetti
… calmly there she lay.
All pain had left her; and the sun's last ray
Shone through upon her, warming into red …

2) Eulogy for Princess Charlotte of Wales
Life is full of death; the steps of the living cannot press the earth without
disturbing the ashes of the dead — we walk upon our ancestors — the globe
itself is one vast churchyard.

3) From *Fly Away, Fly Away* by Christina Rossetti
Come again, come again, come back to me,
Bringing the summer and bringing the sun.

4) From *Hope in Grief* by Christina Rossetti
Tell me not there is no skill
That can bind the breaking heart,
That can smooth the bitter smart,
When we find ourselves betrayed,
When we find ourselves forsaken,
By those for whom we would have laid
Our young lives down …

PART TWO

Chapter Seven

1) From Gaetano Polidori's prefix to Christina Rossetti's *Verses* 1847
As her maternal grandfather, I may be excused for desiring to retain these
early spontaneous efforts in a permanent form, and for having silenced the
objections urged by her modest diffidence, and persuaded her to allow me to
print them for my own gratification.

2) From *Canzonetta* by Gaetano Polidori
Questa rose ch'io ti domo symbol sono nel diverso lo colore del tuo spirit del
tuo core
(Translation: *These roses I give you are a symbol in their different colors of*
your spirit and heart.)

Chapter Eight

1) From *The Girlhood of Mary, Virgin II* (second sonnet) by Dante Gabriel Rossetti
   Until the end be full, the Holy one
   Abides without. She soon shall have achieved
   Her perfect purity: yea, God the Lord
   Shall soon vouchsafe His son to be her Son.

Chapter Ten

1) From *A Pause for Thought* by Christina Rossetti
   I watched and waited with steadfast will:
   And though the object seemed to flee away
   That I so longed for, every day by day
   I watched and waited still.

2) From *When I am dead, my dearest* by Christina Rossetti
   And dreaming through the twilight
   That doth not rise nor set,
   Haply I may remember,
   And haply may forget.

Chapter Eleven

1) From *Three Stages* by Christina Rossetti
   Now all the cherished secrets of my heart, —
   Now all my hidden hopes are turned to sin.
   Part of my life is dead, part sick, and part
   Is all on fire within.

Chapter Twelve

1) From *As I laye a-thynkynge* by Thomas Ingoldsby
   As I lay a-thynkynge, a thynkynge, a-thynkynge,
   Merrie sang the Birde as she sat upon the boughe;
   Lovely Mayde came by,
   And a gentil youth was nyghe,
   And he breathed many a syghe
   And a vowe;
   As I lay thynkynge, her heart was gladsome now.

2) From *Goblin Market* by Christina Rossetti

... no friend like a sister ...

Chapter Thirteen

1) From *So I Grew Half Delirious and Quite Sick* by Christina Rossetti
   When I awoke the sun was at its height,
   And I wept.

2) From *Grown and Flown* by Christina Rossetti
   ... now that leaves are withering
   How should one love at all?

3) From *Somewhere or Other* by Christina Rossetti
   The face not seen, the voice not heard,
   The heart that not yet ...

4) From *An End* by Christina Rossetti
   To few chords and sad and low
   Sing we so ...

Chapter Fourteen

1) From *A Pause for Thought* by Christina Rossetti
   ... It is an empty name
   I long for; to a name why should I give
   The peace of all the days I have to live?

2) From *Three Moments* by Christina Rossetti
   ... she only said:
   "Not this, not this:" and clasped her hands
   Against her heart ...

3) From *Seasons* by Christina Rossetti
   Ice-bound, hunger-pinched and dim ...

4) From *Three Moments* by Christina Rossetti
   The Woman knelt; but did not pray
   Nor weep nor cry ...

Numbers 5 and 6 from *Three Nuns* by Christina Rossetti
5) *But I pressed forward to no goal,*
   There was no prize I strove to win.

6) *I prayed for him; was my sin prayer?*
   I sacrificed, he never bought.
   He nothing gave, he nothing took;
   We never bartered look for look.

7) From *Dream* by Christina Rossetti
   Therefore we parted as we met,
   She on her way, and I on mine;
   I think her tender heart was set
   On holier things and more Divine: —
   We parted thus and gave no sign.

PART THREE

Chapter Fifteen

1) Quote from Christina Rossetti
   Obedience is the fruit of faith. Patience is the early blossom on the tree of
   faith.

Chapter Sixteen

1) From *Symbols* by Christina Rossetti
   I watched a rosebud very long
   Brought on by dew and sun and shower,
   Waiting to see the perfect flower:
   Then, when I thought it should be strong,
   It opened at the matin hour
   And fell at evensong.

Numbers 2 through 6 from *Maude* (short story) by Christina Rossetti
2) *Perhaps there was a degree of truth in all these opinions.*

3) *Yes, I continue to write now and then as the humor seizes me.*

4) *I dare say she is very good ... but that does not make her pleasing.*

5) *Seated between Miss Savage and Sophia Mowbray, she was attacked on*
   either hand with questions concerning her verses. A flood of ecstatic
   compliments followed ... she was so young, so much admired, poor thing,
   looked so delicate ... if only Miss Foster could be induced to publish ...

6) *... never intended to be seen. The locked book she never opened: but had it*

placed in Maude's coffin, with all its records of folly, sin, vanity … and true penitence also.

Numbers 7 and 8 from *Nick* (short story) by Christina Rossetti

7) … *not a thousand miles from fairyland* …

8) … *milk, eggs, mutton, butter, poultry, and cheese … hops and barley for beer, and wheat for bread … orchard with fruit* …

Chapter Seventeen

1) From *Boats Sail on Rivers* by Christina Rossetti
   … a road from earth to sky …

2) From *A Ballad of Boding* by Christina Rossetti
   … in sorry plight, Out of sight.

3) From *Minnie and Maddie* by Christina Rossetti
   Don't wait for roses …
   … primroses
   Blossom to-day …

4) From *The King of the Golden River* (fantasy story) by John Ruskin
   In a secluded and mountainous part of Stiria there was in old time a valley of the most surprising and luxuriant fertility …

Chapter Eighteen

1) Poem written by Gabriele Rossetti for his daughters when they were children
   Christina and Maria, my dear daughters,
   Are fresh violets opened at dawn.
   They are roses nurtured by the earliest breezes.
   They are lovely turtle-doves in the nest of love.

2) From *Persuasion* (novel) by Jane Austen
   "I allow Bath is pleasant enough."
   "… the most tiresome place in the world."
   "Oh. Who can ever be tired of Bath?"

3) From *If the Moon Came from Heaven* by Christina Rossetti
   If the moon came from heaven,

Talking all the way,
What could she have to tell us,
And what could she say?

4) From *If the Sun Could Tell Us Half* by Christina Rossetti
If the sun could tell us half
That he hears and sees,
Sometimes he would make us laugh,
Sometimes make us cry ...

Chapter Nineteen

1) From *The Posthumous Papers of the Pickwick Club* (novel) by Charles Dickens
The hum of many voices, and the sound of many feet...
... music low and gentle, but very pleasant to hear in a female voice,
whether in Bath or elsewhere.

2) From *Persuasion* (novel) by Jane Austen
"I shall never be in want of something to talk of again. I shall always be talking of Bath."

Numbers 3 and 4 from *Remember* by Christina Rossetti
3) *Remember me when I am gone away,*
Gone far away into the silent land;
When you can no more hold me by the hand ...

4) *For if the darkness and corruption leave*
A vestige of the thoughts that once I had,
Better by far you should forget and smile
Than that you should remember and be sad.

5) From *The Bourne* by Christina Rossetti
Underneath the growing grass,
Underneath the living flowers,
Deeper than the sound of showers ...
There a very little girth
Can hold round what once was the earth
Seemed too narrow to contain.

6) From *The Skylark* by Christina Rossetti
The earth was green, the sky was blue:
I saw and heard ...

A skylark hang between the two …

7) From *To A Skylark* by Percy Bysshe Shelley
 … singing still dost soar, and soaring ever singest …
 … sweetest songs are those that tell of saddest thought.

Chapter Twenty

Numbers 1 through 3 from *In the Artist's Studio* by Christina Rossetti
1) *One face looks out from all his canvasses …*

2) *We found her hidden just behind those screens,*
 That mirror gave back all her loveliness.

3) *A queen in opal or in ruby dress,*
 A nameless girl in freshest summer-greens,
 A saint, an angel—every canvas means
 The same one meaning, neither more nor less.

4) From *The Blessed Damozel* by Dante Gabriel Rossetti
 … lean'd out
 From the gold bar of Heaven …

5) From *The Passing of Love* by Elizabeth Siddal
 Love kept my heart in a song of joy,
 My pulses quivered to the tune;
 The coldest blasts of winter blew
 Upon me like sweet airs in June.

6) From *In the Artist's Studio* by Christina Rossetti
 He feeds upon her face by day and night,
 And she with true kind eyes looks back on him,
 Fair as the moon and joyful as the light:
 Not wan with waiting, not with sorrow dim
 Not as she is, but … when hope shown bright.

Chapter Twenty-One

1) From *Ye Have Forgotten the Exhortation* by Christina Rossetti
 Bury thy dead heart-deep;
 Take patience till the sun be set;
 There are no tears for him to weep,
 No doubts to haunt him yet:

Take comfort, he will not forget:—

2) From *Passing and Glassing* by Christina Rossetti
All things that pass
Are woman's looking glass;
They show her how her bloom must fade,
And she herself be laid
With withered roses in the shade …

3) From *Three Stages* by Christina Rossetti
But first I tried, and then my care grew slack,
till my heart dreamed, and maybe wandered, too …

4) From *The World* by Christina Rossetti
By day she woos me, soft, exceeding fair;
But all night as the moon so changeth she;
Loathsome and foul with hideous leprosy
And subtle servants gliding in her hair.

5) From *Heaven's chimes are slow, but sure to strike at last* by Christina Rossetti
Heaven's chimes are slow, but sure to strike at last …

6) From *Dreamland* by Christina Rossetti
She left the rosy morn,
She left the fields of corn,
For twilight cold and lorn
And water springs.
Through sleep, as though through a veil,
She sees the sky look pale,
And hears the nightingale
That sadly sings.

PART FOUR

Chapter Twenty-Two

1) By Mary Carpenter (1807 — 1877) English social reformer
We call then, on Christian women, who are not bound by their pecuniary circumstances to work for their own living … and those who are mothers in heart, though not by God's gift on earth, will be able to bestow their maternal love on those who are more to be pitied than orphans, those most wretched moral orphans whose natural sweetness of filial love has been

mingled with deadly poison.

2) From *Goblin Market* by Christina Rossetti
"We must not look at goblin men,
We must not buy their fruits:
Who knows upon what soil they fed
Their hungry thirsty roots?"

3) By Anna Brownell Jameson (1794—1860) Irish writer, feminist
Send such a woman to her piano, her books, her cross-stitch; she answers
with despair! But send her on some mission of mercy ...

Numbers 4 and 5 from *Goblin Market* by Christina Rossetti
4) *"Come by our fruits, come buy."*
Must she then buy no more such dainty fruit?
Must she no more such succous pasture find,
Gone deaf and blind?

5) *One may lead a horse to water,*
Twenty cannot make him drink.
Though the goblins cuff'd and caught her,
Coax'd and fought her,
Bullied and besought her,
Scratch'd her, pinch'd her black as ink,
Kick'd and knock'd her,
Maul'd and mock'd her,
Lizzie utter'd not a word ...

6) From *Spring* by Christina Rossetti
There is no time like Spring,
When life's alive in everything.

7) From *Look on this Picture and on This* by Christina Rossetti
I wish we once were wedded, — then I must be true;
You should hold my will in yours to do or to undo ...

8) From *On the Death of a Cat* by Christina Rossetti
Who shall tell the lady's grief?
When her Cat was past relief?
... Who shall say the dark dismay
Which her dying caused that day?

Chapter Twenty-Three

1) From *An Apple Gathering* by Christina Rossetti
I plucked pink blossoms from mine apple-tree
And wore them all that evening in my hair:
Then in due season when I went to see
I found no apples there.

2) From *No Thank You, John* by Christina Rossetti
... strike hands as heart friends;
No more, no less ...

Chapter Twenty-Four

1) From *Goblin Market* by Christina Rossetti
Wondering at each merchant man.
One had a cat's face,
One whisk'd a tail,
One tramp'd at a rat's pace,
One crawl'd like a snail,
One like a wombat prowl'd obtuse and furry,
One like a ratel tumbled hurry skurry.
She heard a voice like voice of doves
Cooing all together:
They sounded kind and full of loves
In the pleasant weather.

2) From *At Home* by Christina Rossetti
From hand to hand they pushed the wine ...
They sang, they jested, and they laughed,
For each was loved of each.

3) From *Mr. and Mrs. Scott, and I* by Christina Rossetti
From Newcastle to Sunderland
Upon a misty morn in June
We took the train: on either hand
Grimed streets were changed for meadows soon.

4) From *The Lily Has an Air* by Christina Rossetti
The lily has an air ...
And the sweetpea a way ...

5) From *Parting After Parting* by Christina Rossetti
To meet, worth living for ...

To meet, worth parting for ...

6) From *Hymn to Proserpine* by Algernon Charles Swinburne
Where beyond the extreme sea-wall, and between the remote sea-gates,
Waste water washes, and tall ships founder, and deep death waits ...

Chapter Twenty-Five

1) From *Uphill* by Christina Rossetti
Does the road wind up-hill all the way?

Numbers 2, 3, and 4 from *Goblin Market* by Christina Rossetti
2) *Their mother-hearts beset with fears,*
   Their lives bound up in tender lives ...

3) *White and golden Lizzie stood,*
   Like a lily in a flood, —
   Like a rock of blue-vein'd stone
   Lash'd by tides obstreperously, —
   Like a beacon left alone
   In a hoary roaring sea ...

4) *... loiter in the glen*
   In the haunts of goblin men.

5) From *A Birthday* by Christina Rossetti
   My heart is like an apple-tree
   Whose boughs are bent with thickset fruit ...

Chapter Twenty-Six

1) From *Aurora Leigh, Book One* by Elizabeth Barrett Browning
   She had lived, we'll say,
   A harmless life, she called a virtuous life,
   A quiet life, which was not life at all
   (But that, she had not lived enough to know)

2) From *Echo* by Christina Rossetti
   Come back to me in dreams, that I may give
   Pulse for pulse, breath for breath ...

Chapter Twenty-Seven

1) From *Proverbs 13:12*
   *Hope deferred maketh the heart sick: but when desire cometh it is a tree of
   life.*

2) From *A Smile and a Sigh* by Christina Rossetti
   A burden saddens every song:
   While time lags which should be flying,
   We live who would be dying.

3) From *Goblin Market* by Christina Rossetti
   Cat-like and rat-like,
   Ratel- and wombat-like,
   Small-paced in a hurry,
   Parrot-voiced and whistler,
   Helter-skelter, hurry skurry,
   Chattering like magpies,
   Fluttering like pigeons,
   Gliding like fishes …

4) From *One Day* by Christina Rossetti
   Indeed, when they shall meet again,
   Except some day in Paradise:
   For this they wait, one waits in pain.
   Beyond the sea of death love lies
   Forever, yesterday, to-day;
   Angels shall ask them, 'Is it well?'
   And they shall answer, 'Yea.'

PART FIVE

Chapter Twenty-Eight

1) From *A Death Parting* by Dante Gabriel Rossetti
   And she is hence who once was here …
   In the held breath of the day's decline
   Her very face seemed pressed to mine.

2) From *Mona Innominata I. Agnegation* by Christina Rossetti
   If there be any one can take my place …
   I do command you to that nobler grace …

3) From *In the Artist's Studio* by Christina Rossetti
   And she with true kind eyes looks back on him,

Fair as the moon and joyful as the light:
Not wan with waiting, not with sorrow dim;
Not as she is, but was when hope shone bright;
Not as she is, but as she fills his dream.

Chapter Twenty-Nine

1) From *Monna Innominata, Fourth Sonnet* by Christina Rossetti
... you construed me
... for what might or might not be
Nay, weights and measures do us both a wrong,

2) From *Paradise* by Christina Rossetti
I heard the songs of Paradise:
Each bird sat singing in his place ...

3) From *The Waves of this Troublesome World: A Tale of Hastings Ten Years Ago* by Christina Rossetti
Perhaps there is no pleasanter watering-place in England

4) From *A Triad* by Christina Rossetti
Three sang of love together: one with lips
Crimson, with cheeks and bosom in a glow ...
One shamed herself in love; one temperately
Grew gross in soulless love, a sluggish wife ...

Numbers 5 and 6 from *The Stream's Secret* by Dante Gabriel Rossetti
5) *What thing unto mine ear*
Wouldst thou convey,—what secret thing,
O wandering water ever whispering?

6) *Wan water, wandering water weltering,*
This hidden tide of tears.

Chapter Thirty

1) From *When the cows come home the milk is coming* by Christina Rossetti
And the deer live safe in the breezy brake ...

2) From *Lays of Mystery, Imagination, and humour* by Lewis Carrol
... a dotard grim and gray, who wasted childhood's happy day in work more profitless than play?

Chapter Thirty-One

1) From *Later Life: A Double Sonnet of Sonnets* by Christina Rossetti
All Switzerland behind us on the ascent,
All Italy before as we plunged down
St. Gotthard, garden of forget-me-not ...

Numbers 2 and 3 from *En Route* by Christina Rossetti

2) *"Wherefore art thou strange, and not my mother?"*

3) *Thou hast stolen my heart and broken it: would that I might call thy sons*
'My brother,' call they daughters 'Sister sweet': lying in thy lap, not in
another, dying at thy feet.

Numbers 4, 5, and 6 from *Time Flies, A Reading Diary* by Christina
Rossetti
4) *Wherein lies the saddening influence of mountain scenery? For I suppose*
many besides myself have felt depressed when approaching the 'everlasting
hills.'

5) *Well, saddened and probably weary, I ended one delightful day's journey in*
Switzerland; and passed indoors, losing sight for a moment of the
mountains. Then from a window I faced them again. And lo! the evening
flush had turned snow to rose, and sadness and sorrow fled away.

6) *At a certain point of the ascent of Mount St. Gotthard bloomed into an*
actual garden of forget-me-nots, Unforgotten and never to be forgotten that
lovely lavish efflorescence which made earth cerulean as the sky.
Thus I remembered the mountain. But without the flower of memory could I
have forgotten it?

7) From *Enrica* by Christina Rossetti
We Englishwomen, trim, correct,
All minted in the self-same mold,
Warm-hearted but of semblance cold,
All-courteous out of self-respect.

8) From *Later Life* by Christina Rossetti
So chanced it once at Como on the Lake:
But all things, then, waxed musical; each star
Sang on its course, each breeze sang on its car,

All harmonies sang to senses wide-awake.

9) From *Twilight Calm* by Christina Rossetti
Hark! That's the nightingale,
Telling the selfsame tale ...

10) From *Italia, Io Ti Saluto!* by Christina Rossetti
To see no more the country half my own,
Nor hear the half familiar speech,
Amen, I say; I turn to that bleak North
Whence I came forth—
The South lies out of reach.

11) From *Mother and Poet* by Elizabeth Barrett Browning
When Venice and Rome keep their new jubilee,
When your flag takes all heaven for its white, green, and red,
When you have your country from mountain to sea,

12) From *En Route* by Christina Rossetti
Take my heart, its truest part,
Dear land, take my tears.

Chapter Thirty-Two

1) From *A Sketch* by Christina Rossetti
The blindest buzzard that I know
Does not wear wings to spread and stir ...
He sports a tail indeed, but then
It's to a coat; he's man with men;
His quill is cut to a pen.

2) From *The Bride Song* by Christina Rossetti
Ten years ago, five years ago,
One year ago,
Even then you had arrived in time,
Though somewhat slow;
Then you had known her living face
Which now you cannot know ...

3) Translated from *Il Rosseggiar Dell'Oriente* or *The Rubifying of the East* by Christina Rossetti
Bird of roses and pain, bird of love,
and unhappy: is that song laughter or weeping?

True to the untrue, in a cold land you guard your nest of thorns.

4) From *Memory* by Christina Rossetti
   None know the choice I made; I make it still.
   None know the choice I made and broke my heart …

5) From *The Heart Knoweth its Own Bitterness* by Christina Rossetti
   I used to labour, used to strive
   For pleasure with a restless will:
   Now if I save my soul alive
   All else what matters, good or ill?
   I used to dream alone, to plan
   Unspoken hopes and days to come: —
   Of all my past this is the sum —
   I will not lean on child of man.

PART SIX

Chapter Thirty-Three

1) From *Beauty is Vain* by Christina Rossetti
   While roses are so red,
   While lilies are so white,
   Shall a woman exalt her face
   Because it gives delight?

2) From *Monna Innominata, Sonnet 14* by Christina Rossetti
   Youth gone, and beauty gone if ever there
   Dwelt beauty in so poor a face as this …

3) From *By Way of Remembrance* by Christina Rossetti
   Remember, if I claim too much of you,
   I claim it of my brother and my friend …

4) From *Canzone: His Portrait of his Lady, Angiola of Verona* by Dante Gabriel Rossetti
   I look at the crisp golden-threaded hair
   Whereof, to thrall my heart, Love twists a net …

5) From *Love is as Strong as Death* by Christina Rossetti
   "I have not sought Thee, I have not found Thee,
   I have not thirsted for Thee:
   And now cold billows of death surround me,

Buffeting billows of death astound me, —
Wilt Thou look upon, wilt Thou see
Thy perishing me?"

6) From *The Thread of Life* by Christina Rossetti
And sometimes I remember days of old
When fellowship seemed not so far to seek ...

Chapter Thirty-Four

1) From *A Martyr* by Christina Rossetti
My life and youth and hope all run to waste.
Is this my body cold and stiff and stark ...

Numbers 2,3, and 4 from *The Convent Threshold* by Christina Rossetti
2) *There's blood between us, love, my love.*
There's father's blood, there's brother's blood,
And blood's a bar I cannot pass.

3) *For all night long I dreamed of you:*
I woke and prayed against my will,
Then slept to dream of you again.
At length I rose and knelt and prayed ...

4) *To-day, while it is called to-day,*
Kneel, wrestle, knock, do violence, pray;
To-day is short, tomorrow nigh:
Why will you die? Why will you die?

5) From *Time Flies, A Reading Diary* by Christina Rossetti
The lantern may be placed so as to hide its light; such withholding amounts
not to neutrality but to evil influence: the lantern which does not cast light
casts shadow.

6) From *The World* by Christina Rossetti
By day she woos me to the outer air,
Ripe fruits, sweet flowers, and full satiety ...

7) From *Sweet Death* by Christina Rossetti
So be it, O my God, Thou God of truth:
Better than beauty and than youth
Are Saints and Angels, a glad company;
And Thou, O lord, our Rest and Ease,

Are better far than these.
Why should we shrink from our full harvest …

8) From *Uphill* by Christina Rossetti
Shall I meet other wayfarers at night?
Those who have gone before.

Chapter Thirty-Five

Numbers 1 and 2 from *In the Willow Shade* by Christina Rossetti
1) *Have you no purpose but to shadow me*
   Beside this rippled spring/

2) *A singing lark rose toward the sky,*
   Circling he sang amain;
   He sang, a speck scarce visible sky-high,
   And then he sank again.

3) From *The Winter's Tale, Act 4, Scene 4* by William Shakespeare
   Calendula or the marigold, that does to bed wi'th'sun, and with him rises,
   weeping.

Numbers 5 and 6 from *Caterpillar* by Christina Rossetti
5) *Brown and furry*
   Caterpillar in a hurry,
   Take your walk
   To the shady leaf, or stalk,
   Or what not,
   Which may be the chosen spot.

6) *No toad spy you,*
   Hovering bird of prey pass by you;
   Spin and die,
   To live again a butterfly.

Chapter Thirty-Six

1) From *Mirage* by Christina Rossetti
   Life, and the world, and mine own self, are changed …

2) From *A Shadow of Dante* by Maria Francesca Rossetti
   A shadow may win the gaze of some who never looked upon substance.

3) From a poem by Dante Gabriel Rossetti to mimic William Rossetti's habit of understatement.
My name begins with W.
And hers begins with L,
With details I'll not trouble you,
But I love her pretty well.

4) From *The Portrait* by Dante Gabriel Rossetti
This is her picture as she was:
It seems a thing to wonder on,
As though mine image in the glass
Should tarry when myself am gone.

5) From *What are Heavy?* by Christina Rossetti
What are brief? today and tomorrow:
What are frail? Spring blossoms and youth …

6) From *Annus Domini* by Christina Rossetti
O Lord Jesus Christ, the Bridegroom, I entreat Thee, give us all grace to
hear Thy Voice; that married persons may love Thee in each other, and other
in Thee; and that the unmarried, keeping themselves from sin, may love
Thee without let or hindrance throughout time and through eternity.

7) From *The Face of the Deep* by Christina Rossetti
This world is not my orchard for fruit or my garden for flowers. It is
however my only field whence to raise a harvest.

8) From *Twice* by Christina Rossetti
I take my heart in my hand —
I shall not die, but live …
All that I have I bring,
All that I am I give …

9) From *Lalla* by Christina Rossetti
Darling little Cousin,
With your thoughtful look …
Tender, happy spirit,
Innocent and pure.

10) From *Untimely Loss* by Dante Gabriel Rossetti
Upon the landscape of his coming life
A youth high—gifted gazed, and found it fair:
The heights of work, the floods of praise, were there …

Chapter Thirty-Seven

1) From *Astarte Syriaca* by Dante Gabriel Rossetti
Mystery: lo! Betwixt the sun and moon
Astarte of the Syrians: Venus Queen
Ere Aphrodite was. In silver sheen ...

2) From *Hurt no Living Thing* by Christina Rossetti
Hurt no living thing:
Ladybird, nor butterfly,
Nor moth with dusty wing,
Nor cricket chirping cheerily,
Nor grasshopper so light of leap,
Nor dancing gnat, not beetle fat,
Nor harmless worms that creep.

3) From *The Convent Threshold* by Christina Rossetti
My lily feet are soiled with mud,
With scarlet mud which tells a tale
Of hope that was, of guilt that was,
Of love that shall not yet avail ...

4) From *A Dirge* by Christina Rossetti
And all winds go sighing
For sweet things dying

5) From *Noble Sisters* by Christina Rossetti
'I marked a falcon swooping
At the break of day;
And for your love, sister dove,
I 'frayed the thief away.'

Numbers 6 and 7 from *Hope* by Christina Rossetti
6) *Hope is like a harebell trembling from its birth ...*

7) *Faith is like a lily lifted high and white ...*

8) From *Goblin Market* by Christina Rossetti
She clung about her sister,
Kiss'd and kiss'd and kiss'd her:
Tears once again
Refresh'd her sunken eyes,

Dropping like rain
After long sultry drouth;
Shaking with anguish, fear, and pain …

9) From *Time Flies, A Reading Diary* by Christina Rossetti
… loving mourners followed her, hymns were sung at her grave, the
November day brightened, and the made a miniature rainbow …

Chapter Thirty-Eight

1) From *Called to be Saints, The Minor Festivals Devotionally Studied* by
Christina Rossetti
How beautiful are the arms which have embraced Christ, the hands which
have touched Christ, the eyes which have gazed upon Christ, the lips which
have spoken with Christ, the feet which have followed Christ.

2) From *The Sonnet* by Dante Gabriel Rossetti
A sonnet is a moment's monument, —
Memorial from the Soul's eternity …

3) From *The Moonstone* (novel) by Wilkie Collins
Your tears come easy, when you're young, and beginning the world. Your
tears come easy, when you're old, and leaving it.

4) From *Mirrors of Life and Death* by Christina Rossetti
Stop —
And there's an end,
And matters mend.

5) From *An Old-World Thicket* by Christina Rossetti
The sun had stooped to earth though once so high;
Had stooped to earth, in slow
Warm dying loveliness brought near and low.

6) From *Birchington Churchyard* by Christina Rossetti
A lowly hill … a flat,
Half sea, half countryside …

7) From *A Bed of Forget-me-nots* by Christina Rossetti
She groans not for a passing breath —
This is forget-me-not and love.

8) From *The Woodspurge* by Dante Gabriel Rossetti

From perfect grief there need not be
Wisdom or even memory:
One thing then learnt remains to me, —
The woodspurge has a cup of three.

Epilogue

1) From a private poem by Christina Rossetti published in William Bell
Scott's *Notes*
  My old admiration before I was twenty
  Is predilect still, now promoted to se'entry ...

2) From *My Mouse* by Christina Rossetti
  A Venus seems my Mouse
  ... A darling Mouse it is ...
  Venus-cum-Iris Mouse ...
  In no mere bottle, in my heart.

3) From *I loved you first: but afterwards your love* by Christina Rossetti
  I loved you first: but afterwards your love
  Outsoaring mine, sang such a loftier song
  As drowned the friendly cooings of my dove.

About the Author

 DM Denton is a native of Western New York, where she currently resides in a rural area and cozy log cabin with her beloved cats. Her novels and short stories are poetry in prose, inspired by music, art, classic literature, nature, the contradictions of the human spirit, and wanders into the corners of the past.

Her educational journey took her from a theater and communications major at SUNY Brockport to English literature and history studies at Rosary Hill College (now Daemen College) Amherst, NY, and Wroxton College, England. She stayed in the UK for 16 years in a small village with yellow-stone thatched cottages, a duck pond, a twelfth-century church, and a Jacobean Manor, surrounded by the beautiful hills, woods, and fields of the Oxfordshire countryside.

DM Denton is also an artist who has illustrated the covers and interiors of her own and others' books. Her previous publications released by All Things That Matter Press are full-length historical fictions *A House Near Luccoli, To A Strange Somewhere Fled, Without the Veil Between, Anne Brontë: A Fine and Subtle Spirit*, and Kindle shorts *The Snow White Gift* and *The Library Next Door*. More about DM Denton and her work at dmdenton-author-artist.com and bardessdmdenton.wordpress.com. Find her on Facebook, Twitter, and Goodreads.

Printed in Great Britain
by Amazon

50312802R00169